FIGHT, WIN—OR DIE—AS ONE

The steady hammering of autofire from Tangretti's position made it clear to Thuy that the American was still in the fight.

Thuy reached the banana trees just in time to see an NVA soldier charging at Tangretti from behind. Thuy raised his pistol and fired. The shot went low, catching the Vietnamese soldier just above the kneecap and sending him sprawling. The AK fell out of his hands, and he scrabbled in the mud trying to back away from Thuy.

Thuy didn't have the ammo to waste. He drew his knife and finished the man with one quick thrust. Then he shifted the Makarov to his left hand and pulled a grenade free, tugging out the pin with his teeth and lobbing it into the middle of the nearest cluster of enemy soldiers. It went off with a boom that added to the confusion. Thuy stepped forward, crouching close beside Tangretti with the pistol in one hand and another grenade ready in the other.

The two officers, American and South Vietnamese, would go down together. And they would go down fighting.

Other Books in the
SEALS, THE WARRIOR BREED *Series by*
H. Jay Riker

SILVER STAR
PURPLE HEART
BRONZE STAR
NAVY CROSS
MEDAL OF HONOR
MARKS OF VALOR
IN HARM'S WAY

DUTY'S CALL

SEALS

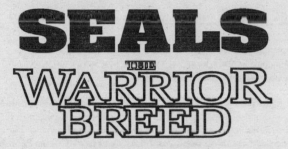

THE WARRIOR BREED

H. JAY RIKER

AVON BOOKS
An Imprint of HarperCollins*Publishers*

AVON BOOKS
An Imprint of HarperCollins*Publishers*
10 East 53rd Street
New York, New York 10022-5299

First Avon Books paperback printing: November 2000

Avon Trademark Reg. U.S. Pat. Off. and in Other Countries, Marca Registrada, Hecho en U.S.A.
HarperCollins® is a trademark of HarperCollins Publishers Inc.

Printed in the U.S.A.

OPM   10 9 8 7 6 5 4 3 2 1

To Commander Roy Boehm, USN (Ret.),
the *real* First SEAL,
and the memory of William H. Keith, Sr.,
former HM/1, USN—
we miss you, Chief.

Author's Note

This is a work of fiction. Indeed, unlike the majority of the books in this series, the events portrayed herein are very much the product of the author's imagination. In earlier books, the actual people and events that played a role in the history of the UDT and the Navy SEALs often served as the models for the fictionalized characters and exploits in the story. While some of these elements are present here, it was necessary to create much more of this novel out of whole cloth.

The simple truth is that very few accounts have yet come out detailing the earliest days of the SEALs in Vietnam. Much of the material remains classified to this day. So there were few handy templates to draw from in creating this story. It represents events that might have happened, rather than those which certainly did. As a result, readers should not think that any SEALs were involved in operations such as those described here. This is not an attempt to expose the secret war in Southeast Asia. The story is no more than that, a (hopefully) entertaining piece of fiction.

Certain characters and events have been taken from real life, but details have been altered. In part this was done for dramatic purposes, but mostly out of respect for those who might not wish to see real people's names or histories used casually in a work of fiction. The fictionalization of these people, places, and events should not, however, be taken as disrespect for the real

SEALs who made the real history of the time. The story of the Navy SEALs is a story of bravery against the odds, and the real-life tales of SEAL heroism would put any mere novel to shame. Our respect should always be for these genuine heroes.

—H. Jay Riker
January 1998

Prologue

Vietnam Veterans' Memorial
Washington, DC
1345 hours

Steve Tangretti stood still, letting the full impact of the Wall wash over him. He had come expecting to be disappointed by the newly dedicated monument, convinced that it would never live up to those grand memorials of other wars. All the descriptions had made it sound like some feel-good effort by artistic liberals to make one last antiwar statement, one last spit in the collective faces of the men and women who had served in Southeast Asia. Tangretti had wanted a proper monument, something as stirring and patriotic as the Mount Suribachi statue near Arlington Cemetery. But now, seeing the Wall for the first time, he had to admit that he had been wrong.

The long, V-shaped structure of black granite with its row upon row of inscribed names stood silent and somber. Tangretti had never been moved by anything quite as much as he was by this sight, at once a bleak reminder of war's cost and a testament to those who had given their lives fighting for their country. There were more than fifty-eight

1

thousand names etched in that black rock, each name a connection with a real person who had fought in Vietnam and never come home to friends or families.

Perhaps, Tangretti thought, there were some people involved in the construction of the monument who really had intended it as a last great antiwar protest. Certainly it brought home the horrific cost of the war. But the Wall was more than that, whether by design or by accident. It was the recognition each of those individual military men and women deserved, late in coming but powerful in the message it sent. The official dedication had only happened three days earlier, as part of the Veterans Day weekend celebrations in Washington. Tangretti had watched the crowds and the speeches on television, but today, at the request of the only son of one of his best wartime friends, he'd come out to see it in person.

He was glad he'd come.

Studying the monument, Steven Tangretti could almost see the jungles of Vietnam reflected in the black granite. A handful of the names on the Wall had a special meaning to Tangretti, though there was nothing special to distinguish them from all the rest in terms of appearance. No ranks or services were identified for any of the names there, so there was no way to pick out the forty-nine men who had been lost from the U.S. Navy SEALs on duty in Vietnam. To find this stretch of the Wall and the one name that had brought Tangretti and his young companion out here today, they'd been forced to check at an information booth that kept files on everyone listed.

That was doubly appropriate, Tangretti thought with an inward smile. It was right for the people commemorated on the wall all to be equals, not divided by rank or service or race or any of the other things that had separated them in life. But it was even more proper that those forty-nine SEALs be anonymous. For years that was exactly what they had strived for, though later on the elite Navy commandos had become famous . . . or perhaps notorious was a better description.

"I found it, sir. Over here!"

Tangretti turned toward the sound of the younger man's voice. Ensign Bernard Gunn was kneeling on the narrow strip of grass beside the Wall, heedless of the damage he was doing to his crisp dress uniform. His look mingled excitement and sadness, and a touch of wistfulness Tangretti had seen in plenty of other young faces over the years.

He started toward the ensign, feeling the weight of every one of his sixty-five years. It was nearly a decade since he had finally accepted the inevitable and retired from the Navy after a career far longer than most, and though he'd been in excellent condition then and had tried to stay fit and active since, civilian life had brought him a full load of aches, pains, and annoying ailments. But Tangretti didn't allow creaky joints to slow him down; nor did he betray any sign of pain in his expression as he joined Gunn.

Wordless, Gunn indicated a spot low on the Wall. Tangretti leaned forward to study the name etched there in the polished black stone.

ARTHUR J. GUNN.

He looked from the name to the young officer beside him, thinking how different this young man was from his father. Arthur Gunn had been lean, slight, with a wiry build and an impression of coiled strength. His son was a big man, constantly battling a tendency toward flab, with a round face and a placid, laid-back manner. He was slower to speak than his father had been, more quietly deferential, and he had a way of sounding thoughtful when he spoke. "Arty" Gunn had been rapier-sharp and quick-spoken, a born leader who could size up any situation and take charge in an instant.

"I wish I'd known him better," young Gunn said quietly. "Seems like he wasn't home much even before . . . well, before that last op."

Tangretti nodded slowly. "I know, kid. Your dad spent a lot of time in Nam, I guess. Damn near as much as I did, one way or another. But that doesn't mean he wasn't thinking about you." His own family had seen precious little of Tangretti during the war. The strain had almost cost him his marriage, and he sometimes wondered if he had done right by his son and his stepson by putting in so much time overseas.

Gunn stood up slowly. "I wasn't criticizing, sir. I just . . . think I would have liked to know him better, you know?"

"He would've wanted the same thing, kid. Believe me." Tangretti fell silent, looking down at the name on the Wall and picturing the man it had belonged to.

"Thanks for coming with me today, sir," Gunn said softly. "It means a lot to me. Dad told my mother once that you were the best damn SEAL he ever knew, even if you were an East Coast puke . . . er, sorry, sir."

Tangretti grinned. "Don't apologize for that, kid. That was high praise indeed . . . coming from a West Coast puke like him."

The younger man looked solemn. "I thought you might want to know . . . I got my orders last week. BUD/S training."

"BUD/S?" Tangretti looked at the young officer through narrowed eyes. The Navy acronym stood for Basic Underwater Demolition/SEAL school, the high-pressure course where only the toughest made the grade. "You're shooting for SEALs, too?"

"Yes, sir," Gunn said, standing a little taller with a conscious effort. "Yes, sir . . . a SEAL. Like Dad."

"It won't be easy, you know. Even after all this time, Hell Week's still a killer. And I've heard rumors—old contacts inside DOD and all—that there won't be as many berths out of BUD/S come this time next year. There's talk about phasing out the UDTs."

"So there won't be a softer billet if I don't cut it in training?" Gunn said, a hard edge in his voice. "Sir, I know I look soft. A lot of people have underestimated me because of my looks. But if I couldn't make the cut as a SEAL I wouldn't want to go UDT anyway. If I can't be in that top percentage, I'd rather be a black-shoe sailor and stay away from Special Warfare altogether. But I *will* make it, sir. Believe me."

Tangretti studied the young officer for long moments before he responded. "You know, I think you will at that, Mr. Gunn. And I've been sizing up potential SEALs for a lot of years, you know. If you've got just half the guts and dedication your dad had, you'll make one hell of a good SEAL."

Gunn's face, so intense just a moment before, creased in a wide smile. "Thanks, sir. Mom always said you told things straight . . . at least when it came to SEALs."

"Your mother is right. I only lie when I'm talking to captains or above . . . or sometimes to civilians. But never to a SEAL . . . or a potential SEAL." He paused, his eyes resting again on the Wall. "I have a feeling you'll make your dad proud, wherever he's gone to."

The younger man didn't reply. For long moments the two of them—one a former SEAL, the other hoping to become a part of the Teams—regarded the Wall and the name of Arthur Gunn in respectful silence.

And the power of the Wall took Tangretti's memories back to Lieutenant Arthur Gunn and their service together as Navy SEALs, a service that had started before Vietnam had been anything more than a vague name, when Tangretti and his newly formed SEALs had confidently expected to go into combat against quite a different foe . . .

Chapter 1

Off San Mariel, Republic of Cuba
0017 hours

Lieutenant Arthur Gunn was treading water with an ease born of long practice, feeling very much alone in the wide, rolling expanse of the Caribbean Sea under a canopy of brilliantly glittering tropical stars. The bright moonlight that struck the ocean surface in an ever-changing pattern of light and shadow made it seem well lit, but despite the excellent night visibility, Gunn had to look carefully to spot the rest of the men who surrounded him swimming in the open expanse of water. With only their heads above water, wearing dark rubber wet suits and camouflage paint on their faces, the SEALs of the recon party were hard to spot even if you knew just where to look.

That was the whole idea behind a nighttime beach reconnaissance. With luck no one would be detected as they swam in to study the Cuban shoreline, then back out to sea for a rendezvous with the USS *Sea Lion*, the submarine that roamed the depths just beneath them.

Close alongside Gunn, a head broke the surface. Pulling away the mouthpiece of his underwater breathing device,

7

the newcomer looked around, taking his bearings, then fixed the cyclopean stare of his face mask squarely on Gunn.

"All right, I'm the last," the new arrival announced. Lieutenant Steve Tangretti sounded irritable. He'd lost the coin toss with Gunn aboard the submarine when they were deciding who would be first to lock out through the escape trunk. "All of you sons of bitches remember your assignments?"

Chuckles mingled with soft-voiced replies from the waiting SEALs. Gunn smiled. "You're the one who's most likely going senile, Gator," he told Tangretti. "None of the rest of us were on Omaha Beach with your NCDU dinosaurs back in the Big One."

"Yeah, and I'd still trade the whole lot of you in for Hank Richardson and a couple more of the old gang," Tangretti growled back. "But you don't always get what you want in this life, do you?" He paused. "Okay, we do this nice and smooth, just like the practice runs. My boys have the beach. You West Coast pukes check the harbor. Go in fast, quiet, and alert, and get the dope we need. Then back out. No contact with the enemy . . . and if *they* find *you*, break it off and get back to the rendezvous. I want live SEALs making reports, not a bunch of dead heroes. Right?"

"Right," someone said. And another SEAL added, "Hoo-RAH!"

"Can it, Jackson," Chief Machinist Michael Spencer growled.

Gunn spoke up. "Make as much of the approach on the surface as possible. Save the tanked air for when we need it. And keep in mind what Marsh was talking about last night. The more you thrash around, the more phosphorescence you'll kick up."

Gunner's Mate First Class George Marsh grunted an

agreement. "Yeah," he said. "And I, for one, have no great interest in being a great big glowing target."

"That's enough," Gunn told him. Marsh was one of four non-SEALs attached to the operation, a part of UDT-12. Because the Underwater Demolition Teams might well find themselves involved in more large-scale operations in Cuban waters if things escalated further, Marsh and three others—two men from UDT units from each coast—were swimming in with the SEALs. Gunn was glad to have them along, since all four were old hands at this kind of work. But some of the SEALs resented them, even though they'd all come out of the UDTs themselves just a few months before. There was a growing feeling that the SEALs were the best of the best, and that "ordinary" UDT men somehow didn't quite measure up to the standard the new outfit was trying to establish for itself.

Marsh had been harping on the problems caused by the tropical phosphorescence ever since they had started their training dives at Key West two days earlier. It was a valid concern, but the swimmers were just going to have to overcome the problem as best they could. That was all a part of the job, and for the first major SEAL operation in the Teams' short history they couldn't afford to let anything keep them from collecting the information they were required to gather. The SEALs had too many enemies in the service as it was, and this trial by fire was crucial if they wanted to keep the new outfit from being shut down before it had even had a fair chance to prove what it could do.

"Let's get moving," Tangretti said sharply. "The sooner we get this done, the sooner we can all crawl back in our racks on the sub."

The SEALs began striking out in different directions, the four East Coast SEALs and all the UDT men following Tangretti, while the eight men of Team One joined Gunn.

The two groups had very different missions to carry out, and the personnel assigned to each group reflected their differing missions. Gunn let the rest of his men forge ahead of him, then signaled Ensign Aengus O'Rourke to hang back with him for a moment. O'Rourke was a thin, wiry native of Ireland who was as zealous in the service of his adoptive country as he was proud of his origins in the Auld Sod. Fiery, stubborn, and a little too impetuous for Gunn's taste, O'Rourke was nonetheless a good officer, well liked by the other SEALs of Team One. He'd been the first man to volunteer when the mission was first being mapped out, and Gunn had picked him even though the unit was really too small to need two officers. After all, if a larger combat mission was warranted later, it would be valuable to have another leader on hand with personal knowledge of the lay of the land.

"Remember the mission, Aengus," Gunn said softly, as the two men swam side by side through the darkness. "This isn't the time for heroics."

"Aye, sir," the young Irishman replied, his voice a musical lilt despite his years in his adoptive Brooklyn home. "You can count on me."

"If I didn't think I could, you wouldn't be out here tonight." Gunn paused. "And, look, Aengus . . . if things go sour for me tonight, you get the rest of the guys out of there. And . . . tell Sally and the kids . . ." He trailed off. His wife had a four-year-old son and a brand-new daughter at home in San Diego, and they were the only things that gave Arthur Gunn pause when he considered the life he'd chosen for himself.

"I'll take care of it, sir," O'Rourke said quietly. "Not that I'll need to. You're too tough to die, and that's the truth of it."

A ghost of a smile touched Gunn's lips. "All right, Aengus, I guess I deserved that one after posting that order about the PTs." There was a small but vocal contingent in Team One who resented the schedule of Physical Training Gunn had put into effect for his SEALs. They both chuckled before Gunn went on. "Now . . . let's get them paired off and head for town."

The officers rejoined the rest of the SEALs, using hand signals to begin pairing them off in the two-man teams who'd practiced together over and over during the rehearsals for the night's operation. Gunn's partner was Engineman Third Class Curt Halvorssen, a big-boned blond from Minnesota who was the least experienced man in the unit. When he wasn't wearing camouflage paint and a wet suit, Halvorssen looked like he'd just stepped off the deck of a Viking longboat, and someone had hung the nickname "Thor" on him after the Marvel Comics superhero. He'd come out of UDT training just a few weeks before the formation of SEAL Team One at Coronado, but his phenomenal marks there had made him an instant asset to the outfit despite his comparative youth and lack of seasoning. Gunn wanted to keep an eye on him tonight . . . but he also thought Thor would make a good man to have at his back.

They swam slowly through the darkness, taking care not to stir up the faint bioluminesence that Marsh had been so concerned about and pacing themselves so that they didn't reach their target too tired to do any good. It was just like one of the endless exercises they'd gone through so many times before, the kind of long-distance swim Gunn had practiced in Underwater Demolition Team Twenty-One long before he'd ever heard of SEALs.

But in the back of his mind he knew that there was a difference. This time, there was a very real danger that the swimmers could encounter hostile forces as they carried out their scouting mission. And if they did, with tensions running high between the U.S. and Cuba, the SEALs could well end up triggering a shooting war.

Maybe even a nuclear war. That was what this operation was all about, after all. It hadn't been announced to the public yet, but the briefings the SEALs had received made it clear just how high the stakes were. Russian "advisors" had been arming Fidel Castro's government with nuclear missiles situated less than a hundred miles from Florida's coastline, and if it ever came to a war with the Communist bloc, those missiles could be hitting American targets before the U.S. had time to react to the threat. It looked like President Kennedy was paying the price for the Bay of Pigs fiasco the previous year.

No decisions had been made yet in Washington, but the president had to keep his options open. That meant being prepared to launch an all-out amphibious assault on Cuba if that looked like the only way to deal with the crisis. And if the Marines had to go in, they'd need all the intelligence data they could get. The Bay of Pigs landing had certainly taught the need for that much preparation, if nothing else.

Beach recon was the job of the Underwater Demolition Teams, and in fact the UDTs from both coasts were standing by to mobilize if the order to attack went in. But before the president could even begin to consider issuing such an order, he had to have as much information as possible on the situation in Cuba. Spy satellites and U-2 overflights had revealed the missiles in the first place, and could give a broad overview of conditions on the island, but there was no substitute for men on the ground to gather the kind of detailed information they'd need to chew over in DC before they could decide if an invasion was worth the risk. With hands poised over the nuclear buttons that could destroy both sides in a fiery showdown, there was no room for error.

So the U.S. Navy SEALs, formed less than ten months earlier, had received their first critical assignment. Steve Tangretti had been one of the principal forces behind the whole concept, and with JFK's blessing he'd started up SEAL Team Two on the East Coast, while Lieutenant Joe Camparelli had taken charge of Team One out of Coronado on the West Coast. The idea behind the SEALs—SEa, Air, and Land Teams—was simple enough. Where the UDTs had long specialized in beach reconnaissance and clearing obstacles ahead of the Marines in amphibious operations, the SEALs were supposed to be elite commandos tasked with Special Warfare duties, the kind of small, highly skilled units the president had been known to favor in the new battlefield of the Cold War. Where the UDTs traditionally went no farther than the high-tide mark on the beach, and were supposed to limit their combat activities to demolition work, the SEALs were intended to be far more flexible. Scouting, raiding, capturing prisoners, blowing up selected targets on the shore or miles inland, the SEALs were supposed to be able to do it all. They were the best of the best, drawn from the toughest men the Navy could find.

And tonight they would see if they could carry out the kind of operation they'd talked about since Tangretti and others had first started pitching the idea.

With the possibility of a nuclear confrontation facing them if anything went wrong, Arthur Gunn wondered if tonight was really the time to test the SEALs in action.

Off Beach "Alpha"
Near San Mariel
0129 hours

It had all led up to tonight!

Lieutenant Steve Tangretti could feel the old, familiar thrill running through his veins as he approached the beach. For a moment his mind flashed back to other beaches, other ops—Normandy, the day his swim buddy Hank Richardson had bought the farm trying to take out German obstacles in the largest amphibious assault ever mounted; Okinawa, where Tangretti and members of his UDT outfit had gone beyond their orders to actually go ashore instead of remaining below the tide line as doctrine required; the beach at Inchon, when MacArthur had given the North Koreans one hell of a surprise with a little help from UDT beach surveyors—but Tangretti forced himself to ignore those memories and focus on the moment.

He'd worked hard to see this day. Tangretti and Richardson had been part of one of the first classes of naval demolition specialists graduated from Fort Pierce in World War II, and they'd gone on to serve not only in the original Naval Combat Demolition Units, but in the first of the UDTs as well. From the beginning they had questioned some of the ideas behind those units, which had been conceived as large support outfits who weren't supposed to engage in combat, although their operations were certain to put them in harm's way when they surveyed a beach or cleared obstacles ahead of a landing. Tangretti still had a souvenir of their first combat op at Kwajalein, a bullet from a Japanese rifle he sometimes wore on a chain around his neck. He'd always thought the UDTs should be ready for more than just support work. It all had seemed so obvious. Small, well-trained naval commando units could investigate a beach, gather information, clear away obstacles both natural and man-made, even carry out small-scale raids as necessary. But the obvious never seemed to appeal to the brass.

Until now, at least. It had taken a new and more lethal world situation and a visionary president willing to consider alternatives to the massive military operations of the past, but Tangretti had finally seen the ideas he'd argued for come to life over the past ten months. The U.S. Navy SEALs were a reality at last, and tonight they'd show just what they could accomplish.

The beach was close enough for Tangretti to hear the pounding surf, and the shore was well lit by the lights showing from a sprawling complex of apartment buildings above the line of the sand. Studying the buildings, he could clearly see people moving back and forth on some of the balconies or behind large picture windows. The lights were bright enough to splash illumination across the beach. He could even see discolorations in the sand that marked lines of footprints. All that light was far from ideal for their mission, and he could only hope that no one would happen to notice the figures of eight American swimmers as they performed their beach reconnaissance.

He hoped the others would take proper precautions as they approached, then shook his head angrily at the thought. Of course they would. All of them, SEALs and UDT men alike, were well-trained professionals. CPO Farnum and Boatswain's Mate First Class Harry Matthews were Team Two plank owners, men he'd chosen personally for the SEALs, and the four UDT men were supposed to do this kind of beach-survey work for a living. They had divided up into two-man teams and spread out, twenty to thirty yards apart. All they had to do now was to get started with the job at hand.

Tangretti paused, treading water, and signaled to Gunner's Mate Second Class Jason Trapford to hold up as well.

Using hand signals, Tangretti indicated that Trapford was to trail behind, remaining clear of the beach, while Tangretti himself made the close-in survey. In most units, the commander of an operation wouldn't be permitted to risk himself that way, but the SEALs weren't most units. Steve Tangretti had started Navy life as an enlisted man, and though he carried an officer's rank and responsibility, he still didn't consider himself a "real" officer. His approach to any situation was strictly hands-on, and he wasn't about to change that technique now.

It had been a long time since the swims at Normandy, Okinawa, and Inchon, but the old familiar surge of adrenaline through his veins was the same as Steve Tangretti started for the sandy shores of his nation's enemies.

San Mariel Harbor
0152 hours

The distant thrum of an engine cut through the night, loud enough to be plain even above the roar of the surf. Arthur Gunn bit back a curse and started to tread water, scanning the darkness for the source of the unwelcome sound.

Halvorssen spotted it first. He touched Gunn's arm and pointed, and Gunn followed the gesture. It wasn't coming from the harbor mouth at all, as he'd first thought. Tricky acoustics had fooled his ears. The boat was actually well out to sea, cruising slowly on a course that paralleled the coast. Searchlights were probing the darkness on either side of the vessel, giving Gunn enough light to get a good idea of the shape of the craft.

It was a Soviet-built Komar patrol boat, a mainstay of Castro's navy. Gunn felt a constriction in his throat. What was that vessel doing out there tonight? It looked as if it was searching for something, but what? Fleeing refugees?

Or American frogmen? Operational security for the SEALs had been incredibly tight from the beginning, but could the Russians have gotten wind of tonight's reconnaissance somehow and passed the word to Cuba? Or had the sub been spotted on sonar as it headed into these hostile waters?

Gunn watched as the boat swept past, several hundred yards away. It passed on, keeping its course and speed constant, until darkness and distance swallowed it up.

Only when he could neither see nor hear it anymore did Gunn let out a sigh of relief. Whether the boat had been looking for something specific or just conducting a random patrol, it hadn't spotted his SEALs.

He gave a quick hand signal and turned resolutely to face the mouth of the harbor once more. SEAL Team One's assignment was to penetrate the sheltered water of San Mariel and check the feasibility of mounting a covert attack on the Cuban naval vessels stationed there—mostly Komars like the one that had just passed, according to recent intelligence reports. A successful recce tonight would mean that, if need be, they could repeat this swim on some other night with a load of explosives that could put those boats out of action.

**Beach Alpha
Near San Mariel
0153 hours**

Tangretti knelt on the shelving sand, waves breaking past him as the rhythmic surf swept past him and over the beach five yards from his position. He held the slate attached to his wrist in one hand, chalking in information on the depth, contour, and bottom composition of this stretch of the shoreline with the other. Though he'd been away from this kind of UDT work for a long time, it was an easy, familiar feeling to be working up a profile of what an attacking force might encounter if push came to shove. He knew the rest of his unit was spread along the beach in both directions, conducting similar surveys. By the time they finished, the SEALs would have a complete picture of Beach Alpha, as detailed as anything their UDT counterparts could produce. That, combined with whatever information Gunn could obtain about San Mariel Harbor and the vulnerability of the patrol boats based there, would make mounting a raid in this area a piece of cake if the president decided to send troops in on short notice.

He paused, cocking his head and listening. He'd thought he'd heard something up on the beach to his left, but now he wasn't sure. Quickly he made a hand signal, ordering the other beach surveyors in line of sight to freeze. Tangretti couldn't help but feel a little jumpy as he contemplated his situation. This wasn't a practice run, nor was it one of the heavily supported operations he'd experienced in years past. A handful of men were bearding Castro right under the bright-lit windows of those towering apartment buildings, and Tangretti felt like hundreds of eyes were staring right at him as he worked.

He was just about to give the signal to get back to work when a shift in the breeze brought the sound to his ears again, plainly this time.

Tangretti didn't even take time to analyze the noise or what it might be. His instincts took over, and he was up, out of the water, and racing across the sand in a crouching run before conscious thought cut in. A patch of low bushes a few yards above the tide line were the nearest cover, and Tangretti was under their protective spread of drooping leaves in an instant. Lying still, he peered out through a gap.

The sound had been the steady clip-clop of a horse's

hooves drumming on hardened sand. He saw horse and rider approach at a slow walk, taking in the man's uniform and the rifle slung over his back. Castro's army still used cavalry patrols to supplement the country's more modern arsenal. On a backward, poverty-stricken island like Cuba, militia and reserve units had to make do with what they could get, even if it was a century out of style in the wars fought between the big boys.

To his chagrin, the horseman drew up right next to the patch of bushes where Tangretti lay waiting, dismounting with a tired grunt. He tied the reins to a branch not a foot away from Tangretti's face, and the SEAL tensed, ready for action. He shifted carefully to get a hand on his knife handle, ready to spring out and strike if the rider saw him. He would probably have to kill rider and horse both, and quickly, since the smell of blood could send a horse wild and raise the very alarm Tangretti was ready to kill to avoid. Even if Trapford or one of the others violated his last order and came to his aid, Tangretti doubted anyone could reach the scene in time to help much. He was on his own.

But the rider didn't seem to notice anything out of the ordinary. He turned and looked out to sea, hands fumbling at his shirt pockets for something Tangretti couldn't make out from his vantage point under the bushes. The SEAL remained poised to act, but forced his thrumming nerves to a semblance of calm.

A flare of light explained what the soldier had sought. The match dropped just in front of Tangretti's face, and a dusty boot ground it into the sand as the rider took a long drag on a cigarette. The SEAL listened as the man muttered something in Spanish, curses by the sound of it, and despite his tension he found himself smiling. The soldier, probably a militiaman mustered to meet the mounting crisis, was a middle-aged, overweight, uncouth specimen, most likely wishing he was in his bed instead of riding patrols across lonely beaches in the middle of the night. Taking time out for a smoke on duty was likely his gesture of defiance to the orders that sent him out onto the beach in the first place.

Tangretti hoped the man would pass on without spotting the SEAL. He didn't want to have to kill him. Ordinary soldiers like him weren't the real enemy, only the pawns who fought, and often died, in the service of other men. Like most of his breed, Tangretti could kill without remorse when duty demanded it, but he hoped it wouldn't be necessary tonight.

At last the man flicked the cigarette into the sand, squashed it with his boot, and said something to his horse in the same half-grumbling tone. The horse tossed his head and neighed a reply as the Cuban untied the reins and clambered onto the beast's broad back. They started off again at the same measured pace as before, and Tangretti let out a sigh.

He checked his watch again—0207. Less than five minutes had gone by since the Cuban had first come into sight, though it had seemed like endless hours.

Tangretti checked the knife in its sheath and crawled out from under the cover of the bushes, creeping carefully down to the water and wading in with slow, deliberate caution to avoid making noise and setting up too much phosphorescence. He swam slowly away from the beach, out toward where he'd left Jason Trapford. No doubt his swim buddy would be worried by now.

As he pushed off from the bottom and started to swim, Tangretti could feel the excitement flowing through him. Dangerous or not, this was what he'd lived for since those first days with the NCDUs back in the war. There was nothing like the feeling of risking it all in the field and coming out alive, of achieving the mission's goals despite whatever obstacles fate and the enemy raised.

He'd been away from it for a long time. Now this first taste of a real operation with the SEALs had left Steve Tangretti hungry for more.

San Mariel Harbor
0227 hours

Arthur Gunn took a deep pull at the mouthpiece of his rebreather and reached out to touch Aengus O'Rourke on the shoulder. O'Rourke turned in the water as Gunn switched on a small waterproof light and used the beam to light up his slate, and the UDT man followed his lead so they could compare their information.

Their tally of the Cuban ships in the harbor matched, and Gunn was pleased to note that O'Rourke had actually taken the time to jot down notes on the condition of some of the vessels. He wasn't sure if he should commend the younger officer on his initiative or dress him down for taking unnecessary risks in surfacing to examine individual ships at anchor in the harbor. On the whole he was thankful he couldn't do either while they stood on the bottom twenty feet beneath the surface. The swimmers had divided up into two groups to make their survey, but both parties had taken note of all the vessels, double-checking each other's work. Everything had gone smoothly; no one in the port had any reason to suspect that eight American SEALs had passed among their ships.

If they'd been carrying limpet mines with them, the American frogmen could have disabled every one of the Cuban ships. Gunn had every reason to feel satisfied, but just then wasn't the time or the place to indulge in gloating. The frogmen needed to get clear of the harbor and head back for the rendezvous with the submarine. Until they were safely out of Cuban waters and on their way home,

Arthur Gunn didn't intend to let his guard down for an instant.

Gunn gave O'Rourke the hand signal to round up the swimmers and return to the rendezvous, and the UDT man gave a sharp nod.

Before he turned away to join the others, Gunn glanced at the looming bulk of the nearest Komar where it rode at anchor, feeling a trace of wistfulness. It was almost a shame the SEALs hadn't come with mines, to leave a calling card behind that would demonstrate just how well they'd pierced the enemy's defenses.

But that would have to wait for some other time, he told himself sternly. This time the job had been reconnaissance, but someday the SEALs would see combat, and when they did Gunn was sure they'd make their mark.

Off Beach Alpha
Near San Mariel
0348 hours

Lieutenant Tangretti checked his watch again and pushed off from shore reluctantly. The beach survey had covered better than four thousand yards of the sandy shoreline, and he knew the others must be feeling just as exhausted as he was. Nonetheless, he wanted to stay, to get just a little more detail in their picture of the beach. The results he'd noted down over the last few hours weren't encouraging, and it bothered him to have to return with a negative report. Of course, it was possible that the others had found better stretches of beach in their surveys, but long experience told Tangretti that everything he'd seen added up to a beach that simply wouldn't be suitable.

What if he'd missed something? Just a little more time might turn up something better. . . .

He realized that there was a part of him that was almost hoping for another encounter with the enemy and forced that thought down. Over the years Tangretti had seen a lot of adrenaline junkies who let their love of danger get them in over their heads. He remembered Frank Rand, an officer he'd served with at Okinawa, and the stories that had gone round the Teams about the man's single-handed assaults on German positions in the Sicily and Normandy campaigns.

Tangretti could also remember a few exploits of his own that hadn't been exactly smart, especially in the months after his best friend's death when his own life just hadn't mattered anymore. Back then he'd been a broken-down petty officer with nothing much to live for. Now he had a wife and two sons at home, and responsibility for the swimmers under his command. He just couldn't afford to push the edge anymore, much as that wild part of him wanted to.

No, they'd spent enough time on the survey. It was time to pack it in. If everything had gone according to plan, Gunn's West Coast pukes were probably already back at the rendezvous point. Their job of counting ships in San Mariel Harbor had been considerably more risky than the beach survey, but not nearly as time-consuming. Tangretti's men didn't have quite as much distance to cover getting back, but they still had to start soon if they were going to make the rendezvous before the hard-nosed skipper of the *Sea Lion* decided not to wait any longer for the reconnaissance party to make it back.

He joined Trapford, and the two men angled across the beach to pick up the other three two-man teams. Farnum and Matthews, the other two SEALs, were at the far end of the line, the last to join up before they all turned their backs on the Cuban coast for the long swim back.

"We're going back underwater," he ordered quietly. "Check your breathing bags before you start. It's a long swim out, but I want us to stay below all the way out to the rendezvous if we can. No sense spoiling a perfectly good op by getting spotted now."

There was a murmured chorus of assent from the others, and Tangretti carefully checked the fittings of his underwater breathing device to make sure he hadn't knocked something loose during the long beach survey. He didn't care for this model of rebreather. It didn't have much endurance, and on a long swim that could mean trouble. But procuring equipment for SEAL Team Two hadn't been easy, and sometimes he'd been forced to settle for second-best . . . even when Tangretti obtained his gear through less-than-regular channels. He'd cut a lot of corners these last ten months, stretching purchasing regs and safety standards to the limit and beyond in order to get SEAL Team Two outfitted in the face of all the opposition the regular Navy bureaucracy could raise against him. Most of the Establishment couldn't understand the needs of an elite naval commando force, and seemed determined to reject the notion that any unit made up of sailors would need parachutes, or assault weapons, or any of a hundred other things Tangretti had known from the start the SEALs would need one day.

Rebreathers had been especially hard to obtain, but they were crucial to the kinds of ops the SEALs were intended to carry out, and Tangretti had finally been forced to go outside the Navy and buy up what underwater breathing equipment he could find on the open market. Even after he'd had them modified—going very much outside of regs again to do it—he hadn't been happy with the results. Especially given the trouble they'd caused from the brass, who'd ordered a full-scale investigation into some of his more dubious procurement ploys once word of the rebreather purchase had gotten out.

Tangretti hoped they'd be worth all the hassle tonight.

Off San Mariel
0405 hours

"Periscope, sir!"

Squinting in the moonlight, Arthur Gunn followed Thor Halvorssen's gesture and made out the faint phosphorescent glow of water rippling past a periscope rising out of the sea like some solitary reed in the midst of a broad river. He offered up silent but reverent thanks to God for getting them safely back to the rendezvous point without incident. The rebreathers were all but exhausted from the underwater work in San Mariel Harbor and the long swim back to the rendezvous point, and Gunn was glad they wouldn't have to use the devices much longer. As it was, it had been a relief to surface and paddle around among the rolling waves, breathing fresh air instead of the stale mixture circulated through the breathing bags while they searched for some sign of the submarine.

"Okay, gang, you know the drill," he said. "Aengus, the line."

O'Rourke produced a hundred-foot length of line from his pack, tying one end to his weight belt and passing the coil to the SEAL nearest to him. Each man in turn passed the line through an eye on his belt, until all eight men were tied together. They'd practiced the maneuver dozens of times in preparation for the mission, but it still made Gunn nervous. Catching a ride with a moving submarine, then diving underwater to a depth of thirty-five feet to find the escape trunk in the sub's hull where they could lock through to safety, with everyone tired out and likely to make mistakes was not Gunn's idea of an easy end to a tricky operation.

They swam to meet the moving periscope, and CPO Spencer managed to hook on with the line as he passed closest to it. The sub didn't slow down at all, and the SEALs found themselves being towed through the water at a slow but steady speed Gunn estimated at about twelve knots. After all eight men had closed in around the periscope, Spencer and Gunn reworked the attachment of the line so that one end was securely tied to the projection. Whatever happened, the sub wouldn't lose them . . . unless, of course, she decided to head for the bottom.

"All right, Aengus," Gunn said. "You lead the way."

"Aye, sir," the Irish SEAL said cheerfully. He, at least, sounded like he was ready to do the whole mission again without a rest, and Gunn shook his head at the boundless energy of young ensigns.

O'Rourke set his mouthpiece firmly in place and grabbed on to the thin wire that ran from the periscope down to the escape trunk set in the hull about thirty-five feet below the SEALs. The Irishman unhooked himself from the line and dived out of sight. Gunn could picture the ensign as he moved down the curve of the hull, trying to locate the escape trunk in the murky water where the bright moonlight didn't penetrate.

After a few moments, Gunn nodded to BM/2 Jackson. "Right. You're next."

Each man in turn plunged underwater. Gunn was the last man in the chain. He headed downward into darkness, holding on to the wire and all too aware of the looming bulk of the sub's hull close alongside and the dangers of an unpredictable surge in the water that could slam him against it. Time seemed to stand still, until suddenly he reached the escape trunk. Gunn swung himself into the opening smoothly. There was some air trapped inside the narrow confines of the lock even when it was open to the sea, and Gunn thankfully tore his mouthpiece free, gulped in a quick breath, and touched the stud of the intercom there. "Securing the lock," he said, closing and dogging the outer hatch as he spoke. "Ready." He paused. "Permission to come aboard, sir?"

On the other end of the intercom he heard the captain of the boat chuckle. "Permission granted, Lieutenant. Welcome home."

Off San Mariel
0447 hours

Steve Tangretti broke the surface and pulled out the mouthpiece of his breathing device, gulping fresh air in deep gasps. The air bag on the rebreather was almost useless, the chemicals that scrubbed the carbon dioxide nearly exhausted. As he'd suspected, this batch of underwater breathing gear wasn't suitable for long-range SEAL missions, and when he got back to headquarters in Little Creek, Virginia, he'd start looking for a replacement system before he finished unpacking his sea bag.

Assuming he made it back to Little Creek, he added with a silent curse. The surveyors had followed a reciprocal course out from the beach back toward the rendezvous point, and by his best estimation they should have reached it by now. But for the last ten minutes periodic checks had failed to reveal any sign of *Sea Lion*'s periscope above the water. And visibility just wasn't good enough to see anything, not even something the size of a submarine, while swimming underwater.

George Marsh surfaced a few yards away, coughing as he removed his mouthpiece. "This fucking piece of shit is no damned good," he announced, punctuating the words with more coughs. The UDT man undid the straps from the breathing device and tossed it away with a contemptuous gesture. "I'd be better off holding my breath."

The other swimmers were starting to come up to join them, and in a few moments they had gathered around Tangretti, treading water. Some of the others had worn out rebreathers, too, and even the ones that were still working weren't likely to last long.

They had perhaps another hour left until daylight. After that, he knew, the sub's captain had orders to sail home regardless of the status of his passengers.

"Why did I ever let them make me an officer?" Tangretti muttered under his breath. He'd never asked to be commissioned, but somehow he'd wound up as a leader instead of a follower, responsible for the lives of these seven men. It was one thing to use his authority to get things done when he was organizing the SEALs back in Little Creek, but making life-or-death decisions was something he didn't want, now or ever.

But the swimmers were fast running out of options, and Steve Tangretti knew they'd have to do something soon.

USS *Sea Lion*
Off San Mariel
0513 hours

The atmosphere was tense in the control room of the USS *Sea Lion*, and Lieutenant Arthur Gunn did his best to remain unobtrusive as he hovered near the aft hatch, watching the captain and crew at work in the narrow confines of the undersized compartment. Every so often he checked his watch. The beach team was over half an hour late, and Gunn was worried. It wasn't like Steve Tangretti to make mistakes. Despite the man's reputation as a free-and-easy wheeler-dealer who would bend any rule or regulation, when it came to operations in the field the World War II UDT veteran was well-known for his competence.

If something had gone wrong on the beach below San Mariel, it could spell trouble. Captured Americans would give Castro a powerful propaganda tool in the current crisis, and could possibly turn the heat up on the Cold War. Dead Americans, if discovered and identified for what they were, could be just as bad . . . and in either event the SEAL Teams would likely be branded as useless if they failed this first genuine mission.

It didn't bear thinking about.

"Conn, Sonar," someone called out over the sub's intercom. *"I have two surface targets right at the edge of my detection range. Bearing is one-niner-two. They're closing."*

Commander Walter Erskine, *Sea Lion*'s dapper captain, picked up the intercom microphone. "Sonar, Conn," he said crisply, "You got an ID on these guys, Patterson?"

"From the prop sounds I'd say it's a pair of Komars, Skipper," the sonar operator replied. *"ETA's . . . fifteen minutes."*

The sub's exec, Lieutenant Commander Hall, spoke up. "I bet we were spotted by that Russkie destroyer on our way in," he drawled. "Probably passed the word to keep an eye out for anything that didn't belong in the neighborhood."

"We spotted a Komar patrolling along the coast near the harbor mouth," Gunn added quietly.

"Wonderful," Erskine said. "And just where is your Mr. Tangretti, Lieutenant?"

"Beats the hell out of me, sir," Gunn replied.

"All right," the captain said at length. "We'll hang tough here until those Komars pass on . . . if they pass on. Drop her down to the bottom and kill the engines. But after those guys are out of range we're getting out of here."

"If we're at the bottom, will they be able to find us?" Gunn asked.

"The water's pretty shallow here, Lieutenant," Erskine told him. "In fact, there's a big outcropping of coral between us and the shore. This is as close in as we can get without tearing the bottom out of the boat, and even out here where we've got enough water we can lie in the mud and still put the periscope up." He paused. "Let's just hope nobody on those two patrol boats spots it before Mr. Tangretti and his boys."

"Amen to that," Gunn said.

Erskine waited a moment, then turned a baleful glare on his Exec. "Well, Mr. Hall, you've got the orders. Let's get cracking!"

Off San Mariel
0516 hours

"It's been half an hour, Gator. Maybe they ain't going to come pick us up."

Tangretti didn't answer right away, but he knew Harry Matthews spoke for the entire bone-weary team. They'd been treading water and swimming in circles for thirty minutes, trying to spot some sign of the missing sub. It would be dawn soon, and with it the end of any hope of a pickup.

"Well, oh Fearless Leader?" Matthews pressed. "Any orders to cover this situation?"

Shrugging, Tangretti pointed out into the Florida Straits. "Swim to sea and drown, I guess," he said.

Matthews looked at him with a grim expression. "I hope you know what a chicken-shit order that is, Gator," he said. "Jeez, I knew being a friend of yours was going to get me killed someday."

That made the rest of the swimmers laugh despite their tired muscles and aching joints, and George Marsh started moving in the direction Tangretti had pointed with a slow, steady breast stroke. "It may be a chicken-shit order, but I guess it's all we can do," he said.

There really weren't any options open, Tangretti told himself bitterly. The gallows humor of Matthews and

Marsh pointed up that stark fact. They could try to swim for Cuba, where they'd be captured or killed. They could remain in place, until exhaustion claimed them one by one. Or they could strike out to sea in a hopeless gesture of defiance. For Tangretti, as for the others, the third choice was really the only thing left to try. He was a SEAL, and if he had to die, at least he'd die trying his best to complete the mission . . . even if he had to swim all the way to Florida.

They kept to the surface, since only three of them could get any use out of their breathing gear, and Marsh had lost his rebreather entirely. Eight men, spread out in a loose line, alone on the open sea.

Then Trapford's voice cut across the night. "Periscope! By God, it's the periscope! Over here!"

They angled toward him, and Tangretti spotted the *Sea Lion*'s scope beckoning like a beacon on a friendly shore. Matthews produced their safety line and they linked together, but it was clear that the sub wasn't moving. Soon they had lashed themselves to the periscope mast, ready for pickup.

But there was still a problem.

Five of Tangretti's men couldn't count on their rebreathers any longer; Marsh didn't have one at all. But diving down to the escape trunk and locking through would take time—four minutes just to flush out the water that was in the airlock at the start of any cycle. There was no way they could hope to get those men down, through the lock, and into the sub if the men were reduced to holding their breaths . . . but would Captain Erskine surface in hostile waters?

Tangretti unhooked the line from its fastening at his belt, and signaled for Matthews and Radioman Second Class Zettel, the other two men who had reported they could still use their rebreathers, to do the same. "We're going down," he told the other five. "Stick with it, and we'll let them know the score."

CPO Simon Farnum looked at him with a sour expression. "Don't you forget about us, Skipper," he said dourly.

"Hey, c'mon, Pete," Tangretti said with a grin. "Would I abandon my rock in a place like this?" Matthews, Trapford, and Farnum all laughed, while the UDT men looked puzzled. They hadn't been there the day the SEALs had first mustered, when Tangretti had picked out Farnum as the outfit's senior petty officer and intoned formally, "Simon, thou art to be called Peter, for upon this rock I shall build my SEALs."

"This is one tired rock, Skipper," Farnum told him with a weary grin. "Don't keep us bobbing out here too long."

The three men dived, following the wire down to the escape trunk. Tangretti entered first, spitting out his mouthpiece and gulping air from the bubble trapped at the top of the chamber. Then he grabbed the intercom microphone and pressed the switch.

"Captain," he said. "This is Tangretti. We're back. We have the information, but I've got five people who can't make it in through this lock. You'll have to surface to pick them up. The ball's in your court. You can drown us, or you can see if you can find another way to get these guys in."

The captain's voice came back a few seconds later, sounding distracted. *"All right, Tangretti, you and whoever else can get in through the escape trunk, do it. We'll see what we can do about the others."*

A moment later a different voice chimed in. *"Conn, Sonar. Those Komars are angling this way, sir. They'll be on top of us in a few minutes . . ."*

Tangretti cursed under his breath.

USS *Sea Lion*
Off San Mariel
0520 hours

George Marsh heard the roar of engines before he saw
anything, but it didn't take long to catch sight of the moving lights in the distance. In the brightening predawn light
Marsh could distinguish the menacing shapes of two
Komar patrol boats to the southwest, still a long way off
but plainly heading in the direction of the sub. Had they
detected the *Sea Lion*, or was it just bad luck that a patrol
sweep was passing through this stretch of Cuba's territorial
waters at this particular moment?

In either event, those boats spelled trouble. Even if they
weren't out hunting the American sub, their crews would
have to be blind not to spot the American swimmers clus-
tered around the periscope, given the rapidly improving
light of the tropic dawn. And a few bursts of machine-gun
fire would take out the frogmen before they could do a
damned thing about it.

He swallowed. *Sea Lion* could still evade if she moved
quickly, but she'd have to cut her losses and strand the
swimmers. Tangretti and the others had enough information to give a report on beach conditions, so that meant the
rest of the party was expendable.

No doubt *Sea Lion*'s captain had the word on the
approaching boats from his sonar operator, and had already
come to the same conclusion, but just to be sure Marsh
slipped his diving knife from his sheath and began rapping
against the periscope mast, spelling out a warning in
Morse code.

They'd done their best, and almost made it out. But the
mission objective had to come first.

Control Room, USS *Sea Lion*
Off San Mariel
0520 hours

"No, sir, my men will not enter until you've secured the rest of the party."

Arthur Gunn didn't know whether to cheer or throw up his hands in despair as he heard Tangretti's rasping voice over the intercom. He couldn't help but admire the man's determination to see all his men safely aboard, but Gunn also knew the mission information had to come first.

Yet there was Tangretti, steadfastly refusing to lock through until Erskine brought all the swimmers in. And all the while a pair of Komars bore down on the sub.

"Damn the man," Lieutenant Commander Hall muttered. "I'd heard he was a loose cannon, but this is ridiculous . . ."

At that moment a staccato rattle echoed through the hull.

"That's one of the guys topside," someone said. "Code . . ."

T-W-O K-O-M-A-R-S I-N S-I-G-H-T, Gunn translated the tapping code. G-E-T C-L-E-A-R.

"Goddamn it, now *those* bastards are giving me orders," Erskine exclaimed angrily. He whirled on the dive control station. "Blow ballast on tanks one and four," he ordered sharply. "Mr. Hall, get some men into the conning tower on the double. Let's get our heroes on board, for Christ's sake. Maybe I'll let them run the boat until we get back to Florida!"

USS *Sea Lion*
Off San Mariel
0520 hours

Marsh continued tapping out his message until the water suddenly surged beneath him. "Hang on, people!" he shouted as metal broke free from the water.

Sea Lion hadn't completely surfaced. Only a portion of her conning tower was out of the water, and the five swimmers were hard-pressed to hang on to the small platform at the top of the sail.

Almost before they could react the hatch clanged open, and the sub's Exec was waving urgently. "Come on! Move it! Move it!"

The SEALs hastened to the open hatch and hurried down the ladder, with Marsh bringing up the rear. When he was through, the Exec slammed the hatch shut behind them, bellowing "Hatch secured!" before he had even finished dogging it shut.

Marsh heard shouted orders, felt the sub moving as it began taking on ballast and diving steeply under full power from the engines, but the sound that carried most clearly was from the intercom.

"If you don't surface this goddamned boat right now," Steve Tangretti's voice boomed like a mad prophet preaching to the faithful, *"someone is going to get killed."*

"All right, Lieutenant, all right," the captain's voice responded, sounding more tired than the SEAL. *"Your people are in. Now why don't you join us? Unless you want to wait for the next bus heading for home?"*

Chapter 2

Situation Room, The White House
Washington, DC
1414 hours

Steve Tangretti had heard of the Situation Room, but he'd never seen it before. Buried under the basement of the White House, the Situation Room housed a complete planning and command/control center where the president could take command in time of crisis. The room was supposed to be safe even in the event of a nuclear strike on Washington, a claim Tangretti, for one, fervently hoped would never be put to the test.

At that moment a cluster of political and military leaders were gathered around a conference table, studying slides made from aerial recon photographs taken by U-2 spy planes over Cuba. Most of the people at the table were members of the Executive Committee appointed by the president to oversee management of the crisis; the rest were military men, like Tangretti, assembled to give EXCOMM the benefit of their special expertise in various areas. He wondered if any of the others felt as tired and disoriented as he was. Forty-eight hours ago he'd been in

Puerto Rico, fresh off the *Sea Lion* with the rest of the recon unit. They'd flown home to Virginia, where an intensive debriefing session had kept them up most of Thursday night. Then a phone call in the wee hours of Saturday morning had summoned him to the White House to be available in case EXCOMM wanted his firsthand knowledge of the San Mariel mission.

He was one of the most junior officers in the room, relegated to a corner of the room with the aides and attachés who had accompanied the big guns sitting at that table. From where he sat, Tangretti could look directly across at a fresh-faced young Air Force captain whose rank was equivalent to his own, seated not far away from President John F. Kennedy and holding a briefcase in his lap. That briefcase was an ominous reminder of why all these men were really here. It was the notorious "football," which contained the launch codes the president would need to authorize a nuclear strike.

The Cold War had never been closer to the boiling point than it was today.

Kennedy coughed as he looked across the table at the Air Force officer who had just concluded his part of the briefing. The president had come home early from a campaign trip in the Midwest on the grounds he was suffering from an "upper respiratory infection" and had to consult with his doctor, and he really did have a mild cold that made his voice husky. But the real reason he'd called off the trip was to deal with the growing crisis in Cuba, a threat very few men outside the Situation Room were aware of.

"So what you're telling me, Colonel," he said in his sharp Massachusetts twang, "is that there is no doubt that these are the genuine article. Is that correct?"

"Yes, Mr. President," the officer replied.

"The Soviets continue to deny that they have missiles on the island," a State Department bureaucrat put in.

"Then the Russkie bastards are lying," someone else said harshly. "You can see from the photos that those emplacements are nearly finished. And once those missiles are fully operational . . ."

"The entire United States is in danger." The voice was almost identical to the president's, with the same accent and inflection, but it belonged to his brother Bobby. The Attorney General wouldn't usually be involved in a national security issue like this one, but Tangretti could see that JFK was giving him the same attention as he had the military men who had already spoken up.

"Exactly." That was the Chairman of the Joint Chiefs of Staff, General Maxwell Taylor. "I cannot emphasize too much, Mr. President, the need to take firm action now, before these missiles are fully installed on the island. If we wait very much longer, we run the risk of being presented with *a fait accompli,* and Khrushchev can just sit back and laugh at us if we try to force him to remove the threat."

"I understand the urgency, General," President Kennedy told him gruffly. "But I still do not like being so limited in available responses."

Secretary of Defense McNamara spoke up. "There just aren't that many options open to us, sir," he said. "Surgical air strikes could take out those positions, but they'd cause terrible collateral damage among civilians as well as putting our pilots at risk."

"I take it we've ruled out invasion as a choice?" The gruff question came from CIA Director John McCone.

"I'll answer that one." That was Captain Joseph Galloway. He wasn't part of EXCOMM, but was present as the Pentagon's resident expert on Naval Special Operations. Tangretti had known him since World War II days, and still remembered how the two of them had seen President Kennedy in that fateful meeting in the Oval Office less than a year ago that had led to the order authorizing the formation of the SEALs. "Our beach reconnaissance at San Mariel indicated that conditions there were unsuitable for mounting an amphibious landing, sir. If we had more time, we could no doubt locate some place suitable, but frankly I don't think we can afford that time. And each recon effort increases the risk of an incident that could heat things up even more than they already are. I think we have to rule out a large-scale military action."

"Thank God for that," Secretary of State Rusk said. "Good Lord, if we sent troops into Cuba we'd be committing suicide. The UN would be all over us, and we'd be giving Khrushchev just the leverage he'd love to have to turn world opinion against us."

"Not to mention the political effects of losing American soldiers." The drawled comment came from the vice president, Lyndon Johnson, who was the nominal chairman of EXCOMM. His mournful features looked even longer and sadder than usual. "If the casualties from the air strikes wouldn't be acceptable, how much worse would it be to lose men on the ground?"

"If things had worked out better last year, we wouldn't need to worry about this mess now," McCone said. He didn't need to mention the Bay of Pigs landing by name to make his point. JFK stirred as if prodded, but didn't answer the comment directly.

"I was never comfortable with the invasion option anyway," the president said quietly. "Or the air strikes, for that matter. Any aggressive action we take runs the risk of escalating the situation out of control. The Soviets are committed to the defense of Cuba, just as we've been to protecting West Berlin. If we push too hard, the whole thing could blow up in our face."

"Mr. President, there's another way to deal with these missiles that wouldn't run any of the risks of these other military options." The words had come out before Tangretti was even aware he was speaking aloud, and there was a sudden silence in the conference room. He could feel hostile eyes on him as the political and military bigwigs glared their displeasure at having a mere lieutenant interrupt their Olympian proceedings.

Kennedy, however, seemed less shocked than the others. "I remember you," he said. "We met last year . . . Lieutenant, ah, Tangretti, isn't it? The man who organized the first SEAL Team."

"Er, yes, Mr. President." He suddenly felt tongue-tied with the spotlight focused on him.

The president turned to his brother. "Mr. Tangretti here is a man who speaks his mind, Bobby. The first thing he said to me when we met was to tell me that he hadn't voted for me." As the Attorney General chuckled, JFK turned back to Tangretti. "I'd be glad to hear your option, Lieutenant. Don't let all this intimidate you. I need all the advice I can get, especially from men who aren't afraid to speak the truth."

"Yes, Mr. President," Tangretti managed. "Er, thank you, sir." He cleared his throat uncertainly, then took the plunge. "I was thinking, sir, that this situation is exactly what you created the SEALs for in the first place. You might remember what we said when you issued the authorization, about how the face of war was changing and there was a new role for Special Operations. Small, elite units that can surgically remove a target without involving large numbers of men or the threat of major escalation."

"A raid of some kind?" Kennedy asked.

"Exactly," Tangretti said. He leaned forward in his seat, growing more excited and almost forgetting just whom he was speaking to. "Those beaches are no good for a major amphibious op. I know, I was one of the guys who did the survey. But SEALs could infiltrate the different target areas, plant explosives, and knock those missile launchers out. We'd be off the island and on the way home before the Cubans even knew we were there. Special Operations forces would be a hell—would be a lot better than air strikes at making sure the damage was confined to the targets in question. A few SEALs would be less likely to take casualties than a massive Marine landing, or even a squadron of bombers. And if we go in without identification of any kind, maybe with foreign equipment, you'd be able to deny that we were American commandos at all." He shot a look at Director McCone. "They might think we were CIA, but we could equally well be Cuban freedom fighters staging another Bay of Pigs–type of op."

There was a long moment of silence. Then General Taylor spoke up. "Nonsense! I'm sorry, Mr. President, that this man is just wasting our time here. The whole idea is thoroughly ridiculous."

"Why is that, General?" the president asked. Kennedy looked at the JCS Chairman with a tired expression, as if wrestling with this problem had simply become more than he could handle. Tangretti thought he could see conflicting emotions at war behind those boyish features. The president was well-known to be interested in the idea of elite Special Operations units. Perhaps he was hoping Tangretti's notion offered him a way out of a no-win situation. But no chief executive could afford to ignore the military advice of his top generals.

"Special Operations units have a place in modern warfare, Mr. President," Taylor said sternly. "They are useful for reconnaissance, for creating diversions, for supporting larger military ops. But no one would seriously consider pitting a few SEALs or Green Berets against the entire island of Cuba! The forces guarding these missile sites would be impossible to penetrate without a large-scale ground-combat element, and the risk of having the entire mission thrown over by a single misstep is simply too great."

Kennedy frowned for a moment, then looked at Galloway. "What do you think, Captain?"

"Mr. President, I think General Taylor may not realize just how good some of our Special Operations forces are," Galloway said slowly. "They have a tremendous potential." He paused. "On the other hand . . . I'm not sure we have the logistics capability to organize a raid along the lines Lieutenant Tangretti proposes. It might not take as long to put together as a full-scale invasion, but it would require time to train and equip the men, assemble the ships and planes needed for insertion, and draw up a detailed plan of action. And from what has already been said, we might not have the time. SEALs, especially, are still a new breed, and a major operation of this kind might still be outside their capabilities . . . not for the reasons the general has given, but because of lack of experience and logistics. I would hope that we could push to develop the ability to act rapidly in a crisis, but I can't say for sure that we're close enough to that point to stake the outcome of this situation on an intervention by SpecOps units." Galloway shot a sympathetic look toward Tangretti.

"I see." The president paused, his eyes also seeking out Tangretti. "I admire your initiative, Lieutenant," he said at last. "If not your discretion. But I do not think we can try your option this time around. Nonetheless, it was a good idea, and I hope that one day we can see your SEALs playing a major role in dealing with national security crises like this one. I'll have my eye on your units, Lieutenant, believe me."

"Thank you, Mr. President," Tangretti said quietly. In another moment he was a nonentity again, forgotten by everyone at the table.

"So where does this leave us?" Bobby Kennedy asked.

It was Dean Rusk who replied. "There's still the idea of blockade . . ."

Old Executive Office Building Parking Lot
Washington, DC
1504 hours

"Wait up, Lieutenant!" Captain Joseph Galloway called as he started across the parking area toward Steve Tangretti. Galloway walked briskly, his coat flapping in time to the gusts of wind that were spreading autumn leaves over the pristine White House lawn. There was a bite in the air, a hint of the winter to come.

Tangretti paused beside his battered blue Oldsmobile and looked up. "Sir?"

Galloway was puffing by the time he joined Tangretti. They were two old warhorses, products of the war with Germany and Japan, but where Tangretti had spent most of his life on active duty with the Teams—UDT and then SEALs—Joe Galloway had been an armchair warrior for most of his career. The captain had been an early advocate of combat demolitions, and somehow ended up working with the near-legendary father of the Teams, Paul Coffer, pushing paper from a tiny Pentagon office while men like Tangretti had been putting his ideas into practice on the beaches of places like Normandy and Iwo Jima. Except for a brief stint commanding a destroyer after Korea, Galloway had proven too valuable a staff officer to escape from the confines of the Navy's bureaucracy, and it showed now in his waistline and his stamina. But though he and Tangretti were poles apart in most things, the two of them had been fighting for the same ideas ever since those first days when naval combat demolitions had been little more than a vague concept embraced by only a handful of farsighted men.

"Sorry I couldn't back you up any better than I did in there, Lieutenant," Galloway said. "But you know that whatever I said, the brass wasn't about to go along with a SpecOps solution."

"Yeah." Tangretti's tone was sour. "I guess some things never change."

"The hell of it is, Steve, that you're right. This really is exactly the sort of op the SEALs were made to carry out. But we're just not ready to mount anything elaborate yet. Recon missions like the one you guys pulled the other day, that's one thing. But until we get the support network put together, and until we get some solid experience under our belts, we'd be crazy to try to pull off something big. Not when one wrong move could lead to missiles flying on both sides."

Tangretti sighed. "I guess you're right, Captain," he said reluctantly. "But I don't know how we're ever going to *get* the experience, or the support network, the way things are going. You're certainly right about the brass. Some of those dinosaurs wouldn't know what a SEAL was for if all of us came with easy-to-read instruction manuals."

"You sound pretty glum. Problems?"

"Just the usual," Tangretti told him. "I can't get anybody to see that we need to stock a full range of equipment so we can handle different kinds of assignments. The damned breathing units we used in Cuba were garbage even after the modifications we did on them. And I've got some chicken-shit penny-pincher on my back who says he'll file charges against me for going outside normal purchasing channels if he finds any more 'irregularities' in the way I've set the Team up."

"I've been telling you that playing the scrounger isn't so easy when you're the CO, Steve," Galloway said slowly. "There are reasons for the purchasing regs, you know . . ."

"Damn it, Captain, I can't get what we need through

channels! There's always some blockhead telling me all the reasons the SEALs don't need the gear I'm asking for. Somebody else always has the priority . . . or they don't 'see the need' for the equipment to go to SEALs. And then they load us down with safety requirements and try to dump gear on us *they* think we can use." Tangretti shook his head. "You remember the antigas suits at Normandy?"

Galloway nodded. During the D Day invasion, the new Naval Combat Demolitions Units were assigned the task of clearing beach obstacles on Omaha and Utah, but someone high up on the SHAEF planning staff had gotten a bee in his bonnet on the subject of possible German chemical weapons being deployed against the Allies. So the NCDU men had been ordered to hit the beach wearing cumbersome suits to protect them from mustard gas. The result had nearly been disastrous. There weren't any German chemical weapons on those beaches at Normandy . . . but the bulky suits had made swimming almost impossible, reduced visibility and freedom of movement, and left the NCDU men easy targets for German sniper fire. A few of them had taken the initiative and stripped off the suits as soon as they could, and according to stories Galloway had heard, Tangretti had been one of the first to do so.

"I gotta tell you, Captain," Tangretti went on, "things haven't changed much in twenty years. The Navy *still* doesn't know what to do with us, whether we're called NCDU, or UDT, or SEALs, or whatever. There's no place in their carefully planned little world for an outfit that can really get things done. And I'm starting to think there just isn't any way to change it."

"Change comes slow in an organization as big as the Navy, Steve," Galloway said softly. "It took the brass years to figure out that aircraft carriers were a good idea, you know?"

"That's just my point," Tangretti said. "It took a disaster to make the battleship admirals see what carriers could do. What are we going to need to get the SEALs accepted? God knows I'll never have any impact even if I explain what we're doing to every damned ring-knocker in the fleet."

"You've got it backwards, Steve," Galloway replied. "Look, at the forefront of any innovation there are always a few visionaries who know what's going to be needed and how to get there. Think of Billy Mitchell back in the twenties. Nobody bought his vision then, but he pushed as hard as he could, and eventually he got a few others to see what he saw in the whole notion of airpower. And when the time was right for carrier aviation, the seeds he'd sown were ready to sprout. Pearl Harbor was a drastic way of showing what carriers could do, and it forced us to build the Pacific Fleet around the carriers that survived instead of the battleships we'd lost. But the point was that the visionaries like Mitchell had already laid the groundwork. When the time is right, the SEALs will be there, and it'll be largely because you hung in there and made things happen . . . just like Paul Coffer and I pushed through the first Teams back in the forties when nobody else thought we needed them. Hell, MacArthur never did understand what the UDTs were for, back in the war. He used them as a bunch of glorified Seabees."

Tangretti was slow to answer. "Well, maybe," he said at last, grudgingly. "But however you pretty it up, I'm running into a brick wall. The paper-pushers are sitting on everything I try to do through channels, and they're threatening me with a stint in Leavenworth for all the 'violations' they're turning up in this investigation. If I thought I could do a damn bit of good, I might be able to put up with some of this shit, but as it is, well . . . Team Two's up and running now. They don't need me now that they're organized. I'm only Acting CO until Lieutenant Colquhoun gets back from

Fort Bragg; then I'm just an aging Exec. And if anything, all the flak I draw is making things worse for the rest of them. Screech Manners is liable to end up in the cell next to mine, just because he's a damn good quartermaster and he's backed me up every time I've needed it. That's not fair to him or any of the other guys on the Team either."

"Are you asking to get out, Steve?" Galloway studied him through narrowed eyes. This wasn't the Steve Tangretti he knew. That SEAL had never backed down from a challenge in all the years Galloway had known him.

Tangretti shrugged. "Yes . . . No. I don't really know anymore. All I know is that I sure as hell want these damned floating accountants off my back, and out of everybody's hair down at Little Creek. Let them count rivets on the *Nautilus* or something. And I'm starting to think a change in scenery would do me some good, too."

"You're valuable where you are, Steve," Galloway said. "Hell, man, you've got Kennedy's eye on you! That's a pretty good thing for the Teams, you know."

"Yeah, and that plus a nickel might get me a cup of coffee," Tangretti replied. "I'm starting to wish I was one of the West Coast pukes, so you know how desperate I'm starting to feel. At least some of them are getting in on the ground floor of this mess over in Vietnam. These advisors they're sending over . . . at least they're doing *something* more than fighting off hordes of bureaucrats heavily armed with briefcases and pencils!"

Galloway couldn't keep from laughing at the SEAL's indignant tone. "Good God, Steve, you just got back from a recce into Cuba! How much more action do you want?"

"One night's swim. Big deal." Tangretti shook his head. "Maybe if I thought we'd get a shot at something more, I'd feel differently, but you heard those brass hats in there. Air strikes and blockades . . . there's no place for SEALs in the stuff they're planning. At least the guys from Team One

who are going over to Vietnam get to do more than just one
or two real ops in a year."

"Look, Steve, I know you're feeling frustrated," Galloway said, "but try to hang in there for a while. Even
though they aren't going to let your boys take care of those
missiles, this Cuban situation could still need SEALs
before everything's over and done with. Whether the president goes for air strikes or a blockade, things'll get a hell of
a lot worse before they get any better. We could still be
looking at a shooting war if either side makes a single mistake, and if that happens, SEALs and UDT will be in the
front lines. So right now your place is right down there in
Little Creek, making sure your boys are ready to move." He
paused. "After that . . . who knows? Let me see what I can
do about all these investigations, first. I have an idea we can
get them interested in something besides your, ah, unusual
supply methods. Beyond that, I'll have to think what's best
for the service. I don't want to lose you as part of Team
Two, frankly. You've been the driving force that got us this
far, and I think there's a lot more good you can do. But if I
see a better way to use you, I'll do what I can to get you a
new slot somewhere. God knows you've earned it."

"Thanks, Captain," Tangretti said. "I know I'm not
quite . . . the ideal officer. But I want to make a difference.
I owe it to all the guys who've gone before me, especially
old Snake Richardson."

"Yeah, I know what you mean," Galloway said. Even
though he'd never been part of the Teams, most of Galloway's career had been associated with UDT and SEALs
in one way or another, and like Tangretti he felt a bond to
all the men who had fought and died to make those units
work. After an awkward pause, Galloway changed the subject. "How's the family, Steve?" he asked. "Ronnie and the
kids handling this Cuba mess okay?"

A shadow passed across Tangretti's face, but he nodded.

"Pretty well, I guess. You know how wives worry. But Hank and Bill are both doing great. Bill's a straight-A student . . . just turned fifteen and he already knows a hell of a lot more than his old man. And Hank Junior's on the wrestling team and the swimming team at school. I'm betting he's going to be a UDT man like his father." Talking about his son and stepson, Tangretti became more animated. But Galloway sensed there was trouble at home and decided to back off. He knew Tangretti was a private person, the kind of man who didn't like to share his personal problems with anyone, no matter how long they'd known him. Outspoken to a fault in most areas, he just didn't talk about the things that meant the most to him.

"Glad they're doing so well," Galloway said. "Look, Steve, you hang in there. I think things'll work out all the way around. No promises, but I'll do what I can to see that we get some good use out of you."

"That's all I ask, Captain," Tangretti said gravely. "You know, ever since that day when Snake and I got called into your office to tell you about Kwajelein, I've felt like I had a stake in the Teams. Me, the orphan boy from the Eytic foster family, helping to make things better for the whole damned outfit. Having you helping me out has meant a lot to me over the years, Captain. If I never thanked you before, I want to now."

"We all do our part, Lieutenant," Galloway told him with a smile. "Anyway, I know you. You offered all those ideas and opinions over the years because that's what you do best—sound off. Just happened I thought some of what you had to say was worth looking into."

"Well, maybe," Tangretti said. "Hey, say hello to that knockout wife of yours for me, will you? And to the kids, too."

"I'll do that," Galloway told him. "I'm going to have to bring Paul down to Little Creek sometime and let him see some real, live frogmen. He never missed an episode of *Sea Hunt*, not since he was seven years old, and he's always talking about diving."

"Well, maybe someday we'll get him for the Teams," Tangretti said. "Can't have too many SEALs, you know." He gave Galloway a crisp salute and opened his car door. Galloway turned away and started across the lot, his mind already grappling with ways to make fresh use of Steve Tangretti's talents.

That was one man the Navy's fledgling Special Warfare service couldn't afford to lose.

Tangretti Residence
Virginia Beach, Virginia
1928 hours

Tangretti clambered out of the Olds, pausing to smooth his dress uniform and gather a briefcase from the passenger seat. As he straightened up, he heard the screen door clatter on the small, shaded porch.

"How did it go, Steve?" The clear voice held an edge that made Tangretti want to turn away, but instead he started toward his wife. She leaned against the railing of the front porch, her red dress fluttering in the passing breeze, watching Tangretti with an expression of guarded concern that made her eyes look troubled. "Is everything okay? What did they want, dragging you away so early?"

"Wasn't much of a trip, Ronnie," he said. "Just a visit to the White House and a meeting with a bunch of brass hats who didn't really want to hear anything out of a mere lieutenant. Another delightful day in the life of a junior officer!"

"The White House? You didn't say that's where you were going when you rolled out of here at the crack of dawn!" Veronica Tangretti looked surprised.

"Hush-hush stuff," he said quietly. "You know how the brass gets about secrets."

"Did you . . . did you get to meet JFK again? Or just some staffers?"

"The president was there," Tangretti told her. "He even remembered me, a little. But it wasn't much of a meeting, if you ask me. Too many people, too many opinions, and by the time it was over nothing much had been decided."

"So you still don't know if . . . you'll be sent somewhere?" Veronica's voice held an uncertain edge. She knew he couldn't discuss some aspects of his work. The SEALs weren't exactly a secret organization, but they were often given classified missions. Early on in his new job Tangretti had explained to her that he couldn't always tell her where he was going or what he was doing, not even after the fact, and she usually respected his silence. But his sudden "training mission" in the Caribbean and the abrupt call to Washington would have alerted a far less intelligent person than Veronica to the fact that something was going on, and any something that involved the SEALs was apt to be difficult, or dangerous, or both.

"I don't really know yet, Ronnie," he said, climbing the three worn steps to join her on the porch. "Odds are I'll be hanging around here for a while, but you never know. There's a chance we might need to deploy again . . . but nothing concrete." He paused, weighing how much he could say to calm her down without giving the seriousness of the situation in Cuba away. "A big chunk of what they told me in Washington was to the effect that my SEALs aren't ready to play in the big leagues, so I doubt I'll be needed again soon." Try as he might, he couldn't quite hide the bitterness that was still gnawing away within him. Even though he'd appreciated everything Galloway had said to him, he still knew deep down that the SEALs could have mounted an effective mission into Cuba, and it irked him to know he was likely to stay on the sidelines—unless something really bad, like a war, broke out because of a misstep in Washington or Moscow.

Some of the worry went out of her expression. "I hope you'll be staying put," she told him softly. "When you got pulled away with so little warning last week, I was afraid . . . well, you know, everybody's been talking that something's up. You know how the gossip is in a Navy town like Norfolk. Nobody seemed to know anything for certain, but there were enough rumors to cover just about any crisis you can think of. And I can't help worrying about where they might send you."

He stepped back and looked at her, his eyes drinking in the sight of her. At thirty-nine, she had kept the slight, slender figure of the WAC he'd first met in Britain before D Day, and her black hair was still as lustrous as ever. But seventeen years of marriage had changed her in other ways, he thought. He could still remember the time this small but perfectly formed young woman had swung a chair to take out a guy twice her size in the middle of a bar brawl in an English pub, but it was hard to think of Veronica Tangretti doing anything of the sort today.

She had fallen for his buddy Hank Richardson back then, and Tangretti had been glad to use some of his skill as a finagler and a scrounger to help them get married even as the final security measures went into effect before Operation Overlord. Veronica and Hank had managed a short weekend honeymoon together, no more, before orders confining military personnel to their respective bases had separated the couple. And then, just over a month later, the separation had become permanent after Hank Richardson had bought the farm trying to clear obstacles on the bloody beach designated Omaha.

Tangretti had brought back the news, though he'd been badly wounded himself and supposedly confined to a hospital bed. And when he'd visited her to tell how her husband died, he'd discovered she was pregnant with Richardson's child.

It had been a rough time for both of them. Tangretti had been shipped to the Pacific to join the UDTs operating against Japanese-held islands, and he'd gone through a bad spell of too much drinking, too many women, and a self-destructive urge to somehow make up for the fact that he'd been spared when his best friend had died. It had taken the support of other frogmen from his UDT to show him he still had something to live for, and somehow he'd turned himself around before the attack on Okinawa and the last days of the war. During the whole time Veronica had stayed in touch, and after the end of the war he'd visited her at her home in Milwaukee to see the son of his dead friend, christened Henry Steven Richardson in honor of the two demolitioneers who had been inseparable in life.

And on that trip Tangretti, on impulse, had asked her to marry him. To his utter amazement, she'd said yes, and the two were married just before Christmas of 1945.

Over the years since, they'd had their ups and downs. There had been so many good times, especially with the birth of their son Bill, and Tangretti knew that he'd been lucky to win this woman. But other times things had gotten rocky. He'd done his best to be a good father to young Hank, but complications had arisen almost immediately. The boy's grandfather was a rich and powerful man in upstate New York who had some strong ideas about how a Richardson should be raised. He had even demanded that the boy's name be changed, from Henry Steven to Henry Elliot—Hank Senior's name—in honor of a prominent family connection, and he'd flatly refused to hear of Tangretti adopting the boy outright. Steve Tangretti, never the sort to knuckle under to that kind of pressure, had been ready to do battle. But Veronica had urged him to give in for the sake of young Hank . . . and for the sizable trust fund in the boy's name, which would be his one day. Tangretti had finally allowed himself to be persuaded, but he had to admit that since then he'd never quite felt the same about his wife again. He still loved her, but more and more over the years he saw in her a streak of caution and a willingness to compromise that was at odds with his own spirit.

Since he'd formed SEAL Team Two earlier this year, that caution had been coming out more strongly than ever. Though she didn't know all the details of what the SEALs were about, she knew enough to know that Tangretti had taken on a high-risk job, one that could place him in danger at a moment's notice. That was something most Navy wives learned to live with, but Veronica Tangretti had good reasons for fretting. And since Tangretti's freewheeling style had brought down the unpleasant scrutiny of Navy auditors, her concerns had grown that much worse. She wanted him to talk about it, to let her into his world so she could help him meet his problems.

The problem was, Tangretti wasn't the kind of man who could open up the way she wanted him to. Part of his work was too highly classified to share, but even the day-to-day problems he had to deal with weren't suitable fodder for discussion, not to his way of thinking, at least. He sometimes wondered if he would have been more open with her if she'd been on his side in those dark days when he was fighting Richardson's parents.

He forced himself back to the present. "You don't need to worry about me, Ronnie," he said, trying to give her one of his winning smiles. "After all, you've got two teenagers underfoot who should worry you a lot more than I do . . ."

She returned his smile, and the effect transformed her weary expression, recalling the lovely girl he'd first met nearly two decades before. "Well, I'm not worrying about them tonight," she said. "Bill's working the whole weekend on his science fair project, and he's staying with Tim Teller so they can get it finished. And Hank's gone to a party with some of his friends and won't be back until midnight . . ."

"Which leaves us with some time alone?" he finished, not quite able to believe it.

"Which leaves us with some time alone, sailor," she confirmed, reaching out to take both his hands and draw him close. "Since you're not going to have to rush off and save the nation for a few hours, let's go inside and find something more exciting to keep us occupied . . ."

With arms around each other, they went into the house.

Chapter 3

Monday, 22 October 1962

U.S. Naval Amphibious Base
Little Creek, Virginia
1015 hours

A knock on his office door made Tangretti look up from the paperwork on his desk. "Come," he said, thrusting aside the requisition forms and guidelines with a feeling of relief. He had earned a reputation for scrounging over the years largely through an almost intuitive understanding of how the bureaucracy worked, but when all was said and done Steve Tangretti didn't like wasting his time studying the fine print and making sure all his carbon copies were filed properly.

The door opened to admit Arthur Gunn. "You wanted me to drop by, Gator?"

"Yeah. Come in, shut the door, and take a load off, Arty." He stood, extending a hand to his counterpart from Coronado. They had become good friends during the temporary deployment by Gunn's Team One platoon to the East Coast, despite vastly different ages, backgrounds, and outlooks. Like Tangretti, Gunn was listed as Executive Officer of his SEAL Team, though Tangretti had been the acting

CO of Team Two for most of its existence owing to Lieutenant John Colquhoun's extended round of advanced training with Rangers, Special Forces, and paratroops. But any
resemblance between the two stopped there. Gunn was
younger, and on the fast track for higher rank, while Tangretti doubted he'd ever rise above lieutenant. And Gunn
tended to be a by-the-book officer, more careful and cau-
tious than the freewheeling older man who'd once earned a
reputation as the best scrounger in the Pacific Fleet.

The West Coast SEAL pulled the door closed behind
him and dropped his slender frame into one of the chairs in
front of Tangretti's desk. "What's up?"

Tangretti didn't answer right away. If there was anything
he liked less than paperwork, it was officers who interfered
when there wasn't any need for it, but he was being pushed
into just that role.

He finally spoke up. "Look, Arty, I was over in the barracks they assigned to your West Coast pukes this morning
to check some inventory."

"And?" Gunn raised a curious eyebrow.

"I noticed a couple of your guys had some . . . art collec-
tions up on the wall."

The West Coast SEAL chuckled. "That all belongs to
Jackson," he said with a grin. "I swear that goof-off must
have been *the* charter subscriber to *Playboy*. You should
see what he has up back in Coronado. This is just his traveling collection."

Tangretti shifted uncomfortably. "Look, Arty . . . you
know I'm pretty easy on most shit. Hell, I remember bunk-
ing with a guy back in UDT-21 during the war who collected women's panties and liked showing them off. And I
like looking at some good T&A as much as the next guy—
long as Ronnie's not around, at least."

"I sense a 'but' coming up," Gunn said dryly.

Tangretti nodded. "*But* I'm having some problems with

the brass just now, Arty. This little shit Howell is giving me hell over requisitions and procedures, and on top of that the new base CO has a real down on frogmen in general and me in particular." He paused. "I think the guy must be married to some uptight little bitch right out of *Gone With the Wind*. Gets a case of the vapors every time she sees anything 'uncivilized.' Captain Barstow's afraid us rude, crude cavemen from the SEALs are going to offend the ladies somehow or other, and he's been coming down on me for everything from my boys using bad language to some chicken-shit order about always wearing T-shirts then we're out doing PTs."

Gunn was frowning. "Look, Gator, I'm sorry your CO is coming down on you, but you can't think his wife's going to be inspecting the barracks! That's crossing the line from harassed straight to paranoid."

Tangretti shook his head. "Doesn't matter. I've already been raked over the coals about untidy barracks a time or two just on general principles, and I know old Barstool's going to explode if he finds out SEALs are decorating their barracks with pornography. Or what he calls pornography, at least." He shrugged. "If it was up to me, Arty, I'd not only encourage Jackson's art collection, I'd try to see if we couldn't charge admission to the gallery. But I can't afford any more trouble than I've already got. Could you ask him to hide the stuff away for the rest of your stay?"

Gunn grinned. "Don't know what kind of a sex life he'll have without his pictures, but I'll talk to him."

"Thanks, Arty. I sure as hell hate to screw around with this kind of nonsense now. I mean, hell, we're sitting on the edge of a shooting war, and I have to worry about whether the barracks are being policed right!"

"Goes with the territory, old man," Gunn said. "Don't sweat it. I've already got a reputation for being a real stickler for the regs on most things. I've just always tried to give my guys a little personal space. But they'll handle it if I have to tighten up on 'em for a few days." He lowered his voice. "Odds are we'll ship out for Cuba again in a few days anyhow, so we'll be out from under your CO one way or another."

"You think it'll be a fight, then?" Tangretti asked him.

"Well, you're the one who got to jaw with the big boys in DC," Gunn said. "What do you think?"

"I wish to God I knew which way things were heading," he admitted. "From the sound of it, Kennedy's probably going to go with a blockade of Cuba to stop any more missiles or equipment from going in. I think the idea of an outright attack scares the politicians to death. Remember the Bay of Pigs mess?"

"Yeah." Gunn shook his head slowly. "Letting all those exiles get ashore and then pulling the plug on CIA air support . . . what a fiasco. Either we shouldn't have started anything, or we should have backed our allies to the hilt once they were committed."

"Point is, Arty, everybody's looking over his shoulders, thinking about the nukes dropping if anybody miscalculates just one move in the game. It throws everything into chaos, not knowing what might trigger the big one. If we invade Cuba, do the Russkies push the button? What about if we just hit 'em with a few air strikes? Where's the critical threshold beyond which we can't take action because it'll mean both hemispheres go up in flames?" Tangretti leaned forward, animated. "I don't think you're gonna win things in this day and age by committing armies and fleets the way we did back in the war. Everybody's just too damn nervous, and you can't always count on the other guy to back down."

"Yeah," Gunn said. "Just look at World War I. Everybody in Europe got sucked into that one because national pride and ambition wouldn't let them sit it out."

"That's why the SEALs are so important, Arty," Tangretti went on. "SEALs and Green Beanies and all the rest of the elite forces, we can do a hell of a lot more than conventional forces, if they'll just give us a chance. We can operate without being noticed, and we can train local forces to do jobs they aren't ordinarily able to do."

Gunn smiled. "You're preaching to the converted, Gator," he said. "I agree with you. But unfortunately the Pentagon and the politicians don't know what to do with us yet. Give them time. They'll figure it out."

"Well, up in Washington they're still talking about handling Cuba with conventional forces. Air strike or blockade . . . and God help us all if somebody on one side or the other screws up. Because then it'll be a shooting war, and you can bet those sons of bitches at the five-sided loony bin will try to use us the way they did the UDTs back in the war. Unless we can start carving a niche for ourselves that nobody else can fill, you can bet your last dollar they'll want us to keep right on doing beach recon and demolitions work, and never figure out just how much more we're capable of."

The SEAL from Team One shrugged. "Yeah, maybe. But I keep remembering what you told me about your first meeting with Kennedy. Maybe he doesn't know that much about military matters . . . but he's open to new ideas. With him in charge, it's just possible that we'll have a chance to get the SEALs settled into that niche you were talking about. Because once people do see what we can do, they'll never forget it."

There was a knock on the office door, and Signalman Second Class William Brown stuck his head in. "Boss? I know you didn't want to be disturbed, but I don't know how to handle this one." The SEAL did extra duty as an unofficial aide and secretary to Tangretti. Usually he could field just about any problem that came across his desk, but today he was looking harassed.

"What is it, Buster?" Tangretti asked.

Brown came in with a bulging folder under one arm. "Boss, some of the guys got hold of a stack of request chits this morning, and this is what came out of it." He set the folder down on the desk in front of Tangretti and opened it up.

Tangretti studied the form for a moment. It was all very official and formal, a request from GM/2 Trapford for permission "to go out and get drunk." Laughing, Tangretti passed the chit across to Gunn. "One thing you gotta say about Trap, he doesn't beat around the bush."

Gunn smiled. "Original, to say the least."

"It gets worse, Boss," Brown said. He pointed to the next paper, this one submitted by Quartermaster's Mate Second Class James Horner. It asked for permission to "go out and get drunk with Trap."

The next sheet in the stack asked that Electrician's Mate Second Class Lou Boyd be granted permission "to get drunk with Trap and Jim." And the others were the same, each adding new names to the list, but all with the same basic goal.

"This is starting to be annoying," Tangretti commented at last. "The whole damned unit wants to go out and get drunk together."

"It's a good joke," Gunn said. "Too bad you can't authorize any of it."

"The hell I can't," Tangretti said softly.

"You're not serious?" Gunn looked shocked. "Cuba's about to boil over, and you're seriously thinking of letting your outfit go out bar-hopping?"

"Cuba's been at the top of our list of problems since we got this bunch of misfits together last winter," Tangretti said. "You West Coast pukes haven't been involved that long, but we've been training for Cuba since day one. Drills. Alerts. Practice missions. We've had special gear packed up and ready to go in case we got a call to go in since I was able to get hold of all the shit in the first place." He paused. "Hell, my guys have been wound so tight it's a wonder they haven't all gone nuts. This shit with the missiles just makes it that much worse."

"Yeah, sure, but—"

"Look, it's a cinch we're not going in tonight, and not likely tomorrow, either," Tangretti said. "JFK hasn't even announced a plan yet, and you can be sure Joe Galloway would've been on the horn by now if they were thinking of another recon run anytime soon. I figure this is the calm before the storm, Arty. If I let these guys go into town tonight and blow off some steam, they'll be that much better when the fur starts to fly. If it ever does. I'm starting to wonder if we're *ever* going to settle things with Uncle Fidel." He leaned back in his chair. "Why don't you pass the word to your guys that they should get a little R&R too? I can slip Jackson the address of a good whorehouse. Might take the sting out of losing his art collection."

"No, thanks, Gator," Gunn said coldly. "You might think it's a good idea, but I don't. My men stay in barracks tonight. I'm surprised you can even think of such a thing. Just a few minutes ago you were sounding off about how everybody has it in for you, and now you're talking about authorizing something that'll land you right in the middle of a whole world of trouble."

Tangretti shook his head. "Hell, no, I'm not going to get in trouble over this." He grinned. "I'll make sure somebody higher up the ladder signs off on the whole idea."

"Come on! You don't actually expect anybody else to approve these chits, do you?" Gunn looked incredulous.

"Fifty bucks says I manage it, Arty," Tangretti told him with a grin. "You a gambling man?"

"Do I look like a sucker?" the West Coaster demanded.

"Face it, Gator, there's nobody left in the Navy who hasn't been warned about your little tricks."

"Well, then, tell you what. If I get Commander Hogan to approve liberty for my guys, you owe me a case of scotch. Deliver it whenever you feel like, Arty."

"*If* the commander approves . . . okay, Gator, that bet I'll go along with."

Tangretti gave him a wicked grin. "Just make sure it's Johnnie Walker, Arty."

The Blackbird
Little Creek, Virginia
1945 hours

"So then Hogan says, 'Okay, Lieutenant, you've got 'til 0800 tomorrow. Just make sure that bunch of animals of yours show up ready to work. Anybody turns up too hungover to do the job, I'll have them on report so fast their heads will spin . . . and you know what that's like for a guy with a hangover!' "

The SEALs gathered around the oversize table roared with laughter, and Quartermaster's Mate Second Class James Horner joined in the chorus that greeted Lieutenant Tangretti's description of his meeting with the CO of Underwater Demolition Unit Two, the Special Warfare organization that served as parent to SEAL Team Two and UDT-21 and -22. What had started as a running joke in the outfit that morning had turned in to a real party, with most of the East Coast SEALs coming together at one of their regular hangouts, the Blackbird Bar on Shore Drive.

"Aren't any of the West Coast pukes coming out, Boss?" Jason Trapford, who had instigated the whole thing, asked. He had to shout to make himself heard over the Patsy Cline number playing on the jukebox. The Team had commandeered four big tables and put them together at one end of the smoky barroom, making for a noisy throng.

"Nah," Tangretti said, taking a long pull at his beer. "I'm afraid Mr. Gunn doesn't quite approve of us rowdy East Coasters."

Somebody laughed. "Always knew those West Coast pukes were a bunch of pantywaists."

Tangretti's reply cut through the noise and instantly dominated the entire SEAL gathering. "None of that, gang. I don't care where they come from, they're SEALs. Remember that! They all went through Hell Week, and they all got tapped for the new Teams, just like you lot. If Arty Gunn wants to play it by the book, that's his business."

"Er . . . sure, Boss." There was a moment of quiet. Everybody knew just how far they could push things with Steve Tangretti.

The lieutenant went on, his voice just loud enough to carry, but commanding more authority than an admiral bellowing orders. "And another thing. I agreed to this little excursion because I figured we could all use a break. But that doesn't mean I approve of any of you getting so shit-faced you can't do your jobs. If we were to get the call to move out tomorrow at dawn for Cuba, then by God I'd expect every last one of you to bounce out of your racks looking alive and ready for action. I've told you this before. I'm the hardest drinker, the toughest barroom brawler, and the horniest damn fucker in the entire Team, and if I can stay clean and sober I damned well expect you bastards to do the same. So . . . everything in moderation tonight, okay? You can drink, screw, fight, or play pinochle, but just make sure you keep your heads on straight. Right?"

"Yeah, Boss," they responded dutifully. With any other officer, the words would have been meaningless, to keep the man happy while they all made plans to do exactly the opposite of what he asked. But the SEALs from Little

Creek had too much respect for Steve Tangretti just to pay lip service to him. They might argue with him from time to time, but once they agreed to do something, they'd die before they let him down.

"Hey, Boss, how come Buster ain't here?" That was CPO Farnum.

Tangretti laughed. "Well, now, that's a great little story," he began. "Seems our friend Signalman Brown figured the whole damned idea was trouble, so he had as little to do with those request chits as possible. Didn't even *think* about filling one out. But when I told him to let everybody know liberty was on, he got this big grin on his face and started talking about how good it would be to get out and have a few rounds." Tangretti paused, looking around the table with a grin on his face. "Well, hell, what could I do? I had to tell him that he couldn't come. He didn't fill out a chit? So he has the duty tonight!"

Next to Horner, Chief Bob Finnegan wasn't paying much attention to Tangretti's story. He nudged Horner in the ribs with an elbow and nodded toward the other side of the bar, his prominent nose like a bobbing pointer. "Hey, Jimmy, get a load of the black-shoe working out of his league."

Horner followed the nod. A fleet sailor was dancing with a good-looking woman whose dress would have cost a month's pay. "What do you think, Hawk?" he asked. "Hooker, or rich girl slumming?"

"Probably a hooker," Finnegan replied.

"Well, hooker or not, what do you want to bet I can charm her away from the kid, huh?"

"I don't know. Unless you flash some big bucks, I'd say she'd take the bird in the hand." Finnegan grinned. "If you'll pardon the expression."

"No way. I'll have her away from that kid in no time flat." Horner shook his head. "Hell, it's the least I can do to protect the poor guy, don't you think?"

"I've always admired your civic-mindedness, Jimmy," Hawk told him. "Tell you what, you score with her without paying, and I'll take your next two night watches. But if you don't, or if she charges for it . . ."

"Yeah, yeah, I know the routine," Horner said. The two of them frequently made bets of the same kind, and Horner usually ended up as Finnegan's personal manservant as a result. But he was a SEAL. He never gave up.

Horner stood and started across the room. His conscience gave him a twinge on the way as he thought about his wife and daughter at home. He loved Lucy and would never do anything to hurt her, but sometimes he cheated on her. None of the women he picked up ever amounted to more than a one-night stand, and they never threatened his abiding feelings for Lucy. More and more, though, Horner realized he was running risks with his marriage by giving in to lust as he did, and he wouldn't really have minded losing the bet with Finnegan. Nonetheless, the pervasive atmosphere within the SEALs was one that encouraged sexual exploits, and Horner felt compelled to be "one of the boys" even when things felt awkward or uncomfortable.

He thrust doubts from his mind as he stepped smoothly behind the sailor and tapped him on the shoulder. "Hey, buddy, how's about letting a frogman cut in, huh?" Like most veterans of the UDT and SEALs, he detested the label "frogmen" hung on them as far back as World War II, but it could be used to advantage from time to time. He'd first decided to join the UDT because of a movie called *The Frogmen,* and the television exploits of Lloyd Bridges as Mike Nelson on *Sea Hunt* had lent even more glamour to his calling. Horner wasn't the least bit hesitant about throwing around that glamour shamelessly when he thought it might be useful.

"Buzz off," the sailor said.

Horner stepped close, separating him from his partner by

sheer physical presence, and drilled a dangerous stare into the younger sailor's eye. "Listen, kid," he said quietly, pitching his voice so that the sailor was the only one who could hear him. "I've been trained in more kinds of fighting than you could ever count, especially with your shoes on. I know hand-to-hand, knives, explosives, rifle, pistol, submachine gun, and booby traps. You don't want to mess with me. Anyhow, didn't you ever hear that us UDT types are crazy? They run us through something called Hell Week to try to break our spirits, and they know that anyone who survives that is certainly crazy enough to play with explosives and swim in enemy waters. Now, I want a dance with the lady here, and you're going to let me have it. Either that, or I'll show you what they taught us about twenty-nine different ways to kill a man without a weapon."

For a moment the sailor stood his ground, but under Horner's icy stare he suddenly blanched and took a step back. "Hey, man, I don't want to start no trouble that'll bring in the SPs," he said loudly. "You want a dance, go ahead."

Horner smiled at him. "Wise choice, kid," he said. Then he turned to the woman as the jukebox switched to a sad Hank Williams song. "My friend here just remembered a previous engagement," he said, turning up the charm. "Would you allow me to fill in for him?"

She gave him an assessing look and smiled back at him. "Why not?" she said in a husky contralto. As she stepped into his arms, she went on, "Is it true? You're really a frogman?"

"Yeah, but if you give me a kiss in just the right place I turn into a handsome prince," Horner told her.

Tangretti Residence
Virginia Beach, Virginia
2003 hours

Veronica Tangretti almost dropped the plate in her hand when the phone rang loudly behind her. She set it down and reached for the handset, thinking it was probably Steve calling—hours after he should have been home—to tell her he'd be late again. Even when he wasn't off on mysterious deployments or errands to Washington it seemed as if he was never home on time these days. This new SEAL unit took all his time, and Veronica was beginning to think of it as even worse than a mistress who competed for her husband's attention. Another woman she could fight . . . but his obsession with the Navy's Special Operations capability was a passion she couldn't understand, much less overcome.

To her surprise, though, the voice on the other end of the line didn't belong to her husband. "Veronica? It's Linda." Linda Farnum was the wife of one of SEAL Team Two's senior petty officers. Though usually officer and enlisted families didn't mingle much, Steve had come up from the ranks, and most of the Tangrettis' social circle was made up of enlisted men and their families. "Is your TV on?"

"What? No . . ."

"Then you'd better switch it on. The president's about to make a speech . . . and the lead-in from the news anchor didn't sound too good." Linda paused. "I'll talk to you later." Before Veronica could respond the line went dead.

"Hank!" Veronica called, heading for the living room. "Put on the TV. Now."

"What channel, Mom?" Henry Elliot Richardson Junior rose from the floor, putting aside his homework.

"Doesn't matter . . . no. Wait, make it CBS." All three

networks would cover a presidential speech, of course, but she wanted to hear Walter Cronkite's coverage when it was over.

"What's going on, Mom?" Bill Tangretti, young Richardson's half brother, asked. He put down a book to look up at her as she perched nervously on a chair. She gave him a distracted smile, thinking how unlike the two boys were. Odds were Bill had finished his homework hours ago and was reading for the fun of it; a glance at the book's jacket confirmed what she'd suspected. It was Tolkein's *The Fellowship of the Ring,* heavy going for most fifteen-year-olds, but typical of her younger son's reading habits. Hank Jr., on the other hand, would rather mow the lawn than read.

But both boys had a lot in common, for all their differences. Like their love for the sea, and their respect and admiration for Steve Tangretti, who'd been a father to both of them.

"Be quiet and listen, dear. It's a presidential speech."

The president appeared somber as the television screen lit up to reveal his image. "Within the past week, unmistakable evidence has established the fact that a series of offensive missile sites is now in preparation on that imprisoned island," he said. Cuba . . . he had to be talking about Cuba. She could still remember the tense days surrounding the Bay of Pigs landing, and the rhetoric that had gone out over the airwaves then. "The purpose of these bases can be none other than to provide a nuclear strike capability against the Western Hemisphere.

"Upon receiving the first preliminary hard information of this nature last Tuesday morning at 9 A.M., I directed that our surveillance be stepped up. And having now confirmed and completed our evaluation of the evidence and our decision on a course of action, this government feels obliged to report this new crisis to you in fullest detail."

So that had been the SEAL "training mission" that had called Steve away the week before. Veronica was sure of it. Some of the rumors floating around the base at Little Creek had hinted of a recon mission of some sort.

As Kennedy continued, Bill caught her eye. "D'you think Dad'll be invading Cuba?" he asked.

Hank answered him before Veronica could respond. "Come on, Tadpole, you know better than that. It's the Marines who mount the invasion. Dad'll be leading the frogmen in to clear the way for them, but once the beaches are secured, the UDT and the SEALs are out of the fighting."

She wondered just how true that might be. Tangretti was always pressing for a more active role for his SEALs. The old Underwater Demolitions Teams' responsibility ended at the high-tide mark, but the whole idea of SEa, Air, Land Teams was to allow naval commandos to exert pressure wherever they were needed.

A stray memory from years before caught her unexpectedly. A quiet little boardinghouse in Weymouth, England . . . the first twinges of morning sickness as she realized she was pregnant with Hank Junior . . . Tangretti, hardly able to walk after being wounded, sitting with his leg propped on a battered ottoman and describing the fighting on Omaha Beach that had led to her husband's death . . .

She'd barely had time to get to know Hank Richardson before he'd been killed on that damned French shore, and yet his death had left such an empty place inside her. Then she'd married Steve, and they'd been together for seventeen years now. How much worse would the void inside her be if he was killed on some godforsaken beach? She could still remember how much she'd worried when Steve was sent to Korea with MacArthur, but after the end of the

Korean War they'd settled down into such a quiet, happy routine. Of course there was always an element of danger for the men of the UDT, but nothing like the threat they faced in wartime.

But then this SEAL thing had come along. Tangretti had been a very vocal part of the movement to create a new kind of frogman, a commando who could do more than just survey beaches and clear obstacles. He'd fought hard to see the new unit created, and ended up in command of one of the two new Teams after he'd impressed Kennedy with his drive and commitment.

Now Kennedy was on her television screen, describing a terrible crisis that could mean war with Cuba or even the Soviet Union, and Veronica knew that if real fighting grew out of the crisis, Steve Tangretti would be in the forefront of the action.

She wasn't sure she could deal with the emotions those simple facts brought to the surface. Steve had already given better than twenty years to the Navy; most sailors were retired by the time they reached his age. Instead, he was just embarking on a whole new career, and knowing him she was afraid he'd stick with his SEALs as long as he could still keep up with them. People said the young sailors just inducted into the unit had trouble keeping up with Tangretti, and she could well believe it.

It was just so *unfair*. She didn't want to lose him, not the way she'd lost Hank. But he simply didn't seem to understand her fear. If anything, she knew, he was annoyed when she tried to talk him into slowing down.

On the screen, the president had gone on talking as she reflected, and Veronica forced her attention back to his words as she caught a change in the tone of his address.

"Acting, therefore, in the defense of our own security and of the entire Western Hemisphere, and under the authority entrusted to me by the Constitution as endorsed by the resolution of the Congress, I have directed that the following initial steps be taken immediately." Kennedy was saying. "First: To halt this offensive buildup, a strict quarantine on all offensive military equipment under shipment to Cuba is being initiated. All ships of any kind bound for Cuba from whatever nation or port will, if found to contain cargoes of offensive weapons, be turned back. This quarantine will be extended, if needed, to other types of cargo and carriers. We are not at this time, however, denying the necessities of life as the Soviets attempted to do in their Berlin blockade of 1948."

A blockade . . . not much scope for action for the SEALs in that. Was that what he'd meant when Steve had told her the brass in Washington didn't plan to use his SEALs?

The president continued. "Second: I have directed the continued and increased close surveillance of Cuba and its military buildup. The foreign ministers of the OAS, in their communiqué of October 6, rejected secrecy on such matters in this hemisphere. Should these offensive military preparations continue, thus increasing the threat to the hemisphere, further action will be justified. I have directed the Armed Forces to prepare for any eventualities; and I trust that in the interests of both the Cuban people and the Soviet technicians at the sites, the hazards to all concerned of continuing this threat will be recognized."

That could mean more missions like the one of the past week, she thought. And "further action" implied that Kennedy was willing to escalate if Khrushchev didn't back down. It was like some strange game of high-stakes poker, with the two players raising back and forth until someone folded . . . or until there was a final showdown. And God help the men who had to back those raises with their lives.

"Third": the president went on calmly, "it shall be the policy of this nation to regard any nuclear missile launched from Cuba against any nation in the Western Hemisphere as an attack by the Soviet Union on the United States, requiring a full retaliatory response upon the Soviet Union."

For years there had been a mounting hysteria about nuclear weapons, but it seemed somehow unreal to Veronica Tangretti. Her fears weren't fixed on a rain of fire from the sky, but on the possibility of her husband and her friends facing another conflict like World War II.

"Fourth: As a necessary military precaution, I have reinforced our base at Guantanamo, evacuated today the dependents of our personnel there, and ordered additional military units to be on a standby alert basis."

Standby alert. The president was getting ready for a real showdown, all right. She had little doubt that the SEALs were high on that list of "additional military units." Was that what had detained Steve tonight? Or something less dramatic, like the trouble he'd been having with Pentagon auditors who didn't approve of his equipment purchases? Either way, it was a sure bet she wouldn't be seeing much of him until this crisis was resolved, one way or another.

Veronica forced herself to pull back from contemplating just what form such a resolution might take. Inside she was a bundle of jangled nerves, but she couldn't let it show. Not in front of Hank and Bill.

She'd have to wait until she was alone in her room, with the lights out and the bed beside her empty, before she could release those hidden fears.

The Stonewall Arms Motel
Little Creek, Virginia
2119 hours

Her name was Carol and she was drunk. Jim Horner
didn't know much more about the woman than that even
after an hour of dancing and drinking at the bar. He was
fairly sure Finnegan's notion had been right and she was a
hooker, at least a part-time one, but after a few drinks she
seemed likely to give away free samples, and that suited
him just fine.

As a tactical operation his moves had been flawless so
far, but Horner's heart really wasn't in it by the time he'd
driven her car to the closest motel, signed for a room, and
gotten her to the door. For one thing, she giggled too much.

But having come this far, he wasn't about to back off.

"Ohh, what a nice place," she said, as he opened the
door and switched on the lights. "Real classy. Most guys
just head for any old dump." She giggled again. "You're a
special one, aren't you, sugar?"

"Nothing's too good for a lady," he answered gallantly.
That made her giggle again.

"Ain't ever been called a lady before, either, sugar," she
said. More giggles. "Except, maybe, y'know, a 'lady of the
evening.' "

He turned away to close the door, then back to her in
time to see her fumbling behind her neck to undo the fastening of her slinky black dress. It fell away, exposing her
to the waist. Her breasts, unhampered by a brassiere,
defied gravity, the nipples stiffening in the cool air.

"What do you think, sugar? Like what you see?" She
cupped her breasts in her hands, then did a bump-and-
grind that sent the dress slithering down her legs to land in
a pile at her feet. Her black underwear only served to
enhance her near nudity, and Horner forgot the giggle and

the voice of his conscience alike. He took off his shirt, and Carol sank to her knees in front of him and reached for the buttons on his fly. The touch of her hands heightened his excitement. "This is where I usually stop to talk about how much it costs for a poor girl like me to get along in the world . . ." She paused, looking up at him with a wicked little grin on her face. "But in your case, I'm still waiting to see if I can find that handsome prince."

As she pulled his pants and underwear down, releasing his erection and stroking it with one soft hand, Horner closed his eyes and savored her touch.

Later, they lay side by side in the queen-size bed, wrapped in the afterglow of their lovemaking. She might have picked up money selling her body, Horner thought as he propped his head on one arm and studied her nude body, but she was no jaded whore. Carol knew how to please a man, all right, but she performed with an enthusiasm that couldn't have been feigned. Most hookers didn't even bother to pretend after a while.

He reached out to touch one perfect nipple, hoping she might be stirred to a repeat performance, when a heavy fist shook the door. "Vice squad!" a harsh voice yelled, and the door flew open. In an instant the motel room seemed to be filled with cops. They surrounded the bed, uniforms and plainclothesmen flashing badges.

Carol screamed and drew the sheet up to cover her exposed breasts, which had the disadvantage of pulling it clear from Horner's side of the bed and leaving him exposed. He felt himself flushing a little, but ignored his own nudity.

"What the hell is this?" he demanded.

The oldest of the plainclothes detectives shrugged. "The night manager recognized your date as a repeat customer. Seems she's been here a few times before with . . . several different escorts."

Horner darted a look at Carol. So, drunk or not, she'd been playing games when she talked about how she didn't usually get to visit a "classy" place like this one. Maybe she was a little more involved in her chosen line of work than he'd thought. Perhaps she really had enjoyed the sex, but planned to slip away later with his wallet.

"Anyway, he called us. Management's been trying to discourage her kind of trade." The cop looked almost apologetic. "Guess you were just unlucky."

Horner gave him a grin. "Not necessarily," he said. "Personally, I think I got pretty lucky, all things considered." He reached for the clothes piled on a chair beside the bed. As he pulled on his underwear and pants, he found his wallet and passed it to the vice cop. "I imagine you'll be wanting my ID."

The detective found his military ID and liberty cards and studied them. "Ah, you're with the UDT."

The SEALs were still considered a secret, and neither of the Teams had separate ID cards. The men still used the same cards they'd been issued when they were part of the Underwater Demolition Teams. Nonetheless, the detective sounded impressed. Once again the magic of "frogmen" was working to Horner's advantage. He might yet manage to escape from the mess without further loss of dignity or other complications. . . .

"Yes, sir," Horner told him, using the same tone he would have used with a senior officer. He didn't want to do or say anything that might turn the man against him.

The detective started to hand his ID back to him, and Horner's spirits lifted. When police took military men in, they kept their papers.

From across the room one of the other plainclothesmen intervened. "Hang on, there, Webster," the second cop called. He was younger, but had the aura of the man in charge. "You remember the directive. The Chief wants to see a crackdown, so we give him a crackdown. I've already called the paddy wagon, and this little boy blue here is just going to have to take what's coming to him."

Horner finished dressing in silence, but inside he was cursing himself. After Tangretti's lecture at the bar, he should have been more careful. But, as usual, thinking with his hormones instead of his brain had gotten him in trouble.

It was going to be a long night.

Tuesday, 23 October 1982

Tangretti Residence
Virginia Beach, Virginia
0315 hours

Tangretti groaned and rolled over sluggishly as the phone jangled on his bedside table. It seemed as if he'd only just got to sleep after a late night at the bar and a blazing row with Veronica. Groggy, he picked up the receiver and tried to force himself to some kind of awareness. Could the shit have hit the fan so soon? He'd missed the president's speech, but surely things couldn't have snowballed so soon.

"Tangretti," he growled. If this was a drunken SEAL playing a practical joke, he vowed silently, he'd see to it the fellow looked back on Hell Week as the easiest time of his life.

"Uh, Boss? This is Horner . . ."

"You'd better have a damn good reason for calling me after 0300, Horner," Tangretti told him. "What's going on?"

"Boss . . . I'm in jail." Horner sounded as if he'd been handed a death sentence. "Cops raided the motel where I ended up with that bimbo I picked up . . ."

"Wonderful," Tangretti said, mustering every bit of sarcasm he could command. "Just wonderful. I suppose you want me to do something about it?"

"Er . . . they set my bail at $38.50, but I don't have that much on me," Horner said. "And I don't think it would be such a good idea to call Lucy to come in and bail me out." He paused. "I figured since I was already in the shithouse, I might as well go in style."

Despite himself Tangretti chuckled. "All right, Horner. All right. I'm on my way."

As he hung up, Veronica sat up in bed beside him. Her look was a mixture of the anger she'd already unleashed on him when he'd arrived late and smelling like a distillery, and apprehension. "What was that?" she demanded. "Was it . . . the base? Orders?"

"No, no, nothing like that," he said quickly. The Kennedy speech had put her on edge. No doubt it had contributed to her getting so mad; usually she didn't get upset if he went out drinking with the guys. "One of my boys got into trouble with the cops, is all. Needs me to go in and bail him out." He swung his legs out of bed. "God only knows how long it'll take to round him up. I might not be back tonight. Sorry . . . it's just something I have to do."

The look she gave him made Tangretti think it would be a good idea if he didn't make it home again.

Police Station
Little Creek, Virginia
0427 hours

Horner slumped on his bunk, wishing he was anyplace else. Even a beach survey under fire from angry Cubans would have been better than this, he thought bitterly. He'd let Tangretti down, he'd let the SEALs down, and he'd let his family down. And what for? A half-sloshed hooker who'd probably planned to rip him off as soon as he'd gone to sleep.

The night had, indeed, been a long one. It seemed to take forever to get through the processing in the police station. The cops had been friendly enough, but once he'd started through the procedure there was no way to get out of it. They'd given him the choice of being turned over to the Shore Patrol or facing the civil authorities, and Horner had rejected the idea of letting the SPs get in on it. Tangretti had enough problems with superiors scrutinizing the SEALs without having one of his men draw official attention from the brass. But the visit to night court where the judge had set his bail had ended his last hope that he might get out of the situation without attracting any further attention to himself. Without bail money, he was faced with the choice of calling Lucy—and then explaining how he'd ended up charged with soliciting a prostitute—or trying to find someone else who could bail him out. Tangretti had seemed like his best bet. He wouldn't be likely to spread it around the way Finnegan or some of the others might, and at that point Horner didn't want any stories circulating where they might get back to Lucy.

So he'd made the call to Tangretti, and then gone back to waiting. His cellmate, a drunk, had made bail soon after they'd brought him back from making the call, leaving him alone in the cramped, spartan jail cell with his bitter thoughts. It didn't help that he'd heard a radio replaying pieces of Kennedy's speech, reminding him that they might be called into action at any time. He'd really screwed up big-time.

Footsteps on the concrete and a familiar laugh made him sit up. Tangretti and one of the cops on duty came around the corner, talking and laughing like old buddies, and Horner felt a tiny feeling of relief. Surely Tangretti wouldn't be laughing like that if he was really angry at Horner?

The policeman opened the cell, and as Horner stepped out Tangretti met him and slapped him on the back. "Come on, son," he said gruffly. "Let's get the hell out of here before they take another look at us and decide we're really on the Most Wanted List."

Horner studied Tangretti for a long moment. The SEALs hadn't been together all that long—only ten months—and he'd only been in UDT for a couple of years before that. There was no real reason for Tangretti to know that much about Horner, or care. Right at that moment, though, Horner felt he'd do anything for the man, even swim the whole distance from Florida to Cuba to blow up Havana Harbor, if Tangretti told him to do it. "You're not pissed at me, Boss?" he asked. "I really screwed up."

Tangretti gave him a lopsided grin. "Son, if you ever get caught doing something I didn't do when you were still in diapers, then you'll be in a world of shit. Until then, don't worry about it, okay?"

"Okay, Boss," Horner agreed. Some of the tension knotting his stomach vanished.

"You got any clothes at your locker back at the Team?" Tangretti asked him.

"Uh, yeah, sure, Boss."

"Well, then, there ain't much sense going home, then. We'll head back to the base. Maybe stop and get something to eat on the way. That way you don't have to say anything to Lucy until you've had time to, uh, consider the account you want to give of the evening's activities. Right?"

"Right, Boss," Horner said.

They left the station and climbed into Tangretti's Olds. Heading down Oceanview Drive toward the Amphibious Base, Tangretti spotted an all-night diner and pulled in.

The two men walked in the front door and stopped dead in their tracks just inside as they heard the familiar song playing on the jukebox, "You're the Reason I Don't Sleep at Night."

The two SEALs broke down, laughing hard enough to draw stares from the waitress and a pair of truckers sipping coffee at the counter.

Chapter 4

U.S. Naval Amphibious Base
Little Creek, Virginia
1127 hours

There was relief in the air at Little Creek this morning, though it was also tinged with a sort of regret. As Tangretti stood before the assembled ranks of his SEALs out on the grinder between the Team's barracks and the headquarters building that housed UDU-2, he couldn't help but reflect on what a difference a week could make.

A week before, when he and Horner had arrived in the wee hours of the morning after the arrest incident, the world had been hovering on the brink of war with Cuba. Though he'd known the SEALs wouldn't be part of the plan to neutralize the Soviet missile sites, Tangretti had been sure they would be seeing action one way or another. He'd expected at the very least to be mounting more recon ops on the Cuban coast, searching for possible invasion beaches or eyeballing the missile sites to bring back better information than aerial-recon photos could reveal. And if things had escalated . . . well, there had been a plan floating around the Pentagon, one he'd only learned about after it was no longer under consideration, to use the SEALs as paratroopers to drop en masse behind an invasion beach and secure the area for Marines.

But although the United States reached DEFCON 2—the highest state of readiness short of actual war—just before the first of several Soviet ships had approached the blockade zone, the prospect of combat had quickly and unexpectedly receded. The Soviets had turned back rather than test the president's resolve, except for freighters that weren't carrying anything related to the missile sites and were passed through the blockade with minimal delay. Only one man had died on the American side, a U-2 pilot shot down on a recon pass, and that casualty hadn't been revealed outside the confines of the Intelligence and Special Warfare communities and the senior politicians they reported to.

By Sunday, the twenty-eighth, the Cuban Missile Crisis had died away, the final nail in its coffin Kennedy's second speech on the subject revealing the arrangements he and Khrushchev had agreed to regarding the dismantling of the missile site and the American declaration that Castro's Cuba was safe from American intervention.

All of which was to the good, as far as most people were concerned. The world could breathe a sigh of relief now that the two superpowers no longer had fingers poised over their nuclear triggers, ready for the devastating war everyone talked about but few could truly comprehend.

But for the SEALs, those feelings of relief were mingled with the knowledge that they wouldn't be seeing action. Even the covert recon ops into Cuba were likely to be curtailed, at least until the incident had faded in everyone's mind. The end of the missile crisis also meant a return to business as usual for the UDT and the SEALs. Gunn's West Coast pukes and their UDT counterparts could return home to Coronado. And Tangretti, who had been convinced that his Team would earn its baptism of fire in Cuba, now found himself wondering where and how his Team would make itself useful. There were training missions scheduled to deploy to NATO countries such as Norway, Greece, and Turkey, but the chance of seeing any real action there was about equal to the prospects of a deployment to Cuba, now.

He considered a bleak future as he waited on the grinder, watching as Gunn's detachment of SEALs and UDT men passed in review in front of the UDU-2 staff. It was a minor ceremony to mark the fact that they could stand down now, allowing Team One to return to the west coast and get back to their own jobs. Most of the East Coast SEALs would be sorry to see their comrades leave, despite the rivalry between the two outfits. The men had trained together, operated together, and faced the prospect of fighting together, and there had been some powerful friendships made these last two weeks.

They waited as Commander Hogan addressed a few well-chosen words to Gunn and his men, and then through a short speech by Captain Barstow that was far more flowery and quite a bit less sincere. At length someone shouted "Dismissed!" and the ranks of SEALs broke up, the West Coast contingent heading for a truck that would take them to the Naval Air Station to catch their transport flight to Coronado, while Chief Rudy Banner started finding work for the Little Creek SEALs to do in his characteristic strident tones.

Tangretti moved to intercept Arthur Gunn, holding out his hand. The other man's grip was firm and hearty. "Hope your lot can handle things now that the reinforcements are going home," Gunn told him with a gentle smile. They walked together, heading for the truck.

"Hope you guys have benefited from serving together with some more experienced men," Tangretti shot back. Despite their respective designations, the East Coasters had created SEAL Team Two exactly three hours earlier than the West Coasters had formed Team One, thanks to the time zone difference between Norfolk and San Diego. Tangretti enjoyed pointing out the difference in seniority between the Teams, something Gunn refused to acknowledge.

"Sorry we didn't get a chance to see some action together," Gunn said.

"Yeah. Things are going to get pretty dull now that we're not allowed to play tag with Uncle Fidel anymore," Tangretti replied. "How about you, Arty? You just going to lie on those California beaches and watch the surfers?"

Gunn shook his head. "Nah. My orders were already cut when they decided you needed my sage advice and assistance here. I've got an MTT assignment. Leaving next week."

"Sounds exciting," Tangretti said sarcastically. Mobile Training Teams were the small bands of instructors who trained Allied forces in American combat techniques, like the ones headed for NATO countries from Team Two.

"Maybe more exciting than you think," Gunn said. "I've drawn an all-expenses-paid vacation in Vietnam, where the students actually get to go out and use the stuff we train them for. Could be . . . interesting, at least. Even if it isn't as much fun as mining Komars or hitting the beaches near Havana." He studied Tangretti for a moment. "How about you, Gator?"

Tangretti shrugged. "Paperwork, I guess. I just heard yesterday that my buddy Peter Howell wants to see me again. That should be good for some excitement. Want to help me plant some C-4 under his chair and see how high he flies when the stuff goes off?"

"I'll pass, thank you." Gunn's tone turned serious. "Look, Gator, you be careful with the bureaucrats. I've heard all the stories about you, about how you can scrounge anything and handle anybody, and my hat's off to you after you pulled that stunt with the commander last week and got your boys that liberty. But don't keep screwing around like that. These Pentagon brass hats have no sense of humor and damned little idea of what we're all about, and they resent guys like you who came up through the ranks. If they see a chance to clip your wings, they'll do it. So don't give them any extra ammunition when they come gunning for you, okay? You old WW-II UDT vets are too rare a breed to waste, these days."

"Thanks for the concern," Tangretti told him gruffly. "But I've handled punks like Howell before, and I'll handle them again. You just remember you owe me a case of scotch, sonny boy."

"You'll get what's coming to you, Gator," Gunn said. They shook hands again before Gunn clambered up into the back of the truck, aided by Ensign O'Rourke. The driver gunned the motor, and the truck was on its way.

Tangretti watched as it drove toward the gates, a little envious. At least Gunn was heading somewhere where combat skills would count for something. All he had to look forward to, it seemed, was purchase orders and audits.

It wasn't quite what he'd envisioned when he first started fighting for the SEALs.

Wednesday, 31 October 1962

U.S. Naval Amphibious Base
Little Creek, Virginia
1440 hours

"Lieutenant Howell's here to see you, Boss."

"Wonderful," Tangretti said, rolling his eyes heavenward. "Okay, Buster, send him in."

He didn't stand to receive Lieutenant Peter Howell. That would have been a courteous greeting, and Tangretti wasn't the least bit interested in extending courtesy to the

man who'd become the bane of his existence over the last
several months. Slim, dapper, and always impeccably
groomed, Howell could have been on a recruiting poster
as the perfect picture of the dynamic young Navy officer.
He'd sprung from a prominent Boston family and attended
Harvard, majoring in business, and had taken NROTC
training in much the way other students might have taken
drama courses or rowed crew. Evidently, though, he'd
found the Navy to his taste, though Tangretti suspected the
young Ivy Leaguer had plans to hook into the Navy's "Old
Boys' Network" before taking a job in some area of the
private sector, such as shipbuilding or shipping, where
naval experience and contacts might really pay off. He
was that kind of man: precise, careful, ambitious, and calculating.

Tangretti had nothing against officers with wealthy and
privileged backgrounds per se. Hank Richardson, his best
friend, had been the scion of a powerful New York family,
and if he didn't get along with Hank's father these days, at
least he had never felt uncomfortable around his swim
buddy. The shared experiences of Hell Week bound the
Navy's frogmen closer together than brothers, and distinc-
tions of class, race, or other essentially trivial background
matters were nothing compared to that strong bond. But
Howell had rubbed Tangretti the wrong way from the first
day he'd visited Little Creek. He wasn't a fighting sailor by
any stretch of the imagination, just a jumped-up little
accountant who enjoyed the power he gained from watching over Pentagon funds and the officers, many of them far
senior to him in rank, who were responsible for spending
that money.

Tangretti looked up from his desktop and its stacks of
paperwork as Howell entered and Brown closed the office
door to give the two men privacy. "I'd damn near forgot it's
Halloween," he said. "Want some candy, young man?"

"That's enough, Lieutenant Tangretti," Howell said, his nasal, Harvard-educated accent jarring after months of listening to the soft drawls of Virginia natives. He sat across from Tangretti, setting his briefcase on the desk and opening it with the same neat, precise movements that characterized all his actions. "We have some very serious matters to discuss, and it would be wise if you dispensed with your usual callous disregard for protocol."

"Right. Fine. Let's just get this over with, Lieutenant," Tangretti said, suddenly tired of fencing. "What's the problem this time?"

"The same problem we've been discussing since July, Lieutenant," Howell said stiffly. "Or rather, problems. So far I've put together enough evidence of irregularities in the areas of procurement and equipment safety standards to take you before a court-martial five times over. You're not simply looking at a reprimand, Tangretti. You could end up in Leavenworth for years if the court finds against you in all these matters . . . and I very much suspect that they will."

"You've threatened me with court-martial before, Lieutenant," Tangretti said quietly. "And with Leavenworth. Is there some specific reason for this little visit, or do you just like to hear yourself reciting charges and specifications so much that you feel the need to rehearse them on me before we actually get around to a hearing?"

"I am trying, Lieutenant, to give you every opportunity to deal with these charges in a responsible manner," Howell said. "So far, you've failed to cooperate with me or anyone else from my office, leaving us with no option but to act on the material we've uncovered thus far. If you wish to offer any sort of justification for your actions, any shred of a reason why we should not prosecute this matter to the full extent allowed under the Uniform Code of Military Justice, you had better come forward with something substantial now. I'll be filing my final report by the end of next week,

Lieutenant, and once the wheels are set in motion I don't think they're likely to stop again until they've ground you right into the ground."

Tangretti shrugged. "So glad to hear you're concerned for me, Lieutenant," he said, an edge of sarcasm clear in his voice. He just didn't care about trying to build goodwill with Howell, not anymore. He'd tried that tack back in the summer, when the investigations had still been in their early stages, but the Harvard man hadn't responded with anything other than lofty disdain. "We've been over this ground before, too, or don't you remember? I've justified myself until I'm blue in the face, but whatever I explain in one session just seems to vanish from the record by the time we get together again. Do you really want to go through this one more time?"

Howell fixed him with a clinical stare, as if he were a scientist examining some particularly ordinary species of insect. "In the past, your 'explanations' have generally boiled down to 'I did it for the good of the service.' The problem I've had with this particular approach all along, Lieutenant, is the fact that you seem to feel that you are the only one who understands that good."

"Not 'the good of the service,' " Tangretti corrected him. "I've been working for the good of the SEALs, and if you can point to anyone better qualified to judge the needs of this unit, I'd certainly like to see it."

"No junior officer in a comparatively minor part of the service can be permitted to set major policy decisions that can influence the entire Navy," Howell said pompously. "You have no right to go behind the backs of Navy purchasing agents to procure what you want, simply because it suits you to do so."

Tangretti leaned forward, slapping the desktop with his open palm. "If things weren't so fucked up in Purchasing, I wouldn't have had to go outside channels," he said, enjoy-

ing the shocked expression that played across the other
man's features at his use of such blunt profanity. "I ordered
a batch of .357 Smith & Wesson Model 19 Combat Magnum revolvers for the unit, and some dead-between-the-
ears commander in Supply replaced the purchase order
with one for the Model 15 Combat Masterpiece."

"So?" Howell shook his head. "If that was what Supply
felt we should ship to your unit, that's what you should
have been willing to use."

"The Combat Masterpiece uses .38 Special ammunition,
Lieutenant," Tangretti said patiently, feeling like he was
lecturing a particularly dull-witted recruit. "Trouble is, we
already had .357 Magnum ammo in stock. Call me old-
fashioned if you will, but I sort of like going into a combat
situation armed with a weapon for which I actually have
ammunition. It makes it so much easier to shoot back at the
bad guys. Or are we supposed to creep up on the enemy
and insert the bullets by hand?"

"A minor glitch," Howell said expansively. "You could
easily have corrected it through channels. The incident
certainly didn't give you the right to bypass Supply
entirely."

"I received a Presidential Priority Two authorization to
build the SEALs as I saw fit," Tangretti said angrily. "If I'd
waited for channels, our recon missions the past few
months would have brought back the old tag about 'naked
warriors,' only this time we really would have had to go in
naked. There was talk about using us as paratroops in the
event of going into Cuba, but Supply never got around to
issuing us with parachutes. I *had* to get them from other
sources, for God's sake!"

"And you promptly ordered them modified to a completely new set of specifications," Howell said dryly. "Cir-
cumventing just about every safety regulation on the
books. Had you paradropped into Cuba, Lieutenant, I sus-

pect that half your men would be dead because their parachutes failed to operate properly."

"Nonsense!" Tangretti said harshly. "The only chutes I was able to obtain were commercial sport parachutes. We needed an airfoil design, steerable chutes we could use for precision insertions. We got together with experts who understood parachute design and made the modifications with their guidance, and we practiced with them down at Fort Bragg for half the summer. Do you think for one second that I'd expose my SEALs to unnecessary danger by giving them untested equipment?" Inwardly, he couldn't help but think of the failure of the breathing devices on the Cuba raid, but those had been tested as thoroughly as possible, too, just not under mission conditions as long or as difficult as the ones they'd faced in the field. Not that he intended to admit the problem to Howell.

"Regulations are not provided as good ideas that you can break when it suits you, Lieutenant, though from your record I see that you've never had occasion to learn that in the course of your, ah, checkered career." Howell picked up a file folder and paged through it. "I suppose you felt the same justification in the matter of the AR-15 rifles?"

"We needed a reliable combat rifle," Tangretti said flatly. "Something rugged enough to survive in any of the conditions we might be expected to operate in. Nothing in our current stocks struck me as filling our needs, but one of my men heard about the new Colt design. It had just come on the market, so I knew the odds were it would take a year or two to get any sort of evaluation from your buddies at the Pentagon, much less actually having them available to purchase through channels. So some of us went to the Colt plant in Baltimore and put the 15 through its paces. It's a superb weapon, Howell. Lightweight, sturdy, handles sand and surf with very few problems . . . I'll bet you anything that it'll end up being a standard infantry weapon when your bureaucratic buddies finally get off their asses and look at them. I got a damned good price on them—better than Supply would have managed from an ordinary procurement contract. So I just don't see what your problem is. It isn't like I wasted money. If anything, I saved money and time both, because if we'd settled for second-best this year, we'd have ended up going to a lot of time and expense reequipping ourselves later on when a decent weapon finally became available. So I really don't understand what it is you want from me?"

Howell nodded grimly. "That's exactly the problem, Lieutenant," he said. "You don't understand. The Navy cannot afford to let wild men like you run loose, acting entirely on your own initiative on matters that need to be carefully weighed and considered. But the sad fact is that you will never change this ingrained disrespect you have for the system, and that means our only alternative really is to remove you from any position in which you could continue to indulge in your proclivity for ignoring the wider picture in favor of your immediate desires." He stood, closing the briefcase. "I really see no alternative but to go forward with a prosecution, and I fear that's what I shall have to recommend to my superiors."

Friday, 2 November 1962

The Pentagon
1022 hours

Captain Joseph Galloway rose courteously as his visitor was ushered in. The new arrival was about his own age, sporting a walking stick with a fancy ornamental head and clothing that probably came from Savile Row or some other upper-crust tailor shop. He walked with a slight but noticeable limp, and his handsome features were marred by the scar tissue visible just above the collar of his starched white button-down shirt. For all of that, though, the man had an aura of command and the calculating look of a predatory bird.

"Thank you for coming, Senator," Galloway said. "Please, have a seat. I wish I could offer you something a little more comfortable, but they keep the Special Warfare people penned up in the slum district."

Senator Alexander Hamilton Forsythe III gave him a brief smile as he settled into the chair and propped his stick against the desk in front of him. "Don't apologize, Captain," he said. "I don't mind roughing it when the cause is a good one." He looked around. "At least you have a bigger office than I did when I was posted here back in '46."

Galloway sat down, trying to decide how to broach the subject that had led him to ask the senator to stop off at his office during his visit to the Pentagon. Even after more years than he cared to remember functioning in the strange world that straddled the Navy's high command and the fringe of the Washington social world, Galloway had never become comfortable in the ways of manipulating others, and most especially he didn't like asking favors of politicians. They tended to be a fickle lot, and many of them demanded far too much in return for their occasional gestures of assistance.

But before he had been a politician, before he had been a staff officer at the Pentagon, Alexander Forsythe had been a UDT officer in the Pacific Theater of World War II. He was known to be sympathetic to the cause of Navy Special Warfare, and he was the only man Galloway could think of who might be able to help with the problem he needed to solve.

"How's Ginny?" Forsythe asked politely. "Still as beautiful as ever?" Back when he was still a Navy commander recovering from wounds received at Okinawa, Forsythe had been one of the scores of guests at Galloway's wedding to his high-society bride.

"I think so," he said. "But I'm biased." He paused. "I was sorry to hear about Margaret. If I had my way they'd shoot every drunk who ever got behind the wheel of a car."

Forsythe looked away. It was only six months since his wife of fifteen years had been killed when a drunk driver had run her off the road on a lonely highway in upstate New York. "If I thought I could get a law like that passed, I'd probably try it," he admitted. "As it is, Allison keeps things pretty lively at home. She's finally accepted what happened to her mother. I wish to God I could." Forsythe paused. "All right, Joe, we've got the regulation small talk out of the way. What say we cut to the chase?"

"As you wish, Senator," Galloway said. "How closely have you been following the SEALs?"

"Not as much as I'd like to," the senator told him. "I did some lobbying for the idea with JFK last year, and I made damn sure the Senate Armed Services Committee understood how important it was to approve their budget when it came up this year. I keep wishing I could take the time to visit Little Creek or Coronado, but there's always one damned thing or another more important coming up and keeping me from following through on it."

"You haven't heard about the investigations into the conduct of the acting CO, then?"

The politician shook his head. "Should I be concerned? If it turns out the SEALs are some kind of giant boondoggle . . ."

"Nothing of the sort, Senator," Galloway said quickly. "Just the opposite. So far the SEALs have proven very effective, although they haven't had the opportunity to show off everything they can do as yet. Still, this recent mess with Cuba . . ."

Forsythe frowned. "Bad business there. I know Khrushchev backed down, but I couldn't help but think there was something a little more positive we could have done. If I'd still had the gang from UDT-21 with me, I'd've thought about taking them in and planting enough explosives at those missile bases to set fire to old Fidel's beard from halfway across the island." He smiled. "But don't pass that on to my constituents. They like to see me as a voice of calm reason, not a wild-eyed ex-frogman."

"That's pretty much the same idea that Steve Tangretti came up with," Galloway told him with a grin. "He's—"

"Tangretti! That old warhorse? Is he still around?"

"You know him, Senator?"

"Know him! He was in UDT-21 when we hit Okinawa. He and Frank Rand pulled me out of trouble after I was wounded. Frank gave me the tracheotomy," Forsythe went on, touching the scar above his tie, "while Gator covered us. What's he doing now?"

"Being investigated," Galloway said dryly. "He's the acting CO of Team Two."

"Knowing Gator, it's either Drunk and Disorderly, Conduct Unbecoming, or fiddling with the books," Forsythe said, smiling as he reminisced. "Back in '45 he was enlisted, not an officer, and he had a real reputation for booze, broads, and being the best scrounger in the entire Navy."

"Well, I'll tell you right off that I don't think the investigations should ever have come this far," Galloway said. "When he was put in charge of organizing the Team he was given Presidential Priority Two authorization to purchase whatever he needed to get the SEALs up and running, and he did a fine job. Unfortunately, Steve's always been the kind who gets things done no matter what, which is fine for a mission against an enemy-held beach but a disaster waiting to happen when you're dealing with the folks in this five-sided squirrel cage. When he couldn't get the equipment he wanted through channels, he went straight to outside contractors and got what he wanted from them. And if the stuff he bought didn't quite measure up to the Team's needs, he modified it . . . but he didn't always stick to the letter of the regs on safety standards. Both items are like red flags in front of a charging bull to the folks in Procurement, so they called in the JAG, and Tangretti's been fighting off charges ever since."

"Just how serious is the threat?" Forsythe asked.

"I've got some sources close to the investigation," Galloway said. "They've got enough evidence to hit him with five separate prosecutions. All of it garbage, if you ask me, but if they convince a court, Steve's career will be sunk. He could even get jail time out of it."

"So . . . what exactly do you want from me?" Forsythe asked. "I want to help Gator out, don't get me wrong. But a freshman senator, even one on the ASC, doesn't command enough power to order a cheese sandwich around here. You must know that I can't simply legislate his problems out of existence."

"I know, sir," Galloway said. "But I thought you might have some ideas about how to get him off the hook. The Navy can't afford to lose a man like Steve Tangretti. A lot of us pushed for the creation of the SEALs, but Steve was the one who took it over the top. He was the one who impressed the president enough to get the final authorization order signed, and—"

"Kennedy knows him, then?"

"They've only met twice that I know of," Galloway said. "Once at the meeting where we got the final approval . . . and again last week, when Steve was at the briefing on the Cuba situation. The president remembered him . . . listened to his scheme for using the SEALs to take out the missiles, even if he did reject it on advice from the Joint Chiefs."

"Hmmm . . ." Forsythe looked thoughtful. "Look, like I said, there's not much I can do from my Senate seat. But if we can bring JFK in on this in a quiet way . . . well, he *is* the commander in chief, after all."

"I considered that," Galloway admitted. "But I don't have the right kind of access."

"Well, I do. I was invited to dinner at the White House for tomorrow night, although I was halfway planning to send my regrets and have a quiet weekend at home. Now I think I'll go and see if I can bend the president's ear in private." The senator smiled. "I heard a rumor that he's making a campaign swing through Norfolk early next week. Maybe he'd like to stop off at Little Creek and see his prize SEALs in person, eh? I can certainly get him interested in doing that much, at least. And if I prime the pump the right way, he might just be inclined to take a personal interest in the welfare of the outfit. And its CO, even if he is still a bit of a rogue."

"Senator, I really appreciate your help. If there's anything I can do for you, ever—"

Forsythe touched the scar on his neck again. "I wheel and deal with the best of them, most of the time, but this is one favor with no strings attached." He stood, wincing a little as his bad leg took his weight. "I owe Steve Tangretti my life, Joe. And it's a debt I'll gladly pay a hundred times over, if I can."

Monday, 5 November 1962

U.S. Naval Amphibious Base
Little Creek, Virginia
1345 hours

"Boss! Boss! He's coming! JFK's coming here!"

Tangretti looked up as Brown burst into the Team barracks, breathless and excited. "Whoa, there, Buster. Slow down," he said. "Yeah, I know, the president's supposed to be on the base today."

"No, Boss, he's coming *here*! He's on the way now! I just saw a bunch of guys in suits coming out of Barstool's office block, and I heard a couple of sailors say the president wanted to see the SEAL barracks before he left."

For a moment, Tangretti felt like cursing. The announcement of the president's plans to visit Little Creek had taken everyone by surprise. Evidently it had been a last-minute notion tacked on to a campaign trip to the Norfolk area. The presidential party had already made the rounds of the rest of the base in a blaze of publicity, touring the Marine barracks, watching the men of UDT-21 drilling on the grinder, even observing the current crop of Basic Underwater Demolition/SEALs candidates enduring a grueling Hell Week exercise down on the beach. But when word of the visit had first been received from on high, Captain Barstow had made it plain that Tangretti's SEALs weren't expected to be part of the day's activities. So Tangretti had gone ahead and ordered the Team to follow the normal routine, which today meant an inventory of weapons and equipment. The barracks building wasn't ready for a formal inspection. Equipment lockers were open, and there was gear stacked along one end of the building where several of the men were busy ticking off each item against their stock records.

Well, he thought, *doesn't much matter if they decide to chew me out over not being ready for the VIPs. They'll have to get in line behind Howell and his vultures anyway.*

"All right, you swabbies," he growled out loud. "We've got company coming. Best behavior, all of you." He fixed a stare on Horner, who grinned at him and whistled a few bars from "You're the Reason I Don't Sleep at Night."

From beside the door, Chief Rudy Banner's gravel voice rang out. "Ten-HUT! Attention on deck!"

"Gentlemen, the president of the United States!" That voice belonged to a staff lieutenant, young and eager, announcing the arrival of their visitors.

Tangretti stood ramrod-straight as the VIP party entered the Team barracks, swirling past Rudy Banner in an untidy mass of dark suits and flashing smiles. Kennedy was the only one he recognized, but he guessed the others were pretty evenly divided between political aides and Secret Service agents. At least there weren't any reporters with them. The media representatives had been sent away after Kennedy had gone to visit Barstow's office, and apparently hadn't been allowed to rejoin the president's tour when they came out again. The government was still sensitive about giving the Navy's elite commandos too much publicity, though the directives concerning the matter seemed to go back and forth from one month to the next.

Kennedy led the way, with Barstow and Hogan trying to match his brisk stride as the president moved down the center of the barracks area, past SEALs drawn to full attention beside their racks. The contrast between the gaudy dress uniforms of the staff officers and the grungy look of the SEALs in working dungarees made Tangretti want to smile at the absurdity of it all, but he schooled his features to remain still and impassive.

Since he wasn't wearing a hat, he didn't salute as

Kennedy approached him. "Well, the outspoken Lieutenant Tangretti," Kennedy said. "I see our arrival has taken you and your men by surprise."

"Yes, sir," he said. "I'm afraid we weren't informed that you'd want to inspect our barracks, Mr. President. We were in the middle of a work detail."

Kennedy gave him a warm smile. "Well, I'm sorry to have interrupted you, but as I told Captain Barstow I thought it was time I got a look at the SEALs firsthand."

"We're proud to have you here, sir . . . even if things are a little untidy."

"I was dining the other night with an old friend of yours, Lieutenant," Kennedy said. "Senator Forsythe. He says you served with him at Okinawa."

"Yes, Mr. President."

"He also told me he couldn't think of a better man to be guiding the SEALs through their first months as a unit." Kennedy gave him another smile. "Now, the fact is, Senator Forsythe isn't even from my party, but I still respect his opinions. I knew him when he was still a junior member of the House, and even if we don't always see eye to eye on policy, I know he's got a lot on the ball. So I'm glad to hear that he approves of you."

"Me too, sir," Tangretti said, allowing himself a half smile. He wondered where all this was leading.

Kennedy glanced past Tangretti at another of the SEALs, Engineman First Class Adam Carmichael, who was standing next to an open crate of AR-15s. "Well, now, sailor, looks to me like you've got enough firepower around here to win a war all by yourselves. Those look like interesting weapons . . . I don't believe I've seen that type before. Tell me about them."

Carmichael stammered, but did as the president asked. "Th-this is the AR-15 combat rifle, Mr. President," he said. "It's a new design, only recently on the market." He picked

one up and held it out so that Kennedy could get a better
look at it. The president studied the weapon for a moment,
then gave a nod.

"What do you think of it, son?" he asked.

The sailor's response was enthusiastic. "It's the best
weapon of its kind available, sir," he said. "All the rest of
this stuff is just sh—er, junk, in my opinion, sir, but these
AR-15s give the best combination of firepower and easy
field maintenance I've ever seen in ten years in the Navy.
We had to go right to the manufacturer to get them, sir, but
by God we found just what we needed." Carmichael
paused. "It's too bad, though, sir, Lieutenant Tangretti set
the whole thing up, and now he's probably going to draw a
court-martial for doing it."

Kennedy glanced down at the rifle, then back at the
SEAL. "Well, now, sailor, don't get too worked up about
something that hasn't happened yet." He looked over at
Tangretti for a moment and smiled again. "Someone who
commands the loyalty of his men *and* the good opinion of
Senator Forsythe is too good a man to be ground under the
wheels of the bureaucracy. Maybe things will work out
better than you think." He paused. "What's your name,
son?"

Carmichael replied with his full rank and name, and
Kennedy made a gesture to one of his aides. The man jot-
ted something down in a pocket notebook, and Kennedy
turned back to Tangretti.

"Senator Forsythe thought I might want to talk to you
and some of your men, Lieutenant. He didn't mention anything specifically wrong, but I thought he was hinting at
some kind of problem down here. You know the impor-
tance I place on getting the SEALs up and into action. I
don't like problems that get in the way of that . . . and I
think this is one occasion where the commander in chief
needs to step in to protect an important project. I'll be

instructing my staff to have a look at this little matter, and I hope you'll be getting some good news in a few days. Meanwhile, keep up the good work."

"Yes, Mr. President," Tangretti got out. "Thank you, sir."

Kennedy and his entourage swept back toward the door, leaving Tangretti to stare after them, hardly daring to believe the visit had even taken place.

Chapter 5

U.S. Naval Amphibious Base
Little Creek, Virginia
1525 hours

"Hey, Boss, will you get a load of this!"

Tangretti walked across the barracks room to join the cluster of SEALs gathered around Adam Carmichael. The commotion when they had come in from mail call had brought him away from his desk and out into the barracks area proper, and he could almost sense the excitement as he approached.

"What's going on?" he asked.

Carmichael held up a heavy manila envelope. "This was in the mail today, Boss," he said. His voice rang with pride. "Just look at it—from the White House, no less! And look what was inside!"

The sailor held up an eight-by-ten glossy photograph. Tangretti studied it, interested. It was a picture of John F. Kennedy, looking sternly presidential, and there was writing across one corner. *To Engineman 1/C Adam Carmichael,* it read. *Always glad to listen to one of our boys in uniform.*

Kennedy's signature completed the short note.

Carmichael was beaming. "He remembered meeting me!" the sailor said, beaming. "What d'you think of that, Boss?"

Smiling back, Tangretti clapped him on the shoulder. "That's pretty damned good, Carmichael," he said. "Who'd've thought a SEAL could get to be best buddies with the president, huh? Just do me one favor, okay?"

"Sure, Boss, anything you want," the SEAL said. "What is it?"

"Well, now that you're a VIP and all, try not to let it go to your head. Just because you're friends with JFK doesn't mean you can get out of Rudy's PT class every morning."

That broke them all up. Physical Training under the stern eye and stentorian voice of Chief Banner was perhaps the least popular part of life for the SEALs in Little Creek.

Tangretti turned away, feeling pleased. He'd suspected Kennedy would do something of the sort ever since he'd seen one of the presidential entourage jotting down Carmichael's name. It was a natural for any politician, especially one as deft at public relations as JFK. No doubt, come election time, Kennedy would be assured another vote from a sailor impressed at his common touch. But Tangretti was glad of the gesture for his own reasons. It was a great morale boost for the SEALs to be reminded once again that the presidential eye was indeed turned their way.

He returned to the office and went back to the stack of reports that had been piling up on his desk over the last few weeks. First the missile crisis, and then the situation with Howell, had put him behind on the routine paperwork the Navy seemed to require more than ammunition to keep its units in fighting trim.

After a few minutes, his phone rang.

"Tangretti," he answered.

"Steve, this is Joe Galloway."

"Yes, Captain. What can I do for you?"

"I wanted to be the first to congratulate you on the news I just heard today, Steve. Peter Howell has been reassigned to evaluate the possible purchase of a pair of fast torpedo boats from the Norwegian government for a Special Warfare project. All plans for further investigations or court-martial proceedings against you or the SEALs have been suspended indefinitely."

Tangretti leaned back in his chair and smiled broadly. "That is good news, sir. Thanks."

"Don't thank me. I understand there was some quiet but rather firm pressure applied from a friend of yours in very high places." Galloway paused. "There's another matter we need to discuss, now that this investigation nonsense has cleared itself up. I saw a report that indicated one of your officers was injured."

"Jack Kessler," Tangretti replied. "Yeah, he had an accident. Broken leg."

"He was slated for an assignment as observer with MTT 4-63," Galloway said.

"Yes, sir. I recommended him for the job myself, a few months back. If I remember it properly, you were asking for someone whose judgment I trusted and who understood Special Warfare."

"Right," Galloway said. "I seem to remember you claiming that you were the only one who really met those specs, but since you couldn't go, Kessler was the next best choice."

"Yeah, well, I probably did say something like that," Tangretti admitted with another smile.

"Well, you'll recall that little chat we had in the White House parking lot last time you were up here. You were looking for a new job. How would you like to fill in for Jack Kessler?"

Tangretti straightened in his chair. "Tell me more, Captain," he said earnestly.

Tangretti Residence
Virginia Beach, Virginia
1845 hours

"Vietnam! Why are they sending *you* to Vietnam?"

Tangretti sat down heavily in the big, overstuffed chair that dominated the living room, heaving out the quiet sigh of a man who knew a fight with his wife was inevitable. "Originally, Jack Kessler was scheduled to go, but then he broke his leg." He forced a laugh, trying to lighten the mood. "Imagine it, he spends more than a month training with the paratroops, jumping out of airplanes damn near every day, and doesn't get a scratch. Then he comes home and trips over his kid's roller skates, and that lays him up."

Veronica perched on the couch and looked at him with fire in her eyes. "That's not the point. Quit trying to change the subject, Steve! You told me Vietnam was the property of the West Coast SEALs, out of Coronado. Why do *you* have to go?"

"Look, Captain Galloway's office wants to do some cross-training between the coasts. We had some guys from Team One here to help out during the missile crisis. Now they think it'd be a good idea if a few observers from Team Two become part of the Mobile Training Team in Vietnam." He paused. "Like I said, Jack was up for the slot, but now he's out of it for a while, so I got the call instead."

"You're the acting commander of the Team, Steve," she said, shaking her head. "I've been around the Navy long enough to know when something isn't being done by the book, and this little deal isn't even anywhere in the *library*."

He shrugged and nodded. "I guess it does look funny from where you are, Ronnie. But it makes sense, some ways. Look, Mr. Colquhoun is due back at the Team next week to finally take command. I've been running things for ten months now, and as long as I stay on as Exec I'll just confuse things. The men will be looking to me, not to him, and that's damned awkward for an officer just taking command. He needs a chance to put his own stamp on the Team without feeling like I'm hanging over his shoulder, second-guessing him all the time."

"Well . . . maybe," she said. "I can see that much. But there are a lot of assignments closer to home that you could have drawn."

"Not as many as you think, Ronnie," he said earnestly. "All the MTTs scheduled for Europe have already been sent for the next six months, so that's out. I suppose they could have posted me to some advanced school or other, but the fact is—in all due modesty—I have a lot to contribute to something like the training program in Vietnam. After all, who knows more about SEALs than I do? The MTT is supposed to train local forces in SEAL techniques and tactics, and if I'm there, I not only can observe how the West Coast pukes do the job, I can also make a few suggestions on ways we might do it better. You know that Joe Galloway still likes to get my opinions on things from time to time. I imagine he's hoping I can evaluate the program in Vietnam and help bring things up to speed there fast. After all, Vietnam's not like Turkey or Norway or the Philippines. There's fighting already going on over there, and they don't have a whole lot of time to experiment."

Veronica frowned at that. "That's just what bothers me, Steve. You'll be going into a combat zone."

"As an *advisor*," he stressed. "From what I hear Americans are being kept well out of the action. I probably run more of a risk of being mugged every time I visit DC."

She smiled despite herself. "If there's fighting going on, trust you to find it," she said. "I know you too well, Steve. You put in for this assignment, didn't you? You can almost always rig things to get your way . . . like getting them to drop the charges and the investigation, after they were so strong to see you in trouble just a couple of weeks ago."

"That wasn't any of my doing, Ronnie," he protested. "Swear to God. Oh, okay, I put a word in Captain Galloway's ear last time I saw him, and I guess he got Senator Forsythe to suggest that the president come and look into things himself . . . but I didn't pull any real strings. Not like I was really operating or anything . . ."

"Yeah. Right. Where do I go to get a lightning rod that'll keep me safe while you're making up all these tall tales? I don't want to be around you when God decides you've lied one time too many . . ."

Tangretti did his best to look innocent, but that just made her laugh louder. At least he'd turned away some of her anger.

"I'm serious, Steve," she said at last. "I know you could get out of this tour in Vietnam if you really wanted to."

"Don't be so sure, honey," he said. "Look, I burned up most of my credit with the brass over these investigations. The president may have made them move Howell on to greener pastures, but I'm not too popular around the Pentagon just now. Even Captain Galloway's probably pretty unhappy with me at the moment. So I don't really know if I could pull any rabbits out of the hat at this point." He paused, shrugging again. "And, frankly, Ronnie, I'd be happier on this assignment than on most anything else I might draw. With Cuba defused, there won't be a lot of work for Team Two. Vietnam's the hot spot right now, the place where a SEAL's talents are going to be put to the best possible use, even if it's only a matter of training our gooks to fight Commie gooks. I need to know that I'm doing a job that's important. Otherwise, they might as well reserve me a place in a rocking chair and retire me."

"You could, you know," she said. "You've already been in longer than most lifers, and you've done your part a hundred times over. We could settle down, watch the kids grow up, maybe make a real life for ourselves instead of always being at the mercy of the Navy. It's not like they're going to fall apart without you, or anything."

"Ronnie, I'd go crazy on the beach!" he protested. "I still have a lot to contribute to the SEALs, and by God I'll keep right on contributing as long as I possibly can! There's no way I'm going to end up playing golf and talking about my aches and pains with a bunch of worn-out old geezers."

"Retiring from the Navy doesn't mean retiring from life, Steve," she said. "I mean, you could get a job with some defense contractor . . . or maybe open a construction business of your own. Your Seabee experience—"

"Was twenty years ago," he finished. "Ronnie, try to look at it from my side. My training is in sneaking up on deserted beaches and blowing things up. That's what I'm good at. Can you really see me as some kind of shill for a defense contractor, wining and dining Galloway or Forsythe to peddle a new weapons system or going over accounts with the likes of Peter Howell? And I'm not cut out to be a business owner, either. I'm a SEAL, Ronnie, and a damned good one. If I lose touch with that, I lose touch with everything that I am."

She gusted a sigh. "I . . . I suppose you're right. It's just, well, how long is this tour overseas? Are we just going to get settled in, and then get uprooted all over again? Junior graduates next year, and Bill's doing so well in the school here . . ."

"Nobody's going to be uprooted," he said firmly. "Nobody but me. From what I hear, dependents aren't being allowed in the war zone except under very special circumstances. And you're right. The kids shouldn't be put through an unnecessary change. The standard MTT tour is six months or so. It wouldn't even be worthwhile for the family to move to the West Coast. I'll be back in time to be there for Hank's big day."

Veronica looked stricken. "Six months . . . you just want to go away for six months?"

"Hey, wait, I'm just trying to look at realities here," he said. "You're the one who was worried about the kids . . . and you ought to be used to sea duty by this time."

"Oh, I'm used to it," she said bitterly. "I still remember how much fun it was waiting for you when you were in Korea. And I also remember all the stories about your liberties—not from you, no, but from other Navy wives who heard their husbands boasting about being with that wild Gator Tangretti, the man who knew every bar and brothel in Japan! Are you really trying to help the SEALs, Steve, or are you trying to hold on to the life you used to have? You're always talking about all the good times you and Hank had together. Maybe what you really want is to have everything the way it was back then, when you didn't have a family to hold you back and you could be just as irresponsible and wild as you wanted!"

He surged out of the chair. "That's unfair, Ronnie!" he said harshly. "Yeah, sure, I did a few stupid things when I was away from home. But I always came back to you, didn't I? I never looked at another woman the way I look at you . . . and if I went out partying with my buddies, it was because that's what we always did. Work hard, fight hard, party hard . . . that's been the way it was since Snake and I were at Fort Pierce. Well, I'm sick and tired of having you load all this guilt on me. If you're not worrying about where I'm going or what I'm doing, you're badgering me about retiring! You knew what I was when you said 'I do' all those years ago, *so stop trying to make me into someone I can't be*!" He started for the door.

"Where are you going?" she demanded.

"I'll sleep down at the Team tonight," he told her.

"Tomorrow I'm supposed to see Joe Galloway in DC. I'll send somebody around to pack what I'll need . . ." Tangretti trailed off, then added, more softly, "I'll call you before I go to Washington tomorrow. Maybe both of us will be a little less on edge by then."

Friday, 9 November 1962

The Pentagon
1502 hours

"Lieutenant Tangretti to see you, sir."

Tangretti stepped past the secretary and into Galloway's office, taking the captain's extended hand.

"Good to see you, Steve," Galloway said. "Park it."

As Tangretti sat down, Galloway went on. "Word has it that you're not going to be living in Kansas after all. I'm glad." He dropped into his chair with a little grunt.

"So am I, sir," Tangretti said with a smile. "Thanks for your part in it."

"Me? I didn't do anything, Lieutenant. This office never gets involved in petty politics." Galloway's expression was a study in blandness.

"Yes, sir."

"Look, Steve, the reason I called you in here today is to explain a few things about your MTT assignment. There are some . . . special circumstances involved, and I want to be sure you know the score before you get on that plane tomorrow." He paused, studying Tangretti through hooded, tired eyes. "If, after you hear what I have to say, you want to ask for a different assignment, I'll see what I can do."

"You know I wanted Vietnam, sir," Tangretti said.

"Maybe so, but you might have second thoughts." Galloway leaned forward in his chair and steepled his hands on the desktop. "First off, Steve, you should understand that this isn't a case of your being handed an assignment you want as some kind of reward for past good deeds. Fact is, removing you from SEAL Two was the only way Lieutenant Howell's office would even consider dropping the investigation, even with the pressure from Kennedy. It is thought in certain circles around here that you should not be used in a command capacity, particularly in any position which gives you purchasing authorization. They say your judgment is questionable at best, and that your motives may be criminal. I don't agree with this school of thought, Steve, but you have to understand that you stepped on a few too many toes this time around. The president may have backed them down from a court-martial, but they'll be looking for other ways to get at you. Getting you the hell out of Dodge for a while was the best compromise all the way around, and if you should decide you don't want Vietnam after all, you'll probably be sent to some equally charming vacation spot—like a training camp in the Bering Sea or a weather station in Greenland. You understand?"

Tangretti nodded. "Yes, sir. I thought that might be the way things were stacking up."

"All right, then. The MTT 4-63 mission to Vietnam." Galloway leaned back, but his scrutiny was no less intense. "Your spot was originally assigned to a j.g. named, ah, Kessler, I believe."

"Yes, Captain."

"Well, we want an East Coast observer with this mission, but putting you in the slot does create some . . . tensions. You're a full lieutenant, and your commission goes all the way back to the mid-fifties, doesn't it?"

"Yes, sir. Fifty-six. I was made j.g. while we were over in Korea in '50."

"Well, that technically makes you senior to the CO of the MTT, Lieutenant Gunn. But this is supposed to be a West Coast show, Lieutenant. You're assigned as an observer, and I want you to keep it that way. Lieutenant Gunn makes the decisions. If I find out you've tried to pull rank on him because of some disagreement or other, I'll come down on you so hard you'll wish Howell had locked you up in some nice, quiet cell instead. You read me?"

Tangretti nodded. "Yessir," he said. "I'm strictly along for the ride. Arty and I worked together on the Cuba thing. I'll give him all the room he needs."

"Good. He'll be glad of your input, I'm sure. But he's in command of the training team, and he makes the final decisions."

"Suits me fine," Tangretti said with a smile. "Never liked being an officer anyway. I'm glad to let somebody else take all the grief anyway."

"Like hell you are," Galloway said. "You can't snow me, Tangretti. The first time I met you and your buddy Richardson you were fresh from a dive off Kwajelein where you two wild men had violated orders and gone up on the beach when you were supposed to remain well offshore. You had a spent bullet from a Jap rifle . . ."

Tangretti touched the chain around his neck. "Still have it, too, sir," he commented with a smile.

"You like to bend the rules to make the Navy go your way, Steve, and to a certain extent I don't blame you. But you have to rope it in. Make many more waves, and you'll go under for sure. And next time you might not be lucky enough to have a president around to save you."

"Understood, sir. I'll behave myself."

"Good." Galloway extracted a file folder from a stack at his elbow and pushed it across the desk to Tangretti. "Now, as far as the MTT operation goes . . . This is all the background material you're likely to need. MTT 4-63 will be the second SEAL training mission to Vietnam. You'll be relieving MTT 10-62, which has been over there since April. Officially, you are there to teach SEAL techniques and tactics to Vietnamese commandos, just as other teams have done for Australia, Norway, Greece, and so on."

"You say, 'officially,' sir?" Tangretti pounced on the word.

"That's right. *Unofficially,* the real purpose of the MTT in Vietnam is to prepare Vietnamese naval commandos for clandestine missions into the north. The spooks over at Langley are in charge of that aspect of things, but they've jumped on board the bandwagon when it comes to using SEAL-trained troops to carry out their special ops." He paused. "Understand me, Steve. American military men are not to be used in direct action against any target in Vietnam. They may defend themselves if fired upon, but right now we are there strictly in the role of advisors and teachers. Nothing else."

"So what is it that the CIA wants us to advise and teach over there, sir?"

"Langley wants to see the government in Hanoi destabilized," Galloway said. "The way we figure it, the Saigon government can take care of the home-grown Communist guerrillas on its own, with minimal support from us, but only as long as we can keep the North Vietnamese from fishing in troubled waters. What we want to do is cut the Viet Cong off from any kind of support that might be coming from the North. So the CIA is working hard to place agents into North Vietnam to stir up a local resistance against Ho Chi Minh and distract the NVA's attention away from the South."

"Sounds like SEAL heaven, Captain," Tangretti said.

"Like I said, the orders for now are for no active American involvement. The president's line on this is that South Vietnam is our sovereign ally, fully able to take care of its own affairs. We supply assistance in the form of advice, training, money, and supplies . . . but we keep a low profile otherwise. The French got themselves kicked out by being too heavy-handed. JFK doesn't plan to see us repeat the mistake." Galloway paused. "For now, the thrust of covert operations is to set up an effective route for smuggling agents and small commando teams into and out of North Vietnamese waters. The core of the Vietnamese forces involved in the operation is the Biet Hai, a commando unit. The name seems to translate as 'junk commandos,' so they're probably more like Marines than SEALs, but the reports from the first training class indicate they're tough customers. There is also a South Vietnamese navy frogman unit, the equivalent of our UDTs, but they're used for more conventional purposes."

"So we teach these junk commandos how to infiltrate along the North Vietnamese coast, then wave good-bye and watch them sail out of the harbor?"

Galloway smiled grimly. "Essentially, that's the job. We've just taken some old torpedo boats out of mothballs and assigned them to operate out of Da Nang. That's where the MTT and the Biet Hai are based. Our hope is that a second six-month training course with SEAL instructors will turn out enough Biet Hai with SEAL-style training to allow them to take over the entire training program next year. After that . . . well, we'll have to see."

Tangretti thought he detected something behind Galloway's bland demeanor. "Okay, Captain, I'll bite. What's the part of this you haven't told me yet?"

The captain looked at him with a neutral expression on his craggy features. "This is not for dissemination, not even to your fellow SEALs, Tangretti. It's the main reason why I'm glad to have you on board, even if it does give me migraines." He smiled thinly. "Right now the president is dead set against direct action by American forces, but there are a lot of factions inside the Pentagon who think it's only a matter of time before we get more involved over there. The South Vietnamese government is too corrupt to hold out very long without being extensively propped up, but the more advisors and support people we send over, the more pressure there is going to be to cover them with troops. Sooner or later that will lead to active fighting, the very thing the president doesn't want. You wrote the book on Special Operations, Steve. What do you say to all this?"

Tangretti pursed his lips thoughtfully. "Instead of building up a large military presence and getting bogged down in a protracted guerrilla war just like the one the French lost, we ought to be looking for ways of intervening with small but effective forces—elite troops. I see where the president wants to make it look as if the Saigon government is handling things on its own, but a little nudge here and there by Special Forces or SEALs could do a lot of good."

"Exactly." Galloway nodded. "I want you to assess the opportunities for employing SEAL platoons in direct action over there, either supporting these Biet Hai operations or carrying out other types of missions that would have an impact on the war over there. If we can convince the president to opt for Special Warfare over a conventional buildup, we stand to save a lot of lives and maybe make Vietnam a showcase for the new kind of war the president is always talking about. That's your real job over there, Steve. I think you're the best man to do it."

"I'll give it my best shot, sir," Tangretti told him. He rose, and the two men shook hands. As Tangretti gathered up the file folder, he looked at Galloway again. "And thanks . . . for everything. It's good to have a job that gives me a chance to do something worthwhile again."

Saturday, 10 November 1962

MATS Transport Plane
Over Nevada
1128 hours

Steve Tangretti put the file folder back in his briefcase and sagged back in his seat, his eyes sore from too much reading and two consecutive nights without enough sleep. He was still elated about the prospect of a new assignment, but at the same time he was suffering a growing depression as he considered the new strains in his marriage.

If only Ronnie could understand!

She'd brought Hank and Bill in to the Naval Air Station to see him as he waited for the transport plane that was set to fly him to the West Coast SEAL home on Coronado Island off San Diego, just as he'd asked when he phoned her on his return from Washington. But while the two boys were caught up in the excitement of it all, sorry to see him leave but eager to hear everything he could tell them about his new assignment, Veronica had been stiff and withdrawn the whole time. Even their parting had been almost formal.

After seventeen years of marriage, Tangretti had expected more. Even after their quarrel, he'd expected her to relent, to say something to let him know that underneath it all she hadn't given up on them. But her eyes had been cold, and when he'd said his final "I love you" her only reply had been, "Good-bye, Steve."

The long flight had given him plenty of time to replay the scene over and over again in his mind, even with the briefing papers available to distract him from the unhappy memory. Was that "good-bye" just a cool send-off, or was there a deeper message in it somewhere? Perhaps she really had reached the end, and he'd get word in a few days or weeks that she wanted out of the marriage. Her family in Wisconsin would welcome her back, he thought. Even the snobbish Richardsons, who had never entirely approved of their son's choice of Veronica as a wife, would likely be so glad to have Steve Tangretti out of their lives forever that they would encourage her to leave him, even help her any way they could.

Well, he told himself bitterly, it wouldn't be the first time he'd screwed up his life, but it would certainly be the worst screwup he'd ever managed. There had been a time back in the war when he'd wanted nothing more than a chance to end it all, but he'd gotten through that bitter period of his life . . . largely because of Ronnie's support. Now it seemed he might actually lose her, and that would hurt.

And what about Hank Junior? He had no legal claim over his stepson. All talk of adoption had been steadfastly blocked by the Richardsons, and if his marriage fell apart entirely, they'd be able to keep him away from their grandson if they so desired. That hurt almost as much as the thought of losing Ronnie. Young Richardson was everything his father had been, and more, and Tangretti regarded the boy as being as much his own son as his buddy's.

It just wasn't fair, having to deal with all this extra baggage *now*.

The hell of it was that he understood a lot of what Veronica was feeling. She worried too much about the danger he was in; this advisor's slot in Vietnam would likely be safer than traffic out of DC on a Friday night. But she didn't have any real way to gauge the risk. All she knew was that he was heading for a war zone, and bullets or shells didn't care if you were an "advisor" or a combatant. She had reason to be concerned about his safety, and reason to be upset over a separation. One of the most difficult things about Navy life was the way it tore families apart every time a sailor had to go on sea duty. Months of coping with life without a husband, of dealing with household crises and financial worries and the health and well-being of kids made it tough to be a Navy wife; and though Veronica was a fine example of that tough breed, sometimes it just got to be too much. It was that much worse for her, too, because for years he'd been employed in posts where they could be together, and over time they'd developed a comfortable routine.

Most ships or units in the Navy supported a "Wives' Club" that organized social events and made sure there was plenty of support among families of the men who served in the outfit, but Tangretti had decreed that the SEALs wouldn't do that. Now he was forced to wonder if he'd been right to make that decree. No one envisioned long overseas deployments for the SEALs. They were elite commandos, intended for raids or short, decisive operations, but perhaps he had underestimated the need for the wives to have some central focus they could rally around when their husbands were in harm's way. At the time he'd been more concerned about the security aspects of a Wives' Club, but maybe he'd been shortsighted. Of course, with or without a club, the wives had their own friendships. Still, it might not be the same.

Ronnie had been right to point out that he could take retirement. He had already served longer than most men who made the Navy their career, and he was fast approaching mandatory retirement. As long as he was useful to the Navy, they'd find ways to let him stay on, but was he just being arrogant to think that the Navy needed him as much as he thought they did?

Maybe she was right. Maybe he really was ignoring reality by clinging to his career so hard.

And she was right about something else, too. Tangretti hadn't always been faithful over the years. In his heart, he'd never felt he'd really been untrue to Veronica. The occasional fling with a prostitute or some casual pickup in a bar somewhere . . . those were meaningless, as far as Tangretti was concerned. It was almost an expected part of life in the UDT, and now in the SEALs, to be able to carouse anywhere, anytime, and leave a string of sexual conquests behind to mark the frogman's triumphant path. Tangretti had been a wild man in World War II, and when Korea rolled around he'd stepped right back into the role with barely a thought or a pang of conscience. Only later had he realized how he could hurt Veronica, but even then he wasn't always able to stay on the straight and narrow.

He hadn't pursued another woman since Hank Junior's sixteenth birthday. As a joke he'd taken the kid to a burlesque house, "to follow in your Dad's footsteps" as he'd put it then, but one thing had led to another and they'd both ended up doing a lot more than watch some fan dancers strut their stuff. And that had been an accident. It wasn't as if he'd set out to cheat on Ronnie. He'd just gotten a little too drunk, a little too rowdy. That was the way those things usually happened.

Nonetheless, Ronnie saw it differently. Maybe, all things considered, he really hadn't been much of a husband to her after all. And maybe he deserved whatever came out of their most recent quarrel.

But Tangretti wasn't a man to back down from a challenge, or he would not have stuck with the UDT for so long, or embraced the new SEALs so thoroughly. One thing a long and eventful life had taught him was that there was always a way out, no matter how tough things might look. He would carry out this assignment in Vietnam, and with style. And when his tour was over, he would win back Veronica Tangretti's heart, even if it turned out to be the hardest campaign he ever waged.

Chapter 6

Camp Tien Sha
Da Nang, Quang Nam Province
Republic of Vietnam
0845 hours

The UH-1 Huey set down on the tarmac with a roar of engines that was deafening for the men inside. Lieutenant Arthur Gunn steadied himself against the open door frame as the helo lurched sideways one last time and then came to rest, back on solid ground at last.

SEALs had to be ready for all kinds of conditions, and able to deploy from any sort of vehicle, whether it be a submarine, an airplane, or a fast-moving ship. Sometimes SEALs had problems with one or another of these delivery methods. Even a mild case of claustrophobia could make locking in and out of a submarine, as they had done in Cuba, a major ordeal, and there were some SEALs who had overcome a fear of heights to master the art of parachute jumping. Gunn's swim buddy in Underwater Demolition training had always been seasick when they practiced in small boats making high-speed runs to drop off or pick up UDT swimmers near a beach.

For Gunn, though, it was helicopters.

It wasn't a phobia, as such; he wasn't afraid of them. Nor was it airsickness, per se. He could fly in anything else, from an OV-1 Bronco to a jetliner, and never have a problem. But flying in helicopters always bothered him. The uneven motion, the clatter of turning rotors, the stink of oil from the engine . . . something about flying in helicopters always made Gunn queasy, and he was always inordinately pleased to get his feet back on the ground.

Still, he paused for just a moment as the engines began to shut down, and glanced at Steve Tangretti. Technically, Tangretti was senior to him, and by age-old Navy tradition the senior was the last in and the first out of any conveyance. On the other hand, Gunn was the actual commanding officer of MTT 4-63. Who took precedence? He wasn't sure.

Tangretti grinned at him. "After you, Alphonse," he said loudly, shouting to be heard.

"If you insist, Gaston," Gunn shot back. Thankfully, he dropped to terra firma, lurching a little on unsteady legs. He waited a moment as the others began piling out, and by the time the last SEAL was clear he could walk again without betraying any sign of his weakness.

At least it was better than being seasick, he thought. A sailor who got seasick was sure to be a laughingstock, but how often did a sailor have to travel by helicopter?

The SEALs walked away from the chopper, looking around like hick tourists hitting the big city for the first time. Trailing behind, Gunn found himself smiling. Two officers and six enlisted men, coming to Vietnam to turn the tide of the war that had plagued this corner of Southeast Asia for years. It seemed like a tall order, but then, these were SEALs.

Tangretti turned and waited for Gunn to draw even with him. "So this is Da Nang," he commented. "It's more than I expected." He indicated the skyline of the city visible to the west of the military compound that had been provided to the SEALs and their trainees, on the other side of the major river that swept down into the magnificent, sparkling blue waters of the South China Sea. Even at a distance Gunn could see the white stucco walls and colorful awnings of some of the buildings, giving the city a surprisingly Western look. It might almost have been transported intact from some Mediterranean beach and set down in the rugged Vietnamese countryside.

"Biggest city in this part of South Vietnam," Gunn replied. "Provincial capital, and a major deep-water port. When the French were here it was called Tourane, and it was a pretty typical colonial city. Lots of money and power concentrated here."

"Well, sounds like you've been doing your homework," Tangretti commented.

"Don't forget, we've already had Team One SEALs here. I've had access to more than just that basic backgrounder they gave you."

Tangretti pointed toward a complex of squat concrete structures close by the helo pad. The contrast with the vista presented by the city was disturbing. "Looks like this place has seen some fighting," he commented. "Hmm . . . that one over there reminds me of a Jap bunker I saw during the cleanup after Okinawa."

"That's probably what it was, once upon a time," Gunn told him. "Don't forget, the Japs took over this whole corner of Asia during the war, and they had to contend with guerrillas trying to throw them out. Then the French came back and ran into even worse resistance. Most of those blockhouses look like they were probably added after the war by the French garrison." He paused. "Now it's our turn. Hope we have better luck settling in around these parts."

"Well, we're not the Japanese Empire, and we're not a

colonial power," Tangretti said. "We're here to help these people."

Gunn shook his head. "The Japs proclaimed the brotherhood of Asians against all the round-eyed foreign devils, and it didn't get them much," he said. "And the French always said *they* were only trying to help. How's a peasant or a shopkeeper going to know the difference between Americans and any other bunch of invaders?"

Tangretti looked thoughtful. "You could have a point there, Arty," he said quietly. "We'd be well advised to watch our step, not throw our weight around too much. Captain Galloway said we want to keep the American presence in the background. Maybe the brass is on to the right notion, just this once."

"Yeah, could be." Gunn looked around. Camp Tien Sha had a makeshift look, all right, a combination of French and Japanese defensive positions, Quonset huts, and tents spread out over a stretch of open ground between the river on the west and the China Sea on the east. "If this is supposed to be our home away from home for six months, I'll sure as hell be glad to get back to Coronado. This isn't a military base. It's more like a reform school for renegade Boy Scouts."

"Ha!" Tangretti's laugh was derisive. "If you think this is bad, you should have seen Fort Pierce when I went through the first NCDU class there! Nothing but tents in a swamp. This is downright decadent compared to that."

"Yeah? Well, I'll take a little bit of decadence, thank you very much."

As they talked, a truck appeared from beyond the complex of bunkers and blockhouses, raising a cloud of dust as it barreled across the open tarmac toward the tiny group of SEALs. A car followed it, an older model French Citroën, black and somehow menacing. As the two vehicles stopped, a trio of men climbed out of the auto. The two from the backseat were Westerners, dressed in civvies and managing to look bland. The third man had been riding in front, a Vietnamese officer in a uniform Tangretti thought was probably Navy, with rank insignia that identified him as equivalent to a lieutenant j.g.

"Gentlemen," one of the two civilians began, his flat tone giving the lie to his friendly words, "welcome to Da Nang. My name is Frank Dexter. This is Mr. Lattimore."

Gunn hadn't been sure if they were State Department, CIA, or possibly even military men who happened to be out of uniform, but the delivery and the way they avoided referring to their organization made him suspect they were from the CIA. If so, the SEALs would be largely answering to them on this tour. He wasn't entirely sure he found that notion comfortable. There was something about working for the "spooks" that bothered him. At heart he was a straightforward naval officer who wasn't at home in the twisty world of international espionage.

"Arthur Gunn," he said. "I'm in charge of MTT 4-63. This is Lieutenant Steve Tangretti, with SEAL Two in Little Creek, who will be acting as an observer with the MTT." A sweep of the arm took in the rest of the SEALs from Team One, dominated by the flamboyantly Nordic figure of Thor Halvorssen and a squat, menacing fireplug of a man, Chief Torpedoman Richard Briggs. "These are my men."

"Excellent, Lieutenant," Dexter said. "If you'll kindly get aboard the truck, we'll take you to the barracks area where you'll be quartered . . ."

"Excuse me, sir," Tangretti interjected. He indicated the Vietnamese lieutenant. "I don't believe I caught this officer's name?"

The two CIA men exchanged glances. "This is Lieutenant Nguyen Thuy," Lattimore said after a moment. "He serves as our liaison officer with the Biet Hai."

Someone chuckled among the SEALs. "Hey, that's a

pretty poor name for a soldier . . . 'No-Win.' " Gunn thought it was GM/2 Jackson, the self-appointed wit of the outfit.

Before he could respond, Chief Briggs growled, "That's enough, sailor."

Tangretti seemed not to notice the byplay as he gave the man a quick nod. "Pleased to meet you, Lieutenant."

"Thank you, Lieutenant Steve," the Vietnamese officer replied.

"That's, ah, Tangretti . . ."

"Get used to being Lieutenant Steve," Lattimore advised him. "It's considered a mark of respect."

"As I was *saying*," Dexter broke in, "we'll transport you to your barracks and give you a chance to get settled in. Tomorrow you can get started working out your training program. Your students won't be ready for anything much until the end of the week."

"All right, SEALs, you heard the man," Gunn said loudly. "Into the truck! Move!"

They tossed their sea bags up ahead of them before swarming aboard, with Tangretti and Gunn climbing up last of all. As the vehicle lurched into motion, Gunn tapped Tangretti on the shoulder to get his attention. "Hey, Gator, stop gawking at the scenery and tell me something."

"What?"

"Why were you trying to piss off our new lord and master? We've only been in Da Nang for a few minutes. You trying for some kind of new personal record, or what?"

Tangretti shrugged. "I didn't like the guy," he said gruffly. "The quiet one, Lattimore, he's okay, but Dexter just rubbed me the wrong way. I didn't think he should exclude the gook that way."

"And is it any more polite to call the man a gook?"

"Hey, Arty, give me a break. I acquired a lot of bad

habits a long time ago, and it's way too late for me to
change the way I talk now. But I don't like some big shot in
a dark suit treating men who are going to be part of my
team like second-class citizens, no matter what their skin
color is."

"Right on, brother." That was contributed by the SEAL
on the other side of Tangretti, Radioman Second Class A.L.
Carter, a wiry little black man from Mississippi. There were
few blacks in the Teams, but like most SEALs Gunn hardly
noticed the man's color anymore. He was a SEAL. He'd
been through Hell Week just like every other man in the
back of that truck. Those were the things that counted.

Wednesday, 14 November 1962

Camp Tien Sha
Da Nang
1125 hours

"All right, people, we've got a lot of ground to cover in
the next couple of days. It might not seem like stuff you particularly want or even need to know, but believe me, if you
don't know what the hell is going on around you, there's no
way you can do your jobs properly. So pay attention."

Tangretti smiled as he listened to the chorus of muttering and groaning from the six enlisted SEALs in the briefing room. Just like his own Team, these were men who
preferred action to words, and they didn't hesitate to let the
two officers know their feelings.

"That's enough," Gunn said. "Now let's get down to it,
shall we?"

Tangretti leaned back in his chair and studied the toes of
his boots as Gunn launched into a briefing on the overall
situation in Vietnam. Back home, he reflected, few people

had even heard of the little country at the edge of Southeast Asia, and those who had probably thought of it as a land of jungles and savages.

In fact, as they had noticed when they arrived at Da Nang the day before, Vietnam was a place of beauty and culture. The French had occupied the entire region—Vietnam, Cambodia, and Laos—during the heyday of Colonialism, when European countries competed to acquire territory overseas and to spread civilization among the peoples they found in remote and backward lands. In Vietnam, the result had been an interesting blend of Western and Eastern cultures, where Buddhist monks walked down streets that might have been on the French Riviera, dodging pedicabs and French-built automobiles, while the air echoed with a cosmopolitan range of languages, Vietnamese, French, English, Chinese, and many others. Out in the countryside, the people were less influenced by the West, and still lived as simple peasant folk in tiny villages where they raised rice, water buffalo, and chattering little children.

The French colonial occupation had never been entirely welcome. There had been some savage fights early on to establish European rule, and the colony had seethed with discontent from time to time. At the end of the First World War a would-be revolutionary named Nguyen Ai Quoc had tried to bring the plight of his people to the attention of the world by arguing for an end to French rule at the Versailles Peace Conference, but to no avail. Later he absorbed Communist philosophy and mixed it into his message, emerging on the world stage under the name of Ho Chi Minh, "He Who Enlightens."

Ho Chi Minh rejected the Europeans, but he was no supporter of the Japanese when they arrived in 1940 proclaiming their Greater East Asian Co-Prosperity Sphere. Recognizing that Vietnam would simply be trading one set of masters for another, Ho's Viet Minh guerrilla resistance had fought the Japanese as hard as they'd previously fought the French. Eventually, the waning tide of Imperial power had forced the Japanese to withdraw. Once again, however, Ho saw his hopes of a free Vietnam dashed by the arrival of French troops, many of them fresh from the battlefields of Europe, determined to retain their long-standing hold on their Southeast Asian colonies.

But this time the resistance to French rule was far stronger. Despite better weapons and experience, the French forces found it hard to make headway against the Viet Minh, who had brilliant leadership in Ho and his general, Vo Nguyen Giap. After nine years of bitter fighting, a French force was surrounded and besieged by superior numbers at a remote town called Dien Bien Phu, where the Vietnamese troops wore down and then overran their opponents in a long and bloody fight.

The defeat convinced the French to pull out of Vietnam. The era of Colonialism was coming to an end, and the expense and trouble of trying to retain a hold on the nation was simply too much for the war-weary Europeans to maintain. In 1954 a treaty was signed in Geneva which arranged for the French to pull out of Southeast Asia altogether. The Communists were granted control of the portion of Vietnam north of the Seventeenth Parallel, with their capital at Hanoi. A "democratic" government was established in the south, under the leadership of President Ngo Dinh Diem, with a call for national elections within two years of the settlement. But when the time came, Diem had balked, and instead of becoming unified the two Vietnams had been completely estranged from one another.

As the years went by it became obvious that democracy in South Vietnam was a concept more talked-about than practiced. Corruption was rife, and the repression of any and all resistance had alienated a sizable fraction of the population. Diem's regime was likened to a Fascist dictatorship, but the West had decided he was preferable to the Communist alternative. Ho Chi Minh was already thoroughly in the Soviet camp, materially and ideologically, and Diem was the only available counterweight to him. But discontent in the South had been growing steadily, and there had already been one serious coup attempt in Saigon against Diem. Shortly after it had failed, with sharp repression afterward to punish the revolutionaries and clamp down even more on anti-Diem elements, a group calling itself the National Liberation Front had emerged. They were supported covertly from the North, and had a decidedly Communist viewpoint. These days they were becoming better known as the Viet Cong.

Now Ho Chi Minh's government was actively committed to reuniting the entire country under the rule of Hanoi's Communist leaders. Since 1954 there had been a steady flow of men and matériel southward, first agents, then arms and supplies, then advisors and small military units, all working to create another guerrilla force that could repeat the triumph of the Viet Minh, this time against the Diem government. The Viet Cong might not be much of a threat by conventional military terms, but they were a dangerous destabilizing influence in South Vietnam.

Communist influence had been spreading rapidly of late all over the world. Tangretti had served in Korea with the UDT, where the Communist North Koreans had come entirely too close to taking over the entire peninsula. The fall of Cuba had alarmed the United States even more, and coup attempts or ongoing guerrilla wars by Communist-backed forces in the Philippines, Indonesia, Laos, and elsewhere had focused American attention on the threat these posed to the West. Tangretti wasn't sure he agreed with the so-called Domino Theory, but experience had shown that the time to stop aggression was early on. If Hitler had been met with resistance when he overran the

Rhineland or marched on Austria, things would have been considerably different, and the same principle could be applied here. It was in America's interest to contain the spread of Communism, so it only made sense to support any opponents of the Communists, wherever they might be found.

Hence the American interest . . . and the presence of the SEALs.

Tangretti found himself wondering about their two-pronged mission. The straightforward training of local forces in SEAL specialties like beach reconnaissance and underwater demolitions was easy enough. Mobile Training Teams had been operating in friendly countries all over the world almost as soon as the SEALs had been established. The first two SEAL officers had visited Vietnam to assess the situation within three months of the unit's creation.

But Tangretti wasn't so sure about the deeper, darker part of their assignment. The SEALs were supposed to prepare their Vietnamese students for a series of very specific missions across the Demilitarized Zone and into the North. In a briefing earlier that morning from the two CIA men, Tangretti and Gunn had been told they were to start practicing these ops as soon as possible, which meant that they wouldn't even have a chance to pass down basic principles to the so-called junk commandos. Of course, there was already a cadre of trained men, sixty-two graduates of the MTT 10-62 class which had wrapped their training with an earlier SEAL unit in September. But the SEALs wouldn't have much chance to assess the level of training . . . and if things started going wrong, they could burn up their reserve of trained manpower entirely too fast.

The Biet Hai were supposed to be elite troops, though in South Vietnam you could never be sure how "elite" was likely to be defined. Diem's regime stressed loyalty to the president over ability and experience at all levels, starting with the senior officer corps and spreading down into the ranks. The president was known to be suspicious of any underling who gathered too much power, or too much popularity, so individual initiative and skill were discouraged. These junk commandos—Tangretti preferred to think of them as an elite Marine unit, something like the new Force Recon troops, rather than as a direct equivalent of the SEALs—could prove to be very good . . . but it wasn't guaranteed, by any means. Further, despite the obsession with loyalty within the ranks of the Vietnamese military structure, there was a growing danger of Viet Cong sympathizers working their way into any unit or organization and feeding information back to their real friends. So there was no way of knowing whether or not the Biet Hai would really be able to carry out the types of missions the CIA wanted them to attempt.

It all struck Tangretti as foolish, anyway. The SEALs were expected to prepare the Biet Hai commandos for missions without having any particular knowledge of the terrain, defenses, or special circumstances of their targets. They'd be able to pass on information obtained by CIA and Naval Intelligence sources, but those items could have been presented directly, without SEALs as middlemen. Nor could the Americans go north to gather their own intelligence data. All in all, Tangretti was very much afraid they would end up just spinning their wheels here. They should have been given permission to stage their own missions, with or without local help. At least then they'd know something of their own capabilities.

If Galloway wanted his input, that was exactly what Tangretti intended to tell him. SEALs weren't about training; they were intended for direct action.

He picked up the thread of Gunn's briefing again.

"Right now, the Biet Hai junk commandos are assigned to a series of camps stretching down the coast over a ten-mile strip from the base of Monkey Mountain—that's this high point on the peninsula overlooking the entrance to the harbor—all the way to the Marble Mountains southeast of the city. The commandos assigned to the individual camps are separated according to their intended specialties. Some are snipers, some are recon specialists, some are being trained as paratroopers. Our lot is based here at Camp Tien Sha, and our training responsibility begins and ends with these men. We'll have sixty-five new students, plus another group of Biet Hai who have already been given training similar to what we'll be carrying out. They will help us with the training program, but will also be subject to being called up for missions from time to time."

"What kinds of missions?" The question came from Machinist's Mate First Class Nicholas Dubcek.

"Recon runs, raids, and infiltrations into North Vietnam," Gunn responded.

"Hot *damn*," Gunner's Mate Second Class Stonewall Jackson said, grinning. Tangretti remembered him as the "art lover" from Team One, a lanky Virginian who preferred to be called "Stone" or "Stoncy" because he found the name his overenthusiastic Civil War buff father had hung on him too likely to draw jokes from his peers. "I volunteer!"

"The orders are that no American goes on any actual combat mission," Gunn said sternly. "We're here to advise and to train, nothing more."

"Well, shit, Skipper. Where's the fun in that?" Jackson looked downcast.

"Look at it this way, Jackson," Chief Briggs rumbled. "It'll give you more time to spend in your rack, or out looking for local pussy."

"Sir?" Hospitalman Third Class John Randolph, who bore the nearly universal Hospital Corps nickname of "Doc," raised a hand diffidently, like a student in a classroom. "Just what are the rules about fraternization with the locals?" He shot Briggs a look. "I'm not just talking about the whorehouses, sir, but about getting out and getting to know the people."

Gunn frowned. "You know that sort of thing is usually discouraged, Doc. Especially given the security situation. Don't forget, our unit is still supposed to be pretty low-profile, so we don't want a lot of casual talk where you might let slip details about the SEALs. And Ho Chi Minh's been slipping a lot of agents south, and getting a lot of local help from the Viet Cong, so you never know if your drinking buddies . . . or your whores . . . are actually enemy agents."

"On the other hand," Tangretti spoke up, "I can't think of a better way to develop our own intelligence network than to start making friends around here. And it seems to me it would be good PR for American servicemen to be friendly, you know? The Frogs wouldn't speak to the locals as equals, either, and we don't want to be lumped in with them, do we?"

Gunn turned an irritated expression his way. "Maybe so, Steve," he said quietly. "But I want to keep things by the book, at least for now. No big binges in the local bars. No chasing after anything in a skirt . . ."

"Hell, sir, most of the women in these parts wear pants," Jackson pointed out with a grin.

"You know what I mean," Gunn said. "Now, about our facilities. This camp ain't much, I'll admit, but it's our home for the next six months. The Biet Hai are responsible for camp security and such, and there are locals in charge of all the administrative and support services. We're the only Americans assigned here at the moment, although there are other Navy men assigned to the boats docked along the waterfront, Rangers, Marines, and Special Forces training the Biet Hai in other camps near here, and some Air Force personnel at an air base at the foot of Marble Mountain on the south end of the beach. But you'll find that we're spread pretty thin here in Vietnam, so this camp, like most others, is run by the locals. Now that's good in some ways, bad in others. Again, we want to be on guard against infiltrators and spies. But it frees us up to do our jobs."

Gunn stood up. "Let's talk about the second component of our job here," he said. "We'll be answering to Lattimore and Dexter. They're the CIA case officers assigned to head up covert operations in these parts, so they'll be handing us assignments from time to time. Now I know there's been talk of SEALs getting into direct operations." He gave Jackson a long, penetrating stare. "But like I said before, the orders I've been given say no American involvement in combat operations. Period. End of discussion."

"Then what will we be doing?" Dubeck asked. "Why put us under these spooks if we're not going to get to join in the fun?"

"More training," Gunn told him. "In addition to putting the new Biet Hai through their paces, we'll be expected to help the more experienced commandos set up for specific missions. We'll help them go through practice runs, advise on operational planning, that sort of thing. But when the time comes for a mission, we hand 'em over to the boat crews and let them go on their merry way."

"Those boat crews are a pretty scruffy-looking bunch," Randolph commented. "Not exactly regular Navy, if you ask me."

"They're not," Tangretti put in. "Uncle Sam's turned over a couple of old PT boats for use by the Biet Hai in their coastal operations out of Da Nang; they're docked down in the harbor, and the crews are quartered nearby. So they're not technically a part of our command, but we will be working with them in training and in helping the junk commandos set up their missions. In fact they'll be the guys we have the most to do with, outside of camp here. But not all of the crewmen are Americans. Each boat has Navy personnel on board, but the spooks have rounded out the crews by hiring mercenary types from all over—Norwegians, French, a couple of Aussies."

Gunn nodded. "That's right. A really mixed bag. Keep in mind the security requirements there, too. It could be important down the line. Basically, don't go shooting your mouths off to anyone, and you'll be in good shape."

"So what you're saying, then, Lieutenant, is that we don't get to go on ops, we don't get to socialize with anyone, and we don't get to have any fun. Does that about cover it?" Carter, the black man with the lazy drawl, didn't bother to hide the sarcasm in his voice.

Tangretti answered before Gunn could reply. "That's about it," he said with a grin. "Now go out there and have a great time!"

That earned him a laugh.

"Okay, you've had your chuckles," Gunn told them. "Now, let's break for lunch and meet back here at 1300 hours to talk about the curriculum. I think we'll have to modify Hell Week a bit. After all, these guys aren't SEALs, and we don't want to flunk out the whole Biet Hai before they even get started. But start thinking about how we hand these guys the essence of BUD/S training in a short course of sixteen weeks. I'll welcome any suggestions you guys might want to contribute. That's it. Dismissed."

The enlisted SEALs were talking loudly as they left the room. As Tangretti started to stand up, Gunn's hand restrained him lightly across his chest. "Look, Gator, you know I respect your opinions," Gunn said quietly. "But don't go contradicting me in front of the men like that. It's not good for morale."

Tangretti frowned. "C'mon, Arty, you know that 'no fraternization' crap isn't enforceable in the first place. And you know I'm right—about the PR value *and* the chance to develop some local intell sources."

Gunn's eyes narrowed. "I thought we all agreed that this was *my* team to run, Gator," he said softly. "You're supposed to be along as an observer, right?"

"Yeah, Arty. An observer." Tangretti tried to stifle a flare of anger and failed. "And I'm going to observe you run this whole damned training mission into the ground if you don't start loosening up a little. These are SEALs, not a bunch of swabbies from the black-shoe Navy. They aren't going to sit back and take a lot of crap from some little tin god of an officer just because he's able to quote all the regs."

"Listen to me, Steve," Gunn said. "This is the only time I'm going to say this, so get it through your head the first time. I saw how you ran things at Little Creek. You're a buddy to your guys. You go out drinking with them, you bail 'em out when they're in trouble. And you join in the fun when it comes to taking on the brass. That's fine . . . it works for you. But SEAL One's been run differently from the beginning. We're a little closer to the regular Navy than you are, maybe. Point is, this is my team, my rules, and if you don't like it, I'll bounce you back Stateside so fast you'll look like an incoming missile and set off all the DEW alarms."

Tangretti fought the urge to keep on arguing. Instead he snapped a salute, although he was indoors and hatless. "Yes, sir! Very good, sir!" he said crisply. "Permission to leave, sir?"

"Cut the crap, Tangretti," Gunn said wearily. "Just do your job, and stay out of my hair, and we can get along just fine. Come on, let's get some lunch, and then you can tell me all about the good old days at Fort Pierce and how we could adapt the original training program for these junk commandos."

Tangretti grunted a reply and followed Gunn out the

door. Inside, though, he was still angry. He'd thought Gunn was a real SEAL underneath his outward spit-and-polish image, but now he was starting to wonder.

SEAL Barracks, Camp Tien Sha
Da Nang
2015 hours

"What I want to know is, what gives this East Coast puke the right to question the lieutenant, anyway? Who does he think he is?"

Doc Randolph turned over in his bunk to lean on one elbow and look at Nicholas Dubcek. "I'd say he thinks he's Gator Tangretti, Nick. One of the first graduates of Fort Pierce back in World War II. Part of the mixed commando force in Korea. The guy who came up with the idea of forming the SEALs in the first place."

"A legend in his own mind," Stoney Jackson added with a grin. He was busy taping up choice pieces of his traveling art collection over his rack, but he had been providing the occasional wry comment along the way. A couple of the other SEALs chuckled in response to his sally.

Randolph ignored him and plunged on. "He's also senior to Lieutenant Gunn, when it comes to that."

"Yeah, but the way I heard it, he's just supposed to be along as an observer. *Not* in the chain of command." Dubcek lit up a cigarette and took a long drag on it. "Seems to me he's throwing his weight around too much, know what I mean?"

"Look, Nick, I like the lieutenant as well as anybody," Randolph countered. "But some of the stuff Lieutenant Tangretti was saying made sense. I don't see any harm in getting to know the locals a little bit. You know, I was kind of thinking I might like to get out in the countryside and sce how they live in the little villages. Maybe even offer them some help with their medical problems. It's a cinch I'm not going to have much to do looking out for this out-fit."

"Yeah," Carter spoke up. "If we don't go into action, there ain't much call for first aid, and if they don't let us go into town to get laid, you don't even get to pull short-arm inspections." The black sailor grinned. "Short-arm inspec-tion" was a euphemism for the periodic genital exams con-ducted to check men for signs of venereal disease.

"Doc probably doesn't like 'em any better than you do, Al," Halvorssen said.

"Probably gives him an inferiority complex," Dubcek said with a smirk.

"Just because you've got problems in that department is no reason to think everybody does," Randolph told him. "I think it'd be great if you guys could leave the local pussy alone for a change, though. Worrying about VD isn't exactly my favorite thing to do, you know, and I'd be glad if I could concentrate on something a little more civilized, just for a change."

"Fine by me," Jackson said. "I get awful tired of hearing that standard lecture about the joys of wearing rubbers."

"Tell me that again when you've got a case of the clap and want me to do something about it," Randolph said sourly. "Look, all I'm saying is that I signed up to see the world, not the inside of a Quonset hut. I just wish the brass would let us out, and I think Mr. Tangretti had a good point."

"You guys ain't missing much by not seeing the place," Chief Briggs spoke up for the first time. "I've seen these parts before, and they ain't worth looking over, let me tell you."

"When were you posted to Nam before, Chief?" Halvorssen asked.

"It was back in '60," Briggs replied. "I was still in UDT-

12 back then. A bunch of us were assigned to deliver some small boats from Yokosuka to the Laotian government in Vientiane. We took those old LCMs and LCVPs all the way up the Mekong River in the middle of summer. I mostly remember heat, rain, and snakes. Seemed like we'd pick up a snake every time we passed under some overhanging branches. After we turned the boats over to Laos we caught a plane to Saigon, hung around there a couple of days, and then headed back to Japan."

"Pretty odd duty for the UDT," Randolph commented.

"Yeah, that's what we said. Lieutenant Camparelli was one of our officers on the trip—this was back before the idea of his being CO of a SEAL Team was even a gleam in anybody's eye—and he always said he thought we were being sent in to get the lie of the land early, so that Washington would have some UDT types who already knew something about Vietnam and Laos in case things escalated out here. I guess there was a pretty good chance of a shooting war getting started back then, even. I heard from some Green Beanies who were stationed in Laos that they'd been in a few firefights that never got any play in the papers back in the States."

"Looks like they got what they were looking for, then," Carter commented. "You guys scouted things out back then, and Mr. Camparelli was over here in the spring setting up this whole MTT shit. And now here you are to lend us the benefit of your vast experience, Chief."

"All my vast experience tells me is that this whole damned place needs to be dried out, air-conditioned, and host a visit from St. Patrick before I want anything to do with it again," Briggs said. "The women I saw in Saigon were all so small I was afraid they'd break if I tried to lay one of them, and the only thing I hated worse than the taste of Vietnamese beer was the taste of Vietnamese food. They've got this fish sauce they pour over damned near everything that makes a Tijuana hot chili pepper seem bland by comparison. They call it 'nuke mom.' And that's just about what I figure it'd do if my mom ate it—nuke her hotter than Hiroshima."

The other sailors laughed.

"But you volunteered to return to this paradise on earth, Chief," Randolph pointed out. "Am I missing something?"

Briggs shrugged. "It beats doing PTs back at Coronado," he said. "And I figured there was at least a chance we might see some kind of action. That was before I started hearing all this shit about how we're under orders to keep out of the fighting."

"You never know, Chief. Things change." Randolph rolled over on his back again, staring up at the top of his bunk. "And whatever you guys think about Lieutenant Tangretti, I've heard he's the guy to be around if you're looking for some action."

Chapter 7

Monday, 19 November 1962

Camp Tien Sha
Da Nang
0530 hours

"All right, listen up!" Lieutenant Gunn waited to allow Thuy, the liaison officer, to translate for him before he continued. "Welcome to Hell Week, gentlemen!"

How many times had he heard those same words, starting with the time he'd first faced a tough UDT instructor at Underwater Demolition School in Coronado as a fresh-faced ensign just five years ago? He was standing on the grinder, the open area surrounded by barracks and other buildings in the heart of Camp Tien Sha. The other American SEALs were lined up behind him, and a small cluster of Biet Hai who'd already been exposed to the tender ministrations of the previous Mobile Training Team were standing off by themselves to his left. The little Vietnamese liaison officer, Thuy, stood beside him, rendering Gunn's speech into his native tongue. In front of the two men, sixty-five trainees from the Biet Hai stood in ranks, wearing the almost traditional BUD/S garb of shorts and T-shirts and looking, as most trainees did as they contemplated the first day of Hell Week, more than a little bit apprehensive. It was enough to make him want to laugh.

Instead he forced himself to maintain a stern expression as he went on. "For the next seven days, you men are going to learn a little bit of what it's like to be U.S. Navy SEALs. You'll be pushed right to the limits of endurance, and then beyond. We have a saying in the SEALs: 'The only easy day was yesterday!' We're going to run you ragged, give you too little food, too little sleep, and too much work. And after you've gone through that for a couple of days things will really start to get tough."

Gunn paused again to let Thuy catch up. Actually, the program had been carefully designed to be a watered-down version of what UDT and SEAL candidates received. He and Tangretti had put in a lot of hours together to tailor the training to these students. It wasn't that the Biet Hai standards were low—they weren't, not by the standards of the Republic of Vietnam's armed forces. The junk commandos were regarded as some of the absolute best the embattled country had to offer. But they still weren't SEALs or even UDT frogmen, not by any stretch of the imagination, and it was no part of their brief to drive out large numbers of the Biet Hai the way instructors winnowed out all but the very toughest men during Basic Underwater Demolition/SEAL school.

Tangretti had complained bitterly throughout the planning stage, saying that there was no future in trying to coddle a bunch of new trainees while spoon-feeding them portions of the BUD/S program. But he'd given in at last. These junk commandos had to be given enough of a taste of the American program, but as many as possible had to finish the course so that they could pass on what they'd learned to others.

And, of course, so they might join the ranks of the advanced class, the ones who would be carrying out actual

missions under SEAL tutelage once the Mobile Training
Team had gotten into the swing of things with the new-
bies.

"Now I want to point out the bell we've set up in front of
the admin hut," he continued when Thuy was caught up.
"Anytime things get to be too much for you, anytime you
decide you can't hack it, all you have to do is ring that bell.
That signifies your request to drop out of the program.
There will be no questions asked, no comments made . . .
and no second chances. I'm not sure how dropping out of
our training will affect your Biet Hai status; that's up to
your own officers. But there are other groups receiving
other types of advanced training, and if you don't want to
stay with us, I'm sure you could find a posting with one of
them."

Actually, Gunn wondered just what the fate of a
dropout might be. Discipline was harsh in the elite units
of South Vietnam's armed forces, though the ordinary soldier or sailor wasn't held to a particularly high standard.
The junk commandos, though, had received plenty of
attention from the Diem government, where the reaction
to any sort of failure or poor performance was swift and
sharp.

Well, it wasn't his problem, he reminded himself. They
weren't going to try to drive anyone out, but by the same
token they weren't going to force anyone to stay in the program if he really wanted out.

"You've all met the members of my SEAL training
team," Gunn went on after a moment. "They are here to act
as your senior instructors. I suggest you obey them
promptly and without question whenever they give you an
order. In addition, members of your own Biet Hai unit who
went through a similar course with our predecessors last
year will also be working as instructors. Remember that the
whole idea of this training program is for us to pass on our

skills not just so you can carry out new types of missions or operate in different ways than you've been used to, but also so that you can earn some nice cushy jobs training other junk commandos in these same techniques. So remember that you'll get the chance to treat your mates down the line just as nasty as we're going to be treating you!"

He would have expected American trainees to laugh, but even after Thuy finished translating there was hardly any reaction in the ranks—a few smiles, and a couple of muttered comments. Otherwise, his new students just kept on staring at him with wide-eyed, intent expressions. Was it a problem with the translation, or did these junk commandos just have a different sense of humor than he was used to playing to?

"This first week of training is going to be intensive. There will be plenty of physical activity and too little sleep. You'll be pushed hard, and the training will be virtually nonstop. Later on, after Hell Week, we'll settle down into a little less difficult routine, giving you a couple of days a week to train with your regular Biet Hai outfits." That had also made Tangretti argue with him, but it was necessary to rotate instruction between the new junk commandos and the ones who had already graduated the basic course but needed advanced training and mission preparation. It did make things hard for the SEAL training team, though, and Gunn understood Tangretti's irritation at having to stretch their meager resources so thin.

"So, expect to work your butts off, gentlemen. I want each and every one of you to give your very best. Obey orders, learn what we're here to teach, and you'll do fine. Otherwise, you can look forward to spending a lot of time performing unpleasant extra physical training. Chief Briggs!"

The squat, powerful senior NCO stepped forward. "Sir?"

"What say we start these guys off easy . . . say with a

run down the beach? Three miles should do it . . . first time out, at least."

"Aye aye, sir," Briggs responded. He turned toward the Vietnamese students. "LEFT FACE!" he bellowed. "FOR-WARD, DOUBLE-TIME! Move it! Move it! Move it!" Even with the language barrier there was no mistaking those orders, and the new class was quickly on its way.

Gunn stepped back and allowed the chief to take charge. He glanced at Tangretti, who was waiting silently off to one side, a little apart from the Team One SEALs. He knew Tangretti was still sulking a little over their confrontation after the first briefing session, and over their subsequent clashes mapping out the training program, but Gunn didn't intend to back down from his position by so much as an inch. Tangretti was one of the finest men the Navy's Special Warfare programs had ever produced, but he was also pigheaded, opinionated, and prone to strike out on his own anytime he felt like it. In a combat situation that was known as "initiative" and was encouraged as long as it led to success. But in the day-to-day operations of the peace-time Navy it could cause serious trouble. The problems Tangretti had gotten himself into over purchasing were good examples of why such officers were unsuited for the dull routine of administration.

He hoped it wouldn't be necessary to request Tangretti's transfer out. The man knew more about the UDT and the SEALs than virtually anyone, and he had some good ideas. Once he'd decided to join in the planning for the training course he'd made some excellent suggestions despite his differences of opinion in the ways some key points should be handled. Gunn wanted to be able to keep on tapping into that fertile brain as they went on . . . particularly when they had to start supporting the Biet Hai operations north of the DMZ.

But he'd also been warned not to let Tangretti take over

the whole operation. Captain Galloway had warned him to be on guard. Like Gunn, Galloway plainly liked Tangretti, but was well aware of his limitations.

Gunn let out a sigh. Time would tell, he supposed, whether or not his "observer" from Team Two would be an asset to MTT 4-63.

Or a liability.

Thursday, 22 November 1962

China Beach, Near Camp Tien Sha
Da Nang
1338 hours

Tangretti sat atop a tall sand dune the SEALs had nick-named "Magic Mountain" and watched as the trainees toiled through yet another set of drills. Today they were working on an obstacle course that had been set up all along the stretch of sandy beach that lay to the south of the high bluff that held Camp Tien Sha. Most of the active instruction was being carried out by the Biet Hai graduates of MTT 10-62, leaving the seven SEALs able to pull back and observe the proceedings. The clipboard resting on the sand beside Tangretti already included a number of short notes that would wind up in his next report to Joe Galloway on the subject of how the MTT program might be improved.

He had a lot of ideas on that point, and he planned to out-line every one of them to the brass when he had a chance.

Watching the Vietnamese commandos tackling the obstacle course made him smile in fond memory. Tangretti and obstacle courses went back a long time together since the one he'd first encountered in boot camp when he first joined the service. Back then he'd wondered why sailors had to deal with such things at all—it was so obviously the

realm of the grunts and dogfaces, not the sort of conditions
you were likely to encounter at sea. But that boot course
had paled by comparison to the one they'd devised at Fort
Pierce when he and Snake Richardson had trained for the
NCDU. Paul Coffer and Joe Galloway and some of the
most fiendish instructors ever gathered in one place and
given free rein to inflict torture upon a hapless band of
trainees had built a playground that took full advantage of
the marshy conditions of the little Florida camp. And running that course really had helped to prepare him for combat conditions. The lessons he'd learned in the hot, muggy
Florida sun had served him well on the shell-torn beach at
Normandy.

Since then he'd been required to recertify as a combat
swimmer three times, and each new course of training had
added some new and different wrinkles to the old favorites.
Tangretti hadn't experienced the new program put in place
since the creation of the SEALs, but he was sure that the
new BUD/S course lived up to the proud old tradition.

The obstacle course here was as watered-down as the
rest of the training program, but it still included some
tough physical challenges that would stretch the Biet Hai
right to their limits. The UDT O-course had twenty-six different obstacles the men had to get through. This one had
only eighteen, but they were still tough. From Tangretti's
vantage point he had a good view of two in particular, the
Belly Robber and the Slide for Life.

The Belly Robber was a series of logs mounted chest-
high in a complicated pattern which the trainee had to
weave his way through, over and under. From there he ran
to the improvised tower known as the Slide for Life, where
a pair of lines angled down over a long, muddy pool of
water. The trainee had to climb a rope to the top of the
tower and then slide down one of the lines to the ground
below. Tangretti had never liked having to go through that

particular obstacle. He hated climbing ropes, and he had never really mastered the art of the slide in a way that would win the full approval of any of the instructors who ever monitored his progress in any of the variations of the O-course he'd ever run. While he'd always made it in his own fashion, Tangretti had endured far too many chewing-outs over his sloppy performance on the Slide.

It was a particular pleasure, today, to know that he didn't have to show off his lack of skill, only watch and evaluate as others did it.

Tangretti watched one Biet Hai trainee hit the rope and start his climb to the top of the tower, only to lose his grip partway up and fall with a *thud* that made Tangretti wince even at his distant vantage point. He recognized the recruit, a Vietnamese villager named Duong, and shook his head. Duong was perhaps the clumsiest of the trainees—popular legend made him the clumsiest in the entire armed forces of the Republic of Vietnam—and was, by local standards, big, slow, and not too bright. Stoney Jackson had nicknamed him "Doberman" after the out-of-shape, innocent corporal of the old *Sergeant Bilko* show, and the tag was apt. But for all of his shortcomings, Duong had one thing that endeared him to the SEALs. He was determined.

The commando picked himself up off the ground and was back on the rope in an instant, but once again he didn't manage a good enough grip and he again lost his hold and fell.

By that time he had attracted the attention of one of the Biet Hai instructors, Le Xuan Chinh. A fiery, excitable little bantam-rooster type, Le made up in volume and anger what he lacked in height, and today was no exception. Crossing to where the hapless Duong was once again rising from the sand to take another run at the obstacle, Le ripped into the larger man with a torrent of verbal abuse. The tirade was in Vietnamese, but the meaning was clear.

But Duong didn't react at all. He just stood there, taking it all, with an expression of acceptance on his broad peasant face.

In ordinary UDT training, Tangretti wouldn't have thought twice about the incident. Verbal harassment was a big part of what Hell Week was all about. Instructors rode the trainees mercilessly, calling them every name they could think of, threatening them with dire consequences for their many misdeeds and obvious lack of any redeeming ability or quality, letting the trainees know that not one in four of them was likely to see the end of the training anyway, so why not quit now and save the government the time and money it took to prove that their sorry asses didn't belong in the UDT. He was sure the same conditions still prevailed in the BUD/S version of the program.

But that was back in the States, not here. One of the things they'd finally agreed on when Tangretti and Gunn had set up this program had been to keep the verbal harassment to a minimum. The object wasn't to drive trainees out in droves, as it would have been with the SEALs, it was to give as many of the Biet Hai as possible the experience of something like SEAL training without the ruthless elimination typical of American frogman training. As Gunn had said, it required a delicate balance. Tangretti still wasn't convinced it was the right approach, but it was the policy they'd laid down, and all the Biet Hai instructors were supposed to know it just as well as the SEALs.

He was already starting to get up when Le Xuan Chinh's assault turned abruptly physical. Le's hand lashed out in a sudden slap across Duong's face. Still the peasant didn't respond. Tangretti knew that if he'd been struck that way he probably would have retaliated—and no doubt ended up at captain's mast for "striking a superior officer." Duong's dogged acceptance of everything Le threw at him just made the big peasant seem that much stronger. He could easily have flattened his smaller tormentor with a single blow of one powerful fist, but he didn't even change his expression.

Tangretti trotted down the long, gentle slope of the dune and hastened to the site of the confrontation. It had already drawn other onlookers, mostly other trainees who hesitated to interfere with an instructor. But Nick Dubcek arrived just about the same time as Tangretti did, shouting loudly for Le to stop. The Vietnamese instructor didn't even seem to notice, though, so thoroughly consumed by his rage at Duong.

"Ngung lai!" Tangretti roared. It strained his limited knowledge of the language. *"Ngung! Stop, damn it! Ngung lai!"*

When he was similarly ignored, he took the Biet Hai by the shoulder and pulled him away from Duong. Le Xuan Chinh twisted free of his grasp and turned on him, one hand straying toward the knife on his belt, until Dubcek grabbed him in a full nelson. There was a long moment of tense silence before Tangretti signaled Dubcek to release the little man.

"I think that's about enough," he said quietly.

"Xin loi," Le said, visibly taking control of himself. *"Toi xin loi.* I am sorry, Ong Steve. I . . . *gian,* angry . . ." He paused, breathing hard. "This peasant should not be in Biet Hai. Too much *phan* . . . how you say it? Too much shit between his ears."

Tangretti fixed him with his best SEAL stare. "Listen to me, Le. I don't care how angry you get at any of these men, you keep that temper under control. If I hear you've been slapping around any of these men, I'll personally kick you so hard you'll land on the wrong side of the DMZ. You got it?"

"Toi hieu," Le answered, slipping back into Vietnamese again. Then he seemed to realize it, and added, "Understand. I understand, Ong Steve."

"You'd better," Tangretti told him. He decided not to mention the man's attempt to draw his knife. Taking official notice of that could cause too many problems, and anyway it had been clear that the excitable little commando had completely lost it by that time. But he would have to remember to mention the man to Thuy and Gunn. After a short pause Tangretti turned, ready to ask Duong if he was all right, but he remembered that the peasant's English was even worse than Tangretti's Vietnamese. "Who speaks English here?" he demanded. When one of the trainees stepped forward he ordered him to check on Duong's condition and let him know he wouldn't be subjected to any more of Le's abuse. Then he raised his voice to a proper parade-ground bellow. "All right, you squirrels! Back to work! You've got an obstacle course to get through! Move it!"

He exchanged grins with Dubcek and headed back for the sand dune, while behind him the trainees returned to their work.

China Beach, Near Camp Tien Sha
Da Nang
1545 hours

Lieutenant Arthur Gunn passed the line of weary-looking trainees being herded up the steep road that led to the camp at the top of the hill by their instructors. He tapped the jeep's horn twice and gave a casual wave to CPO Briggs, then turned off the road and onto the sandy stretch of ground at the edge of the obstacle course.

Tangretti was still on the low rise of Magic Mountain,

but he'd turned his back on the obstacle course and was staring out across the clear blue waters of the South China Sea. Gunn stopped the jeep and climbed out, walking slowly up the slope to stand beside the other SEAL.

"What a view," he said quietly.

"Yeah," Tangretti agreed. "You'd hardly believe a place this nice could be so close to that rathole up on the mountaintop."

Gunn chuckled. No one cared much for Camp Tien Sha. The base was nothing but a crazy amalgamation of cast-off buildings and equipment left by previous occupation forces, and it was all too clear to the SEALs that it had only been assigned to the training class of Biet Hai because no one wanted anything to do with the place. And although it overlooked the same sea, the view across a jumble of rocks and old Japanese blockhouses just couldn't approach the scenic beauty of this quiet little cove with its breathtaking curve of white sand set off by the bright blue of the ocean beyond. The Americans had taken to calling it China Beach, and Gunn, for one, was looking forward to every chance they could get to keep on using it as their main training area. The Silver Strand back on Coronado had nothing on China Beach for atmosphere, that was certain . . . you could almost visualize the place as a remote tropical resort catering to elite jet-setters rather than Navy frogmen from two different countries.

"Pity nobody thought to put a base camp down here," he said "I wouldn't mind making this place our permanent headquarters."

Tangretti nodded, then looked up at him. "You probably didn't come down here just to talk about the scenery. Something up?"

The other lieutenant gave a shrug. "Nothing much. I wanted you to sit in with me when I go over the progress of the class with Thuy after chow. Hell Week's almost over, after all, and it's time we started looking ahead to the next phase of this god-awful mess."

"Hell Week. Yeah, sure." Tangretti looked sour. "If you ask me, this stuff barely rates as 'Heck Week.' If those were UDT candidates we were working over, er, with, they'd all be dead on their feet, hallucinating, and barely able to hoist a beer at the end of the day."

Gunn laughed. "Heck Week. I like it. Maybe we should try to persuade 'em back home to downgrade BUD/S so that our guys only have to go through heck to get in, huh?"

"Not even as a joke, Arty," Tangretti said quietly. He stood up slowly, meeting Gunn's eye with a serious expression. "Look, I know we've been clashing over this ever since day one, but you know what I think about this watered-down sorry excuse for a training course. It doesn't do a damned thing to weed out the unfit, and it doesn't help morale the way Hell Week does for UDT and SEALs."

"Yeah, I know." Gunn frowned. "Trouble is, look what we've got to work with." He jerked a thumb over his shoulder in the direction of Tien Sha. "The Biet Hai would make good enough commandos, I guess, even if they don't measure up to all of the standards we've set for SEALs. But they don't have the equipment or the facilities to be a really first-class fighting force. I mean, the outfit got the name 'junk commandos' because they started off doing their operations off old-fashioned junks, sailboats, for Christ's sake. And I don't think any commando unit's too good that doesn't make the officers train alongside the men. You know morale's going to suffer. But so far Thuy's the only officer I've seen, and he mostly steers clear of the training."

"I understand he did go through the course that 10-62

ran over the summer," Tangretti said. "At least that's what I heard on the grapevine."

"Well, then he's a better man than most of the other Biet Hai officers," Gunn said. "Point is, they've got a lot of shortcomings as far as our methods of training are concerned right from the start. Now add to that this silly directive about making sure they're all able to spread the benefit of our training after we're gone, and while you're at it toss in this nonsense about splitting our time between the basic and the advanced classes. There's no way we can do the kind of job we'd do if we were back home. So we have to make compromises."

"They won't thank us for it when they get in a firefight somewhere and they only have part of the whole package of SEAL trade secrets to draw from," Tangretti said. "But I guess we just have to do the best we can with what we've got."

"That's the spirit, Gator," Gunn told him. He paused. "I hear you guys had some trouble out here today."

"Nothing much. That fruitcake Le Xuan Chinh got carried away dressing down Doberman. You talk about shortcomings of the training program. That's one little hot dog who never would have made it through Hell Week, I guarantee you."

"And yet his record's pretty good. He did pretty well with 10-62. Good diver and a crackerjack fighter. If he could just keep his temper, he'd be one of the best men in the advanced class."

"Trouble is, he's a talented amateur, not a professional commando. There's a difference. I know the government likes having all these gung ho types in their elite unit, but give me a bunch of professionals who check their passion at the door anytime."

"This from you?" Gunn grinned. "You've got more passion for your work than any ten other SEALs, Steve. That's why you're so damned hard to work with—because you won't compromise when you're sure you're right. If that isn't passion, I don't know what is."

Tangretti gave him a lewd grin. "If you don't know what passion is, Arty, then I'd be a little concerned about where the two kids came from. Know what I mean?"

Gunn laughed. "Hey, I thought everybody knew. The stork brought them!" He clapped Tangretti on the shoulder. "Come on, Steve, let's mount up and head back to the stables. I want a good meal in me before I have to take on all that bureaucratic mumbo jumbo with friend Thuy."

Together, they climbed down the sand dune to the waiting jeep.

Admin Hut, Camp Tien Sha
Da Nang
2012 hours

"Man, I thought we'd never get through all that shit," Tangretti said, stifling a yawn. "I thought it was just the good old US of A that ran on forms in triplicate, but I think these RVN guys have found a few tricks our bureaucrats haven't figured out yet."

"Yeah, it was pretty bad, all right," Gunn said. "Sorry to put you through all that."

"No you're not. Misery loves company, and you knew you were going to be pretty damned miserable going over those reports with Thuy."

"Well, after all, you're supposed to be observing what we're doing here so you can pass on our vast wisdom to the rest of your East Coast pukes." Gunn yawned this time. "Look, I'm turning in. Don't forget, we've got the IBL races tomorrow."

"Oh, joy." The IBL—Inflatable Boat, Large—was a key part of a late Hell Week exercise that required the trainees to do a marathon raft trip. For the MTT program, Gunn had decreed that the other six SEALs would be a part of the exercise, handling their own boat right alongside the ten Biet Hai boat teams. Gunn himself would supervise from the shore, something Tangretti had been riding him about from the time the evolution had first been announced. "Well, see you tomorrow, oh great and powerful one. I'm going to take a little walk around the compound and get the blood flowing after all that exciting administration we were doing. If I don't see you before we start in the morning, enjoy your day of rest while your humble servants toil."

Gunn grinned. "I intend to. With all the trainees and all the rest of you guys out of my hair, it might actually be peaceful around here tomorrow!"

The younger SEAL turned to head for the hut that they jokingly called the Bachelor Officers' Quarters. It was exactly the same as any of the other barracks buildings, but only the two SEALs and Lieutenant Thuy were housed there, spread out among the stacks of bunks. Tangretti watched him for a moment, glad that the breach between them was at least starting to heal, then turned and walked briskly toward the grinder.

He spotted the slender figure of Lieutenant Thuy on the far side of the open ground. Another man in an ARVN uniform was with him, talking volubly and gesticulating as wildly as any of Tangretti's Italian relatives. Curious, Tangretti angled across the grinder toward the two.

"Something wrong, Lieutenant?" he asked as he approached.

Thuy turned to meet him. "Nothing . . . serious, Ong Steve," he answered, but his expression looked strained.

"Some of my men got into an altercation at a bar in town. The military police have arrested them, and I must go in to take care of the matter."

"Want some company?" Tangretti could hardly believe he was making the offer. A few minutes ago he had been looking forward to some serious rack time to rest up for the IBL race. But he had been wanting to see something of Da Nang ever since the SEALs had arrived, and even a short trip into town would be a welcome relief from the boredom of Camp Tien Sha.

At any rate, Thuy looked like he could use some support. Tangretti thought of the incident with Horner back in Norfolk and suppressed a grin.

"There is no need to trouble yourself," Thuy began.

Before he could go any farther Tangretti interrupted. "Look, I'm not trying to horn in on your territory, Ong Thuy," he said quickly. "I just thought I'd like to ride along. I doubt I could be much help . . . but I'd be glad to pitch in if I can. Mostly I'd just like some fresh air."

Thuy smiled. "In that case, you are welcome, Ong Steve," he said. He turned back to the ARVN soldier and spoke in fluid Vietnamese. The man nodded, saluted, and motioned for them to follow.

He had left a jeep parked not far away. Tangretti climbed into the back, while the two Vietnamese took the front seats. It was an ancient vehicle, probably World War II surplus foisted off on America's ally in some foreign aid program. But like most of its kind the battered old jeep was still tough and reliable, and if the drive to Da Nang was bouncy and loud, Tangretti still found it exhilarating.

The city was brightly lit at this time of night, and the night life was in full, hectic swing. Tangretti was surprised by the cosmopolitan flavor of the city streets. He tended to forget that Da Nang had been a major city of the French colonial period, and it retained the flavor of a sort of imitation Paris even after nearly a decade without the French presence in Vietnam.

On the way, Tangretti took Thuy's mind off his wayward soldiers by telling him about the night he'd been called to bail out Horner, and Thuy laughed politely when he wound up with the punch line of the jukebox playing "You're the Reason I Don't Sleep at Night." The Vietnamese lieutenant seemed to appreciate the fact that there were some things that truly were universal to the military services of all nations. The ability of enlisted men to get into trouble that called for the intervention of their superiors seemed to be a universal constant.

The headquarters of the local branch of the ARVN's military police, the Quan Cahn, was located in the heart of the city. Inside, the place had much the same look as Tangretti would have expected to find in any Shore Patrol or MP establishment—or, indeed, of any small, overworked, understaffed police precinct anywhere. A civilian woman at the main desk listened patiently to Thuy's explanation of their presence, then pointed wordlessly to a narrow bench by the door. Tangretti and Thuy settled down to wait.

After a wait that might have been twenty minutes, but felt more like twenty hours to Tangretti, they were finally ushered into the office of an aging Quan Cahn captain. He seemed surprised to see Tangretti, but smiled, nodded pleasantly enough, and greeted him in fair English. Naturally the Quan Cahn would have plenty of people who spoke the language of their allies, given the number of incidents involving American servicemen that were likely to come across the captain's desk every week.

The bulk of the conversation, though, was in Vietnamese, which left Tangretti out of things. As Thuy and the captain exchanged lengthy, rapid-fire statements, he resolved to find a chance to learn more than just the basics he had already picked up. It would be very hard to operate with the freedom he was accustomed to if he couldn't sling the local lingo, as he'd previously learned in Korea. Tangretti also made a mental memo to recommend that all future SEALs posted to Vietnam be given at least some training in the language, customs, and general background of the country before being assigned to the country. Most of the Mobile Training Teams didn't require such, any more than regular military personnel in overseas stations needed it, but work as intensive as what the SEALs were doing really required that language barriers and differences in culture be eliminated wherever possible.

If the SEAL role in Vietnam expanded as Tangretti felt it should, such a program would be almost essential. SEALs involved in active combat duty, especially covert action, would find at least a smattering of the Vietnamese language very useful, both in the field and for gathering and evaluating intelligence information. He had certainly believed it worthwhile to have plenty of men assigned to the Cuba missions who could speak Spanish, and this was just an extension of that same idea.

Finally, the captain broke into a lengthy harangue, finishing up by calling an NCO in and giving him a string of curt orders. Thuy motioned for Tangretti to come with him, so the two followed the noncom deep into the heart of the Quan Cahn building, winding up at a holding cell. There were five men there, and Tangretti recognized two of them as Biet Hai instructors from Camp Tien Sha. The others looked familiar, but he couldn't place their names.

Again there were heated exchanges in Vietnamese, with Tangretti able to follow only a little of it. The senior of the prisoners, an NCO named Huan Van Nim, seemed to be describing a bar fight in considerable detail, with occasional interruptions and corrections from the others. Thuy lost patience after a few minutes and gave them a tongue-lashing that Tangretti could understand from tone and volume alone, without recognizing any of the actual words. It was the first time he had ever seen the usually self-possessed little officer lose his temper, and it made all the prisoners draw back and look ashamed. The phrase *"Xin loi"*—Tangretti knew that one, it meant "Sorry"—was repeated several times, but Thuy didn't seem interested in apologies.

Much to Tangretti's surprise, Thuy broke off the meeting and led him out of the holding area. At first he assumed they would wait for the men to be released into Thuy's custody, but that wasn't the case. Soon they were out of the building, on the sidewalk, with Thuy still looking like a thundercloud waiting for a chance to rain.

"Want to share the experience?" Tangretti asked mildly. "When are they being released?"

"They may not be," Thuy said, still angry. "At least not for a while."

"What's the problem?"

"The problem is that the owner of the bar those water buffalo broke up is very likely to file charges against them. It isn't much of a bar, from what I've heard, but the owner is . . . powerful. Many connections. Captain Huynh refuses to release the men into my custody until he knows what action the owner will take."

"So if the owner doesn't choose to press charges . . ."

"The men will be free to return to the camp. Otherwise, they'll likely face severe disciplinary action. Much worse than the offense warrants. But when you deal with someone who has political connections, such things happen."

"Don't I know it," Tangretti said fervently. "Okay, the next step's pretty clear, then. We go to see this well-connected bartender, or whatever he is. Maybe he'll listen to reason."

Thuy shook his head slowly, smiling. "I fear you may be optimistic, Ong Steve," he said. "You don't know what you're up against."

"Neither does he," Tangretti told him.

Chapter 8

Thursday, 22 November 1962

Le Parroquet Verde
Da Nang
2308 hours

The little bar showed every sign of recent remodeling, despite an air of seediness that pervaded the dingy little place. Tangretti suspected that it had looked something like a Parisian bistro in an earlier incarnation, back when Da Nang had been the colonial city of Tourane and the French had been the foreigners of the moment. Now the place looked more like a run-down nightclub, complete with a stage where a pretty young Vietnamese girl in a star-spangled bikini was dancing vigorously to the blaring tones of a jukebox playing "Blue Suede Shoes" loud enough, Tangretti told himself, that it could probably be heard in Hanoi. The Vietnamese were adapting to the slow but steady increase in the number of Westerners, especially Americans, in their country. The bland-faced Vietnamese man behind the bar had an eye patch that made him look like a pirate, and there was a motley-looking green bird in a cage hanging near the cash register that reinforced the appearance, and was presumably the source of the bar's name—in English, it would be the Green Parrot.

It was located in a bad part of town. Tangretti didn't have to know Da Nang well to know that much. It was on the fringe of the city's waterfront area, where there were few streetlights, plenty of dark alleys, and enough women in tight, revealing clothes striking up poses on the sidewalks to entertain a significant portion of the Seventh Fleet, should it come calling. Tangretti and Thuy had been forced to hire a cyclo, a tiny motorized version of the ubiquitous pedicabs that were the chief form of transportation in town, to get to the bar from Quan Cahn headquarters, since the jeep and driver that had brought them in from Camp Tien Sha were both military police assets that Captain Huynh couldn't afford to waste on a Biet Hai problem. The driver of the ersatz taxi hadn't seemed too happy to be heading for Da Nang's waterfront district this late, and Tangretti was inclined to agree with his viewpoint. He wished he'd thought to go back to his quarters to get his diving knife, at least, before volunteering to come into town with Thuy, but it was too late for second guesses now. Thuy had a pistol on his hip, and Tangretti hoped that and SEAL unarmed combat training would be enough if they should run into trouble.

After reaching the bar and paying the driver, the two men had entered and found a quiet booth in the darkest corner of the little bar, sitting with their backs to the wall and their eyes on the activity around them. There wasn't much of a crowd in the place, just a handful of Vietnamese men gathered around the bar chatting up a woman who was probably an aging hooker, and a couple of men who looked like they were from the crew of the French merchant ship that had been tied up in the harbor for most of the week. The bartender, a waitress, and the girl in the bikini were the only staff in sight. Despite the new theme to the joint, Tangretti seemed to be the only American around.

There were a few signs of the earlier fight still visible to Tangretti's practiced eye. In a business that aimed to crowd as many tables and booths into the available floor space as possible, the telltale gap near the door that led into the back almost certainly marked a table that had been broken during the brawl. There was glass scattered on the floor close by, too, and a garish painting of a reclining nude hung somewhat askew on the wall. Still, it didn't look like much of a bar fight, not by Tangretti's standards.

Of course, he reminded himself with a tiny inward smile, he was known as a bit of a connoisseur of barroom brawls.

He and Thuy had agreed to bide their time before approaching the owner. They watched, and exchanged a few low-voiced comments when the noise from the juke-box let them talk.

"I don't get something," Tangretti said. "If this joint is a regular hangout for military types, why is it they're coming down so hard on your boys? Most places would turn a blind eye . . . either because they like their customers, or because the servicemen have made it clear what they'd do if any goddamned civilians start pushing them around."

Thuy smiled. "You do not have all the facts, Ong Steve," he said. "In this case, it is a rather poorly kept secret that the owner of this bar is, in fact, a colonel in our Special Forces who also has some very powerful political connections. He has very little to fear . . . and I am afraid he is not likely to be friendly, either. Not to the Biet Hai. I have heard that you Americans sometimes have . . . interservice rivalries? Is that the phrase?"

"If you're being polite, yeah. That explains a lot."

They were interrupted by the waitress, who took their drink orders with the blank-faced indifference of someone who'd seen more than her fair share of life. A few minutes later she was back with their drinks, Tiger Beer for Thuy and a glass of something that was supposed to be imported scotch for Tangretti. He took one sip and set it down on the table, studying it suspiciously.

"If that's Johnnie Walker, than I'm the Master of Ballantrae," he said. "I smell a rat." In fact, he thought he could smell something other than a rodent, and taken in combination with the inferior liquor passing itself off as genuine scotch in his glass that smell gave him some ideas of the way these people ran their business.

It was just possible it could get him some leverage, too, if he worked things right.

The next time the waitress came by, Thuy asked to see the owner. She shook her head and pointed to the man behind the bar. After she'd moved on, Thuy filled in the blanks for Tangretti. The owner wasn't around, but the eye-patched bartender was the manager of the dingy little joint. He would have to do. Tangretti nodded. He'd expected that this well-connected Army officer would want to keep a low profile where his side businesses were concerned. That, too, could be useful.

A few minutes passed before they saw the waitress take over behind the bar so that Eyepatch could join Tangretti and Thuy. Seen close up, he was even more villainous-looking than he appeared from a distance, with a twisting scar running up his cheek to disappear under his patch. He sat down and looked from Thuy to Tangretti, finally fixing his one-eyed stare on the American and speaking in fair English.

"You wanted to see me for something?" he asked.

Tangretti shrugged. "Actually, I'm here for the atmosphere. It's Lieutenant Thuy here who wanted to talk with you."

Eyepatch shifted his look to the Vietnamese officer.

"I am an officer of the Biet Hai," Thuy said, speaking in English for Tangretti's benefit. "I understand some of my men caused some trouble here earlier."

"Trouble? I'll say there was trouble. The five of them beat up another soldier, from the Luc Luong Dac Biet, and in the fight they smashed a table and some chairs."

Thuy nodded. "So they told me," he admitted. "But they also told me that it was the other man who started the fight, though I did not hear that he was in the hands of the Quan Cahn."

The manager shrugged elaborately. "That is not my business," he said. "For all I know he is in the hospital. It was no fair fight."

"Although as I heard the story he claimed that one Luc Luong Dac Biet soldier was worth any five of the Biet Hai, and set out to prove the fact on my men," Thuy responded blandly. "I was also told that he was very drunk, and in fact fell on the table himself after taking a swing at one of my men."

Tangretti hid a smile. The Luc Luong Dac Biet were supposed to be the ARVN's answer to America's Green Berets, an elite Special Forces unit touted even more highly than the junk commandos. But in fact their reputation was decidedly different from the claims made for them by the government. Tangretti had heard it said that their initials, LLDB, actually stood for "Look Long, Duck Back," though one Special Forces sergeant he'd seen in California en route to the Mobile Training Team had referred to them instead as "Lousy Little Dink Bastards." And this wasn't just a case of the casual racism of American fighting men, either. By all accounts the LLDB had been doing a very poor job every time they came up against the Viet Cong, although they still held a high opinion of themselves.

And the bar's owner was an LLDB colonel, it seemed. Perhaps the local unit used it for a hangout, and resented the Biet Hai intrusion. Certainly there was now a conspiracy to protect the drunken commando who'd triggered the whole mess by pinning the blame on Thuy's men instead.

"I did not see much of the fight," Eyepatch said stiffly. "I only know that your five men were all involved and that they are responsible for the damage done to my bar."

"Not your bar, certainly," Tangretti said quietly. "Surely it belongs to . . . a certain colonel. One who would prefer it if the LLDB wasn't at fault."

The manager examined him with an uncertain look in his eye. "Just what is an American doing involved in this? What is your interest?"

"Like I said, I'm here for the atmosphere," Tangretti said with an easy smile. "Also, my unit's involved in training the Biet Hai, and I'd kind of like to keep them out of trouble the night before an important exercise. But I don't want to step on Lieutenant Thuy's toes if I can help it."

There was a pause while Eyepatch seemed to consider this. Then he looked again at Thuy. "I suppose that an . . . arrangement could be made for your men. If you cared to make sure that the damage they caused was taken care of—and providing the owner approves—there is no reason why your men should have to continue in Quan Cahn custody." He paused for a moment with a thoughtful expression before saying something else to Thuy in rapid Vietnamese.

The Biet Hai lieutenant blanched and spluttered an angry reply.

"Whoa, there, partner," Tangretti said, laying a hand on his arm. "Take it easy."

"This . . . this *krait* wants more money than this bar is worth for his cooperation, Ong Steve!"

"Calm down," Tangretti said. He turned back to the manager. "Look, would you give us a couple of minutes to talk about your offer? I'm sure we all want to work something out that will be satisfactory to everybody, don't we?" He smiled again, and Eyepatch gave a reluctant nod and left the booth.

"I am a poor man, Ong Steve," Thuy said. "I could not afford to pay this bribe even if I was willing to stoop to that kind of corruption . . . and I am not. Nor would I accept money from you to bribe this man, if that is what you are going to suggest as a way to 'work something out.'"

"Don't worry, I'm not particularly rich either," Tangretti told him. "And I'm not about to go feathering this guy's nest, not if I can help it."

"Then I do not see any way to handle this."

Tangretti grinned. "I had another arrangement in mind, actually." He stood up and walked across to the bar, turning his most charming smile on the manager. "Look here, friend, I think I might have a counteroffer for you. Now just suppose that I could put you and your boss in touch with a Marine gunny sergeant I know who is in charge of disposing of weapons and equipment that aren't needed by the Marines any longer. I heard he's been assigned to the naval base at Subic Bay in the Philippines, and I'll just bet he's looking for a few markets where he can sell off some of this gear and make himself a little profit."

"So?"

"So . . . even the stuff the Corps doesn't want any more is pretty good compared to the World War II castoffs I've seen the ARVN using. Wouldn't your colonel like to be able to get a better class of equipment for his unit? Or perhaps he'd know some better way to make use of it, something that would also be profitable for him."

And so the negotiations began.

Half an hour later, Tangretti and Thuy were heading back out to the jeep. "Ong Steve, I don't think I have ever seen anyone handle a situation like this quite the way you did. This sergeant—he is real?"

"Hell, yes. Gunnery Sergeant Hank Markham. I've known him since Korea, and he's one of the smoothest operators you'd ever care to buy from—if you're looking for somebody who's not too fussy about the source of his inventory. He really is at Subic Bay, and I'd lay odds he can get a lot of gear for our friend in there."

"I thought you said you didn't intend to bribe the man?" Thuy demanded. "Yet you are willing to be part of this illegal arrangement?"

Tangretti smiled. "First of all, I don't regard this as a bribe—just a way of generating a little goodwill between allies, as it were. I figure old Hank's going to peddle the merchandise one way or another, so it might as well do us a good turn here as end up in the hands of some bunch of backwoods revolutionaries living in the hills outside Manila. And it's not as if the stuff's likely to be all that much better, really, than the gear the ARVN already has. Markham's shifty, but he generally sells off the stuff that really is due for retirement anyway."

"Won't this come back on us later, then? Do you think these men are so gullible they won't realize this?"

"Oh, Eyepatch in there knows it already. I let him know pretty much what to expect. But I also let him know that I knew a few things about *his* little operation, too, and I think he decided this deal was the most face-saving way out of a bad situation."

"*His* operation? I do not understand, Ong Steve."

"Our boy with the bad eye isn't just watering the drinks, he's brewing them up in the back room," Tangretti said.

"My uncle Vincenzo used to make a better grade of bathtub gin than that when he was supplying for a speakeasy in Chicago during Prohibition, and I used to run my fair share of unauthorized stills in my younger days. Remind me to tell you about the booze I used to cook up on the APD I was assigned to before Inchon. I imagine the real stuff is going on the black market, and they're using the rotgut they brew here on the paying customers." He grinned. "From his reaction to my comments on the subject, I'd say the whole setup is One-Eye's idea, and the colonel doesn't know about it. Which makes our friend vulnerable."

"You . . . blackmailed him?"

"That's such an ugly word. Let's just say that we understand each other. I won't make a stink about the liquor—and even if the colonel *does* know about it, he wouldn't like it at all if I pulled some strings and brought in health inspectors and such on the grounds that this joint should be declared off-limits to American servicemen. And I offer a little deal with Sergeant Markham as a carrot to go with the stick. In exchange, your men are free, and Eyepatch here will even help me out if I ever have to get some information or find a good deal he can set up, or whatever. Everybody's happy."

Inwardly, he was thinking just how useful the evening's work had been. In one stroke he'd helped out the Biet Hai, won the genuine friendship of Lieutenant Thuy, and established a useful new contact at the Green Parrot. He'd have to see how he could get Gunn to relax the restrictions on fraternization—or find a way around them, if he had to—so that he could exploit the little bar to the fullest potential.

It was nice to be back in his element again. For Steve Tangretti, Vietnam was starting to look like a place he could really come to enjoy.

Thursday, 29 November 1962

China Beach
Near Da Nang
2221 hours

Tangretti was buried in sand, all but his head and arms covered. In the dark, he doubted he could have been spotted even with an infrared scope, at least not until the enemy was right on top of him. He had been there for hours, motionless, though it went against his usually restless and impetuous nature just to lie still, waiting and watching. It was damned uncomfortable, lying in the sand for so long, but the discomfort helped Tangretti stay alert.

Darkness made it almost impossible to see anything, though his eyes had adjusted to the available light levels enough to distinguish his surroundings in various shades of gray. More importantly, his ears could pick up the regular pounding of the surf along the beach. Somewhere in the distance, a motor throbbed, and he smiled grimly. Soon the waiting would be over.

Hardly breathing, he continued to listen to the night, until he heard an irregular splashing that sounded in counterpoint to the natural noises of wind and wave. Tangretti squinted against the darkness and thought he could make out something dark moving against the white surf.

The raft beached less than a hundred yards from Tangretti's position, and four figures bounded free and fanned out across the beach. They were good, he had to give them that much, good within the limitations of their conventional warfare training. They weren't bunching up to make a single good target, and each man was covering his section of the perimeter with single-minded attention to his job.

But one of the figures passed within ten yards of Tangretti and never spotted him. The SEAL smiled. That mistake would cost him.

He freed his knife and surged up from his hiding place, sand streaming from his body as he charged his chosen victim. With an ease born of long practice Tangretti seized his man from behind and held the knife to his throat.

"You're dead," he hissed in the man's ear.

His opponent obligingly sat down on the beach, and Tangretti went through the motions of wiping his rubber blade on the man's shirt. The Biet Hai commando looked up at him with wide, unbelieving eyes, but said nothing.

Well, he was dead, after all, at least for the duration of the exercise.

The other three junk commandos hadn't noticed the loss of their comrade yet, and Tangretti took advantage of the situation. He moved silently down to the beached raft, an IBS—Inflatable Boat, Small—drawn up above the tide line but otherwise left out in the open. Shaking his head sadly, Tangretti dropped to his knees beside the raft and checked the beach carefully in all directions. The Biet Hai had already moved out of sight, continuing their practice mission by moving inland according to the mission profile they were supposed to follow. With the beach to himself, Tangretti dragged the IBS away from the landing point, concealing it behind a small sand dune. Then he collected his rifle, a Chinese-made Type 56-1 knockoff of the Russian AK-47 that was commonly used by the North Vietnamese army. He positioned himself at the place where the boat had been beached and settled down to wait again.

It didn't take long for the three commandos to make it back. They were moving fast and professionally . . . at least until they caught sight of Tangretti.

"Bang," he said cheerfully. "Or, as my kid's Sergeant Rock comic books used to say when simulating automatic weapons fire, 'budda-budda-budda.' "

The senior NCO, a big man for a Vietnamese national, stared at Tangretti for a long moment, then let out a barking laugh. "You are one *dien cau dau* son of a bitch, Ong Steve," he said in a mix of English and Vietnamese. "How did you do it?"

"Superbly," Tangretti deadpanned, which provoked another laugh. The first "casualty" had joined his comrades, and all four were managing to look shamefaced at being outmaneuvered by the American.

Their leader's name was Li Han. He held a rank equivalent to a chief petty officer, and he was one of the few Biet Hai of mixed race. For the most part the junk commandos were all of pure Vietnamese extraction, but Li was different. His father had been one of the many Chinese who lived in Saigon, but his mother had been the daughter of an American missionary. He spoke English fairly well, as well as French and Vietnamese, and was a well-educated, soft-spoken man. Nevertheless, he was also one of the deadliest commandos Tangretti had ever encountered outside the ranks of the SEALs, despite his being caught in the SEAL's trap.

"I would not have believed it if you had told me you could defeat us so easily, Ong Steve," Li Han said.

"That's what they're paying us the big bucks for," Tangretti replied. "Lesson one. Always send in a swimmer recon first. Two men should scout ahead of the raft, and make a *thorough* job of it. Your raft doesn't come ashore until your swimmers have signaled it's safe. No compromises. No shortcuts. If you'd had your supercargo with you, I could probably have taken you all out with a burst of autofire before you even got off the raft."

Tangretti hunkered down, and the others crouched in a half circle in front of him. "Second, never, ever leave your raft out in the open. If you can't leave someone to guard it, then you should be damned certain you've got it well enough hidden to keep any casual visitors from spotting it. Hide it in the bushes, bury it in the sand . . . I don't know, paint it to look like a water buffalo if you have to, but hide it. Otherwise, you could lose your extraction ticket."

"I should have done that," Li Han said. "I suppose I let my guard down because this was just an exercise . . ."

"Never treat an exercise as anything less than the real thing," Tangretti said. "Never. You'll always fight the way you practice, so if you're sloppy in training, the odds are you'll be sloppy in the field, too." He paused. "Final point. Keep your eyes on each other. Now I'm not saying any of you should try to do your teammate's job—you need to stay focused on what you have to do, and trust your buddy to do his job. That's the whole point of being part of a team. But teammates also back each other up when they get in trouble. You've got to go out there each time you're on a mission knowing with absolute certainty that the guy guarding your back is going to be there for you, and he has to know that you'll be there for him, too. That's the real secret to an elite fighting unit, gentlemen, the knowledge that every member of the team is your brother. You might fight with him, steal his girl, rob him blind in the weekly card game, whatever, but when you go into action you're all looking out for each other. I should never have been able to pick off one man and then set up an ambush on the rest of you. Not if you'd been working as a team."

Li Han nodded slowly. "I understand, Ong Steve," he said. "We will think about these things, and when we try this again we will do what we can to act on them." There was a murmured assent from the others.

"That's good," Tangretti said. "Because you've only got another week or so before your big mission, and you'd better be ready for action when the time comes. There's no second chances when you're up against the enemy."

Friday, 30 November 1962

Le Parroquet Verde
Da Nang
2115 hours

"The word is that you made my best team look foolish last night, Ong Steve. I hope you aren't ready to give up on the Biet Hai because they showed up so poorly."

Tangretti leaned back in his seat and took a sip of Tiger Beer. "Trust me, Ong Thuy, they didn't do as poorly as they may have thought. I'm afraid a lot of people get taken by surprise by SEALs." He was thinking of the training mission they'd run during the early summer on the island of Vieques off Puerto Rico, when SEALs from Team Two were assigned to mount a recon and raiding mission against a Marine unit. The SEALs were supposed to slip ashore and plant a series of simulated explosive devices, while the Marine task was simply to stop them. But although the jarheads had full knowledge of the coming raid, they'd badly underestimated the unorthodox way of thinking that the SEALs cultivated routinely. The frogmen had hidden in plain sight by stripping to their trunks and mixing with civilians sunning themselves on the beach, even waving like goofy tourists when a Marine helicopter had passed right overhead. Later a few of the SEALs had put their fatigue uniforms back on and walked brazenly right into the Marine camp, where they took in a movie while listening to their opponents speculating on what the secret new Navy unit might be like and how much trouble they'd have penetrating the Marine perimeter to carry out their mission.

No, Thuy's men hadn't performed all that badly. They just didn't quite have the right mind-set for conducting unconventional warfare the way Tangretti had learned it over the years, right from the day he and Snake Richardson had violated orders and personally examined a Japanese-held beach when they were supposed to remain well out in the water and observe from a distance. The Biet Hai would learn, though. Tangretti thought that learning the essence of unorthodox solutions to tactical problems might be better than all the Mobile Training Teams might do in the way of showing off new equipment or new demolitions techniques.

Tangretti was sitting with Thuy in the same booth they had occupied the first time, sampling their drinks and taking in the activity in the little bar/nightclub. Tonight it was more crowded, and there were a few tables occupied by men of the LLDB, but they were apparently on notice to ignore Thuy and his American friend. So far there hadn't been any sign of trouble. The music was still loud—tonight it was Bill Haley and the Comets—and the dancer, a different girl from last time, was wearing even less. All in all, though, there wasn't anything particularly interesting or exciting about the evening.

Still, Tangretti found himself taking no little pleasure in being here. Gunn had reaffirmed his orders regarding SEALs fraternizing with the locals outside the call of duty, but Tangretti had simply reinterpreted the order to suit his own desires. After all, he was building better relations with the Biet Hai liaison officer, as well as doing some private scouting for better sources of information. It always gave Tangretti a secret thrill to be able to put one over on the system, even when the system was represented by someone he regarded as a friend, like Gunn. After all, he'd pulled a few fast ones on Snake Richardson back in the old days, and there'd never been a better buddy than Snake.

Thuy leaned close to Tangretti. "You see that man at the bar. The one in the peasant clothes?"

Tangretti spotted the man and nodded. "What about him."

"That is no peasant," Thuy said. "He is a major in the

Viet Cong. Responsible for half of what the Communists do here in Da Nang."

"What?" Tangretti was incredulous. "You can just point him out like that? How is it he's able to show his face in the city? Why doesn't somebody pick him up?"

"Well, we know who he is . . . but we have no real proof of it. He makes his living driving a cyclo, or so it seems. But there are rumors . . . stories . . ."

"So the guy just comes and goes as he pleases? The police don't even try to stop him? Or the Quan Cahn?"

Thuy shook his head. "If they picked up every person who was suspected of being Viet Cong, Ong Steve, the jails would fill up fast. But unless he's foolish enough to do something to get himself caught, there is little we can do."

"I don't understand this war you're fighting, Thuy," Tangretti said, exasperated. "Ever since I got here I've been hearing all about the fighting, but I've never seen anything of it. There are supposed to be VC up in the Marble Mountains overlooking China Beach, but they let us go about our business and never bother us. And now I hear that a Viet Cong officer just comes and goes as he pleases right here in a major city, and you don't lift a finger to stop or capture him!"

Thuy shrugged. "I do not make the rules by which the war is fought, Ong Steve."

"Well, why don't *you* do something about it? Put the man under surveillance. Follow him and take him prisoner when he's off by himself somewhere . . . or let him lead you to wherever his VC are hiding. Do *something*, for God's sake."

"This is not my area, Ong Steve," Thuy said, frowning. "The Biet Hai are maritime commandos, not Intelligence operatives. Or police."

"Remember what I was telling you about taking people by surprise, Thuy?" Tangretti said. "Well, friend, I think this is one time you might want to do it. Stop waiting for orders and take the initiative. If you could set up a tight enough surveillance on this character, you might crack open the whole VC cell in this part of the country."

"We would not eliminate that many Communists, Ong Steve. They would scatter, and then regroup, as they always do."

"Ah, but think of the intell you might get! Thuy, the most important asset a military unit can have is intelligence information. Preferably fresh, accurate, and detailed. Now you can leave it for the official spy types if you want. But I guarantee you this, the information you can get from sources you control will always be better than what some other agency hands you."

Thuy sat still for a long moment, as if digesting Tangretti's comments. Finally, he looked the SEAL in the eye. "Exactly what would you do in this situation, Ong Steve? How would you handle it?"

Tangretti smiled broadly. "I would start by putting in a phone call to your boys at Camp Tien Sha. Get a couple of them out here in civilian clothes to keep tabs on your suspect. Have him tailed for a while, changing your surveillance teams as often as possible so he doesn't catch on to the fact he's being followed. Then . . . Well, just see where he goes, who he sees, what he does. And when you think the time's right, just swoop in and you've got him."

Thuy rose slowly. "I will try your 'initiative,' Ong Steve," he said. "Perhaps my superiors will see the value in your ideas. I trust you will argue the case with the same eloquence should they decide, instead, to have me court-martialed for exceeding my authority."

"Hey, come on, Thuy, a court-martial is no big deal. I've been threatened with them lots of times, but I've always beaten the system one way or another. Live dangerously . . . and think about the rewards, not the dangers. Pull this off right and you'll be getting a medal, instead."

Thuy shook his head doubtfully, but headed for the public phone near the rest rooms all the same.

Tuesday, 4 December 1962

CIA Station
Da Nang
1430 hours

It was the first time Tangretti had visited the CIA headquarters building in downtown Da Nang, and he didn't know whether he should be impressed or amused. From the looks of the place, it had been a small villa belonging to some rich Frenchman during the colonial period, an oversize, overelegant building sitting on a parklike piece of land thoroughly hemmed in by the city's recent growth. Considering the relatively small size of the CIA presence in Da Nang—the two officers in charge had only a few specialists and support staff—the ostentatious surroundings were entirely too much. Especially for a group that prided itself on secrecy as much as El Cid. He was reminded of the jokes that had been current back in World War II about the predecessor of the CIA, the infamous OSS. It had been an article of faith among servicemen that the initials had actually stood for "Oh So Social" because of the haughty attitudes and expensive lifestyles of the upper-crust types who made up the bulk of the outfit's personnel. It seemed that some things hadn't changed over the years.

He was sitting at a large oval table in what had probably started out as a formal dining room before the Agency had taken over. Now it was a conference room, with room for a large staff meeting and a large map of Vietnam dominating the wall under Dexter's seat at the head of the table.

"So it seems we owe Lieutenant Thuy and his people a

considerable debt of gratitude," William Lattimore was saying. He was seated next to Dexter, both of them impeccably dressed in the trademark dark suits that seemed to be the uniform of the day for CIA operatives in the field. Tangretti, wearing his usual olive drab fatigues, felt distinctly underdressed. Not that he was likely to start dressing up just for a meeting with the resident spooks.

"The Biet Hai not only brought in a Viet Cong major and several of his people, they also nailed a spy who was placed right here in this building," Dexter put in, looking sour. "One of my file clerks. We're only now beginning to get an idea of how much she was able to pass on to the Communists."

"Sounds like you guys need a better security setup," Tangretti commented, not bothering to hide a smile. After seeing firsthand the cavalier attitude of the two CIA men toward the local population, including Thuy, he was glad they'd been taken down a peg. One thing Tangretti had always despised was anyone who underestimated an enemy's capabilities. Men got killed that way—usually men like his SEALs, rather than the rear-echelon wonders who made the mistakes in the first place. "I would've thought that a pair of CIA agents would be a little more conscious of security."

Dexter fixed him with a piercing stare. "Officers, if you please, Lieutenant."

"What?"

"In the CIA, Lieutenant," Lattimore jumped in, "we use the word 'agent' to refer to our local assets. Agency representatives are referred to as 'officers' or 'case officers,' never as 'agents,' if you please."

Lieutenant Gunn spoke up from the opposite side of the table from Tangretti, ignoring the byplay. "Does any of this affect our mission?" he asked. "We've been rehearsing for that Biet Hai landing op next week. Has it been compromised by this?"

"We don't believe so," Lattimore said. "The mission remains a go for the moment. Unless we discover something that might indicate she passed on those plans, we want this thing to go down as planned."

"I'm not so sure that's such a good idea," Tangretti said. "Even if your clerk didn't get hold of the mission specs, I'd say there's pretty good odds there are other spies around here you haven't found yet. Might be a good idea to change things around just to keep the bad guys guessing."

Lattimore shook his head. "This op is too time-sensitive," he said. "Saigon set it up, and they want action now." He glanced at Thuy, who was beside Tangretti. "I believe your superiors have already discussed this with you?"

"Yes, Ong Frank," the Biet Hai lieutenant said. "Provided the transportation is still available, my men are ready to go in as planned. Assuming their instructors are satisfied with their preparations." He glanced at Tangretti.

He shrugged. "I want to see another run-through to see what they made of the last critique," he said. "But I'd say they're as ready as they'll ever be." He was tempted to find an excuse to derail the mission, just in case there really had been information leaked to the enemy, but that wasn't the way Tangretti worked. He might twist almost anything to get his way, but he never made a false assessment of the capabilities of the men under his command. That was an ironclad rule he'd set for himself early on.

Besides, there was no way to judge if a delay really would be a good idea. More time would just give the VC a chance to plant new agents in the Agency headquarters, or somewhere else where they could discover the Biet Hai mission and transmit details to the North. When literally anyone might be a secret Cong sympathizer, the odds were even that a spy was going to end up in a sensitive position. The best security in the world would still have trouble keeping them out, and from what Tangretti had seen so far the American presence in Vietnam didn't have particularly good security yet. There was a general mind-set that this wasn't a real war, just a collection of advisors letting Saigon call the shots. That was something that was sure to wind up in one of his reports to Joe Galloway. Until the Americans in Vietnam started treating this more like a real war, they were asking for trouble.

Gunn was frowning. "One question I did have, sir," he said slowly. "This little operation in town that bagged the major and the spy. If it was a Biet Hai show, why weren't my SEALs at least informed of it? We could have screwed them up by pulling a night practice run, or assigning those particular men to some other duty around the compound. It's not that I want my finger in every pie . . . I just like to know what's going on so we don't trip over each other."

Dexter looked at Thuy, then at Tangretti. "According to Lieutenant Thuy's report, Mr. Tangretti helped him plan it all," he said slowly. "I assumed it had your okay, Lieutenant."

Gunn turned an irritated stare on the other SEAL, who shrugged. "This was all in the nature of an improvisation," Tangretti said. "The opportunity presented itself, and Lieutenant Thuy used his initiative. I saw no reason to involve anyone else in what amounted to a very unofficial operation."

"I see," Gunn said tightly. "Very well, since the results turned out to be worthwhile, I don't see how I can take any sort of disciplinary action. Not *this* time. But I hope in the future you'll consult with me before coming up with any similar acts of 'initiative.' "

Dexter cleared his throat. "If we might get back to the subject at hand, gentlemen?" He leaned forward, steepling his fingers on the table. "There is the matter of final preparation for the Biet Hai mission. I feel it might benefit the Mobile Training Team program if a SEAL accompanies the mission going north . . . with the understanding that no American is to be involved in the actual operation ashore. Mr. Tangretti? I was assuming that you would be the best person for the job, but if Lieutenant Gunn lacks confidence in your ability to follow orders . . ."

Chapter 9

Friday, 7 December 1962

Patrol Boat *Adder*
Off the DMZ
2127 hours

Officially, the battered old torpedo boat didn't have a name, only a hull number; it didn't exist on any official records, and answered only to the Central Intelligence Agency Tangretti and the other SEALs had hung names on both of the boats, however—*Adder* and *Boa*—and the designations had stuck. The boat crews, the junk commandos, even Lattimore from the CIA HQ in Da Nang had all started using them.

Adder was on the prowl, working her way up the coast past the Demilitarized Zone and into North Vietnamese waters. In the blackness of the tropical night, Tangretti could see very little beyond the dimly lit confines of the well deck, and he knew the boat would be hard to spot as it crept slowly northward, keeping well offshore in the Gulf of Tonkin. But the irregular throb of the ancient engines bothered him. Perhaps these were the most readily available craft the United States had been able to provide to their Vietnamese allies, but neither boat was particularly good for stealthy approaches to enemy beaches. They would have to stay farther from shore than a newer, quieter boat, which meant a longer raft trip for the four Biet Hai commandos and their companion, a Vietnamese Intelligence agent who had been introduced only as Bui.

He had managed to persuade Gunn and the CIA officers to let him accompany the Biet Hai mission after all, although Gunn was still mad enough over his involvement in Thuy's spy capture to have given him another lecture full of warnings of what would happen to him if he didn't stay exactly where he belonged, on the deck of the *Adder*, throughout the entire operation. It would have been easy enough, he thought, to circumvent Gunn's restrictions, but Tangretti told himself firmly not to try. He had to win back some part of Gunn's trust, if he could, and the Biet Hai would be better served if they relied on themselves rather than having him tagging along to confuse the issue.

Still, it was a terrible temptation to try to join the operation. He hadn't realized how very boring the MTT assignment was getting until he saw the four junk commandos getting ready for their covert foray ashore. Then it had hit him . . . he really was just along for the ride. Only a month in Vietnam and he was already beginning to feel as if those heady days of the recon work off Cuba had happened a whole lifetime ago.

Now that the watered-down version of Hell Week was over, the SEALs were turning their attention to the other reason they were in Da Nang, the advanced training and planning support of the Biet Hai teams that had graduated from the course run by MTT 10-62, their predecessors. They were needed to conduct covert operations on the other side of the DMZ, and it was up to the SEALs to help them get ready for these dangerous missions. Practice runs like the one Tangretti had "ambushed" and long sessions going over plans to meet every possible contingency were now interspersed with the rest of their training duties, and tonight was the culmination of all that extra work.

The training program had given Tangretti a new respect for the junk commandos. They might not be SEALs, but they were tough and disciplined. Even trainees like the clumsy peasant Duong had the kind of spirit that made for a superb fighting man, and he was beginning to think their trainee class could have taken a shot at the real Hell Week, rather than what they were still jokingly referring to as "Heck Week." Tangretti was beginning to suspect that more Biet Hai might have come through BUD/S training without ringing the bell than a comparable number of American sailors. Of course, all of them had already been through Vietnamese-based commando training, and they were part of an elite and highly motivated unit to start out, but it went beyond that. These junk commandos were a lot tougher than they looked, and for the most part the Biet Hai had proven to be stolid, determined, physically and emotionally strong men who accepted every order, every challenge, with a fortitude that had won the respect of all the SEALs in MTT 4-63. A few had dropped out in the face of the intensive training program, but not many. And those who remained were damned good men.

As for the advanced students, the ones passed to carry out missions like the one tonight, they seemed to know their business exceptionally well. Even though Tangretti had managed to surprise them a time or two, as in the ambush on China Beach, he found them considerably more adaptable than many an American combat outfit the SEALs had dealt with in the past year.

Once Tangretti had seen what the Vietnamese commandos could endure, he'd found himself gravitating toward them. He had arrived in Vietnam expecting typical Third World fighting men, ill trained, poorly disciplined, indifferently led. Instead he'd found men every bit as deter-

mined as the best of the UDT, men who could very well
have made it through the regular SEAL training program
handily. So he'd started getting to know them as individu-
als, and his respect for them had only grown on closer
association.

The four Biet Hai men aboard *Adder* had been hand-
picked by Thuy, Gunn, and Tangretti for the first foray
above the DMZ. They were among the very best of the
graduate Biet Hai, equally good at serving as instructors
for the new class and at the simulated combat ops the
SEALs had been supervising. Li Han, their leader, struck
Tangretti as a particularly intelligent and competent leader
of men, a tough NCO type who might easily earn himself a
field commission. A few words from Tangretti had sufficed
to make Li tighten up his team so that their second dress
rehearsal had gone almost flawlessly, thoroughly redeeming them after the earlier fiasco with the SEAL.

Li was lounging near Tangretti in the well deck, wearing
nothing but swim trunks and carefully sharpening a
wicked-looking knife on a small whetstone. In the darkness, Tangretti couldn't quite make out the tattoo on his
chest, the one that read *Sat Cong*. "Kill the Communists"—it wasn't exactly the ideal decoration to sport when
going ashore in Ho Chi Minh country, Tangretti thought.

Many of the Biet Hai sported the tattoos, though. They
were fanatically opposed to the Communist regime in the
North and to the prospect of a takeover by the Viet Cong in
South Vietnam. If they were captured, those tattoos would
condemn the men to death, but they didn't seem worried at
the prospect.

"So, Lieutenant Steve, are you coming ashore with us
tonight?" Li asked, showing white teeth that contrasted
with the camouflage paint that covered his face and body.

"Wish I could," Tangretti said. "But this is supposed to
be your show, tonight."

The junk commando laughed. "My men, they know how much you want to get out and kill something, Lieutenant Steve. The Biet Hai understand the feeling. We would kill all the Communists, if we could, but we would be glad to save a few for you."

"It's not so much that I want to kill anyone," Tangretti told him. "But I wish I could get into some kind of action."

"Ah, you are in this for the sport, then?" Li shook his head. "This is something we don't understand about your SEALs. The ones who trained my class were the same way."

"What don't you understand?"

"For you Americans, especially you SEALs, fighting is like a game. You want to match yourselves against an enemy, to prove you are more clever or more skilled. This isn't the way it is for us, you know."

"No?"

The Biet Hai commando showed his teeth again, but this time the smile was predatory. "No. We fight for our people, Lieutenant Steve. When the French were here, we fought to be free of them. And from the Japanese before that. But many of us did not fight to put Ho Chi Minh and his ideas into power. We wanted what you Americans take for granted. Freedom. A government that protects our rights. A field we can call our own in the country, or a job where we can earn money for ourselves in the city. These are things the Communists would deny us, just as the French did before. Our fight isn't about proving ourselves to anyone, Lieutenant Steve. It is about killing, or being killed, in the hopes that one day our families may be as free as yours are in America. So we kill the Communists, and one day perhaps there won't be any of them left to threaten us."

Tangretti nodded. "I suppose that's the . . . most effective way of taking care of the problem," he said. "But do you really have anything like the freedom you want now? I mean, I've heard some nasty things about the government in Saigon, some of them from your own men."

Li shrugged, a surprisingly Gallic gesture. "President Diem's government is not very . . . popular, these days. Someday it will probably fall, and be replaced by something better. But at least Diem and his ministers keep their corruption to themselves. They do not spread it to every level of government, setting political agents and tax collectors with armed guards to force everyone to pay 'each according to his ability,' like the Communists do."

Tangretti chuckled. "I wish more of your countrymen felt that way. All the unrest over government abuses down in Saigon has made things easy for Ho's people. Recruiting has been awfully easy for the VC."

"Ho Chi Minh is a powerful name, even in the South," Li told him. "Remember that he was the one who finally drove the foreigners out, and that was no small thing. He has been shrewd since then, and commands much support on both sides of the Zone."

"Ruthless bastard, too." That was Sean Kelly, the Australian mechanic who acted as the *Adder*'s engineer. He was a middle-aged cynic with a sour outlook on life and a gift for spreading gloom, but he was also one hell of a good mechanic. "Squashes dissent in the North a hell of a lot more effectively than Diem and his mates do in the South."

"True enough," Li said. "But it may be we can balance that out by missions like this one."

Kelly sat down next to Tangretti and drew out a pouch of chewing tobacco. He took a pinch and put it in his mouth, then held it out for the others, but no one accepted the offer. As he worked the chaw, Kelly looked across the deck at Bui, the Vietnamese agent, who spoke no English. "You really think you're going to beat old Uncle Ho at 'is own game, mate? I was in these parts ten years back, when the Frenchies were in charge, and I've been watching. The Viet Minh and the Viet Cong, they've got motivation. They'll die for Uncle Ho, because he's given them a dream to rally 'round. But Diem? He's just a politician. No offense to you, mate," he said with a sidelong glance at Li, "but it's easy to talk about freedom and a better life. Harder actually to get people to fight for 'em. You need leaders, symbols. When we threw out the Brits a century back, it wasn't mining rights and better prices that won us the fight. It was the Eureka Stockade for us, like it was the Alamo in Texas. Symbols and leaders, those're the keys. And right now you folk just don't have 'em."

"We will," Li said quietly. "Believe me, Mister Sean, we will."

Kelly left to tend his engines, and Li went into a huddle with his teammates to go over last-minute preparations for their mission. That left Tangretti alone in the well deck to ponder the conversation.

For all his gloom, Kelly had a good point. South Vietnam was still very much a nation divided against itself, vulnerable to the kind of infiltration and destabilization the Communists excelled at. Was the North equally vulnerable? Tangretti doubted it. If it had gone the same way as Cuba, the cult of personality built up around the leadership would make their voices powerful, and as long as they had some demon to pin all their misfortunes on—like the United States—people would willingly suffer hardships in the name of furthering their patriotic struggle. The Diem government could send their agents north time after time, but they probably wouldn't make much headway. There might be discontent in places, but a combination of fear and fervor could do a great deal to keep discontent from turning into actual resistance.

That meant that missions like this one probably weren't

worth the effort being expended to mount them. A few small revolutionary cells might spring up, but they wouldn't gather much support, and they were likely to be terribly fragile. If anything, Hanoi would probably welcome the chance to see such would-be liberators rise up so they could be identified and crushed, the way Castro had used the abortive Bay of Pigs to solidify his hold on Cuba.

But what, Tangretti wondered, should the Americans and the South Vietnamese be doing instead? Most importantly, how could the SEALs make a real impact, if the job they were doing was doomed to fail?

He didn't have an answer yet, but he'd find one.

The helmsman cut back on the throttles, and the engines subsided to a low grumble. Tangretti saw some lights on the distant shoreline that seemed to be moving, but realized it was the torpedo boat changing course that caused them to appear to be creeping forward. *Adder* had reached the prearranged drop-off point, and the boat was slowly moving in toward the coast.

North Vietnam. It was hard to believe that was an enemy country over there. In the darkness, the loom of the land was barely visible, more felt than seen. Yet that was Ho Chi Minh's territory, implacably hostile to each and every one of the men in the small, aging patrol boat.

Lieutenant Franklin Woods, the skipper of the torpedo boat, clambered down the ladder from the bridge and approached the junk commandos. "All right," he said, addressing Li Han, "we're in position. It's up to you guys now." He sounded bored, as if there was nothing special about cruising into enemy waters in the middle of the night. Perhaps, Tangretti thought, that was just how he felt. The two of them had gotten drunk together a few nights back after the second of the mission rehearsals, and exchanged war stories over a couple of bottles of scotch. Woods had a lot in common with Tangretti. Both of them were mustangs who had earned commissions out of the ranks. In Korea, Woods had served on a torpedo boat much like the *Adder*, taking charge when a mine had blown a hole in the side of the vessel and killed the CO. Somehow he'd brought the boat and crew out of the mined waters, earning a Silver Star and a commission in the process. But there hadn't been much of a future for him once Korea was over and done with, and he'd wound up in the Reserve, approaching retirement, when he'd been approached to take the current assignment. Woods was technically on detached duty with the South Vietnamese Navy as an advisor, but in fact served as an officer in the CIA-run "navy" based in Da Nang. It seemed to suit him.

Tangretti watched as two of the boat crew joined the Biet Hai in preparing a large rubber raft and getting it over the side. Bui, the intelligence agent, climbed down into the raft, and was joined a moment later by two of the junk commandos, Truong Ky and Huan Van Nim—both of whom Tangretti recognized from the holding cell at the Quan Cahn headquarters after the incident at the Green Parrot. Li Han and the fourth Biet Hai commando, a small, wicked-looking pirate named Tran Nhat, completed the team. They cast off and began rowing the IBL toward the distant loom of land along the western horizon.

In no time, darkness swallowed them up, and Tangretti joined the crew of *Adder* in settling down to await the return of the Biet Hai team.

Beach Red
North of the DMZ
2235 hours

Li Han emerged from the water cautiously, eyes and ears tuned to the night. Under the waxing moon there was just enough light to make out the shadows of trees looming above the beach less than thirty yards away. Within the jungle, the night was virtually impenetrable, and Li Han had the uncomfortable feeling that anything might be lurking there, even the entire North Vietnamese Army, safe from detection. The memory of the American SEAL's mock ambush during the rehearsals for the mission had kept haunting him, and perhaps exaggerated his fears. But fear could be a good thing when it made a man more careful.

The pounding surf that surged around his ankles made it hard to hear anything else, but he thought he detected a few birdcalls nearby. That was a good sign, he thought.

He crept carefully toward the tree-line, a shadow among darker shadows, quiet and as close to invisible as his training allowed. Once he was in the underbrush he felt better, and he paused to assess his surroundings more closely now that he was safely under cover. He checked the knife strapped to his leg, his only weapon until the raft arrived.

Somehow it was hard to grasp that he was in enemy country. Less than a decade ago, all of Vietnam had been a single country, under French domination, admittedly, but one united nation in arms against the colonial oppressor. In those days Li Han had been a young guerrilla fighter, and for a time his militia unit had served not far from this stretch of beach, fighting the soldiers of the French Foreign Legion in the weeks leading up to the Viet Minh siege of Dien Bien Phu.

Many people had tended to forget that the Viet Minh had not fought alone against the Europeans. They had been only one of many groups committed to the liberation of the country, although it was true that under Ho Chi Minh and General Giap the Viet Minh had achieved all the most visible successes in battle. Still, Li Han resented the way that all the credit went to the Communists for the end of colonial rule. He had done his part in that war . . , and he hadn't done it so that someone like Ho Chi Minh could impose a new kind of tyranny on the nation.

One day, this would all be one Vietnam again. And Li Han vowed that it would be a free nation, free not only of the Communist dictatorship of the North, but also of the repressive regime that now ruled in Saigon as well. There had to be a way to make the country stand proud and strong among the nations of the world.

He spotted Tran Nhat a little ways down the beach, crouched under a spreading tree and scanning his surroundings with the same care Li Han was using. Tran Nhat was a good man for an operation like this, tough and ruthless. Back in Da Nang he was a brawler, a carouser, and a womanizer, and there were stories about the little commando's bloodthirsty record that could make the blood run cold. But though he had the reputation of a callous killer, he was also a man who came back from his missions.

Tran caught sight of Li Han and gave a crisp hand signal that indicated everything was clear on his section of the beach. Finishing his own assessment, Li Han returned the gesture, then signaled for the other man to keep watch inland while he returned his attention to the sea. He produced a flashlight from his pack and made the agreed-upon signal that indicated the beach was clear for the raft to land on.

It wasn't easy to pick the raft out of the darkness, but Li Han was able to make it out as it moved in toward the beach. Soon it was negotiating the surf, and he ran out to assist Truong and Huan as they struggled to reach shore.

Bui, cold and aloof, did nothing to assist the Biet Hai. Once the raft was safely above the tide line he stood up, stepped onto the hard sand, and started inland without a word. Li Han took his weapon, a World War II vintage M-1 Grease Gun, from Huan, passing another on to Tran Nhat before he signaled for Huan to remain with the raft. Then he and Truong set off after the agent. Li Han was aware of Tran Nhat shadowing them, keeping out of sight as he paralleled their course through the trees, all according to the routine they'd been rehearsing for over a week now. The idea for keeping one man out of sight had been yet another good suggestion from the American, Tangretti, who was always ready to share his expertise without ever seeming as condescending as most of the other American "advisors."

Ahead of them, a light flashed three times, the prearranged signal for the rendezvous. Bui gave a satisfied nod as they angled toward it, with the two Biet Hai trailing him at a slight distance. It might have been taken as a sign of respect, but Li Han considered it a matter of prudence. There was no sense in bunching up and presenting a better target.

They came out of the trees and into a small clearing, where the light of a battered old lantern illuminated five men in the traditional *ao baba* dress of Vietnamese peasants. They carried a motley assortment of weapons, from an old Japanese Arisaka rifle to a Russian-made Kalashnikov that they had evidently acquired from a North Vietnamese soldier who no longer required it, and they all had the suspicious look of men who lived outside the bounds of society. Without seeing any sign of other people, Li Han was sure there were more hidden around the clearing, watching.

"Giai phong!" The oldest of the five, a wizened little man who looked like he might have fought the first French invaders sometime in the previous century, stepped for-

ward. It was the challenge they'd been briefed to respond to: *Liberation*.

"*Sat Cong*," Bui replied, betraying no emotion. When Li Han and his comrades uttered the phrase, it was with relish, or anticipation, or anger, but the spy from Saigon simply recited the password matter-of-factly.

There were smiles from the reception committee. "We were getting worried," the old man said. "You are late."

When Bui didn't respond, Li Han stepped forward. "Never mind that," he said. He jerked a finger in the spy's direction. "Our orders are to see this man delivered to your *dai uy*. Then we return to the sea."

"I am Van," the old man told him. "I am the *dai uy* of this band." The term *dai uy* had many meanings, from tribal chief to village elder to captain, but in any event it meant that Van was the leader of this band of partisans. Li Han wondered how many more were in the unit. He had a feeling he was already looking at the bulk of their manpower, which meant that Bui would have his work cut out for him in trying to build an anti-Communist resistance unit out of these men.

"*Khong duoc khoe*," Li Han responded. "Good. Then I will leave him in your hands. We will—"

At that moment he was cut off by the sound of a rifle shot, and a shouted "*Bo Doi! Bo Doi!*" from the trees beyond the clearing. Northern soldiers—and close by, if that firing was any indication.

"*O phuc kich!*" someone else called, "Ambush!" In an instant the five guerrilla fighters were scattering, weapons in hand. Li Han gripped Bui's arm, forcing him down into a crouch as more gunfire erupted in the night. Truong had dropped to one knee behind a tree and had his M-1 Garand ready, but so far there were no targets in sight.

They had been caught by the North Vietnamese Army, Li Han thought. The "secret" rendezvous had turned out to be something less than secret after all, and it had turned into an ambush. The question now was how to extricate his men from the closing jaws of the trap . . . and whether he should still try to carry out the mission as he did so.

He rejected that idea immediately. In this chaos, there was no way of telling if the guerrillas could get themselves out, let alone Bui. Li Han strongly suspected that Van's outfit hadn't been very large to start with, and the odds were that the NVA ambush had been possible only through the aid of one or more traitors in Van's ranks. There was no way he'd entrust Bui to any of them now, even if he could find them again in the middle of the chaos that had engulfed this lonely stretch of jungle.

"We will fall back to the beach," he said quietly. "Truong, you will escort Bui. I will remain here to cover your withdrawal, then join you."

"I should stay, Ong Li," Truong began. "You—"

"I have the submachine gun," Li Han said sharply. "And the responsibility for getting you out. Now go! That is an order!"

Reluctantly, Truong left his position and ran to join Li Han and Bui. The spy hesitated for a moment, as if he wanted to argue the decision to retreat, but seemed to think better of it as he caught sight of Li Han's expression. As the spy and the commando started for shore, Li Han scanned the tree-line, listening to the sounds of firing that were coming closer with each passing minute. He checked his SMG and found a fallen log he could drop behind for cover.

A moment later uniformed figures burst into the clearing, and Li Han let loose a long burst from the Grease Gun. Two of the newcomers caught his fire square in the chest and were flung backwards, falling heavily into the underbrush. A third squeezed off a shot from his AK-47 before his face blossomed dark gore and he fell. Shouted orders and expletives mingled in the jungle behind them as more soldiers focused on Li Han's unexpected intervention in the fight.

Li Han fired again as another group of uniformed North Vietnamese charged him. But someone was taking control over the men, because this time he was aware of covering fire coming from behind one of the trees, and he thought he could hear movement in the jungle off to his left. No doubt the enemy was trying to work some men in behind him to cut off his retreat to the beach. But with the suppressing fire coming from his front, and the soldiers who seemed willing to risk his fire in a frontal attack, there wasn't much Li Han could do. He could stay put, be encircled, and die. Or he could try to run and die.

He wasn't pleased with the options open to him.

At that moment a new thunder of automatic fire ripped the night to his left, and he could hear the screams of pain and surprise from the men who had started to outflank him. Li Han grinned as he quickly switched to a fresh magazine for his SMG. The American *co van my*, Tangretti, had been right when he suggested one man from the Biet Hai team remain hidden during the approach to the rendezvous. That had to be Tran Nhat making his presence felt.

He took advantage of the momentary confusion to spray an uncontrolled stream of bullets at the enemy position across the clearing. Then Li Han was on his feet and running, feeling the bullets streaking past him like angry insects. He ran a zigzag course, crouching low, and was quickly able to reach the shelter of a massive rubber tree.

After a moment Tran Nhat materialized out of the undergrowth like a ghost, his pleasure in his deadly work apparent from the gap-toothed grin that split his homely features. Tran changed magazines quickly, then pointed toward the beach. Li Han nodded, waited for a count of three, and then sprinted into the jungle. Behind him he heard Tran laying down a fierce covering fire.

He found a spot with good cover and stopped there, readying his weapon. After a few moments Tran appeared once again, running. Li Han opened fire into the underbrush beyond him, not caring now if he hit any targets so long as he forced the North Vietnamese troops to think twice about pressing their pursuit.

The leapfrog retreat continued until the two men reached the beach, where Huan and Bui waited in the raft while Truong covered the beach from a sniper's position. The Biet Hai commandos raced to the raft and shoved off, all of them piling aboard and grabbing paddles as they hastened to escape to the security of the empty sea.

The mission had been a failure. Li Han could only hope it wouldn't be repeated.

Patrol Boat *Adder*
North of the DMZ
2358 hours

"I'm telling you, that's gunfire I'm hearing," Tangretti said, cocking his head as he strained to catch the distant sounds carried on the night wind. "They've run into something nasty."

"Hell, even if it really is gunfire you're hearing, you don't know it has anything to do with them," Frank Woods replied, sounding testy. "Some of the gooks could just be shooting off a few rounds just for the hell of it."

"Come on, you don't believe that any more than I do," Tangretti growled. "Li Han's boys ran into trouble. We should swing inshore and check things out."

"No way, friend," Woods told him bluntly. "That's not just against my orders, it's against everything the spooks who run this show have been preaching ever since they started this little program. This is supposed to be a gook show, first to last. We provide the transportation. Other than that, we stay out of it . . . and out of the line of fire. And that's exactly the way I want it, thank you very much."

"You'd abandon those men to the North Vietnamese?" Tangretti asked. He was thinking of that *Sat Cong* tattoo on Li Han's chest. "Just turn for home and forget them?"

"Hell, they're just gooks," Woods said with a shrug.

The callous comment made Tangretti's blood boil. Sure, he'd used the same kind of epithets often enough, and he could remember a time when he'd been offhand about the suffering of the Koreans and Japanese he'd seen during the Korean War. But these men were different. He's watched them during training, gotten to know Li Han and some of the other junk commandos as fellow warriors, as comrades in arms . . . as friends. They were far more than just anonymous "gooks" to be dismissed out of hand.

"Well, if you won't go in to help, I will," Tangretti said harshly. He started to unbutton his shirt, ready to swim for shore if he had to.

Woods shook his head. "No way, Lieutenant," he said. "Those orders apply to you just as much as to me. And since I'm the lucky guy saddled with the responsibility of commanding this tub, the boys from the Company will hold me responsible if you break the rules. You go ashore and create an incident, and I'm up on charges right alongside of you—assuming you survive and make it to a court-martial."

Tangretti paused, his shirt dangling from one hand. "This is supposed to stop me?" he asked with a nasty smile.

"Well, if that doesn't, then this"—he slapped the butt of the pistol holstered on one hip—"will just have to do instead." There was a dangerous glint in the man's eyes.

For a long moment Tangretti tried to stare him down, but Woods held firm. A long time back the SEAL had learned how to read people, and what he read now on the torpedo-boat skipper's set face said the man meant what he said.

And even if he didn't . . . well, he was right about the orders. Tangretti might disagree with them, but disobeying could have some far-reaching consequences. If he was captured, or killed and his body recovered by the NVA, Hanoi wouldn't hesitate to get all the propaganda value they could out of proving that the Americans weren't the mere advisors they claimed to be. And that would ratchet the conflict in Southeast Asia up another few notches.

Lieutenants didn't make decisions that could suck the nation into entire wars. That, as the saying went, was way above Steve Tangretti's pay grade.

At any rate, there wasn't much that one man, even a SEAL, could do ashore at this juncture. By the time he made it to land Li Han and his people would either have escaped, or they'd be dead. There was no middle ground. No matter how much Tangretti's whole being screamed out for him to do something, *anything*, the potential results just didn't justify the risks he'd be running.

Tangretti let out his breath, though he hadn't realized he'd been holding it. "All right, Frank, you win," he said. "But I don't have to like this."

"I want to do something too, Steve," Woods said softly. "Sometimes you can't, no matter how hard you wish you could. Now put your shirt back on and forget we ever had this conversation."

Time passed. The boat, barely under power, circled slowly through the agreed rendezvous with a nervous crew and passenger listening for further sounds from shore, but the gunfire had faded out. The strain was getting on everyone's nerves, even the outgoing Australian, Kelly.

At last Tangretti spotted movement in the dark waters, hard to pick out even under the moonlight. He tapped Kelly on the shoulder and pointed, and the Australian nodded. "Got something out there, Skipper," he said quietly. "Looks like a raft."

"Small arms ready," Woods ordered tersely. "Quindoy, man the fifty."

A swarthy little Filipino sailor nodded acknowledgment and hastened to the machine gun mounted on the bow of the torpedo boat. He stripped off the protective cover and started to load the weapon. Other sailors had produced rifles and pistols. Tangretti, unarmed, stayed where he was, watching the raft as it approached *Adder*.

"Cowboy!" a familiar voice called from the raft. It sounded like Li Han, and it was the challenge they'd agreed on for the rendezvous tonight. It wasn't likely that Ho Chi Minh's people would recognize the word.

"John Wayne!" Tangretti replied. Around the deck, the sailors relaxed. The helmsman brought the boat in close to the raft and killed the engines, and Tangretti and Kelly started helping the Vietnamese aboard.

Bui was first out of the raft, and even his normally expressionless face looked harried. Li Han climbed out last, and took Tangretti's hand with a firm, friendly grasp. "Thank the Lord Buddha that we made it back, my friend," he said. "I wasn't sure if I'd get a chance to see that long nose of yours again."

"What went wrong?"

"Ambush," the Chinese commando told him. "Somehow, they knew we were coming. They hit us just as we met with the cell leader."

"Time for a debriefing later," Woods called down from the bridge. "Right now we'd better get the hell clear of enemy waters before they send coastal patrols out looking for us." He turned toward the helmsman. "Let's *chogie*, Mr. Haviland."

Tangretti smiled at the order. Woods was reverting to his Korean war days, using an old Korean expression that meant "let's move." The helmsman pushed the throttles forward, and as the boat rose up on a plane he swung the wheel hard over and headed south, toward Da Nang.

Tangretti let the four junk commandos sprawl in the well deck and rest. For himself, he crouched near the ladder to the flying bridge, staring toward the hostile shore, already busy composing the report he knew he had to make to Joe Galloway.

He'd been sent to Vietnam to make recommendations. Now he had a few to make, and he didn't plan to pull any punches.

Chapter 10

Camp Tien Sha
Da Nang
0938 hours

"You in charge here?"

Gunn looked up from his cluttered desk at the burly American CPO looming in the doorway of the Quonset hut. "Yeah. Lieutenant Gunn. What can I do for you?"

"We're here to start work down on the beach. I gotta have your signature on these orders before I can tell the boys to go to work." He thrust a clipboard at Gunn.

"Just what is this about? Nobody told me anything about this."

The petty officer shrugged. "I got orders to come down here and do some construction work on your beach," he said. "Piers, a floating dry dock, barracks, some rec huts, the works. You're either lucky or have some good connections, Lieutenant, 'cause the Seabees are stretched thinner than a Scotsman's rubber right now."

Gunn crossed the hut and brushed past the man. A small convoy of vehicles was drawn up near the camp entrance, with a swarm of sailors in faded dungarees milling among them. He looked back at the petty officer. "I really don't know anything about this, Chief," he said. "Who put in the request?"

"I did, Arty," Tangretti announced, appearing from around the corner of the Quonset hut with a smile on his face. "Merry Christmas, a few days early."

"What? What's this about, Steve?"

"Well, you know, I've been thinking. You know this camp here hasn't exactly offered much in the way of accommodations. You said so yourself. So I thought we should design ourselves a place that has what we need, and I put in a call to a buddy of mine with the Seabees."

"You should have discussed it with me, Steve," Gunn said.

"Look, Arty, I just wanted to do something constructive—no pun intended. We've got the training course rolling smoothly, and there ain't much else to do these days, so I thought I could turn my hand to getting us a better base to work out of. It didn't take much, and it'll be worth the effort. You'll see."

"Hmm . . . maybe." Gunn had to admit that the facilities they'd been using were a far cry from what they needed. There weren't enough buildings to conduct indoor classes efficiently, and they had a long hike to get down to the beach for practice swims. Moreover, they had to take trucks down to Da Nang harbor to reach the PT boats moored there. During "Heck Week" it was good for the trainees to have the extra exercise involved in getting around, but now it just wasted time and effort they could better use for more useful purposes. "What exactly did you have in mind?"

"Well, I thought China Beach might be the place to set things up," Tangretti told him.

Gunn rubbed the bridge of his nose thoughtfully. It was a good choice, he had to admit that much. With a couple of finger piers and the floating dry dock the Seabee had mentioned, they could handle the PT boats directly out of the SEAL base anytime they needed them, whether it was for a CIA mission north of the DMZ or a practice run with the trainees. The beach itself afforded ample room for fieldwork, even if they did put up some buildings. And of course everybody was agreed that China Beach was just about the best piece of real estate around Da Nang when it came to scenery—and even SEALs could appreciate that, stranded thousands of miles from home and family. It was a tempting prospect.

"Do we have permission to put this stuff up down there, Steve?" he asked.

Tangretti grinned broadly. "C'mon, Arty, who do you think you're dealing with? I got Lattimore to sign off on it, and Thuy said the Biet Hai would be glad to accommodate us any way we needed. It's a done deal . . . unless you think I've gone too far and want to throw the book at me."

"I ought to," Gunn admitted sourly. "Sometimes I think you sold your life story to the guys that made that Bilko show. One scam after another."

Tangretti adopted a hurt expression. "Ah, come on, Arty, that's not fair." He grinned. "I only use my talents for good, instead of evil! When have I ever turned a profit out of one of my deals, huh?"

Gunn gave him a long, flat stare. "Never . . . that any of us know about," he said. "Look, I wish you'd gone through channels on this. But I've got to admit it sounds like a pretty damned good idea." He turned to the Seabee and accepted the clipboard and pen, scrawling his signature across the bottom of the paper. "Okay, Chief, tell your boys to do their worst."

"Aye aye, sir," the CPO replied. As he started toward the nearest truck, Tangretti fell in beside him and clapped him on the back. "Hey, Chief, if you get the rec rooms set up today, how about letting me buy you a drink. I was in the Seabees back in '42, out in the Pacific . . ."

Gunn shook his head and went back into his office. Steve Tangretti couldn't help being an operator, he thought. It was just a good thing that he was usually on the same side as the rest of the Americans in Da Nang.

Usually.

Friday, 21 December 1962

CIA Station
Da Nang
1129 hours

Once again Tangretti found himself in the CIA's lavish villa offices in Da Nang, and once again he regarded his surroundings with a dubious eye. The meeting wasn't in the conference room, but rather in a small but exquisitely furnished second-floor bedroom that had been converted into an office. Dexter and Lattimore were sitting across the desk from him, studying him with eyes that gave away nothing, and Tangretti wondered why he'd been summoned. There was a third man in the room as well.

"Lieutenant Tangretti, this is William Colby," Dexter told him. "He's the chief of Far East operations. Mr. Colby flew up here especially to talk to you."

Tangretti looked at the man, another of the nondescript "suits" he'd come to expect from the CIA. Colby nodded, but didn't speak.

"How's the work going at China Beach, Lieutenant?" Lattimore asked casually.

"Just about done, sir," Tangretti answered. "Those Seabees really know how to get things moving. Thanks again for granting the request. I'm sure the training program will go a lot smoother in the new quarters."

"By all accounts it was going pretty well already," Dexter commented. He leaned forward in his chair. "But right now we're concerned with the other aspect of the SEAL presence here."

Tangretti gave a brief nod. "The Biet Hai missions above the DMZ."

"Exactly," Colby said. "The mission you accompanied failed completely. Not only were we unable to get the South Vietnamese agent into place advising a resistance cell, but it seems likely the cell itself was killed, captured, or so thoroughly dispersed as to be useless to rely on for any future activities."

Lattimore spoke up. "I suppose an 'I told you so' is on your mind right about now, Lieutenant," he said. "You did suggest that we postpone the mission after the discovery of the VC spy here."

"I'd love to say the magic words, Mr. Lattimore," Tangretti said with a smile. "Fact is, though, I don't think the failure of the mission had anything to do with spies down here."

"No?" Dexter was frowning, as if Tangretti's comment disappointed him somehow.

"No." Tangretti leaned back in his chair. "The NVA trap was concentrated on the rendezvous point with the resistance people. If they had known what the rendezvous was all about, they would have posted some of their people in a position to intercept the Biet Hai, either on their way in or, more likely, to cut them off from the sea once they were already ashore. They didn't. Whatever intell they had must have been based on the resistance cell, not on the Biet Hai activities."

Colby was smiling. "You see, gentlemen? I told you he

was more than a typical grunt. Mr. Tangretti here has a real
flair for this kind of work." He looked straight at the
SEAL. "Would you have any interest in a full-time position with the Company, Lieutenant?"

"Me? Working for Crap In Action?" Tangretti laughed.
"Sorry, that was uncalled for. But I'm a SEAL, not a spy.
Thanks anyway."

Dexter was flushing, but whether it was at Tangretti's
derogatory play on the Agency's initials or Colby's evident
championing of the SEAL he couldn't tell. Colby himself
seemed more amused by Tangretti's comment than angered.

"Well, I'm glad to see you agree with the assessment our
people made. We were afraid the leak came from this station, but like you we concluded otherwise." Colby paused.
"That's not what we asked you to come here and talk
about, though. You sent a report to Captain Galloway in
Washington a week ago. He passed it back to us with his
endorsement of the points you made. We'd like to discuss
your observations."

"Yes, sir," Tangretti said. He'd hoped to be able to avoid
dealing directly with the CIA on this. His report, based on
what he'd learned on his ride with the Biet Hai, was
intended to focus entirely on the role of the SEALs in Vietnam. He didn't feel he had any special insight to offer the
CIA officers, beyond the basic fact that the program for
stirring up anti-Communist groups in North Vietnam
needed to be rethought from the ground up.

"What we're interested in, Tangretti, is your conclusion
that the infiltration operations are of only marginal effec-
tiveness," Dexter put in. "How exactly do you come to that
line of thought?"

"Sir, I've been giving this a lot of thought," Tangretti
said slowly. "It seems to me that trying to offset Viet Cong
pressure in the South by stirring up trouble in North Viet-

nam isn't the most effective use of manpower . . . and it doesn't answer your basic problem, in the long run."

"Explain," Colby said.

"Well, set aside the question of whether or not you can actually create an effective resistance against Hanoi. That's something we don't know much about. But the Viet Cong are already established in this country, and short of a major revolution against Ho Chi Minh, I think it's pretty likely that Hanoi's going to keep supporting them. A few resistance cells won't distract enough of their attention to make them give up their interest in the South."

"You seem to think that we're not going to get anything more than a few isolated resistance cells," Dexter said, frowning. "Our experience elsewhere has shown that you can always build a strong antigovernment movement in a Communist country."

"Yeah . . . like the anti-Castro forces at the Bay of Pigs," Tangretti commented. "Look, you guys are the experts in the spook department. You could be right. But I think that right now you don't know enough about the situation north of the DMZ to predict how much help you can expect locally. The way I see it, you've been putting the cart before the horse. You need to be doing some aggressive recon work in North Vietnam, not setting up a network of agents trying to stir up antigovernment feeling."

"We have excellent intelligence-gathering capabilities, Lieutenant," Colby said.

"Aerial recon, that sort of thing, right?" When Colby gave a reluctant nod, Tangretti went on. "I'm talking about the kind of on-the-ground intelligence that you'll never replace with all these high-tech gizmos. Trained observers getting a feel for the country, not just watching troop movements but seeing how the locals react."

"That kind of information can be supplied by our

agents," Colby protested. "But you don't seem to think they're enough."

"Oh, I'd keep putting your agents into the North," Tangretti told him. "But I'd cool down the partisan-building work and focus on learning more about enemy activities. That is, if you want to do some good in the South, as well as preparing the way for overthrowing Ho down the line."

"What do you mean?" Dexter asked.

"Look, sir, I was a Seabee before I was in the UDT, and if there's anything I learned from those days it's just how complicated supply lines and logistics are." Tangretti looked from one man to the other. "If you want to weaken the VC, you have to cut off their sources of supply. The North is sending them weapons, ammunition, advisors, food, you name it. You can do a lot more damage to them down here by finding how those supplies are coming into the country and putting a stop to it. That's where the intelligence-gathering comes into it. First learn where the supplies come from, then how they're getting here. That puts you in a position to shut them down, which throws the Viet Cong back on their own resources. Diem's troops can handle peasants armed with sticks and rocks, no matter how much of the military budget he's skimming off the top to redecorate his villa or pay his relatives."

Dexter frowned again, but Tangretti thought he saw a ghost of a smile flit across Colby's face. "You may have a point there, Lieutenant," Colby said. "But it seemed to us that you were mostly trying to persuade Captain Galloway to turn your SEALs loose on direct-action operations. How much of this is just you looking for an angle that'll let your men into the fighting?"

"I won't deny that the thought occurred, sir," Tangretti said with a smile. "But I think it's a legitimate argument even if you leave the SEALs out of the picture. Look, what you need is several parallel lines of operations here. First,

you need to gather information from north of the DMZ—
both the logistics and the political and social situation up
there. Second, you have to start taking action to shut down
the enemy supply lines. I'd bet they're moving an awful lot
of it by sea. If we can slip torpedo boats into their waters,
there's no reason they can't be sailing right past our patrols
coming south. Foreign-flagged cargo ships, fishing
boats . . . hell, even big sampans could carry some supplies
in. As far as I know, there hasn't been much effort
expended on coastal patrols so far."

Dexter shook his head. "We haven't seen any activity
that would support that theory, Tangretti. There isn't nearly
enough traffic along the coast to permit the kind of supply
effort you're talking about."

"Well, what about shipments by sea to Cambodia, and
then overland or down the Mekong River?" Tangretti
demanded. "Or cargoes could be transferred to smaller
boats out of Cambodia and brought in from the south.
Nobody's looking in that direction." He spread his arms.
"The point is, we have to find out just what's going on out
there. Your agents can do that from inside North Vietnam,
and they'll still need something like the current system to
put them in place. But I think you should be looking into
some more aggressive recon work at the same time, the
kind of thing the SEALs have been practicing to do for
almost a year now. I may be prejudiced, sir, but I'd think
you could place more reliance on the information we could
bring back."

"You think the Vietnamese are unreliable?" Colby
asked. "Inferior, maybe?"

Tangretti smiled at him. "Far from it. But I always
believed the best way to find something out was to go and
have a squint at it myself. When we were preparing for Normandy, we had access to all the charts and all the accounts
of French refugees and fisherman and such who knew the

coast, but we still sent in Scouts and Raiders to reconnoiter the beaches in person. They brought back soil samples and detailed drawings and maps and such so that we were absolutely sure we had the best possible picture of what was waiting for us. And even then we didn't get it all right." He shrugged. "I like these Biet Hai guys a lot. They're good. But their interests aren't necessarily ours. Their own attitudes are likely to slant the information they bring back, whether they're aware of it or not." He turned toward Dexter. "When the president withdrew support from the Bay of Pigs operation, and left all those Cuban freedom fighters high and dry, did he make the right choice?"

"Hell, no, he didn't," Dexter replied.

"Well, maybe if he'd known more details of the situation as it unfolded, he might have made better decisions. I got to see the missile crisis firsthand, and it looked to me like the advice he was getting was heavily weighted in favor of politicians and hidebound senior military people. Oh, they paraded their aerial photographs and their statistics and their intelligence reports in front of him, but they knew he didn't really know all the details. Is that how you want to manage operations here? With your information filtered through sources you don't control and can't adequately assess for reliability or bias?"

"For a SEAL, Lieutenant, you seem to do a lot of thinking beyond the tactical operations you're supposed to concentrate on," Colby commented.

"Sir, I learned a long time ago that most of the guys giving the orders didn't have the faintest idea what they were doing," Tangretti said bluntly. "I saw so many screwups at Normandy that I lost count, and one of them killed my best buddy, Snake Richardson. The way I figure it, it's up to guys like me to find ways to keep guys like them from killing off guys like him. If that means going outside the chain of command to find better ways to get things done, then that's exactly what I'm going to do."

"An admirable attitude," Colby said, smiling slightly. "So you think we should send your SEALs in to gather intelligence data north of the DMZ? Aren't you afraid that direct involvement in the North will lead to an escalation of the war? Our purpose so far has been to limit American involvement and let the South Vietnamese bear the brunt of the fighting."

"If the SEALs were gathering intelligence in the North, Mr. Colby, they'd never come in contact with the NVA," Tangretti told him. "On the other hand, you might prefer to use the SEALs for other things, if you're happy with the information you can get from the Biet Hai or your agents in place. *I* wouldn't be, but everyone knows I'm never satisfied with anything I didn't have my hands in from the beginning." He paused. "You'll need to organize somebody to start taking action against the VC supply lines. That could mean raids in the North—which the SEALs could do, or the Biet Hai, or whatever—or it could mean pinching off the supply lines at this end, by finding where they're being brought in and attacking the Viet Cong there. Lots of possibilities."

"Using Americans for direct action against the Viet Cong could have even worse repercussions than employing them north of the DMZ," Dexter commented. "The Diem regime is already unpopular enough. I'm not sure we would want to be perceived as lending active American support to repression of the local dissident element."

"Maybe not," Tangretti said. "Look, all this comes from my report to Captain Galloway, and one of the things he's interested in is my view on how SEALs could best be utilized over here. I'm not trying to set foreign policy. These are just the areas where I think the SEALs might be used if our lords and masters—you gentlemen, for instance—decided to let us do what we've been trained to do."

Colby looked thoughtful. "Well, you've certainly given us some food for thought, Lieutenant. Your observations are certainly of considerable interest. But for the moment, I fear we're bound by *our* lords and masters, who have their own ideas about how to manage this war. And until they say otherwise, I'm afraid you'll have to be content with training your Vietnamese counterparts and hanging out at your fancy new digs down on China Beach."

"All I can say, sir, is it's one hell of a strange way to run a war," Tangretti told him, rising. "I feel as if I'm on a package-vacation tour somewhere, instead of being in a war zone."

Lattimore gave him a grin. "Well, enjoy it while you can, Lieutenant. Wars have a way of taking some unexpected turns, and your cushy life on the beach could vanish if things heat up around these parts." He paused. "One thing we have decided on that I think will please you. We're impressed with the way you've been developing information from the locals. I think you can look for a relaxation of the rules on fraternizing with the locals in future, and I intend to continue allowing your people to hitch rides with the torpedo boats out on ops from time to time—provided you continue to use some restraint when it comes to getting involved in actual confrontations with the North Vietnamese. I'm afraid Lieutenant Woods wasn't at all pleased with your behavior, you know, although we're inclined to understand your feelings in the matter. Just remember that we cannot afford to have Americans actively engaged with the enemy, not as long as the president remains set on the rules of engagement that have been laid down so far." He shrugged. "Perhaps in light of some of your recommendations today this will change in time, but it's important that no one push the envelope too far just yet."

"I understand, sir. I'm glad to know you won't be recommending a court-martial for me, or some other unpleasantness." Tangretti smiled grimly. "That's usually the way people react when I get creative, you know."

"Oh, we considered it, Lieutenant," Colby told him, and though the tone was bantering, there was something in his expression that told Tangretti he was serious. "But we decided we didn't want to waste an officer with useful ideas . . . and at least some of your ideas may well prove to be useful."

He left the villa wondering if he'd shared a few too many of his "useful" ideas with the CIA men.

Tuesday, 25 December 1962

SEAL Barracks
China Beach
2015 hours

It didn't feel much like Christmas at China Beach.

Steve Tangretti could remember other holidays spent far from home and family, especially when he'd been with the UDT in Korea worrying about how Ronnie was dealing with all the problems of being on her own and trying to raise two young boys single-handedly. Back then Veronica had still been relatively new to the problems of being a Navy wife, and Tangretti had spent plenty of sleepless nights thinking about her. Christmas had always been the very worst.

It seemed as if things should have changed with the passing of years. But even though they were both older and more experienced, there were new problems to be dealt with now. He knew Veronica was up to the challenges of keeping the family together while he was overseas . . . he just wasn't sure that she wanted to anymore.

He glanced around the spartan room that served him as Bachelor Officers' Quarters at the new China Beach SEAL compound. The SEALs had picked up the local usage and started referring to their quarters as "the hooch," but whatever it was called, it still remained something less than impressive. The room wasn't much, small and drab, with just enough room for a bunk, a locker, a tiny shelf overflowing with books, and a small desk and chair off in one corner. He shared a bathroom with Gunn, and had additional space to call his own in the office in the compound's admin hut.

There wasn't much in the room to personalize it. Tangretti didn't go up for the pinup pictures that made Jackson such a legend from Little Creek to Da Nang; his walls were bare, aside from a map of Vietnam that hung above the desk. The books were the only really distinctive things, an odd assortment of Vietnamese and French language books, military field manuals, a few novels by Mickey Spillane and Harold Robbins, and his tattered old copy of *The Bluejacket's Manual.* Not much to reveal the man, he thought. And certainly nothing to reveal the time of year. No Christmas tree or decorations to brighten the room with holiday cheer. Tangretti hadn't felt much like bothering, though he'd dutifully helped the rest of the SEALs put up a tree in the main part of the barracks and had joined them in decorating it with ornaments he'd scrounged from a Catholic mission in town in exchange for talking some of the SEALs into helping with some building repairs the previous weekend.

No, he told himself, there's not much Christmas spirit in here this year. And he didn't feel much like celebrating. The mission to Vietnam was turning out to be little more than make-work. He was beginning to think he could have done better going to one of the NATO countries, or even taking his chances by fighting the brass hats who wanted him out

of his old slot at SEAL Team Two. At least then he might
not have gone through the whole mess with Veronica.

The thought made him look down at the watch he'd left
sitting on the desk beside the recorder. It had been one of
Ronnie's Christmas presents from a year ago, a rugged
new timepiece that was advertised as "genuine, waterproof, shockproof." She'd given it to him as a joke, saying
that the description reminded her of her favorite frogman.
That had been in the heady days just after he'd learned of
the president's decision to create the new SEALs and make
Tangretti a part of it, before the unending cycle of work
and strain had come between them.

This Christmas he hadn't even tried to shop for anything
to send home. In his last letter he'd told Veronica he didn't
have the free time, and listed a few ideas for what to give
the kids in both their names.

Yeah, some Christmas . . .

Sighing, Tangretti forced the glum thoughts from his
mind. He switched on the old tape recorder and raised the
microphone to his lips, trying to sound upbeat and cheerful
as he started to speak.

"Hey, gang, it's the Oldest Living SEAL here. I saw this
tape recorder on sale in Da Nang when I went downtown
the other day, and I thought it would be a great way to
write letters back and forth. You know how lousy I am at
actually sitting down and writing something. This is a lot
easier, and I'll really be glad if you can send me a tape
back so I can hear some friendly voices."

He paused the tape, wondering for a moment just what
kind of friendly voices he'd get to hear if his family did
tape a reply to his letter. He was sure that Bill and Hank
would both be excited at the idea of taping messages
instead of writing, but Veronica was still an unknown.
She'd written him twice since he'd arrived in Da Nang, but

both letters had been concerned with problems at home that she needed to tell him about—the cost estimate on repairing the roof by the patio door in the family room and concerns over whether Hank should spend Easter vacation with his Richardson grandparents instead of going to Wisconsin with Veronica and Bill, as originally planned. In each case Tangretti had detected a coldness in those uncomfortable letters, and he was worried that it would only get worse as time went on.

Hence the tape. When he'd seen the old reel-to-reel machine in a corner in a shop in town, Tangretti had instantly seized on the idea of sending taped letters Stateside. It made for a more personal touch, and perhaps the feeling of being in a conversation instead of just reading the poor scribblings of a man who had never been much of a letter-writer anyway might overcome some of the barriers that had gone up between Tangretti and his wife. He hoped so, at least.

He started the tape again. "Vietnam is a strange place," he said. "The people here aren't anything like the Koreans or the Japanese I saw back in '50. For one thing, there's a lot of different kinds of people in Vietnam, which makes for a strange mix. I've made friends with a guy who's part-Chinese and part-American, but who thinks of himself as a patriotic Vietnamese. And there are a whole bunch of tribes that live out in the wild country, Montagnards, Nungs, Cambodians, you name it. A lot of the Americans over here talk about the Vietnamese as all looking alike, but to me it seems like there are a lot of differences there that we don't see unless we look really close. I guess I started noticing because I watch the trainees so closely, so I get a different view than your average soldier or sailor."

Tangretti leaned back against the wall behind his rack. "I couldn't tell you what the North Vietnamese are like, because we're never anywhere near them. It's really a funny way to run a war, if you ask me. Not only are we kept out of the line of fire, we're so far from the fighting that we might as well be on vacation in the Riviera or something. I've seen more action on liberty cruising through the Norfolk bars." He chuckled. "We have this really beautiful stretch of beach here where our new SEAL compound is set up, and the other day I went out for a run. I must have been all the way to the south end of the beach, where the foothills of the Marble Mountains come down close to the shoreline, when I suddenly realized I didn't have any weapons on me. There's all this talk about the Viet Cong guerrillas infiltrating South Vietnam, and I'm out there without so much as my trusty old diving knife! But there just isn't any need. The Cong have apparently decided that American advisors aren't in season, so they don't even hassle us with sniper fire. Like I said, a strange kind of war."

He hoped that would settle some of Veronica's concerns. It was true enough. The war barely touched the Americans outside of Da Nang, and except for his foray with Li Han's team Tangretti hadn't heard a shot fired in anger since his arrival in Vietnam.

"It's just a shame, as far as I'm concerned, that these people are in the middle of this fight," he went on. "Even though we're not seeing much of it from where we sit, it's certainly thrown the whole country into a turmoil. If these folks could settle their differences and get the country moving again, I think they'd have something wonderful. They're friendly, industrious, enthusiastic, and intelligent, nothing at all like the way a lot of our 'advisors' think of them. I was as guilty as anyone, I guess. When I first got here I was calling them 'gooks' and 'slopes' the way I did when I talked about the Japs or the Koreans. Old habits die hard, but I've been trying to clean up my act. I'm really impressed by what I see here, a mixture of the French influence and a local culture that is suited to the place in a way ours will never be. Yet they're amazingly adaptable, too. In the couple of years since the advisors started pouring in, Da Nang has already developed an entire subculture devoted to separating American servicemen from their paychecks by offering them all the comforts of home. There are bars that play country-and-western music, movie houses that show films like *Casablanca*, burlesque houses that might have been lifted right out of Chicago or New Orleans. Twenty years ago I wouldn't have given it a second thought, but now when I see how smoothly the locals are absorbing everything they need to know to get along with us, I find myself wondering if that isn't their real strength. Because the changes they make don't touch the underlying culture. They adapt and survive, but they keep right on being themselves. I think they'll outlast President Diem and his strong-arm tactics, Uncle Ho and his Communism, and anything else that descends on this country, and in the end they'll be the same people they always were.

"It's that quality of rolling with the punches, taking whatever life throws at them and coping, that really makes me feel for these people. All the troubles they've had here are like a prolonged version of Hell Week. They're just being trained to survive, and they keep meeting the challenge. I admire them for that, and I really want to do what I can to help them."

He paused the tape again, then went on when he thought of a story that the family might enjoy. "I'm not the only one who thinks that way, either. For a while, we had a no-fraternization order that Arty Gunn was enforcing strictly, but word from on-high persuaded him to loosen up last week. So right away Doc Randolph, who's a hospital corpsman, decided he wanted to work with some of the locals, you know, give checkups, do first aid, that sort of thing. Da Nang has plenty of doctors and a couple of hospitals, but a lot of the peasants who live outside the city might as well be on the moon for all the good that does. There are people who live only a few miles outside of town who have never left their villages, and Doc thought it would be a great idea to make the rounds in a jeep, stop at different villages, then move on when he'd taken care of things. Arty signed off on it, and Doc got some support from a Frenchman who runs a mission on the outskirts of Da Nang who was willing to contribute medical supplies and a guy to drive and translate—although the fact is that Doc's already starting to pick up the local language, better than any of the rest of us.

"So the first time out Doc loads up his jeep with supplies, and he and his driver head on out, planning to swing through three or four villages and be back that evening. He left us a detailed plan so we could track him down if he needed to, and drove out of the compound at the crack of dawn. I mean, we're talking oh-dark-thirty here. Doc wanted to put in a good, solid day of it."

Tangretti smiled to himself, remembering the incident. "Well, came nightfall, and Doc wasn't back. Arty was storming up and down the barracks calling him every name he could think of—even though his vocabulary isn't up to my standards in the swearing department, he knew some good ones—and when he wasn't cursing he was worrying out loud. We were all starting to get concerned, let me tell you. Some of the guys got the notion that maybe the Viet Cong had grabbed him to question him or something, even though we hadn't had any trouble with them before. Well, next morning we went out loaded for bear, all of us in two jeeps with enough weaponry to march up to Hanoi and oust Uncle Ho if we'd wanted to. We decided our best bet was to trace his planned route backwards so we'd meet up with him somewhere along the way, or get news of him, but the first village we visited, the one he was supposed to

reach last on his rounds, hadn't seen or heard of him. Ditto
for the next one, and the one after that. By this time we
were all ready to tear the place apart, I kid you not. Ronnie,
you know how you say the SEALs scare you sometimes?
Well, that morning they scared *me*, and I was as bad as any
of the other guys! We figured one of our own had been
taken, and by God we weren't about to let the bastards who
did it get away with it. Not on our watch!

"So we reached the village that had been first on Doc's
schedule, and the first thing we saw was this old jeep he'd
been using parked right in the middle of town. We all piled
out of our jeeps in a hurry, and you could hear all the bolts
being pulled back on our weapons as we made a circle and
got ready to blow the living daylights out of anything that
so much as looked cross-eyed in our direction. Good old
quiet, stick-in-the-mud Arty had a pistol in each hand and a
gleam in his eye. I swear he was just about to give the order
to open fire when a bunch of villagers swarmed out of a
hooch, with Doc Randolph leading the way. His jaw
dropped when he saw us, and Arty went from gung ho to fit
to be tied in about a heartbeat and a half."

Tangretti paused for effect. "Well, before Arty could say
anything, we heard a baby bawling in the hooch Doc had
just come out of. And Doc just looks at us and shrugs.
'Sorry I didn't make it back last night,' he says. 'Fact is, I
ended up having to spend the whole day here. Guess I was
kind of popular, once they realized I was there to help. And
just when I was getting ready to leave, this woman went
into labor. But I think she must have been in the military.'

"Gunn walked right into it, 'How's that?' he asked Doc.
And Doc just grins. 'Well, she was in labor all night and
most of this morning. Typical case of hurry up and wait, if
you ask me.' "

Tangretti went on, relating other anecdotes, rambling on
as he talked about this and that but hardly paying attention

to what he was saying. After a time he decided he'd filled enough tape. He only hoped it would make the good impression he wanted.

"Ronnie, this next bit's for you, so if you want to chase the kids out now, you can. You kids behave yourselves, listen to your mother, and stay on the straight and narrow, or you'll be answering to one angry SEAL when I get back." He paused. "Ronnie, I've been thinking about the things you told me about in your last letters. I guess you handled the roofing job without me. I'm sure the contractor you called was the best guy for the job. I remember Simon Farnum mentioning the guy one time. I think he was a Seabee back in the war, and he still gives breaks to Navy families . . . and he does good work. So you made the right call there. But I'm concerned about this offer of money from the Richardsons. You know I don't want to take money from them. If you could talk to the contractor, I'm sure he would cut you some slack, maybe give me a chance to get home and work out some kind of deal that would get us the money. But taking it from the Richardsons . . . I just feel like they'd hold it over our heads until the end of time."

He took a deep breath before going on. "And that, of course, leads us to the big one. You know how I feel about Hank Junior's grandparents. But . . . look, Hank's graduating next spring, and he'll be going out on his own one way or another. College, or the Navy, or a job, or whatever. Seems to me he has to start making up his own mind about things, so if he's as excited by spending time up in the Hudson Valley as you say he is, I guess that's his call to make. All I ask is that the Richardsons stop trying to tempt him with that trust fund they keep dangling in front of him. If you could tell them, diplomatically, to let him go his own way, I don't see why he shouldn't spend Easter week with them. I know you wanted to have him with you when you saw your folks in Milwaukee, but he's been there plenty of times before. Again, that's just my take on it. By now all my information's probably as outdated as some of the stuff that turns up here from our so-called Intelligence experts."

He hesitated a moment, then plunged ahead, feeling strangely unsure of himself. He was a hardened, veteran Navy frogman, used to taking risks and enduring unimaginable hardships, but Tangretti still found it hard to face the woman he loved when things were bad between them. Even this taped message was hard for him. "Ronnie," he went on at last, "I really am trying to be more flexible about things. I'd rather Hank Junior didn't get the spoiled-rich-kid bug from those grandparents of his, just like I don't want us to start getting dependent on running to them when we get in a bind. But I'm willing to let Junior off the leash now that he's growing up. And . . . there's other stuff I'd change, too, if I could. I hope you'll let me try.

"This place has really impressed me, but it's nothing without you here to share it. I know now I made a big mistake signing up for this tour, not because of any danger, but because it took you away from me. I'm counting the days until April when the tour is up and I can be with you again. I hope you'll feel the same way when the time comes.

"In other words, sweetheart, I love you. I miss you. And I want to be with you again soon." He switched off the tape recorder and leaned back, feeling completely drained, like he'd just done a long swim and a dangerous beach recon in enemy territory.

He hoped this mission, above all others, would turn out to be a success.

Chapter 11

Saturday, 26 January 1963

SEAL Recreational Building
China Beach
1826 hours

The jukebox by the bar was playing a Kingston Trio number, a modern version of the old sailing song "Early in the
Morning." Tangretti sat in a corner, nursing his first beer of
the day, listening to the music and watching Carter and
Jackson playing a game of pool. The Quonset hut set aside
as a recreational area for the China Beach facility was surprisingly large, and seemed even bigger due to the small
numbers who were generally to be found there. For the
most part it was limited to the SEALs themselves and
occasional guests they invited to join them from one of the
other American compounds around Da Nang or off ships
that dropped anchor in the port from time to time. The Biet
Hai rarely fraternized with their instructors, though Thuy
spent some time there with Tangretti when they didn't head
for the Green Parrot or other bars in town. The SEALs
called it "The Clubhouse," and spent most of their off-
hours there.

This evening the place was more empty than usual.

Randolph was away from the compound on one of his circuits through the countryside, and Dubcek had gone with him. Gunn and Briggs were working late going over the results of the latest simulated combat mission by some of the Biet Hai.

It looked as if it was going to be another long, dull night.

Life at China Beach had become predictable in the last few weeks. The training of the Biet Hai recruits went on as before, but with "Heck Week" long past, the training was focusing on technical matters—demolitions, the use of aqualungs and other SCUBA gear, and basic techniques for infiltrating small groups of men into enemy territory with a minimum risk of being discovered. It was exactly the same sort of thing Tangretti had done with Team Two SEALs at places like Fort Pickett in Virginia, Roosevelt Roads in Puerto Rico, or in the jungles outside Panama City in the months after the formation of the Teams. Only the students were different.

The other Biet Hai operations—the kind that had produced his meeting with the three CIA men before Christmas—had dried up, although they still ran through practice missions every few days just to stay sharp. The rumor mill had it that the failure of Li Han's mission, coupled with several similar incidents on other ops, had mightily displeased the Biet Hai's lords and masters in Saigon. Tangretti felt sympathy for whoever was in overall charge of the junk commandos. He would have to answer to President Diem and his unpleasant brother Ngo Dinh Nhu, who weren't likely to tolerate failure even when the whole idea behind the missions, at least as far as Tangretti was concerned, was plainly unworkable. Where the CIA stood in the whole matter was open to question. There had been no announced change in policy, but Tangretti suspected the Agency was taking stock of the situation, perhaps even mulling over some of what he had said, before trying to persuade the South Vietnamese to move ahead with incursions into the North once more.

In the meantime, though, it was clear that things were escalating for America as far as South Vietnam was concerned. Activity at American sites around Da Nang had increased since Christmas, and Tangretti had heard that U.S. strength in-country had passed the eleven thousand mark by the beginning of the new year. That, he thought, was an awful lot of advisors in a small place like Indochina, and there was no end in sight for the ongoing buildup.

Just the night before, he had watched a Navy APD, the USS *Weiss,* dropping anchor in Da Nang harbor. The sight had brought back memories of days gone by, in World War II and the Korean War, when Underwater Demolition Teams had traveled aboard such ships on their way to action. Tangretti had wondered if there were any UDT men aboard the *Weiss,* but so far the rumor mill had been surprisingly silent about the new arrival. That suggested the ship had come under the auspices of the CIA, like so many other Navy outfits in Da Nang.

The sight of the ship in the harbor had made Tangretti feel a little bit wistful. For the first time in a long time he was wondering if he had done the right thing to trade in his old life with the UDT for the new unit, the SEALs. The action he had craved so much while stuck behind his desk in Little Creek seemed to be eluding him just as much here in Vietnam. Had he done right, that day in JFK's office, when he'd accepted the responsibility to build the new Teams?

He looked down at the letter on the table in front of him and silently shook his head. Nothing had been right with Ronnie since that day, it seemed, and this letter was only the latest proof of just how badly he'd screwed things up. Tangretti picked the two sheets of paper up, thought of crumpling them in one hand and pitching them at the trash can a few feet away, but then thought better of it. Carefully, he folded them up and tucked them inside the money belt he wore under his uniform.

Tangretti's attention was momentarily distracted by laughter from the pool table, where Carter had once again cleaned the table without giving Jackson so much as a chance to hold a cue stick. Jackson took the loss with good grace, waving a wad of money and promising drinks for everyone.

"Does that include us?" a new voice demanded from the door of the hut. Deep and gruff, it had a vaguely familiar ring to it, but Tangretti couldn't place it right away. It had been a long time since he'd heard that particular voice . . .

He squinted at the figures silhouetted against the bright afternoon sunlight leaking through the open door. There were six or eight of them crowding through the door, wearing Navy whites. The man in front had an officer's cap, but Tangretti couldn't see him clearly enough to distinguish rank or branch of service. He only knew that he should have recognized the man. Tall, with broad shoulders and heavily muscled arms, he gave an impression of size and strength that belied his grizzled hair. Tangretti's first thought was of Popeye the Sailor . . .

"Good God!" he exclaimed out loud. "Bill Wallace? Is that you? I didn't know they let relics like you stay on in the Navy!"

William M. Wallace took a step forward, squinting into the gloomy corner and managing to look even more like Popeye in the process. "Tangretti? Gator Tangretti? Nobody told me you were hanging around these parts. I figured a big-shot commando like you would be living it up back in some Virginia country club."

Standing, Tangretti closed the gap between them, holding out a hand. As he approached, he caught sight of Wallace's rank insignia.

Lieutenant Commander Wallace grinned and took his

hand. "What's the matter, Gator? Surely you're not suddenly intimidated by rank? You never used to be!"

"Just didn't expect to see you got bumped up another
notch . . . sir," Tangretti told him. The grip was still as
strong as he remembered it, and the smile that creased
those granite features was genuine.

"Hey, guys," Wallace said, half-turning toward the men
behind him. "Want you to meet an old buddy of mine. He
was in the first class I taught back at Fort Pierce during the
war, and he was part of my UDT outfit in Korea. Now he's
one of these newfangled Navy animals, a walrus or a pen-
guin or whatever it is they call them!"

"That's SEAL, Commander," Tangretti told him. "And
I'll thank you not to forget it. We may be new, but we're on
our way up."

"Whatever," Wallace said. "Damn, it's good to see you,
Gator."

"Yeah. C'mon, I'll buy you a drink." He motioned the
big man toward the table where he'd been sitting. The rest
of Wallace's companions found seats elsewhere, except for
two who headed for the pool table and immediately chal-
lenged Carter and Jackson to show their skill.

Wallace settled into the chair across from him. "How's
Ronnie and the kids?" he asked. He'd been the best man at
Tangretti's wedding.

"Good," Tangretti said, a little stiff. Family matters were
weighing heavily on him this morning, thanks to the letter
that was tucked inside his money belt. He didn't really
want to talk about Ronnie today. "Alice?"

"More beautiful than ever," Wallace said with a grin.
"And that accent of hers still drives everybody crazy." The
UDT man had married a girl from Cornwall during the
war. "You'd hardly believe she has a daughter who'll be
starting at USC next year."

Tangretti smiled. "Emma, right?" When Wallace nodded, he smiled. "See, I didn't forget after all. Bet you're the proud poppa these days, huh?"

"You'd better believe it, Gator," Wallace said. A young Vietnamese boy who worked at the SEAL club took their order, and there was a long moment of silence before Wallace spoke again. "Something I really want to know, Gator. Why the hell did you leave the Teams?"

"It's like this, Commander," Tangretti began.

Wallace held up a beefy hand. "Nobody here but us Teammates, Gator," he said quietly. "I'm still just plain old Bill Wallace, you know."

"Yeah, sure . . . Bill." Tangretti had never been one to pay much attention to mere rank, but Bill Wallace was a man who had earned his respect long before either one of them had become "an officer and a gentleman." Wallace had been a CPO when they'd first met, back at the Combat Demolitions school at Fort Pierce. They'd both been stationed in England, and took part in the Normandy invasion, but Wallace had never been as close a friend as, say, Hank Richardson. Wallace had earned the Navy Cross and a commission for his part in D day. During the period when Veronica, widowed and pregnant, had been alone and friendless in wartime England, Tangretti had written him from the Pacific Theater and asked him to look after her. Wallace, newly married himself, had been glad to help. The Wallaces had brought Veronica home when Bill had taken a job on Joe Galloway's staff at the Pentagon in the last months of the war, and he'd helped her find a place to live and a War Department civilian job. Later, Tangretti had served under him in his first combat command, during the Korean War, but Tangretti had quickly moved on to a special demolitions unit, an early experiment that had been a forerunner to the SEALs. Wallace had been a good friend, but Tangretti had always felt that he hadn't entirely understood Tangretti's decision to look for something more than

the UDTs offered. "Fact is, Bill, I was never too happy
with the limitations they placed on us back in the war . . .
and in Korea, too, at least at the beginning. Remember all
those damned fishnets?"

Wallace laughed. "Yeah. I can still see those bloody
things in my nightmares." One of the most common assignments handed to the Underwater Demolitions Teams during
the Korean conflict had involved raids to destroy North
Korean fishing nets and so limit a major source of food to
the enemy. It had been quite a comedown from the days of
the Teams spearheading landings on the Normandy beaches
and against the Japanese-held islands of the Pacific Theater.

"Well, I'll tell you something, Bill," Tangretti said.
"When George Atkinson recruited me for that Marine/UDT
unit, I knew I'd found what I was looking for right from the
very beginning. Back in WW II Snake and I griped about
the idiotic ideas the brass kept foisting on us—you know,
the Stingray drone tanks that were more dangerous to our
side than the enemy, and those antigas suits we wore going
into Normandy, and the nonsense about staying below the
tide line when we did a beach survey. That damn near
screwed my team at Okinawa, you know. Thing is, the outfit Atkinson was running was a hell of a lot better. Marines
would grab a perimeter and protect it while the UDT boys
went in and blew up a target. It worked, too. Trouble was, it
was still too heavy on the conventional warfare shit. I mean,
I was glad those Marines were there and all, but it always
struck me that we could handle these ops on our own if we
just trained our guys to fight as well as survey beaches and
blow things up. So I started agitating after we got back from
Korea . . . and somebody finally thought the best way to
shut me up was to let me try."

"Somebody, yeah," Wallace said. "Scuttlebutt says you
have the ear of JFK."

Tangretti shrugged. "I've met him . . . three times now.

And I guess I made an impression on him. But it was guys like Joe Galloway and Mike Waverly who really carried the ball."

"Modesty, Gator? I'm not sure I'm ready for that." Wallace laughed.

"Now look here, Bill," Tangretti said, holding up a hand. "I'm just a poor old orphan boy trying to get along . . ."

"Yeah, right," Wallace said. "You know, I still wish I knew how you pulled off all those little cumshaw deals at Pierce. Like 'finding' those oars so your boat crew would have better equipment . . . and in the middle of Hell Week, at that!"

Tangretti gave him a blank look. "Sir, I don't know what you're talking about, sir," he said. Then he grinned. "Those were the days, weren't they, Bill? Good old Fort Pierce, garden spot of south Florida." He paused. "So . . . what the hell are you doing here, anyway? Don't tell me the UDT is joining into this whole 'advisor' gig now, too."

Wallace shook his head. "Naw, the same old UDT routine, I'm afraid," he said. "They just bucked me up to Exec of Team Twelve—"

"Hey, congrats," Tangretti put in. The boy arrived with their beers, and he held his up in a toast.

Wallace just shrugged. "The way I figure it, I only got the job because I'm the oldest relic in the unit who's still only a lieutenant commander. I'm not exactly on the fast track, you know."

"Hey, I know the feeling." Both men had started off from the enlisted ranks, earning their commissions as a result of service in the front lines. Mustang officers like Wallace and Tangretti could rarely expect the kind of rapid promotion that went to the Annapolis graduates or the well-connected ROTC men, like Peter Howell. But the Navy needed them, nonetheless.

"Anyway," Wallace resumed, "Twelve's Det Bravo is

assigned to operate out of Subic Bay. Somebody higher up the ladder decided our charts of Vietnamese beaches need to be updated, so Bravo Detachment drew the survey duty, and I flew in from Coronado to take charge for the duration."

"Beach surveys, huh. Great fun." Tangretti looked at him speculatively over his beer bottle. "So you guys are on the *Weiss*?"

"Yup. Just like old times."

"Where you headed? North? Or south?"

"South, of course," Wallace said. "You don't think anyone would seriously propose we survey beaches north of the DMZ, do you? I mean, it's not like we'd ever be using them, or anything."

A fleeting picture of the failed night op aboard *Adder* passed through Tangretti's mind. "I just thought maybe somebody back home was starting to get the idea that North Vietnam's the real enemy," he said. "Hell, even if we just sent in some guys to cut their fishnets, it might show them we mean business."

"Not gonna happen, Gator," Wallace said. "No, we're going to survey the coast from here right on down to below Saigon. UDT teams below the surf line, Marines doing recon into the jungle above the beaches. The old familiar song."

"Well, sounds like you'll at least be earning your pay. I'm not sure we're doing as much here. Seems like the whole training thing is starting to run out of steam, and they sure as hell aren't using the SEALs for anything we were created to do. Maybe I should have stuck with Underwater Demolitions after all."

"That's what I was thinking," Wallace said, taking a swig from his bottle. "On the other hand, you guys have a nice, cushy place to live here, and we're crammed into an APD with a bunch of leathernecks who want to get even with every UDT guy who ever planted a sign on an invasion beach that said 'Welcome Marines.' Guess we all have our crosses to bear, huh?"

At that moment, sitting with an old buddy who brought back memories of the good old days when Gator Tangretti and Snake Richardson had raised hell together at Fort Pierce, Tangretti would gladly have taken up those particular crosses.

Monday, 28 January 1963

CIA Station
Da Nang
1608 hours

They had assembled in the CIA Station conference room again, but this time it was a larger meeting. It was chaired by Dexter and Lattimore, but in addition to Gunn and Tangretti there were several other American servicemen there, including Bill Wallace, a Marine Force Recon major named Corbett who was Wallace's opposite number in the beach-survey operation, the skipper and exec of the *Weiss*, and Nguyen Thuy. After several hours they had been over every aspect of the UDT/Marine mission, and Tangretti had been growing restless as he wondered why the SEALs and the Biet Hai were even represented. Then Dexter had dropped a bombshell, and in the merest instant the atmosphere in the conference room had turned as thick as the jungles above China Beach.

"Sir, I have to protest this in the strongest possible manner," Lieutenant Gunn was saying. "What you're proposing is going to completely alter the whole concept of our training program. Not to mention the fact that you're interfering with my command!"

"Now, Lieutenant, I don't think we're asking all that

much here," Lattimore said, the essence of sweet reason. "This is merely an extension of the advanced training you were already conducting. We merely feel that it would be best to perform the work away from Da Nang."

"Viet Cong activity has been increasing these last few months," Dexter put in, not bothering to sound as conciliatory as his partner. "In the interests of security, we require a less-exposed site, someplace where we can be sure there will be a minimum chance that the nature of our training will be exposed prematurely. After that spy incident last month, I should think it's clear why security should be emphasized."

"Just what in blazes is this additional training you're proposing, anyway?" Gunn demanded hotly.

Dexter hesitated a moment, then shrugged and nodded to Lattimore.

"Commander Wallace's men from Det Bravo can carry out the beach surveys along the South Vietnamese coast with a minimum of difficulty, with the assistance of Major Corbett's Marine Recon unit to provide beach security," the junior CIA man said. "Purely routine, but it's something we're badly in need of. Our charts are getting out-of-date, and I feel sure some of you gentlemen, at least, will remember the trouble outdated charts caused during the Korean conflict."

Tangretti nodded at that. Back in Korea, the U.S. occupation force hadn't bothered to make their own maps, relying instead on local sources. But the new Republic of Korea hadn't done a very comprehensive job of mapmaking themselves, using old Japanese charts while changing place names in the interests of national pride and a hatred of all things Japanese. The results had given rise to chaos when the war broke out. Inaccurate charts of the Inchon invasion area, for instance, had been a major problem, especially for the UDT men who had spearheaded the operation. Tangretti had been one of them. It had taught him a valuable lesson: Never go into an operation without good intelligence. And, preferably, intelligence gathered by your own men, or at least by someone who could be trusted to do his job right.

Wallace was also nodding. "We're in better shape here than we were before Inchon," he said. "But I'd be glad to have some up-to-date beach surveys, just in case."

"Exactly," Lattimore said. "Now, the problem we have is this. The UDT and Marine survey is fine for South Vietnam . . . but it leaves us with very poor information on what's north of the Demilitarized Zone."

Gunn frowned. "Are you suggesting that the Pentagon might decide on an invasion of North Vietnam?" he demanded. "That would be an enormous escalation."

"Nothing like that is being actively considered at the moment, Lieutenant," Dexter told him. "Let us call it a . . . contingency plan. I'll be frank. The government is concerned over the lack of progress against the Communists over the past few years." He shot a look at Thuy before continuing. "The Diem regime has been doing everything possible, but so far it simply hasn't been enough. The Cong are making progress in their infiltration of the South, and it is plain that they are being supplied and supported by Hanoi at every turn. We can't allow the status quo to continue. Ultimately, if our hands remain tied while Ho Chi Minh remains free to do whatever he wants, we'll lose this fight."

Lattimore spoke up. "There are many different plans under consideration at home. An increased commitment of American ground forces to the fight against the Viet Cong here is one. So are air strikes to disrupt the North Vietnamese ability to supply their allies. We still have hopes of infiltrating our own people into enemy territory, although those plans are currently on hold while the Diem government reconsiders its options in the matter. But we'd be foolish not to at least consider the possibility of combat operations in the north."

"Damned straight," Wallace said. "Everything I've heard since I got briefed for this mission tells me we could take out Uncle Ho anytime we wanted to if we'd just make the decision to go in and kick some serious ass."

Lattimore smiled thinly. "That's a political decision that's got to come from a few levels above *my* pay grade, Commander," he said. "Conventional military action is not the only option, of course. An increase in covert action is also possible." He glanced at Tangretti. "But that, too, requires additional intelligence information regarding the north. The point is, we need to keep all of our options open. Which means we'd be happy if we could get some beach surveys done north of the DMZ . . . without using your UDT men for the job. President Kennedy is still adamant about limiting our involvement to an advisory role and avoiding anything that would expose American servicemen to direct contact with hostile forces."

"So instead you want to use some of my SEALs?" Gunn said. "Isn't that going against presidential policy as well?"

"Not exactly, Lieutenant," Lattimore said, smiling wanly. "Look, we all know how you folks feel about the CIA, but I assure you that this station, at least, keeps its operations within the limits set by the guidelines we receive from our superiors. Active operations in North Vietnamese waters, as before, are to be carried out by the Biet Hai. Your role in this is just what it has been all along, gentlemen. You are responsible for joint planning of the operations, and for making sure the Vietnamese swimmers are fully trained for the jobs we give them."

"Such as?" Gunn was still sounding inclined to be belligerent.

"I understand you and Lieutenant Tangretti both had recent experience in doing covert beach recon work from a

submarine," Dexter responded. "That's the kind of operation we're going to require to do these surveys, but the Biet
Hai training program to date hasn't included locking in and
out of submerged submarines. So we need some of your
people to provide that training, and it is best done somewhere out of reach of enemy spies so that no one will know
that we're mounting an effort involving swimmers
deployed from a sub. Hence our modification to your current operation."

"Just where is this new training program being set up?"
Tangretti put in, his first contribution to the meeting.

"Subic Bay," Lattimore said. "The submarine USS
Perch has been refitted to support clandestine amphibious
operations, and is arriving in the Philippines next month,
part of the resources available to Commander Wallace and
Det Bravo. But the UDT doesn't need *Perch* to handle its
mission. They can work just fine off the APD. So *Perch*
will be used for covert insertions of the Biet Hai once the
SEALs have certified them as ready for the ops."

Gunn was still frowning. "The whole purpose of the
Mobile Training Team program is to put in a small team
capable of doing intensive training into a specific country.
I'm not happy about the idea of suddenly taking away part
of my unit and sending them to an entirely different country. Don't we have an MTT in the Philippines that could
handle this?"

"Not at the moment," Lattimore said. "And it would disrupt *their* scheduled training program just as badly to suddenly get a load of students from here, so even if we *did*
have a team on the ground at Subic, this would still land in
your laps."

"Face it, Arty," Tangretti said. "Our lords and masters
have made up their minds, and we're not getting out of this
one. We might as well lie back and enjoy it."

Dexter frowned. "The disruption to your team's work

will be kept to a minimum, Lieutenant Gunn," he said primly, pointedly ignoring Tangretti's comment. "We feel that two SEALs would be more than adequate to conduct the Subic Bay training, provided both are experienced in submarine insertions. We were thinking that Lieutenant Tangretti would be the obvious choice to head the detachment. Which of your men would you recommend to join him?"

Gunn glanced over at Tangretti, then shrugged. "They're all qualified," he said after a moment. "You have any preference, Gator?"

"How about Doc Randolph?" Tangretti suggested. "He slings the lingo pretty well, and I kind of like his style."

"He won't thank you for taking him away from his medical rounds in the villages," Gunn said. "But you can have him, I guess. Dubcek and Briggs have enough first aid between them to take over his classes."

"I'll leave it to you to work out those details," Dexter said. He turned to the Vietnamese officer. "Thuy, I'd like the final list of the men selected for the recon team as soon as possible."

The Biet Hai lieutenant nodded gravely. "It will be finished this afternoon, Ong Frank."

"Good," Dexter said briskly. He passed a file folder across the desk to Tangretti. "That's settled, then. Everything that's been worked out so far on the project is covered in this summary. Read it over. We'll have briefings for you and Randolph before you leave for Subic, Lieutenant Tangretti. In fact, I'll want the two of you here tomorrow afternoon at two. And you, too, Commander Wallace. We'll be needing to liaise with your command at Subic for the duration of the training, as well as for the missions themselves."

"Aye aye, sir," Wallace said, almost as if he was addressing a real superior officer. Tangretti gave a curt nod.

Lattimore spoke up. "I trust this will prove a reasonably

short assignment, Lieutenant, so that you and your man Randolph can rejoin Lieutenant Gunn quickly. I'm sure none of you wants a prolonged disruption to your lives."

Tangretti caught Dexter watching him assessingly and found himself wondering just how much the CIA men really wanted to avoid disrupting the SEALs' lives.

Tuesday, 29 January 1963

Le Parroquet Verde
Da Nang
0224 hours

The Green Parrot was crowded, filled to capacity with a mix of Vietnamese and foreigners watching the stripper onstage gyrate to the beat of "Rock Around the Clock." Between the music and the shouts of encouragement and whistles that accompanied the girl's toying with her bikini top, it wasn't easy to hear anything, but Tangretti and Wallace managed to keep up a shouted conversation as they worked their way through their drinks.

The bar was a regular port of call for Tangretti anytime he went out for a night on the town in Da Nang. The manager of the place had long since dropped any animosity he might have been harboring over Tangretti's low-key blackmail that first night when he and Thuy had come to get him to ignore the bar fight Thuy's men had been in. Now Tangretti was a welcome regular, and he had spent plenty of time developing the place into a sort of regular base of operations for his activities in town.

Early on he'd learned that Thuy's information about the bar's real owner was accurate. Colonel Tyugen Van Hung was a highly placed officer in the ARVN, a brother-in-law of the local provincial governor, who had some impressive connections to the Vietnamese military, the government, and—most important as far as Tangretti was concerned—the local black market. He rented out rooms by the hour on the floor above the bar and got a piece of the action from the girls who enticed the customers upstairs. The man was also rumored to have some links to the Viet Cong as well, and the SEAL was sure it must be so. Over two decades and across more of the planet's surface than he cared to think about, Tangretti had encountered entrepreneurs of the same stripe over and over, and perhaps the one thing they all had in common was an instinct for keeping open ties to both sides of any given political fence. That way they could be sure of flourishing no matter who was calling the shots from the capital.

He had set up connections with several local black marketeers to ensure that the SEALs at China Beach had a ready supply of life's essentials, especially booze. He'd also acquired some of the medical supplies Randolph used for his traveling clinic through the same contacts. They knew him at the Parrot, and regarded him as a profitable associate, so he always got the best table and the fastest service when he dropped by.

Tonight, though, he wasn't at the Parrot on business. Tangretti and Wallace had spent the afternoon at the China Beach rec center, then headed into town to have dinner at a restaurant Tangretti had discovered. Afterward it had just seemed natural to start bar-hopping, much as the SEALs did back in Norfolk, and Tangretti had gravitated to the Parrot as their final stop after visiting a string of other bars in the heart of the city.

Neither man was feeling any pain by that time. Wallace, for the most part, had stuck to Tiger Beer, which was somewhat milder than the Ba Me Ba brand they had started on back at China Beach. Tangretti, though, had been inclined to mix his drinks more, and at the moment was nursing a tumbler of *ba si de,* a home-brewed whiskey that made him think again of his uncle Vincenzo's bathtub gin.

"I tell ya, Bill," he said, taking another sip. "I tell ya, I just don't know what t'do 'bout Ronnie anymore." Tangretti could usually hold his liquor, but tonight's prolonged drinking bout with his old friend had loosened his tongue, and perhaps inevitably his family troubles had come pouring out soon after they'd settled down at the corner table of the Parrot. "I mean, I send her this long Christmas tape, tryin' ta answer all the things she's been gripin' about in her letters, tryin' to help out any way I can. And I get back a tape Junior made tellin' 'bout his plans to spend time with his granddad in New York an' all, but the only thing I get from Ronnie is a letter that says I should quit bein' so pat . . . pat . . . patricise . . . *patronizing*, damn it! I just can't win either way. Either I ain't around t' help with all the decisions, or I'm bein' too fucking *patronizing* and tryin' to run her life from over here."

"Nobody said marriage was easy, Gator," Wallace said sagely. "I've been through some rough spots with Alice, too."

"Y'fight much?" Tangretti asked.

Wallace looked embarrassed. "Not . . . fights, really. When she gets mad, Alice just gets all . . . I don't know, British, on me. You know, that superior Limey routine, looking down her nose at the savage colonial. Drives me crazy . . . but when she's doing the whole bit, somehow I can't pick a real fight with her, no matter how much I'd like to, because that's just what she seems to expect." He shrugged. "So things just get chilly for a while, until we find a way to work things out."

Tangretti drained his glass. "Wish that was all Ronnie did. I get so damned tired of it sometimes, I just don't know what to do. I mean, I love her, y'know? But she doesn't understand me, not even after all these years, and I don't know what to say or do that would put things right . . . unless I take retirement like she wants. And that'd kill me. I'm not ready for a rocking chair and a shawl."

"Yeah, that's a real problem," Wallace said. "I've been in even longer than you, Gator, and sometimes I don't know if I'm ready to hang up my flippers either." He finished his beer and set it down on the table a little too firmly, making it wobble. "Then there are other times I look in the mirror and wonder how it can be that twenty years have gone by since they tapped me for Fort Pierce, and I start thinking I'm too goddamn old to do this anymore."

"Not me. I've got plenty of years left in me yet. And, y'know, I don't know what I'd do as a civ . . . as a civilian." Tangretti shook his head. "I've spent my whole life in the Navy, since I was old enough to sign up. Learned how t'build things as a Seabee and how to blow 'em up with the UDT, and there ain't a helluva lot more I know how t'do. So what am I going to do with my life, Bill? Ronnie says I should get a job in construction or something. But I've been running the goddamn SEALs, for Chrissakes! I don't have the money or the talent to run a business of my own, but I'll be damned if I'd take orders from some boss like Snake's old man."

"Yeah," Wallace agreed, grinning broadly. "The way I hear it, you sure as hell haven't been taking orders from anybody in the Navy much, so why take 'em from a civilian?" He looked down at his watch, squinting uncertainly. "God, Gator, is it really after 0230? I haven't been out bar-crawling this late since that time in Cornwall with Frazier and Kaminsky. You know, when the bobbies ended up chasing us?"

Tangretti chuckled. "Yeah, Snake was always sorry we missed out on that one."

He started to raise his hand to signal one of the wait-resses for another round, but Wallace stopped him. "I gotta get back to the ship, Gator," he said, standing care-fully. "Not as young as I used to be, you know? At least I'm too damned old to be bar-hopping. You want to share a cyclo?"

"Naw, I'm not ready to crawl back to the compound yet," Tangretti told him. "Sure you won't stick around? We could maybe get the local cops t' chase us, for old times' sake."

"Sorry, Gator. But I'll see you tomorrow ... oh, yeah, make that this afternoon ... for that briefing with the spooks." A little unsteady on his feet, the big UDT man threaded his way toward the door, leaving Tangretti alone.

But he didn't stay that way for long.

"You want company, sailor?" He looked up to meet the eye of a petite and very young Vietnamese woman with long, dark hair and a cheerful smile. She was wearing a form-fitting dress, pale blue in color with a deep, plunging neckline. Before Tangretti could answer she slid into the chair next to his. "I show you very good time."

Tangretti looked her over slowly, alcohol and fatigue and emotional turmoil all combining to blur his judgment and pique his lust at the same time. A small voice in the back of his mind reminded him faintly that he had vowed not to let himself stray again, but the rest of him just wasn't listening. A good time, he thought, was exactly what he was looking for tonight, even if it had to be with some underage whore. The hell of it was, if he ignored her Asian features, she reminded him all too vividly of Veronica ...

He silenced the nagging voice of his conscience and smiled at the teenage prostitute. Below the table, he slipped his wedding ring off his finger and tucked it into the money belt he wore under his whites. That was an old habit, a way to keep from thinking too much about what he was doing when he fell from grace and cheated.

"Sure, honey," he said. "Let's talk about good times."

Chapter 12

Tuesday, 29 January 1963

**Le Parroquet Verde
Da Nang
0545 hours**

Tangretti awoke slowly with a throbbing head and a taste in his mouth that he remembered all too well from past binges beyond count. It was still dark, except for the intermittent blinding glare of a street sign flashing on and off somewhere outside the window, which had neither curtains nor shades. For a long moment he was disoriented, unsure where he was or indeed even who he was. All that was real was his hangover, and a heartfelt desire for death to come swiftly and end the pain.

Hell Week ... Maybe this is what it's supposed to feel like after Indoctrination Week is over. They sure did come up with enough ways to torture us out there. I wonder if Snake feels as shitty as I do right now?

There was something wrong with that thought, and after a long minute he realized that Snake was dead, killed fighting the Nazis on Omaha Beach. Tangretti had taken to drinking far too much since then.

Where the fuck is this, then? Noumea? Hollandia? All

these dreary Pacific ports ran together after a while. So much for the glamorous South Seas . . .

He shook his head slowly, and immediately regretted it. That wasn't right either. That had been a long time ago, back in World War II.

The name "Vietnam" registered in his foggy brain, followed by "Da Nang." His mind came into a sort of fuzzy focus, so that he remembered parts of the previous night. He'd been out bar-hopping with Bill Wallace, trying to drown his sorrows and forget about how sour things were going with Ronnie. They'd ended up at the Green Parrot . . . Wallace had called it a night, but he'd wanted to stay for another drink or three . . . then the girl had come to the table.

The girl. Tangretti hadn't thought anything could make him feel worse than he already did with the hangover, but memory of the girl did. Guilt did battle with nausea for an eternity and finally won out. He'd promised Veronica he wouldn't cheat again, but that's exactly what he'd done last night.

And with a girl who probably wasn't as old as Hank Junior . . .

He groaned aloud. *Of all the stupid fucking stunts,* he thought harshly. *You are one sorry bastard, Tangretti.*

Slowly, he swung his legs out of the bed and sat, cradling his head in both hands and considering the possible benefits of amputation as a way of getting rid of his headache. Of course, that wouldn't do the stomach any good. An errant memory of liberty in Yokohama during the Korean War surfaced. Some UDT men had been talking about the old samurai tradition of committing suicide, and one well-read pundit in the group had described the procedure in gruesome detail. The samurai used his short sword to disembowel himself, and a second cut off his head to complete the process. Tangretti could still see the whole party crack up when he'd offered the comment that perhaps it wasn't honor that compelled *hara-kiri* after all, but just too much *saki* the night before.

Slowly, he gathered his wits and took a sort of impromptu roll call of his various body parts. All of them answered present or accounted for, though a couple seemed a little doubtful. Tangretti stood up, glancing down at his nude body and noting with dismay that there seemed to be even more gray in his chest hair than ever. He was beginning to look positively grizzled, nothing at all like his self-image of the man he'd been twenty years ago when he first reported to Fort Pierce for NCDU training.

Looking slowly around the room, he saw his clothes strewn untidily about, and that made him shake his head again. He really had been shit-faced last night, he decided. Even roaring drunk he usually adhered to a lifetime of Navy habits, folding everything neatly and stacking it together somewhere if he couldn't hang things up. That girl must have been a hot number, to make him that eager. . . .

Sau Thi. That had been her name. Funny, he couldn't remember that much about her, now. She'd been young, and pretty, and her petite figure and long dark hair had brought up visions of Veronica, which had made him feel guilty at first, but then inflamed his passion. Tangretti had a brief flash of memory of Sau Thi straddling him, riding him with a wild abandon that Veronica had never given in to, even in the early days of their marriage. He had been thinking how much he wished that it really was her, instead of this teenage whore, making love to him as if there was no tomorrow.

He bent down with exaggerated care to pick up his underwear from the floor and put them on, cringing as each movement set off his hangover again. Now it *was* tomorrow, and Tangretti realized there was no sign of the girl anywhere in the room. She must have left after the combination of booze and sex had finally carried him off. Why, they hadn't even dickered over a price. . . .

Tangretti crossed the cramped room in three swift steps and checked the top of the dresser beside the door. One stray sock lay there, but nothing else. Not his money belt, or his wallet, or his watch . . . none of the things he would have left there as he undressed. An emotion somewhere between worry and anger gripped him, all but driving away the hangover symptoms as Tangretti searched the rest of the room with the same precision he would have shown conducting a beach survey, gathering up stray articles of clothing as he went.

His personal effects weren't in the room. The little bitch had robbed him while he slept!

He got dressed, keeping up a steady stream of muttered curses. Steve Tangretti, the master scrounger and scam artist, had let some bimbo young enough to be his daughter make off with his wallet, all his money and identification, everything. The watch Ronnie had given him . . . that brought back the guilt in full force.

And his money belt was gone, together with his wedding band and the letter from Ronnie he'd been carrying around inside. That was even worse than losing the watch, he thought glumly, a violation. The knowledge that his little escapade had lost him his wedding ring was almost symbolic of how he'd screwed everything up in a single night of pure stupidity and blind lust. And cold as that letter had been, he couldn't bear to think of it in some stranger's hands, though God alone knew what a petty thief of a whore would do with a letter from home.

When he jerked the door open savagely and left the room, he found the answer to that question, at least. The letter lay crumpled up against a dingy baseboard.

That was a symbol, too, he thought. A symbol of what he was allowing his marriage to become.

CIA Station
Da Nang
1349 hours

Lieutenant Commander William M. Wallace studied his old friend as Tangretti entered the conference room, the last to arrive. The SEAL looked distinctly bedraggled this afternoon, which was surprising. Wallace could remember a time when Tangretti could put away seemingly endless quantities of liquor, yet still be chipper enough to do a deal or recon a beach the next morning without giving any sign of wear and tear.

Well, he thought, *I guess that proves that our bunch is starting to get too old for this shit.* He was starting to look forward to the notion of retirement now that he had nearly thirty years of service under his belt. The Navy had given him a great career, but Wallace believed there came a time when any old warhorse had to admit that he should step aside to give the new generation a chance to take up the burden of defending the nation.

"Well, Lieutenant," Lattimore said from the head of the oval conference table. "I'm glad to see you decided to honor us with your presence."

"Sorry I'm late," Tangretti said, his voice carrying a ragged edge to it. "Had a bad night and a worse morning. Got robbed, and spent some time trying to track down the thief."

"Any luck?" Wallace asked.

Tangretti shook his head slowly. "Nothing but bad. None of my contacts in town knew anything. Or so they claimed."

Lattimore's expression was one of pinched disapproval. "When we relaxed the regulations on fraternization, Lieutenant, we were hoping you'd have the sense to move in a slightly better set of circles. Your . . . associates at the

Green Parrot are not exactly the kind of people we like American officers to be seen with."

"Oh, So Social," Tangretti said, his voice so soft that Wallace was probably the only one who could hear the comment. Wallace hid a smile at Tangretti's quiet jibe. He'd never been impressed with the CIA or their OSS predecessors, either.

The SEAL favored Lattimore with a wan smile. "I suppose you've got a point," he said in a normal tone of voice. "But on the other hand they're better connected than the folks you and Dexter hang out with," he said. "Well, actually, they probably have a lot of the same connections, at that. The upper crust usually owns the businesses that front for the black market, and they have plenty of VC on their payrolls, but they don't like to admit it and it takes a lot more hard cash to get them to open up. I like to deal a little closer to the source."

"Even when they rob you?"

The smile turned wicked. "Especially then," Tangretti told him with a savage edge to his voice.

There was a moment of silence before Lattimore cleared his throat uncomfortably. "Yes, well, if we can get started, then." He looked around the table, and Wallace followed the movement of his eyes as the CIA man studied the others in the room.

In addition to Wallace and Tangretti, the Navy was represented by Doc Randolph and one of Wallace's UDT men, Lieutenant junior grade Howard Simms, who had volunteered to act as Wallace's liaison to the SEALs while they were in the Philippines. Lieutenant Thuy and Li Han were there from the junk commandos, while Lattimore was handling the briefing without the support of the other CIA man, Dexter, today.

"Ong Thuy, do you have the list we asked for yesterday?"

The little Vietnamese officer nodded and passed him a

piece of paper. "Here it is. We selected twelve of our best swimmers, plus myself, though my commander wondered if it should not be a larger group."

Lattimore shook his head. "Thirteen sounds like about all we can handle. Wouldn't you say so, Lieutenant Tangretti?"

The SEAL shrugged. "I guess so," he said. "Too many more and you'd have to do split classes when we started practice diving off the sub, and with just Doc and me to do the training I don't see how we could stretch ourselves thin enough to do multiple classes."

"Good point," the CIA man said. He passed Thuy's list to Tangretti. "You've seen how most of these men perform in training already. Any problems?"

Tangretti scanned the list in silence for a long moment before responding. He glanced up at Li Han. "You're on the mission too, then?"

"Yes, Ong Steve." The half-Chinese commando nodded.

The SEAL gave him a quick smile. "Good. Li Han, I'll be especially glad to have your little band of cutthroats along for the ride. You guys don't need to survey a beach. You can just frighten it into submission." He paused while Randolph and the half-Chinese NCO chuckled. When he spoke again, his tone was serious. "Thuy, are you sure about Le Xuan Chinh? I'm a little surprised to see him on your list."

Thuy's face was a study in uncertainty. "You have some objection to him?"

It was Tangretti's turn to look uncomfortable. Wallace recognized that look. It was the one Tangretti had always given him back in Korea when he was senior NCO on Wallace's UDT, when he didn't approve of some plan or order but didn't want to publicly second-guess a superior. "Not . . . not an objection, necessarily," he said at length. "It's more a feeling . . . gut instinct. I got the idea that he was trying a little too hard. He really lost it that time he was chewing out Duong on the obstacle course, to the point that I'm not entirely sure he knew where he was or what he was doing. It's never a good idea to have men on critical missions who can't stay in control."

"He is a good man, Ong Steve," Li Han spoke up. "I've been in action with him many times against the Cong. He is . . . determined, yes. Dedicated. A very good fighter."

"Hmm." This time it was Randolph speaking. "I had to patch up one of the other guys after Le Xuan Chinh got a little too rambunctious in knife-fighting practice one time. Took ten stitches to patch the wound."

Thuy looked sheepish. "It is true, he has sometimes lost control in a fight. His wife was raped and killed by a squad of Cong, and since then he loses himself in pure instinct when he fights. But he is a fine soldier. We would all trust him with our lives in a combat situation."

Shrugging, Tangretti pushed the list back across to Lattimore. "Your decision, Ong Thuy," he said quietly. "Your neck, too, come to that. Just make sure he knows that the ideal beach recon doesn't involve fighting. You want to slip in, get your info, and slip back out, and never, ever let the bad guys catch you. Eh, Commander?"

Wallace nodded, smiling, remembering. "Damn straight. Right out of NCDU training, Fort Pierce, Class Number One."

"Those were the days," Tangretti said. He looked at Lattimore. "After going over the briefing material you gave me yesterday, I think the one problem I've got with all this is the time factor. You're not giving us a whole hell of a lot of time for training before you want this survey work to start. And any work involving SCUBA is tricky. I'd be a lot more comfortable with a couple more weeks, preferably with an indoor tank for the first few practice runs."

"I'm sorry, Lieutenant," the CIA man said. "We haven't got that kind of facility in the Philippines, and it just isn't practical to ship the junk commandos all the way to Coronado for a couple of weeks of training. Anyway, the schedule's not something we have any control over. These beach surveys have a high priority, and between Mr. Colby's office and Saigon, I don't think there's any way to get a delay approved."

"That's pretty much what you said the last time," Tangretti said coldly. "You know how that turned out."

"Yes, I do," Lattimore nodded. "And believe me, I don't like this any more than you do. But those are the parameters we have to work with. I'm sure that if anybody can get the training done in that time period, you can."

Wallace smiled as he caught the look that flashed across Tangretti's craggy features. Sometimes, he thought, a man's own good press was his worst possible enemy.

CIA Station
Da Nang
1512 hours

"Good job, gentlemen. Thank you all."

Tangretti stood up with the others as Lattimore signaled the end of the meeting, but the CIA man stopped him with a touch on his arm as the others started toward the door. "Stay a moment, Lieutenant," he said quietly.

"Catch you guys later," Tangretti said. He watched the others go out with a wistful feeling. They'd spent hours going over the planned beach surveys Thuy's men were supposed to conduct and discussing the training needs that went with those plans. In the end, they hadn't added much to the written briefing material he'd gone over before, and they hadn't done anything to relieve his concerns about the tight timetable the training program would require.

After the door closed, he looked at Lattimore, who remained seated at the conference table. Tangretti sat down again, as the door on the other end of the room opened to admit Dexter, who nodded curtly to Tangretti and joined them at the table.

"Lieutenant," the senior CIA man said quietly, "there are aspects to the planned recon mission north of the DMZ which were not included in your earlier briefing material, and which for various reasons we would prefer to keep confidential for the moment. This means that anything we discuss here is not to go beyond these walls except as specifically authorized. Can you give us your word that this will be the case?"

Tangretti frowned. "I may have a reputation for not playing things by the book," he said, feeling affronted, "but I know how to keep my mouth shut regarding operations."

"We know that," Lattimore said. "It's just that we don't particularly need any more confrontations with Lieutenant Gunn over the proper utilization of SEALs. Whereas we believe that you take a more . . . flexible view of things. And can help us carry out an important mission that we feel needs a delicate touch."

"Nobody's ever accused me of having *that* before," Tangretti said with a smile. "What are we talking about, here?"

"According to the file we requested on your activities in Cuba on your last assignment, you were part of the covert beach recon mission during the missile crisis last year," Dexter said.

Tangretti said nothing. He did meet Dexter's look with a blank stare.

The CIA man frowned at him. "Yes, that was a secret operation as well. Believe me, Lattimore and I have the appropriate clearance."

"I'm aware of your clearances, sir," Tangretti said noncommittally. "I'm just not sure what Cuba has to do with here and now."

"If we understand properly, the Cuban operation was

two-pronged," Lattimore said quickly. "Beach surveys on
one hand, and a recon of the harbor at San Mariel on the
other. The plans for the Biet Hai mission call for something similar, though we didn't discuss it this afternoon."

Dexter stood up and walked to the large map of Vietnam
that dominated one wall. His finger stabbed at a point just
above the shaded area that represented the Demilitarized
Zone. "The port of Dong Hai," he said. "It's not a very
large city, by any means. Primarily a fishing town, before
the French left. Lately it's become something more."

"In 1961," Lattimore said, "five North Vietnamese operatives were captured aboard a fishing boat on a beach near
An Don. Under interrogation one of them, an NVA lieutenant, revealed that he had been slipping in and out of
South Vietnam by boat for a long time . . . the trip where
he was captured was, in fact, his seventeenth. Dong Hai
was the port of origin for these missions."

Dexter picked up the commentary. "It is our belief that
Dong Hai has become a major base for North Vietnamese
covert operations directed at the south. You may recall our
conversation last month, in which you suggested that men
and materiel were being smuggled into this country by sea.
We dismissed the notion at the time, but after reviewing
some of our information at Mr. Colby's urging we now
agree with your thoughts on this. While the Ho Chi Minh
Trail is still the major thoroughfare for NVA assistance
coming south to the Viet Cong, a second and fairly significant amount is moving by sea, disguised as harmless fishermen." He gave a rare smile. "It seems the NVA has been
doing with great success what we haven't been able to.
Their agents are infiltrating by boat with documents, messages, that sort of thing, to coordinate VC activities in the
coastal provinces."

"It's been a long time," Tangretti said. "Information
gained in 1961 isn't exactly hot news."

"Agreed," Dexter said. "But we do have specific intelligence information of much more recent vintage in which the town of Dong Hai plays a significant part."

"According to information recently passed on by some of our agents in the north," Lattimore said, "there are plans in train for the Viet Cong to step up pressure in the northern provinces of the RVN. We believe that the new American airbase at Dong Ha—don't confuse it with Dong Hai, this is a town in Quang Tri province—is to be a principal target. According to our sources, there are plans for extensive sabotage of various facilities throughout the Quang Tri area, but the airbase concerns us in particular because of the American lives at risk."

Dexter spoke up again. "Our agents have passed on information that indicates the NVA will be shipping in large quantities of explosive, handheld rocket launchers, and similar munitions for use by the VC in carrying out these acts of sabotage. The timetable for this shipment is fairly well established, and so is the route. We believe that the munitions will be arriving aboard fishing boats coming in to the beaches of the Quang Tri province beginning shortly after the twenty-first of next month. And the port of origin for those shipments is to be Dong Hai."

"If we could take out that shipment, it would be a serious blow to the VC plans for stirring up new trouble in Quang Tri province," Lattimore added. "This mission has already been discussed with Lieutenant Thuy, and he has agreed to attempt to locate and destroy those munitions. We feel that this survey mission provides us with the ideal opportunity to deal with this situation covertly. If it could be worked in as part of the beach survey, we'd be killing two birds with one stone."

"Hmm." Tangretti frowned. "I don't know. San Mariel required a division into two units. Lieutenant Gunn led the harbor mission." He paused. "And it was strictly designed to assess the chances of crippling the Cuban patrol boats stationed there. This sounds considerably more difficult . . . and more risky. You'd be exposing your Biet Hai men to more danger than you'd get from a regular survey mission. And that could compromise your secrecy."

"We're aware of the risks," Dexter said curtly. "We're also aware of the fact that the Biet Hai might not be able to handle this on their own."

Tangretti raised an eyebrow. "Are you suggesting American involvement? I thought that was a no-no."

"Lieutenant, ordinarily we'd be absolutely scrupulous about adhering to the president's guidelines," the junior CIA man said. "We don't want to be in the position of authorizing any American nationals to take part in the beach recon missions north of the DMZ. It is a Biet Hai operation."

Dexter broke in. "Nor are we authorizing anything of the sort. But, should an American SEAL with a notorious habit of bending his orders to suit his own needs decide that it might be a good idea for him to assist his Biet Hai friends on this difficult mission, we would not be at all inclined to look into the matter in any detail. Of course, should you see fit to undertake such an . . . unauthorized observation trip in the course of the survey project, we'd expect you to use discretion to avoid giving the North Vietnamese any proof of active American involvement in operations on their beaches." He paused, then cleared his throat. "Or in the harbor at Dong Hai."

Tangretti smiled sourly. "So you expect me to, uh, act on my own?"

"You've been known to do it before," Lattimore said blandly.

"But you're not authorizing anything . . . or ordering."

"Of course not," Lattimore replied. "We're not even urging or suggesting. Nonetheless, in light of our conversation last month . . . we tend to agree with your assessment that the Agency needs more resources of its own. The current climate in Saigon isn't exactly . . . conducive to confidence. The future of the Biet Hai is in serious doubt. We can't even be sure which way their brass is going to jump now. Who can tell how they'll act if they decide they have to placate Diem's brother? They might start sanitizing information to give everybody what they think they want to hear . . . or they might just get uncooperative because they damn well don't care. We need to know this operation has been carried out, preferably by a firsthand account of what happens from someone we can count on."

"At the very least, we want you to ride hard on the Biet Hai who undertake this particular part of the mission," Dexter put in, pacing irritably up and down one side of the conference room and reminding Tangretti of Bogart's portrayal of Queeg from *The Caine Mutiny*. "Whether or not you go in yourself is your own decision to make. But frankly we're concerned over the ability of these Biet Hai to carry out the mission—or to give us accurate reports even if they do. You seem to work well with Thuy and some of the others. That's the real reason we wanted you to head up the training at Subic Bay . . . so you could continue to work closely with them, get a sense for whether or not they can do the job, and lend a hand—entirely without official sanction, of course—if you think you need to."

"It's still a damned tough mission to pull off," Tangretti told them. "And I'm even more concerned than ever over the schedule. I'm going to want some practice time with whichever team Thuy decides to assign to Dong Hai, to try and develop a plan that'll get us useful information without exposing anyone too much."

"Time is something we can't give you," Lattimore said. "Look, getting the Biet Hai assigned to the beach-survey project was tough enough. Like I said, the future of the whole unit is in doubt . . . the rumors we've been hearing about Saigon losing confidence in the junk commandos are all true. Fact is, our esteemed President Diem's brother much prefers the LLDB. They're picked men—picked for their sound political ties, not for being crazy enough to run around with 'Kill the Communists' tattooed on their chests. Nhu wants to expand the role of the LLDB, and he's been busy bad-mouthing the other South Vietnamese commando outfits to anybody that'll listen."

"We'd rather work with the Biet Hai," Dexter added. "They're more reliable, or they have been up until fairly recently, and frankly we'd rather not deal with Nhu's people any more than we have to. He's poison. So we have to move while we still have a Biet Hai to work with. Once the project's in progress we don't expect the ax to fall, but give Nhu time enough and he'll find a way to get the Biet Hai off the job and maybe turn the beach survey over to his precious LLDB."

"Who, of course, haven't been trained in any aspect of naval ops," Lattimore added.

"At least we can count on Thuy and his men," Tangretti agreed. "I doubt any of the guys in the field are likely to be involved in any of the politics."

"Don't be so sure of it," Dexter growled. "Politics is everywhere in this cesspool of a country, Tangretti. Diem and Nhu and their cronies are losing us this fight. We've been backing the wrong horse, but it's too late to do anything about it."

"I thought you boys from the Company specialized in taking care of problems like that," Tangretti gibed.

"Never say that!" Lattimore said harshly. "Never even *think* it! We have to handle this whole Vietnamese station with kid gloves, Tangretti. That's why we have to be so careful about avoiding American involvement in covert ops. The Commies are already claiming that Uncle Sam's stage-managing everything in Southeast Asia. We have to make damned sure there's nothing to bear out those claims. It's essential that this war be seen as a Vietnamese matter, not a case of the big bullies from America trampling on poor downtrodden Asians. That would do an incredible amount of damage to our position here. There's enough pressures turning people to the VC as it is, without giving them any more fuel for the claim that we're just another version of the French colonial empire come to exploit the country for our own ends." He paused. "We keep our hands off the politics, and we keep our hands off the active combat ops."

"Officially, at least," Tangretti said dryly. "I understand the arguments. Not that they carry a hell of a lot of weight anyway. Whether we're really here as advisors or not, you know the propaganda's going to go against us. And from everything I've been hearing, Diem's just making it that much worse all the way around."

"You've got that right," Dexter said. "We aren't allowed to take any action to interfere in local politics, but I for one wouldn't be too upset if somebody got the guts to kick him out and put in a government we might actually be able to work with. Diem may share all our objectives, but his tactics . . ." He trailed off.

Lattimore took up the conversation. "In any event, Lieutenant, we can't let political problems cut off all of our local assets. So we need you to pull this off for us without rocking any boats. And don't expect us to bail you out if you do something stupid and draw attention to yourself. The Agency isn't going to admit anything if you get hauled up on charges. You get our drift?"

Tangretti nodded. "We never even had this meeting, Mr. Lattimore." He paused. "Just how much of this nondiscussion should I share with Petty Officer Randolph?"

"None of it," Dexter told him. "He still belongs to Lieutenant Gunn's unit, and you are still, strictly speaking, out-

side the chain of command. So you can't legally order him
to accompany you on a mission, especially since you aren't
authorized to go on it yourself in the first place. And given
Gunn's resistance to other parts of our agenda, I wouldn't
want you to give him any further reasons for being disturbed by our activities."

"So he's just there for training," Tangretti said, nodding
again. "Fine. You can be sure that I'll leave him out of anything that I'm not officially doing for the next few weeks."

"As long as we understand one another, Lieutenant,"
Dexter said. "Now, suppose we get down to specifics. Lattimore, break out the reports on Dong Hai so we can show
the lieutenant what we need to learn there."

SEAL Barracks
China Beach
1722 hours

Bill Wallace listened to a torrent of angry words, feeling
uncomfortable. He was sitting in the chair by Tangretti's
desk in the SEALs' quarters, trying not to sneak looks at
his watch. He felt he should try to help his old friend, but at
the same time he found Tangretti's problems hard to relate
to . . . or to sympathize with. The UDT man had dropped
by Tangretti's quarters to let him know he was going to
have to pass on another night on the town, since the captain
of the *Weiss* had invited Wallace and Major Corbett to dinner. The UDT man had caught Tangretti in a foul mood,
and had listened as he poured out a more detailed version
of the previous night's fiasco.

"I'm telling you, Bill, I'm at my wits' end," Tangretti said
at last, finally stopping his restless pacing to drop heavily
on the end of his bunk. "That little bimbo just disappeared.
I couldn't find anybody who'd even admit to seeing her."

Wallace frowned, then gave a shrug. "You know how it goes, Gator," he said, knowing he didn't sound very concerned but not knowing how else to make his point. "I've lost count of the number of times one of my men's come to me with exactly the same story, and it always ends up the same. Cops can't do anything about it. Nobody in the area knows anything useful. Military authorities can't do much more than just post warnings, or declare a joint off-limits if it seems to be turning up in too many different reports as a trouble spot. Face it, she's gone, and so's the stuff you lost."

"It really burns me up," Tangretti said. "Not the money. Hell, I go through more money than that on a good night's binge. But losing the watch Ronnie gave me . . . that really bugs me. What do I tell her? That I let some little whore steal it from me while I was sleeping off another carouse? I promised her I'd stop that shit . . ."

"But you didn't, did you?" Wallace shook his head. "Gator, as long as I've known you I don't think I've ever seen you more than two steps ahead of trouble, and something like ninety percent of it is usually something you've brought on yourself."

Tangretti looked away. "Yeah. I know. But, damn it, Bill, I could really use a level head to help me figure this out. I don't want to lose Ronnie—"

"Then, for God's sake, Gator, start thinking with the head to hang your hat on instead of the one in your pants!" Wallace said sharply. "Nobody forced you to get in bed with that whore. And if you really cared for Veronica the way you always say you do, you wouldn't chase every skirt that walked past." He stood up. "Sometimes I'm damned sorry that I ever helped get you and Ronnie together after the war. She could've done a lot better for herself with Snake's folks in New York. Maybe they didn't like it that their kid married a middle-class girl from Milwaukee, but they'd've looked after her for Hank Junior's sake . . . and she would've been spared all the heartache you've put her through."

Tangretti was off the bed in one fluid motion. "Damn it, Bill, I thought you'd understand if anybody would!"

"What's to understand? I've been married to Alice longer than you've been with Ronnie, and I've never fooled around on her. Oh, I go out boozing with the boys, and I talk a good game, but there are some things I draw the line at. And cheating on Alice is one of them. You moan about how she doesn't understand you, Gator, but you can't possibly understand *her* if you keep on acting like her feelings don't count for shit!"

For a moment he thought Tangretti was going to hit him. Then the SEAL seemed to collapse in on himself. Suddenly he wasn't the tough, cocky commando anymore, just a man who looked stretched past all endurance. "Maybe you're right, Bill," he said heavily. "Maybe I'm just getting what I deserve. But . . . I do love her. I just . . . I just don't seem to be able to control myself, sometimes. Like last night."

"Look, Gator," Wallace said slowly. "Look, you've always said that you don't trust a Teammate who can't stay in control. Seems to me that what's good enough to apply to a mission ought to be good enough to take into a marriage, too. You've got to start thinking before you jump into things . . . thinking about what you're doing to Ronnie, and to yourself, for that matter. I know you. You're the toughest, most stubborn bastard who ever put on a pair of flippers. Once you make up your mind to do something, there's nothing short of an A-bomb going to stop you from doing it. Well, start using that stubbornness for something besides antagonizing the brass, just for a change. Use it to patch things up with Ronnie, and then *keep* them patched." He walked to the door. "I'm sorry if you think I was rough on you, Gator. You know I wouldn't waste my breath on anybody I didn't think was worth yelling at. And I'd like to keep right on yelling until I got you to turn over a whole new leaf, but Captain Gressman expects me at 1830 hours, and I've heard he wants to revive keelhauling as the punishment for people who keep him waiting."

"Yeah," Tangretti said. "Yeah, you'd better get moving." He paused. "Thanks, Bill. Thanks for telling me things straight."

"No charge, Gator," Wallace said, his hand on the doorknob. "Keep your nose clean . . . and try not to do anything I wouldn't do, okay?"

Chapter 13

U.S. Naval Base
Subic Bay, Republic of the Philippines
1305 hours

The truck looked like it had been around when MacArthur staged his famous return to the Philippines, and the way it lurched and bucked on the twisting roads only confirmed Tangretti's poor opinion of the creaky old vehicle.

The Biet Hai and their American advisors had taken an Air Force MATS transport flight from Da Nang to Clark AFB near Manila, a long, bumpy ride in the company of a flight crew that was evenly divided as to whether the Navy or the Vietnamese represented the lowest form of life on the planet. On the ground at Clark, Tangretti had asked for transportation to the naval base at Subic Bay, only to be assured that the one scheduled run between the bases that afternoon was this one truck, very nearly too crowded to hold all of the new arrivals from Vietnam at once, returning empty after delivering some misdirected supplies to Clark. The two Navy enlisted ratings driving it were happy to take Tangretti and his companions, but they'd warned him it wouldn't be a very comfortable ride. Cramming thirteen

Biet Hai and three American sailors into the back of the truck turned out to be no easy thing.

But they had persevered. "Hey, you think this is bad, wait until you get aboard the sub," Tangretti had told them. "Consider this as good practice for the weeks ahead." The Biet Hai had mostly accepted the crowding with good humor, although Le Xuan Chinh, sitting right at the back of the truck, had seemed moody and uncomfortable. He spent most of the trip staring fixedly out the back, as if lost in some other world.

At last the truck wheezed to a stop, and Tangretti leaned out the back past the Biet Hai to peer around. They were at the gate of the naval installation at last. The driver was talking to a Marine sentry while another walked back toward the rear of the vehicle. He seemed surprised to encounter a crowd of passengers aboard, but he looked over a copy of Tangretti's transport orders and reluctantly admitted they had a right to pass through his gate.

Once within the confines of the base, Tangretti unloaded the tired travelers and left them in the care of Lieutenant Thuy and Doc Randolph. Howard Simms, as Wallace's representative and something of a native guide, accompanied Tangretti in search of the base admin building.

It took time to work their way through the layers of bureaucracy that were a standard part of a major base like Subic Bay. Tangretti had almost forgotten what it was like. He'd been able to run a virtually independent operation at Little Creek, despite the problems he'd suffered from cranky base commanders and offended officers' wives, and these last few months at Da Nang the SEALs had been left almost completely to themselves, rarely even interacting with other Navy units stationed around the city. So it was something of a shock to be back in the realm of the black-shoe navy again.

But Tangretti had spent many years learning exactly

how to make the system work for him, and while they had to put in some time to secure what he needed, the job went smoothly and painlessly. When he was done, he had temporary quarters for the Biet Hai unit in the compound set aside for UDT-12 Detachment Bravo, and permission to draw on base stores for the supplies and equipment they would need for the mission ahead.

The two Americans rejoined the others and marched them across the base to their new home. Leaving the Vietnamese to get settled in, Tangretti and Randolph let Simms conduct them on a quick tour of Det Bravo's corner of the Amphibious Base. It wasn't long before they encountered a familiar face.

"Hey, Lieutenant! Long time no see!" It was GM/1 George Marsh, the UDT diver who had been part of the Cuba operation. He met them as they were about to enter the rec building, hurrying to join the three men and hailing Tangretti with a voice like a foghorn. "Never figured on seeing one of you East Coasters invading our space here in Flip-land!"

Tangretti took his hand, glad to see the frogman again. "Boy, you don't stay in one place very long, do you? First Little Creek, now Subic. Don't you ever actually hang around Coronado?"

"Not if I can help it." Marsh smiled, an unfamiliar expression for the diver who had been known as the biggest pessimist on two coasts. "All that swimming we did in October reminded me what I joined the UDT for in the first place, Lieutenant," he said. "I had a shot at instructor for the new BUD/S class, but I told 'em I wanted to get out and start seeing the world again."

"Well, it's good to see you. Do you know Doc Randolph?"

Marsh shook his head, then clasped the corpsman's hand. "Another East Coast puke, Doc?"

"I beg your pardon, my good fellow," Randolph responded in an exaggerated, phony English accent, pulling himself up to his full height and looking like the very essence of offended dignity. "I am a Coronado man through and through, and anyone who suggests otherwise, sir, will receive a sound thrashing."

They entered the building, a less-makeshift version of the Clubhouse at China Beach. Inside, Simms found them a table, and while they waited for a Filipino waiter to fetch them a round of drinks the conversation continued at breakneck speed.

"You should have gone with Commander Wallace," Tangretti told Marsh. "He's supposed to be doing some good old-fashioned beach surveys for the next few weeks. The quiet kind, where nobody's expecting you to swim with a bad breather or chasing you in patrol boats."

"Yeah, I was hoping to pull that detail," Marsh told him. "But so was every other swimmer in Det Bravo. I was the new guy on the block, so I guess they thought I'd be better cooling my heels back here with the rest of the stay-at-homes."

"Well . . ." Tangretti paused, glancing over at Simms. "Look, George, I could use you for a special project, if Lieutenant Simms here will okay it. How would you fancy giving a little diving instruction for a few days?"

"Great!" Marsh said, rolling his eyes heavenward. "I turn down an instructor's job at Coronado and travel halfway around the world . . . and I get offered another instructor's job."

"Perhaps someone's trying to suggest you should be an instructor," Randolph offered.

"Yeah." Marsh looked at Tangretti. "What's the matter? A bunch of your East Coast pukes forget how to swim?"

"Not exactly. I've got thirteen South Vietnamese commandos who need to learn the basics on submarine deployments fast. We're up here to meet up with the *Perch* for some practice dives before they get down to business."

"These guys have any experience?"

"Not in lock-outs," Tangretti said. "But they've all had basic SCUBA training, according to their officer."

Marsh nodded. "Okay, I'm game. If it's all right with you, Mr. Simms?"

The liaison officer smiled. "My instructions from Commander Wallace were, and I quote, 'Let this bum have anything he wants, as long as he doesn't try to sell the base.' If you need Marsh, sir, I don't see any problem in assigning him to you for the duration."

"Good." Tangretti smiled and raised his beer bottle. "Here's to instructors everywhere," he toasted. "Those who can, do. Those who *really* can, teach."

**SEAL Compound
China Beach
1425 hours**

"Look, Lieutenant," the civilian said insistently, "I'm not looking to cause you any trouble here. I just want to do a story on the activity in the Da Nang area, and your outfit is a part of it. If I could just have a few minutes of your time . . . maybe hang around and watch your guys work one afternoon . . ."

Arthur Gunn studied the man for a long moment, leaning back in his chair and trying to manage an air of casual indifference. Jack Torrecelli was a stringer for one of the wire services—Gunn didn't know which one, and frankly didn't care—working out of Saigon covering the problems in Southeast Asia. The man had arrived unexpectedly at the airbase in Da Nang a couple of days earlier, making a nuisance of himself among the Air Force people there. That suited Gunn well enough. Like most Navy men, he was glad to see another service cope with problems as long as they stayed clear of his bailiwick. But now, it seemed, Torrecelli had decided to transfer his unwelcome attentions to the Navy instead. And, specifically, to the SEALs.

"Mr. Torrecelli . . ."

"Call me Jack, Lieutenant," the reporter interrupted with a grin. "Everybody does."

"*Mr. Torrecelli*," Gunn repeated, pointedly, "surely there are plenty of more interesting things going on in Da Nang than the activities of a handful of bluejackets on a training mission. We have it very quiet here. My people haven't seen any Viet Cong—at least, none that we know of—and we haven't been close to any kind of action. Our job is simple training, and the most excitement we've had since we got here was the day the Seabees installed these buildings and we got to move out of the first quarters we were assigned to up at Tien Sha."

"I'm covering lots of different aspects of life in Da Nang, Lieutenant. But the folks back home are just as interested in stuff like that—you know, what life's like in Vietnam as they are in genuine war stories. A profile on your unit—"

"Is not something my men and I would welcome, frankly," Gunn said irritably.

"You people have something to hide, maybe?" Torrecelli said, raising an eyebrow. "Rumor has it that you guys are some kind of elite covert-ops unit. You been sneaking across the DMZ or something?"

Gunn bit back a curse. "It's just that kind of comment that makes our people reluctant to deal with the press," he said, forcing his voice to stay calm and even. Reaching into his top desk drawer, he extracted a clipping of the *Los Angeles Times* his wife had sent him shortly after Christmas. "Stuff like this: 'A tough American-trained team of Republic of Vietnam frogman-commandos is being prepared for combat operations against Communist coastal facilities, according to highly placed sources in Saigon. Eight U.S. Navy instructors, designated as MTT 4-63, have been overseeing the final training of these commandos from a base at Da Nang, where sixty-five of their students are about halfway through their sixteen-week training course. The training program includes classes in long-distance swimming, underwater demolition, and commando combat . . .' Well, it goes on for several more paragraphs, talking about the Vietnamese commandos and how they're so dedicated to their cause that they wear *Sat Cong* tattoos, and so forth. And this is just one of several stories I've seen in the same vein, Mr. Torrecelli."

"So? Is it inaccurate? Libelous? What's your beef?"

"My beef, Mr. Torrecelli, is that the story spells out a lot of things that it would be better not to put out for the whole world to see. Such as the location of the training facility. The designation of my unit. The size of the Vietnamese class. The possibility that they will be going into action against Communist bases—which means North Vietnamese facilities, of course. This stuff is bad enough. How much more detail would your next story bring out? The names of the commandos? Or of my people? A list of the targets the Biet Hai might want to hit after the training is over? The United States may only be participating in an advisory capacity, Mr. Torrecelli, but the fact is that these people are fighting a *war*. And you don't go publishing details about a country's war effort just so you can boost a newspaper's circulation. Commando units are supposed to operate covertly. Telling everybody in sight, including the enemy, all about who they are and where they're training and what they're learning to do, that's just plain stupid."

"Come on, Lieutenant, we're not going to publish battle plans. This is a piece for the folks back home, telling them what a good job their son Tommy's doing over in Vietnam.

It's a boost for you guys, to help people see what's going on and why. You'd think we were going to send our stories in to Ho Chi Minh himself, the way you're carrying on!"

"Are you really so naïve as to think the articles from our wire services back home don't get back to the enemy sooner or later?" Gunn shook his head. "You might be writing for the 'folks back home,' but sooner or later everything you put down on paper has the potential of being included in some Hanoi Intelligence officer's morning briefing. And I don't much like the notion of having my men identified as being linked to the training of the junk commandos getting ready to hit Communist bases. Someday some Viet Cong soldier's going to decide that makes my boys viable targets, and then we move from being advisors to being in the thick of things." He gave a thin smile. "There are those in my command who wouldn't mind seeing some kind of real action, but I object on principle to having their wishes granted through some other guy's agenda."

"Sounds pretty paranoid to me, Lieutenant," Torrecelli said, sniffing disdainfully. "Whatever happened to the right of the people to know the truth? To the whole idea of a free and democratic press?"

Gunn shrugged. "First off, I never heard that the right of the people to know anything outweighed the rights of other people—specifically *my* people—to have a fighting chance to stay alive and do their jobs. Freedom of the press means that I'm not allowed to pull a gun on you and tell you what to put in your next story, nor am I able to censor whatever you decide to write. But it doesn't obligate me to cooperate with you just because you flash press credentials, not if my cooperating with you goes against the best interests of my unit, my mission, or legitimate national interests."

"Now, look, Lieutenant, there are plenty of generals and admirals who've agreed to let me do my work. Why is it some lieutenant can tell me to go to blazes?"

"Hey, if generals and admirals want to talk to you, great. Go bother them. But I've got better things to do. Get out of my office and off my compound before I assign some of my Biet Hai trainees an exercise in ejecting unwanted outsiders."

The reporter rose and stalked out of the room. A moment later Chief Briggs appeared in the doorway. "Your guest didn't look happy, Skipper," he said. "Anything wrong?"

"Just a little difference of opinion between the Fourth Estate and the SEALs, Chief," Gunn said. "Unfortunately for Mr. Torrecelli, we won." He paused. "Look, Chief, pass the word to the rest of the gang to keep their guard up around him if they spot him hanging around. That's here *or* in town. I don't want anybody shooting their mouths off and giving him any excuse for writing anything more about what we're doing here. You got it?"

"Sure, Skipper. You know the guys know better than to talk about what we do."

"Yeah. But remind them anyway." Gunn leaned back in his seat. "I don't like the notion of the SEALs getting any publicity. We're supposed to be a covert-ops unit, and press coverage isn't exactly what we need to get the job done."

Briggs laughed. "Yeah. Next thing you know we'll be coming ashore to do beach recons and getting a mob of reporters asking questions and demanding interviews in the middle of the op."

"I wouldn't be surprised," Gunn said with a chuckle. "Anyway, make sure you remind the others of that talk we had back when we were getting the outfit put together last year. We keep a low profile, we do our job, and we don't go around drawing attention to ourselves."

That had been one of the first rules laid down in the creation of the SEAL Teams. Destined from the very beginning for covert operations of all kinds—reconnaissance, sabotage, infiltration and exfiltration of Intelligence agents and other people who wanted to avoid contact with the enemy, surveillance, and the like—the SEALs were still regarded as a clandestine unit. The dive off Cuba, for instance, had been carried out in absolute secrecy; as far as anyone outside a very small circle was concerned it had never happened at all. Gunn and most of his fellow SEALs were convinced that was the way to go, that the very existence of the unit was something better left unsubstantiated. They could do their job far better if men like Torrecelli weren't discussing their activities in print or on the nightly television news.

There were a few dissenting voices, of course. The total anonymity that shrouded the SEALs seemed to be carrying secrecy a bit far, according to a few of the more outspoken men. Like the UDT before them, SEALs didn't have a specific area of specialization that identified their purpose. You weren't a SEAL Second Class or a Master Chief Frogman, you continued to hold whatever rating you'd held before entering the Basic Underwater Demolition school, so that you'd be a torpedoman or an electrician's mate or a gunner all through your career, and never once be identified by your real job. Nor did the SEALs have special insignia or distinctive clothing to mark them apart from others. When the unit had first formed there had been some who'd wanted to adopt a black beret, in the style of the Army Special Forces green beret headgear, but that move had been quickly squashed by the men at the top of the SEAL hierarchy, led by Steve Tangretti.

Now the "Green Beanies" were getting plenty of attention as they operated in Vietnam, helping to build defenses and spread humanitarian assistance through the countryside. That kind of publicity did the unit a lot of good; if the SEALs were more visible, Doc Randolph's traveling medical clinic would have given the Navy a similar boost. But Gunn wondered what would happen if things took a more deadly turn. Would the highly visible Green Berets draw more than their fair share of hostile interest?

All in all, he was happy with the unwritten policy of SEAL reticence, he decided. SEALs weren't defined by the headlines they gathered or the glory they earned. In fact, if they did their jobs right they might well never have their clandestine missions publicized. To a SEAL, what mattered most was doing the job, and doing it well . . . out of patriotism, and out of dedication to the other guys in the Teams. The opinions of reporters and civilians and even other servicemen didn't matter to most SEALs . . . only the opinions of other veterans of Hell Week. That was as true of the quiet ones like Thor Halvorssen as well as it was of brash extroverts like Tangretti.

And Gunn wouldn't have it any other way.

Thursday, 7 February 1963

MacArthur's Return
Olangapo, Republic of the Philippines
2246 hours

"So, Doc, what do you think of our students, eh?" Tangretti asked, grabbing a bottle of Budweiser from off the waitress's serving platter before she had a chance to set it down. He looked her up and down approvingly. The MacArthur's Return bar catered heavily to the servicemen stationed at the American bases near Manila, and most of their staff were young Westerners rather than native Filipinos. This girl looked like she'd just come off the farm in Minnesota, a tall, blond farmgirl type with prominent breasts emphasized by the plunging neckline of her uniform. Despite his experience in Da Nang, despite Wallace's advice, Tangretti couldn't help but wonder if he should make a move on her before the night was through. The smile she gave him as she passed out the rest of the drinks made him think she might just be interested.

It had been a long day spent on practice dives with the Biet Hai commandos, checking their general skill with SCUBA gear. Despite the rush by the CIA to get them to the Philippines and through their training, they wouldn't actually be able to begin learning to dive off of a submarine until the USS *Perch* arrived, and it turned out that she wasn't due at Subic Bay until the weekend. So Tangretti had decided to put the Vietnamese through their paces in order to get an idea of how much they already knew before he started throwing new ideas at them. Things had gone well enough . . . until the day had been capped by the arrival of another angry letter from home which had reached Da Nang just after he'd left, and had been forwarded to him by Arthur Gunn.

Ronnie had decided to accept the money for the repairs to the house from Hank Junior's grandfather, against everything he'd said against it.

Her letter had left him drained. It wasn't just the question of the money, but rather her angry paragraphs telling him exactly how she felt about being left to manage at home on his meager pay, trying to make the best possible decisions for the whole family while he second-guessed her from overseas and cared only about his precious Navy career. He might have left the service, she pointed out, for a high-paying civilian job that would have given them enough to get by on without the need to beg from Hank Junior's grandparents, but instead Tangretti was determined to keep on chasing glory and adventure as if he was still a free-wheeling enlisted man with no ties and no responsibilities.

His response had been almost instinctive. He'd rounded up his friends and proposed a sally into the nightspots of

Olangapo, the town closest to Subic Bay. Tonight the voice of his conscience was hardly audible in the back of his mind at all. He was on his own, half a world away from all the problems of home and family, and all Steve Tangretti wanted to do was get thoroughly drunk and keep himself from thinking about any of his problems by whatever means he could find.

He forced his attention off his problems as Doc Randolph took a swig of his Schlitz. "They did a good job today," the other SEAL said. "They're better than I was when I had to qualify for diving."

Tangretti chuckled wryly. "Well, they've been through something that could pass for Hell Week. After that, anything seems simple."

The hospital corpsman looked away, and Tangretti felt a flash of embarrassment at his tactless comment. It was easy to forget that there were a handful of men like Doc who had become SEALs without going through the regular BUD/S training course. And in a tight-knit community like the SEALs, it was hard to win acceptance without the common ground of Hell Week.

He'd argued against allowing anyone into the new unit, back in the early days when they were first putting together the SEAL concept. Tangretti had been part of the very first class that went through the original version of Hell Week, back at Fort Pierce in Florida in the summer of 1943. He'd seen firsthand how being pushed to the limit and beyond had not only weeded out the men who weren't ready for the dangers of underwater demolition work, but also caused the ones who made it to draw closer together despite widely differing backgrounds and characters. His best friend, Hank Richardson, had been raised in a wealthy New York society setting, an officer and not a little bit of a snob. Yet after surviving Hell Week together Tangretti and Richardson had recognized the essential truth that cut through all the bullshit of class, money, and breeding. They'd respected and liked each other because each one knew what the other was capable of enduring.

That bond had remained central to the Teams when Naval Combat Demolitions Units had given way to the UDT, and Tangretti's intention when he'd first submitted his ideas for an elite Navy commando force to Captain Galloway had been to use only the very best of the best—the top graduates of UDT training—to staff the SEALs. But the combat status of the new outfit made someone higher up in the chain of command demand that hospital corpsmen be integral to each SEAL platoon. The problem was that the SEALs were an all-volunteer outfit, and there was no guarantee that enough trained corpsmen would volunteer to fill out the required establishment. The other option would have been to send selected SEALs through hospital corps school to get the needed medical backgrounds, but that was one of the most difficult schools to get into, requiring top marks in school and a strong academic bent. As a senior officer had put it to Tangretti one time, it was unlikely that very many men would possess the rare combination of talents that would make both a good SEAL *and* a good corpsman.

So they had decided to assign corpsmen to the SEALs on the same basis as the Fleet Marine Force medical personnel. Corpsmen volunteered for the duty and received much of the same ongoing training as the SEALs—dive school, Ranger school, jungle warfare, and all the rest—but they came to the unit as outsiders who didn't have that critical BUD/S training program under their belts. They'd never lived through Hell Week.

For the most part nobody cared. Tangretti hadn't even thought about Doc's background until after the crack about Hell Week. For the most part the corpsmen were accorded the genuine liking and respect that almost always went with their calling. After all, a hospital corpsman was the guy who would patch up his comrades in action, and plenty of ordinary enlisted guys like Doc held down independent duty responsibilities on small ships that made them the equal of full-fledged doctors. Tangretti still remembered the OR tech who had saved his life during the Inchon landing in Korea, running his own operating room without the supervision of a doctor for thirty-six hours straight.

But he tended to forget that Doc and his kind were far more aware of the difference between them and the "real" SEALs.

He dithered a moment, wondering whether to apologize or just pretend nothing had been said, when he was saved by the other man at the table, Lieutenant Ngyuen Thuy.

"Like you, I wish we had more time to practice each of these techniques, Ong Steve," he said diffidently. "This training is going very rapidly . . . perhaps too much so."

Tangretti shrugged. "I'm not the one who drew up the timetable," he said. "That was handed down from on high by the Prophet Dexter. Seems they want to rush this whole beach-recon thing through so they can impress the powers that be in Saigon with the new role for the Biet Hai."

"Politics . . . ain't they wonderful," George Marsh commented.

"The thing that bugs me is how you guys are getting the short end of the stick," Tangretti said, taking a swig of beer. "I don't see why the bigwigs in Saigon have got such a downer on for you."

Thuy gave him a thin smile. "I fear that the Biet Hai has not been . . . political enough. Our ideal is to kill the Communists, not to bow and scrape to the president or Ngo Dinh Nhu. Unfortunately, bowing and scraping is often necessary. Some of our senior people did not realize that in time, and they have angered the president's brother sufficiently to draw unwelcome attention to our unit."

"I know the feeling," Tangretti said, thinking again of Peter Howell. If it hadn't been for *his* connections—Galloway, Senator Forsythe, and even the odd regard he'd won from President Kennedy in a handful of brief meetings—Tangretti's unwillingness to play politics might easily have condemned the SEALs to being disbanded before they had a chance to find their feet. "So you're looking for a way to impress Saigon."

Thuy nodded. "I believe the American expression is 'Nothing succeeds like success,' Ong Steve," he said with another fleeting smile. "I am sure the Biet Hai can have an impact on the Communists, if we are only given a chance to show how much we can do. So far, though, we have been too much hampered by restrictions from above. Restrictions created by people who do not know what we are capable of." He paused. "Forgive me, but we were never intended to be pawns for your CIA. They are perhaps the worst of them all, as far as misusing the Biet Hai goes. It sometimes seems that they hardly know what their own agenda might be, much less how to use our unit to accomplish the missions they need. We could do much more if we were able to function on our own terms."

"I hear you," Randolph said, nodding. "I feel the exact same way about the spooks. I mean, who knows what they're really after, anyway? They come up with a lot of fancy plans, but they won't go the whole distance to carry any of them out."

"That's politics getting in the way again," Tangretti told them. "It's the price you pay for having a civilian authority controlling the military and the spies. I saw it back in Korea, when MacArthur tried to run things to suit himself and Truman stepped in to fire him. But the CIA's different.

They don't necessarily recognize civilian authority, at least not deep down, where it counts. They'll give lip service to the political bosses, but they'll also try to figure ways around the orders they disagree with." He hid a smile, thinking of the way Lattimore and Dexter were using him for their "unofficial" mission.

"Like that Bay of Pigs fiasco," Marsh said. "Yeah."

"So what you end up with is the spooks trying to run their secret operations without letting anybody higher up guess what they're trying to do, and imposing all sorts of restrictions to cover their own tails . . . or when they have no other choice, because somebody has them on the spot. Bay of Pigs might have worked if the president hadn't yanked the air support at the last minute . . . at least the Cuban invasion force might have been able to disengage and pull out when things went sour. But Kennedy had to make the decision he made . . . the CIA had tried to trick him into committing more than he thought we could afford to commit. Same thing could happen over here, if people aren't careful."

"Sounds like it's already happening, if you ask me," Randolph said. "Only this time it's the Biet Hai who are getting the shaft. You'd think the spooks could at least try to cover for them with the president and his crowd in Saigon. But from some of the stuff I've been hearing, it sounds to me like the Agency's ready to throw them to the wolves."

"Exactly. That is the way many of us feel. And I am afraid our time is running out. I only hope this operation will give us the chance we need." Thuy took a sip of rice wine, an air of fastidious care to his every move. Tangretti had trouble believing that this was the same Lieutenant Nguyen Thuy who had been at the forefront of his commandos in every training exercise back at China Beach. With his men, he was as gung ho as any Marine. But on his

own his manners and attitude were exactly what might be
expected of an officer and a gentleman.

That was the way everyone wished Steve Tangretti
would behave, but it simply wasn't in the cards. He'd been
an enlisted man too long to learn to play a new part now.

"I am afraid we will be disbanded—or worse—if we do
not soon demonstrate to the president and his people that
we can be useful against the Communists," Thuy went on.
He paused, then raised his glass. *"Sat Cong!"*

There was something in the intensity of his voice that
made Tangretti study him even harder. "You sound a lot
like Li Han when you say that, Ong Thuy," he commented.
"Don't tell me you sport one of those damned tattoos."

"But I do," Thuy told him. "I certainly do."

Randolph raised a quizzical eyebrow. "Somehow I never
took you for the tattoo type," he said.

"It is the custom of the Biet Hai," Thuy said, though
Tangretti thought he could read something more behind his
eyes. "Do you not have customs of your own, in your Navy
SEALs?"

Tangretti and Randolph exchanged glances and laughed.
"Yeah, one or two, I guess," Tangretti said. "I hope you
don't take offense, or anything, but Doc's right. There's the
hairy apes with the broad shoulders and the weak minds
who get tattoos. I got a couple back in the old days before
they told me I had to behave myself and be an officer. And
then there's the guys like Doc, here, who're too brainy to
want a tattoo."

Randolph held up a hand. "Hey, wait a minute, you're
making me sound like some kind of goddamned wimp. I
just know too much about what can go wrong at the kind of
tattoo parlors most sailors hang out in, that's all."

Tangretti chuckled. "That's what I mean. Too smart.
Thing is, Thuy, I'd've put you in the second category, custom or no custom."

The Vietnamese lieutenant looked away for a moment. "Perhaps I was . . . once. My father did very well under the French. He ran an import/export house out of Haiphong, and handled some fat contracts from the French army as well. Father saved a lot of money, and when I turned eighteen he sent me to school in your country. Berkeley. I was only gone a few months when Giap cornered the French at Dien Bien Phu. But when they surrendered, it turned everything upside down for us."

"Haiphong . . ." Randolph paused. "Your family's from the North, then?"

"Yes. When the country was partitioned, my family wound up in the North, under Ho Chi Minh. The Communists began stamping out capitalist ventures like my father's, nationalizing everything useful and simply wiping out whatever they didn't think they needed. In a matter of weeks my family was poor, and my father offended the wrong people and ended up on a proscription list. They tried to flee, but soldiers were close behind. The family was captured near the border, my father, mother, and my little sister, Hiep Mai. Mother and Hiep Mai were abused and raped, and Mother was killed when she struggled too hard."

"God," Randolph said softly. "You hear about stuff like that, but you never think it's real . . ."

"It was real," Thuy said. His voice was flat, as if all the emotion his story should have held had long since been drained out of him. "Somehow, Father escaped with Hiep Mai, and they made it to the border, where an ARVN patrol found them. But there was a firefight, and Father took a bullet in his back. He was paralyzed, and died a few months later. I came back as soon as I could, and found Hiep Mai in a refugee camp outside of Saigon, but I was too late to help Father. And I'm not sure if Hiep Mai will ever forgive me for not being there when they needed me."

He paused. "I joined the Navy because I had a background in the ships that served my father's business. But when the chance came to join the Biet Hai, I took it, because that was the best way I could see of getting a chance to kill as many of the Communists as I could. And I wear the tattoo, not just because it is something everyone does, but because it says what I believe in most . . . killing the bastards."

Tangretti watched Thuy take another sip of rice wine, feeling a new respect for the young Vietnamese officer. Outside the SEAL compound at China Beach he had been encountering a growing feeling among the American servicemen in Da Nang that their ARVN counterparts were inferior in every respect. The Vietnamese were all too often regarded as lazy, cowardly, or incompetent, and the nicknames the Americans hung on them left no doubt as to the depth of their scorn. One of the latest making the rounds, "dink," was derived from *dien cau dau*, the Vietnamese word for "crazy," but the epithet had taken on a life of its own. He'd been guilty of calling the locals "gooks" or "slopes" early on, himself, a holdover from his Korean War days. But Tangretti, along with the other SEALs, saw the Vietnamese differently now that he'd had time to study them.

It was true that the ARVN was riddled with corruption and incompetence, especially in the upper echelons, where the politicians had the most influence. On the other hand, after his dealings with Howell back at Norfolk, Tangretti didn't see that the USN was exactly efficient or honest. He rather suspected that military organizations were basically the same the world over, with enlisted men and junior officers trying their best to get along under senior officers and bureaucrats who made their lives the sheerest hell. The only real difference was in the extent of the rot at the top. Under President Diem, the Vietnamese military was in pretty bad shape, but that didn't mean that the men in the field were uniformly bad. It was plain that Nguyen Thuy, for example, was as dedicated as they came. Perhaps the desire for revenge had driven him, still drove him, but he was a professional fighting man now. Someone Tangretti could respect.

"All that was, what, ten years ago?" Randolph was asking. "That's a long time to live on hate." He paused for a moment. "How's your sister getting along now?"

"Well enough," Thuy said. "She is a hostess at a bar in Saigon . . . waitress was almost the only work she could get out of the camp, but she's worked her way up to a better position now. We get by."

Tangretti and Randolph exchanged glances again. From Thuy's tone, Tangretti guessed there was more to the story than that. Plenty of waitresses—and hostesses—in the seedier Saigon bars supplemented their income "entertaining" the customers. Had Hiep Mai drifted into prostitution? For a moment he had a vivid mental image of the girl from Da Nang, Sau Thi.

"What I really regret, though," Thuy went on after a long moment of silence, "is that I never realized how quickly you can lose everyone and everything that is dear to you. When I said good-bye to my parents, it was a casual thing, because I assumed they would be waiting for me on the dock in Haiphong when I sailed home in triumph from the United States. And I carried the image of Hiep Mai in my mind as she was when I left, hardly more than a little girl." His voice had suddenly turned bleak. "When I came back, Mother and Father were gone, and Hiep Mai had lost her innocence, and nothing I could do was enough to bring it back." The Biet Hai lieutenant fixed Tangretti with a sharp stare. "And that, Ong Steve, is why I wear the *Sat Cong* tattoo. Because I would gladly kill every Communist from Saigon to Hanoi, even though all those deaths would still not be enough to balance the scales with what they took from me."

Unbidden, a mental image of Ronnie and the boys sprang to the forefront of Tangretti's thoughts. The conversation around him moved on, but he was no longer listening to the byplay. He was thinking of how close he'd been, earlier, to forgetting Wallace's advice and following the selfish impulses that had led him astray so many times before.

What would he do if he lost his family? He might return to Little Creek to find Ronnie gone, and Bill and Hank Junior with her, leaving him an empty house . . . an empty life. Senator Forsythe, who had everything, had lost his wife in a car crash. But it might not take a tragedy like Thuy's or Forsythe's to rob Tangretti of his loved ones. He could do it all by himself.

He couldn't afford to keep pushing Ronnie farther away every time they fought. Someday, he might just push too hard and lose her forever. Steve Tangretti had battled bureaucrats and entrenched senior officers and every other obstacle imaginable to put his SEALs into business. Surely he could put the same effort into meeting Ronnie halfway . . . and the best way to begin was to stop playing the ostrich. He couldn't keep burying himself in booze and broads just because he was uncertain how to deal with his family anymore.

Starting tonight, he vowed, things were going to be different.

Chapter 14

Monday, 11 February 1963

USS *Perch*
Off Subic Bay, Republic of the Philippines
0932 hours

"All right, who wants to be first?" Tangretti said, surveying the knot of Biet Hai commandos crowded around the escape lock of the USS *Perch*. She was a submarine similar in most respects to the *Sea Lion*, the sub the East Coast SEALs had trained on and mounted covert ops from in the waters of the Caribbean. It was hard to believe that it had been less than a year back, now. For Tangretti, his three months in Southeast Asia had stretched out until it sometimes seemed like an entire lifetime.

"I will try it, Lieutenant Steve." That was Li Han, the half-American commando from the fiasco on Beach Red before Christmas. He and his three companions from that op were part of the twelve-man unit selected for the North Vietnam beach-survey project. Nguyen Thuy made it thirteen, and Tangretti sometimes wondered if he was superstitious enough to be worried by that ominous number.

"Okay. Remember what I showed you earlier, Li Han." He gestured to the escape trunk. "George Marsh is outside waiting, and Doc'll be in there with you, so if you get into any trouble, there'll be plenty of help close at hand."

Li Han gave a curt nod and stepped forward, lowering his face mask and checking the fit of the mouthpiece on his aqualung. All of the Bict Hai swimmers had some SCUBA training, but nothing nearly as thorough as UDT and SEAL divers received, and none of them had ever tried swimming off of a submerged sub before. Tangretti could still remember the first time he'd tried it. Emerging underwater, it was easy to get disoriented, and the looming presence of the hull was a constant threat. He'd heard of men accidentally running into a sub's hull and knocking themselves unconscious. So the SEALs were taking no chances during the first few practice dives from the *Perch*.

Located above the sub's main deck, the lock-out chamber was a cramped compartment barely large enough to hold three or four standing men at a time. During these early practice runs Tangretti had decreed that only two men would pass through the lock on each practice dive, one of them always an instructor. Doc Randolph climbed the ladder that led up through the watertight hatch above, with Li Han following. His progress was a little awkward thanks to his swim fins. One of the sub's crew followed the two divers to swing the hatch shut and dog it tightly below them.

Tangretti could picture the junk commando standing with Doc in the small, dim-lit airlock, waiting as seawater rushed into the chamber. When it reached a depth of about five feet, it would be above the level of the side hatch that opened to the outside of the sub. For most American divers, the water level would be about neck-high in the chamber when the flow of water was shut off, and the tall Li Han would find it no problem either. But Tangretti found himself wondering if all of his charges would be able to handle the lock-out process as easily. Some of them were much shorter than their American counterparts.

He heard the pump stop, and knew that the lock was mostly filled by water. There was a short pause as air was forced into the chamber to raise the pressure to match the two atmospheres outside the hull. Only when the pressures were equalized could Li Han kick open the side hatch and exit the sub, where George Marsh was waiting as the dive safety man to help him avoid obstacles and find the line that ran from the hatch to a buoy on the surface.

The day's training was easy. Li Han was making the ascent in daylight, and using his SCUBA gear. As time went on the Biet Hai commandos would start practicing more dangerous kinds of evolutions, such as exiting in darkness and using the "blow and go" technique of swimming to the surface without their breathing gear. Remembering the way the SEALs had run out of air on their return from San Mariel in the Cuban recon op, Tangretti was more convinced than ever that it was smart to use their breathing equipment as little as possible, although "blow and go" could be dangerous if proper care wasn't exercised. Of course, the Vietnamese would be using aqualungs instead of the rebreathers the SEALs had found so troublesome off Cuba, but Tangretti wasn't sure that was much of a trade-off. The Vietnamese equipment was older, not much different from the original Cousteau aqualung design from the late forties. Its air capacity didn't give it any more endurance than the rebreather, and there was the added problem of telltale oxygen bubbles that could give swimmers away to an observant enemy.

His mind once again flashed back to that night they'd scouted the Cuban coast, and Tangretti shook his head slowly. He was very much afraid this beach-recon project was going to run into trouble—a lot of trouble—before it was all over. The restrictions being placed on them from above were going to be a problem, he thought grimly, with the CIA being forced to rely on the Biet Hai instead of using people who were better able to get the job done. Much as he liked the junk commandos, Tangretti knew they didn't have the same level of training, equipment, or solid support to carry out their intended mission.

They just weren't SEALs. That made all the difference.

CIA Station
Da Nang
1530 hours

"Ah, Lieutenant Gunn, come in and have a seat, won't you?"

Gunn regarded Bill Lattimore warily, but closed the office door behind him and sat in the proffered chair. "You wanted to see me?" he asked, voice carefully neutral. Most of his dealings with the CIA to date had ended up in decisions he hadn't liked, and he had no reason to believe that was going to change now.

"I've been in contact with Commander Wallace, and with Lieutenant Tang, the new Biet Hai liaison officer who is replacing Thuy," Lattimore said. "It struck us that the current UDT beach-survey work gives your SEALs an excellent opportunity to conduct some training in that subject for your new class of Biet Hai—some actual hands-on experience. And the addition of the Biet Hai would, in turn, speed up the survey work by giving Commander Wallace more men to draw on. We thought you might mix Biet Hai trainees in with experienced UDT swimmers." He smiled disarmingly. "What do you think of the idea, Lieutenant?"

Gunn shifted uncomfortably in his chair. "Frankly, sir?"

"Of course," Lattimore said. His smile broadened. "Pretend you are Mr. Tangretti, and give us your views in full."

"Well . . . I'd like to hate the idea," Gunn said slowly. "It's yet another assault on the program we worked out, and it moves my trainees out of where my men can keep a close eye on them." He paused. "But . . . well, it has its good points, too. Sorry as I am to admit it, getting some actual beach-recon work in would be good experience. From everything that was covered at the briefings last month, it sounds to me as if you aren't expecting any significant trouble."

Lattimore leaned forward. "I'll be honest in turn," he said. "During the initial surveys right around Da Nang, we had a few reports of sniper fire. But it was mostly meant for harassment, as far as we can tell."

"Hmm." Gunn frowned. "Of course, if the VC realize that there are Biet Hai involved, it might increase the risk of hostile contact. Commander Wallace might not be too pleased at that. His men would actually have an increased risk of running into enemies."

"He's aware of it," Lattimore said. "And he has already indicated that he's willing to risk it. Fact is, I think he feels that the increased speed of the survey is worth whatever additional risk there might be in mixing the Biet Hai in."

"Are you proposing this as a long-term project?" Gunn asked. "I mean, the survey work was projected to take two or three months. The MTT goes home in April. That really would mess up the rest of the training schedule if we spent the whole remainder of the tour on this."

"No, we're only talking about helping out for a few weeks. No more than a month." Lattimore hesitated. "I'll keep on being honest here, Lieutenant. We have an ulterior motive in setting this up. In addition to the beach surveys, we're asking Commander Wallace and Major Corbett to help us on a related project. We're trying to get a feel for the extent and nature of North Vietnamese penetration into the South. Most reports tend to put the most emphasis on the Ho Chi Minh Trail, but we're interested in seeing what kind of activity the Commies are mounting by sea, down the coast. So Major Corbett's men, in addition to providing beach security, will also be poking around looking for signs of NVA and VC activity when they start working in the northern provinces, and the UDT men will be keeping their eyes out for suspicious sea traffic, signs that beaches have been used to off-load supplies, that sort of thing. It's the period when they'll have these added responsibilities that we will want the Biet Hai to lend a hand."

"So . . ." Gunn nodded. "I wondered if there wasn't some Company agenda in all this. "But I still don't see any overwhelming objections."

"Excellent. The major area we want to study is the Quang Tri province, immediately south of the Demilitarized Zone. There are beaches in the region around Dong Ha, our northernmost airbase, and we suspect that these may be getting a lot more use than we previously believed was likely. It's not only the closest stretch of coast to North Vietnamese waters, it's also a key strategic position. The DMZ is well defended and closely watched, to prevent the NVA from moving supplies directly into the country across the Ben Hai River and the Seventeenth Parallel. It would be natural for the North Vietnamese to try to outflank the DMZ by stirring up Viet Cong activity just to the south. So we need to see just how much infiltration they may be attempting in that area, and what kind."

"Makes sense," Gunn said. "But you say the Biet Hai are just there to take some of the burden off the UDT men?"

"Exactly. Major Corbett's Marines and the men from Det Bravo will do that portion of the recon work. We will also be employing the two torpedo boats—*Adder* and *Boa*, I believe your people call them—to sweep the area offshore and report the movement of fishing boats and other coastal traffic. The Biet Hai will concentrate on the standard beach-survey work. A simple training exercise, nothing more."

"And my men?"

"Will travel with them, of course. I'm sure that you and Commander Wallace can best determine how they should be used, but I would imagine you could continue some of your training work aboard the APD, and have your SEALs accompany the beach-survey teams to supervise the trainees as needed."

Gunn gave a reluctant nod. "I think it will work well enough," he said slowly. "Doesn't sound like it violates any of the guidelines I signed off on when we pulled this assignment."

"Good," Lattimore said, smiling again. "I'm glad to see you aren't quite as quick to suspect the Agency of wrong-doing as you've been in the past, Lieutenant. Thank you for your cooperation in this."

"Oh, don't be so quick to thank me, Mr. Lattimore," Gunn said. "I suspect El Cid of lots of things. I just figure that this time out none of them is likely to get any of my people killed for no good reason, so I'll go along with you. No offense."

"None taken, Lieutenant," Lattimore told him. "As long as you do your job, you're free to regard us any way you want to."

Friday, 15 February 1963

Off Subic Bay
1431 hours

Hospitalman Third Class John Randolph took a series of deep breaths, saturating his lungs with oxygen as the pressure inside the airlock slowly rose to match the two atmospheres outside the hull. Unlike the Biet Hai, Randolph had performed this operation many times before. But experience didn't completely eliminate the knot he felt forming in his stomach, or keep him from thinking about everything that could go wrong.

There were those who thought that Navy frogmen were just plain crazy, taking risks no sane man would ever consider, heedless of any danger. That just wasn't true, not for the UDT that most people knew about, and not for the SEALs few outside a select circle had ever heard of. The fact was, Navy divers trained thoroughly and intensively, learning everything they needed to know about every aspect of their dangerous profession. They knew the risks they took better than anyone, but they were also taught not to let those risks keep them from doing their jobs.

The light above his head flashed green as the pressure equalized, and Randolph took a last deep breath before pulling his face mask down over his eyes and breathing in through his nose to seal it tight against the water. He turned to his companion, the big NCO named Li Han, and pointed downward. The Biet Hai's eyes glittered behind his own mask as he nodded, and the two of them simultaneously crouched down in the small airlock chamber, ducking their heads into the warm water. With practiced ease Randolph kicked open the hatch and exited the airlock. The water outside was clear and brightly lit by sunlight slanting down on the surface, and he quickly caught sight of Lieutenant Tangretti in a wet suit and aqualung clinging to a handhold nearby. Tangretti was the safety diver today, responsible for making sure the other swimmers got clear of the sub and on their way to the surface without suffering any accidents or becoming disoriented.

As Randolph emerged from the airlock, Tangretti's hand grasped his, guiding the corpsman to the line tied off around a cleat set in the sub's hull not far from the hatch. The line ran up to a buoy floating on the surface, where the waiting raft was tethered. With filtered daylight, Randolph didn't really need the assistance, but at night it would be another matter entirely. For the purposes of the exercise they weren't leaving any step out.

Randolph flashed the lieutenant a quick thumbs-up signal and saw him turn to assist Li Han. The SEAL started pulling himself up the line hand over hand, keeping his pace measured and deliberate. As he made the ascent, he forced himself to hold his head back and exhale steadily, though it went against every instinct to blow out precious air while underwater. The *Perch* was submerged to a depth of sixty feet, and traveling to the surface too fast from a pressure of thirty pounds per square inch created a definite danger of an embolism forming from air entering the bloodstream. Air bubbles could cause a stroke or heart attack even in a healthy young commando. As a hospital corpsman, Randolph was even more aware of the dangers involved than most SEALs, so he treated the procedure with all the respect and caution it deserved.

Eventually, after the ascent procedure was second nature, the Biet Hai would be taught to go up without the safety line, inflating life jackets as they exited the sub and rocketing to the surface at an incredible rate. But that was something that would have to wait for experience and a more exact knowledge of just how quickly to release the air from their lungs according to the speed of their ascent. Breathing out too slowly increased the embolism threat, but exhaling too fast on the way up would leave the diver without enough air to complete the trip to the surface. Even this basic version of the evolution was challenge enough.

As he approached the surface he could feel the air in his lungs running out. His chest was starting to ache, and he cursed inwardly as he realized he hadn't allowed for his slower ascent when he expelled the air on the way up. It was a stupid stunt, exactly the kind of thing that might be expected from a Hell Week reject. But Randolph fought down the rising panic and kept his head, releasing the line and propelling himself upward with powerful kicks. His head broke water a few yards from the raft, and he gulped in air as he bobbed in the uneven swells, treading water.

After a moment he started swimming slowly toward the raft. George Marsh's homely face peered down at him. Randolph met his gaze and gave him a watery grin. "I feel fine," he said. It wasn't just a greeting. A symptom of embolism that was easy to test for was the inability to pronounce the letter *f*, so Navy divers had evolved that simple three-word phrase as a quick check of their condition after any ascent. Had they been in a training tank on land, Randolph would have given himself a quick physical check and then stood at attention for five minutes, since another symptom of an embolism was an inability to stand still without coming down with a bad case of the twitches. But those tests were impractical in a rubber raft.

Randolph wished they'd been able to work with a training tank and a thorough course of ascents under controlled conditions on land, but with the time constraints and the lack of proper facilities at Subic Bay had forced Lieutenant Tangretti to condense the training to focus entirely on practice runs off the sub. Like the lieutenant, Randolph hoped that the timetable that had been foisted off on the Biet Hai commandos wouldn't turn out to be a dangerous mistake.

Marsh offered him a hand, and Randolph clambered into the IBS beside him. A few moments later, a telltale string of bubbles formed in the water close by. Moments later Li Han erupted from the water alongside the raft like a breaching whale. He grinned as he took a few deep swallows of oxygen, then spoke. "I feel fine," he said in his carefully enunciated English. The mercenary looked at Tangretti. "But I know now that I am not a fish."

He and Marsh helped Li Han out of the water and into the raft, and Randolph gave the commando a quick check

while they waited for the next candidate—or victim, as
Marsh put it—to arrive.

USS *Perch*
Off Subic Bay
1452 hours

"Next two men, into the chamber."

Le Xuan Chinh stepped forward at the order from the
American UDT officer, Simms, swallowing hard but otherwise masking his uncertainty. Lieutenant Thuy, his designated partner, stopped him at the foot of the ladder and
double-checked his equipment: mask, weight belt, life
vest, and SCUBA tank. Then the wiry little commando
stepped back, and Le returned the favor by double-checking his gear.

"All right," Thuy said in Vietnamese when he was
through, "time to go."

Climbing the ladder awkwardly in his swim fins, Le
reached the top all too quickly and clambered awkwardly
through the hatch, with Thuy following close behind. An
American enlisted man followed them up, sealing the
hatch in place below them. The metallic clang as it swung
shut was ominous, echoing in the little airlock.

Then it was silent, and that was more ominous still.

For nearly a week now Le had practiced alongside the
others, but each time it had been a little bit harder to climb
into the airlock and wait for it to go through the ponderous,
slow cycle. He had never admitted to anyone just how edgy
enclosed spaces made him, but the fact was that Le Xuan
Chinh found it almost unbearable. But he was determined
not to give in, not to admit that he might not be able to do
what his comrades seemed to handle with such ease, so he
clenched his teeth and climbed the ladder each time he was

told to, forcing himself to go through with each drill in turn. He would conquer his fear, no matter how hard it was to do it.

Standing still, hands clenching and unclenching slowly, he listened as the rumble of machinery started up and the pumps engaged. Water began to pour into the chamber, rising quickly to his ankles, his shins, his knees . . .

Le breathed deeply, as he had been taught. The American, Tangretti, had said it was important to saturate his lungs in the chamber by hyperventilating. That was one thing that wasn't hard for Le to do. The problem, in fact, was to keep from hyperventilating until the hatch was dogged tight and he was ready to cycle through the airlock. He had heard that a later step in the training would require several men to lock through at the same time, rather than just two, and he wondered if that would be easier, or harder. Having more men to see him would shame Le into repressing his fears even further, but on the other hand it would be even more cramped. The walls would press in that much more.

The water swirled past his waist, now, and Le kept his eye on the red light near the top of the chamber. He found himself wishing, as he invariably did as he waited through this long-drawn-out part of the drill, that the Americans had provided better lighting in this "escape trunk" of theirs. It wasn't completely dark, of course, but it was dim enough to make the shadows seem to close in around him.

He breathed more deeply still, taking in great gulps of air as the water rose over his chest. Shorter than most Americans, shorter even than many of his fellow junk commandos, Le had less time before the water level rose too high to permit him to stand. He bobbed up as the water continued to rise, and now the claustrophobia was all the worse because the small bubble of air at the very top of the chamber was all his senses perceived of the space around him. Beside him, Thuy seemed to be taking everything in stride. Fortunately, his companion was paying Le little heed.

There was another pause after the water ceased to enter the airlock, while air was forced into the chamber. He kept on breathing fast and deep, trying to ignore the discomfort caused by the increased air pressure. His ears popped, and a moment later the light finally flashed from red to green. Le Xuan Chinh set his mask and ducked down under the water. He kicked at the outer hatch, but it did not give way as it should have. Le tried again, harder this time, but it seemed to be stuck fast.

Now his panic was rising fast as he felt trapped by the unyielding steel. Le lashed out with both feet, felt the hatch give slightly, but still it seemed impossible to open. Desperate, the commando turned in the chamber and rammed a shoulder into the hatch. It popped free suddenly, and Le's momentum carried him out into the open water.

He was disoriented and still not able to think clearly as a result of the waves of panic that continued to batter at his sanity. A hand suddenly gripped his shoulder from behind, and without thinking he responded as he had been trained to do, by ramming an elbow straight back. The hand released him, and Le turned in the water to lash out again at whoever had attacked him.

The swimmer gestured frantically, but Le's whole world was reduced to fear and instinct. He grabbed at the other's face mask, and as it came free he knew it would temporarily blind his foe with stinging salt water. Disoriented, the swimmer jerked away from Le, and as he flailed in the water he rammed straight back into the unyielding metal of the submarine's hull.

But at that moment there was another man there, grappling with Le. A hand groped at his chest and pulled the ring that caused his life jacket to inflate. Le Xuan Chinh pushed him away roughly, and then began to rise fast as the life jacket's canister of air made the vest swell to full inflation. He didn't see what happened to the other man, and within moments the pain in his chest and a feeling of dizziness overwhelmed him.

Le Xuan Chinh never even realized it when he made it to the surface.

Outside USS *Perch*
Off Subic Bay
1458 hours

Tangretti was mentally cursing as the Biet Hai shot toward the surface, but he didn't have time to pay further attention to the injured Le Xuan Chinh. His immediate concern was for Thuy, who had collided hard with the hull and was floating, facedown, a few yards away. With powerful strokes of hands and feet Tangretti propelled himself alongside the Vietnamese lieutenant. Thuy showed no signs of seeing him, no signs of consciousness at all, and Tangretti swallowed a lump in his throat. If that fool Le had injured his friend, an air embolism was going to be the least of his worries once the SEAL caught up with him.

Tangretti pulled his mouthpiece free and put it in Thuy's mouth. A wave of relief washed over him as a stream of bubbles formed; the Vietnamese lieutenant was still able to breathe on his own. Holding his breath, Tangretti let Thuy continue to draw air from his own aqualung while he checked the fittings on the Biet Hai's own tanks and mouthpiece. Only when he was sure nothing had been damaged in the fight did Tangretti replace his mouthpiece with Thuy's own. Then he half guided, half dragged his friend back toward the open airlock hatch.

Inside, he stood up so that his head was in the air pocket at the top of the chamber, spitting out his mouthpiece and clawing the mask free of his face before hitting the intercom button. "This is Tangretti," he said. "Suspend the lock-outs. I have a casualty who needs medical attention. Get this goddamned fish tank pumped out pronto and have corpsmen ready."

Only after he'd switched the intercom off and heard the welcome sound of the pumps beginning to force the water back out of the airlock did Tangretti breathe a sigh of relief, relax, and start thoroughly and loudly swearing.

IBS
Off Subic Bay
1458 hours

"Ong Doc! Over there!"

Randolph turned in response to the urgency in Li Han's voice. He was in time to see a body surge out of the water some distance away from the raft, well clear of the lifeline. With a muffled curse the corpsman rose to his feet, balancing against the uneven motion of the raft, and executed a smooth dive over the side. He swam rapidly toward the floating figure.

Reaching the man, he noted that the victim's life jacket was inflated, so that he floated faceup with his head clear of the water. But a quick check showed the Vietnamese commando wasn't breathing on his own. His pulse was thready, and already he was twitching involuntarily. Randolph grasped the collar of his life jacket and began to tow him back to the raft, all too aware of the seconds that ticked by inexorably.

Li Han and Marsh helped him heave Le up into the raft, then aided him over the side. Randolph knelt in the bottom of the IBS over the victim, pulling his head back and checking for obstructions in his throat before he began to administer mouth-to-mouth resuscitation. After a few moments, the commando began to cough and sputter, bringing up a great gush of seawater from his mouth and nostrils. He was alive, at least.

Randolph could only hope that he would stay that way.

USS *Perch*
Subic Bay
1630 hours

Sick bay aboard the *Perch* was tiny, as cramped as the rest of the old World War II–era submarine. There wasn't much room for Tangretti along with the beds and the medical equipment, a sick-bay attendant, and Nguyen Thuy, but the SEAL squeezed into the compartment anyway and looked down at the man in the bed nearest the hatch. "How're you doing, Ong Thuy?" he asked.

The Vietnamese officer's dark eyes looked tired as they met Tangretti's. "My head feels like it has been used as a drum," he said stiffly. "Think of the worst hangover you ever had, and then imagine having it when the jukebox at the Green Parrot is turned up to its full volume, and you have an idea of how I feel. Except that in this case there is no pretty girl around to take my mind off things."

Tangretti smiled. "I doubt I can wrangle a visit from a girl, but I'll give it a shot if you want."

Thuy started to shake his head, but stopped abruptly. "No. Thank you anyway, Ong Steve." He gave a thin smile. "I am not sure I would remember what to do with one anyway, at the moment." His expression turned serious again. "But you can tell me about Le Xuan Chinh. Is he all right?"

"An embolism and a bad case of the twitches," Tangretti said. "But he'll be okay, according to the docs." The sub's doctor, a lieutenant, had said as much, but Tangretti had been happier to hear it from Randolph. Even though a corpsman didn't have a medical degree, Tangretti had always placed his trust in them. That was doubly true when the corpsman was also a SEAL. "Doc Randolph save Le's life out there, Ong Thuy," he added. "I had to get him clear and up to the surface, so I inflated his life jacket, and he lost consciousness on the way up. Li Han told me that Doc gave him mouth-to-mouth when they found he wasn't breathing."

"Doc . . . is a good man," Thuy said carefully. "But not the only one. You saved my life, did you not, Ong Steve?"

"Just doing my job," Tangretti told him. "I'm just mad I didn't do something about the little bastard before he went berserk on us."

"Not his fault, Ong Steve . . . or not entirely. The hatch stuck when we tried to get it open, and Le panicked. He seemed nervous before the airlock filled, so perhaps the problem with the hatch was not the only thing that pushed him over the edge."

Tangretti nodded. "I have a feeling he's got a touch of claustrophobia," he said. "Worst enemy of a diver. It might not show in ordinary dives, but working around a sub can really screw a guy up if he's a claustie. We try to screen them out in BUD/S training, but I guess that's something that the Biet Hai never did with Le." He shrugged. "Just be glad we abandoned the old notion of sending divers out through the torpedo tubes. I tried that a couple of times back in the early days of sub lock-outs, and it gave me a case of the screaming meemies . . . and I've *never* had problems with enclosed spaces."

"I am glad he was not worse injured," Thuy said. "But I imagine he will have to be scratched and sent back to Da Nang."

"Absolutely," Tangretti responded. "He won't be doing

any diving for a while, and even if he could, we sure as hell don't need a claustie when we start our surveys."

"And what do the doctors say about me, Ong Steve? Will I be flying home with him?"

Tangretti fixed him with a deep stare. "Do you want to?"

Again the Vietnamese officer gave an abortive shake of his head, wincing before he said, "No, not if I have a choice. I need to be on this mission."

The SEAL smiled. "Well, you're in luck. Doc told me that if you get some rest and try not to let anybody slam your head against steel-plated hulls for a few days, you should be right as rain."

"That is good. I hope that I am up and around in time to qualify with the others. Right now, I fear, I am not exactly measuring up to your high standards, my friend."

"Hell, no," Tangretti told him. "You're a genu-wine, waterproof, rustproof, shockproof, oversexed, underpaid, big-mouthed, certified, glorified frogman . . . just like Doc and me. You handled yourself pretty damn well out there in a bad situation. Couldn't have been better if you were a SEAL, Ong Thuy." He grinned. "So take care of yourself. They'll transfer you to the hospital over at Clark AFB after a while, but you should be back with the rest of us in a few days. Just in time for things to start getting exciting."

Chapter 15

Sunday, 17 February 1963

USS *Perch*
Gulf of Tonkin
2216 hours

"All right, Mr. Tangretti, we're in position. Time for your part of the show."

Tangretti nodded and bent over the narrow chart table. Across from him, seeming too large to be a submariner, Captain Ronald Lichter jabbed a blunt finger at a tiny cross marked on the map. Lichter wasn't as big as he looked—Tangretti topped him by a good four inches—but he was a squat, powerfully built man who looked more like a stevedore than a Navy officer. His gravelly voice and no-nonsense manner added to that impression.

"We're on the bottom, right about here," he said, tapping the chart again. "Well inside territorial waters, I might add, which doesn't make me too happy."

"How do you think I feel?" Tangretti said. "I'm swimming in to the beach, for Christ's sake, and you can't get a hell of a lot more territorial than that."

Lichter looked up, studying him for a long moment. "Yeah, well, I don't like that too much, either, Lieutenant, but my orders say to cooperate with you in every way possible. So I'm cooperating. Just remember that the other part of the orders talks about not risking my boat unnecessarily. Hanging around North Vietnamese waters waiting for a bunch of slopes to finish a moonlight swim on the beach is pushing it, as far as I'm concerned."

Tangretti glanced up at the third man at the chart table, Lieutenant Thuy. A flash of irritation crossed his mind at Lichter's epithet, but after a moment he remembered the harangue he had given to Gunn the day they'd arrived in Da Nang about old habits of speech dying hard. Had four months working with the Biet Hai really changed him that much?

The Vietnamese lieutenant met his gaze and gave him a faint smile that managed to be just so slightly world-weary. Thuy had recovered from his accident with Le Xuan Chinh and rejoined the other junk commandos in plenty of time to practice all of the techniques the SEALs had taught them. He had a clean bill of health from the Air Force doctors at Clark—Subic Bay didn't support a Navy hospital, to Tangretti's loud-voiced chagrin—and he seemed eager to get into action.

He suppressed an answering smile and nodded gravely instead. "We'll do our best to keep from putting your boat in any danger, Captain," he said. Inwardly he was wishing he was still working with Commander Erskine of the *Sea Lion*. Though elegant in appearance and speech, Erskine had been much less fussy about the beach recon off Cuba than Lichter was about this one.

"All right. You can commence your operation whenever you wish. Just be sure you're back here on schedule. Got it?"

"Aye aye, sir," Tangretti responded. "Come on, Thuy, let's go get dressed for a swim."

It took less than ten minutes to get ready and join the

Biet Hai commandos already assembled in the compartment below the airlock. The eleven Vietnamese looked like something out of Tangretti's UDT past, stripped down to swim trunks and SCUBA gear, armed with knives and slates attached to their wrists for making their beach-survey notes. They were the very image of the classic "naked warriors," and Tangretti approved of their looks as he studied them. Back in World War II it had taken the Navy a long time to realize that the work the UDTs did went best when the swimmers weren't weighed down by too much gear. It was a growing problem that Tangretti had been trying to deal with back at Little Creek, finding a way to get a raiding party into action with enough equipment to hold their own in combat without weighing them down so heavily they couldn't stay fast and mobile inserting into and extracting from the target area. He'd reviewed designs for specialized SEAL assault craft and underwater SEAL Delivery Vehicles that could carry men and equipment, but so far the SEALs hadn't settled on anything definite.

Tonight they'd do things the old-fashioned way. Most of the outfit would swim in, as the SEALs had done at San Mariel. But George Marsh, who was acting as the dive safety man, had already left the sub to deploy an IBS on the surface, which held the heavier gear they might need—weapons, a radio, and other gear intended for the part of the team that would be working above the high-tide mark. That was the best compromise he'd been able to come up with when he and Thuy had been planning the mission back at Subic Bay.

It took Tangretti a moment to realize that a twelfth figure was waiting among the Vietnamese, identically dressed but standing out because of height and skin color.

"Just what the hell are you doing here, Doc?" he asked sharply. "Nobody said anything about you going on this op."

Randolph gave him a lopsided smile. "The same could be said, oh illustrious leader, about you," he responded. "I figured you'd be going in, and I was right. So I thought I'd better come along in case you needed backup—or a patch up job."

"No way, Doc," Tangretti said, shaking his head. "You know it's against orders for us to get involved in direct action. If I do it, it's on my own head. But I can't allow any other American to go."

"Look, Lieutenant, you've already got a hole in the Biet Hai with Le Xuan Chinh gone. And the plans call for part of the team to make a deep recon around Dong Hai instead of sticking to the regular survey job, so that's going to bleed off some more people you can't spare. You *need* me out there."

"We'll manage," Tangretti growled. "You stay."

Randolph shrugged. "Well . . . okay. I guess I can spend the time writing up my report to Lieutenant Gunn." He paused. "Sir, is there one 's' or two in 'disobedience'?"

"You wouldn't . . ."

"*You* would."

Tangretti's eyes locked with the corpsman's. After a long moment, he shrugged. "It's your funeral, Doc. I'll tell you what the boys from El Cid told me. I ain't ordering it, I ain't sanctioning it, and I don't know anything about it if you get caught—by the bad guys *or* the brass back home. You get my meaning?"

"Yes *sir*," Randolph said. "You won't regret it, Lieutenant."

"Regret what? You're not here, never were here, won't ever be here." Tangretti looked at Thuy. "Well, Lieutenant, shall we get this show on the road? Before any more volunteers show up to confuse the issue?"

"First four men into the airlock," Thuy said crisply. "Li

Han . . . Tran Nhat . . . Truong Ky . . ." He paused. "Ran-dolph. *Move!*"

Tangretti's mouth was dry. The mission was under way.

Beach Green
Near Dong Hai,
Democratic Republic of Vietnam
2343 hours

The IBS bucked wildly in the rolling surf as it approached the beach. John Randolph cursed under his breath and held on tight to his paddle, trying to maintain control over the raft that seemed to have developed a mind of its own. He wasn't alone. He could hear one of his Vietnamese boat mates repeating the word *"phan"*—shit—over and over again. Some things were the same in any navy.

The raft touched bottom on the rapidly sloping sand, and Randolph dropped his paddle into the bottom of the boat and vaulted over the side into the warm water. It swirled around his legs, strong enough to knock an unprepared man down, but Randolph kept his balance. On the other side of the boat, Huan Van Nim emulated the corpsman's move promptly. The other two boat crewmen were slower getting out and helping to lift and drag the raft out of the water.

Two more shapes materialized out of the night, Tangretti and the big Chinese commando, Li Han. They had done the first recon swim up onto the beach, and used a lamp to signal the "all clear" to the boat. Now they helped manhandle the raft up on the beach. Presumably Thuy and Tran Nhat, the other two swimmers in Tangretti's party, were deployed somewhere out of sight, guarding the approaches to the beach.

Adrenaline sang in Randolph's veins as they got the raft

above the water mark and started checking over the gear stored inside. *This* was what he was meant to do!

His father had been a petty officer in the Hospital Corps during World War II and Korea, rising to the rank of chief and holding down a slot on independent duty aboard an LST. It had been a responsible post. Independent duty corpsmen handled all the medical duties aboard a small ship that didn't rate a doctor, which meant that Chief Thomas Randolph had essentially held the lives of every man aboard in his hands for weeks or months at a time.

When John Randolph had turned eighteen, joining the Navy—and the Hospital Corps—had been inevitable. He had a family tradition to live up to, and a natural aptitude for it. Largely self-taught, the younger Randolph had been a serious, studious type, and scored high enough on his placement tests to ensure the Hospital Corps billet he wanted. It wasn't until after Corps School and training as an OR tech that he'd discovered the one thing he wasn't cut out for.

Randolph wasn't good at being patient.

He was highly skilled, well motivated, and good at his work, but during his first duty assignment as one of the operating room technicians aboard an APD he found that he was mostly just plain bored. By the time the cruise was over, Randolph was busy bombarding the people at BuPers with letter after letter requesting every kind of duty he could think of that might get him free of the boring routine. He'd even requested a transfer to FMF, the Fleet Marine assignment most corpsmen dreaded because it meant becoming part of a combat platoon, but it was refused with all his other attempts at reassignment.

Then he heard through the grapevine about a new unit that was being formed from the Underwater Demolition Teams. His APD assignment had thrown him into contact with a detachment from one of the UDTs, commanded by a lieutenant named Camparelli. When he learned that

Camparelli was to head up the new SEAL unit on the West Coast, Randolph had gotten in touch with the man. The lieutenant had remembered him—Randolph had assisted on a tricky piece of surgery after one of the UDT men had been injured during a training exercise off Dutch Harbor in the Bering Sea—and was glad to include him on the list of corpsmen who would be attached to SEAL Team One.

Randolph had never regretted his decision to join the Teams. The SEALs had more action in a few weeks of training than most sailors experienced across an entire career. But ever since he'd joined up, he'd been haunted by the fact that he had never been through Hell Week, never seen any real action to prove that he was really worthy of being a part of the SEALs.

Now, perhaps, he'd have that chance to show what he was made of. He smiled to himself as he thought of the look on Tangretti's face when he'd as much as blackmailed the lieutenant into letting him come. Lieutenant Tangretti was the kind of man who could appreciate a gutsy move like that.

Randolph just hoped he'd be able to carry through, now that his chance for action had come.

"Okay." Tangretti's gruff voice interrupted his reverie. Randolph looked up from the Soviet-made AK-47 he'd been checking over as his mind had been drifting, and focused on the lieutenant's words. "Randolph, get the radio set up. We'll let our lords and masters know we're here."

"Okay, Boss." Randolph put down the weapon and started to assemble the PRC-74, a large radio that could be referred to as portable only by someone who was feeling charitable. It had to be big, though, because it had range enough to reach across the DMZ. Usually radios of this type were issued to the Vietnamese Mobile Strike Forces, which operated independently far from regular bases and needed the communications range. This one had a scrambler system built in, which added to the weight.

After he had it hooked up, its antenna deployed, and the batteries warmed up, he signaled to Tangretti. "Secure net's ready, Lieutenant," he said.

Tangretti picked up the mike. "Bearclaw, Bearclaw, this is Alligator. Do you copy?" He repeated the call three times before there was finally a reply, heavy with static.

"Alligator, Bearclaw." It was Lattimore's voice, which surprised him. The PRC-74 didn't have the range to reach Da Nang. The CIA officer must have come north to somewhere near the DMZ to monitor the operation. *"Reading you three by three. Report."*

"Bearclaw, insertion completed. Location is Beach Green. Preparing to deliver our package."

"Understood, Alligator," Lattimore told him. *"Report on completion of mission."* There was a pause. *"Godspeed, Alligator."*

"Alligator clear," Tangretti responded, putting down the microphone. He gestured for the others to gather around him. "Okay, let's go over it one last time. Thuy?"

"Three groups," the Vietnamese officer said tightly. He sounded as keyed up as Randolph felt. "Six swimmers in the water, paired up to do the beach survey. Mung is in command there. Beach security will be commanded by Nim. They are to form a perimeter on the beach and monitor for the approach of an enemy. Orders are to avoid contact unless absolutely necessary, and to avoid attracting any unnecessary attention should they be forced to take action against an enemy. Knives are preferable to firearms. Staying low is preferable to both, unless the enemy is about to discover the swimmers or endanger the mission in some other way."

Tangretti interrupted him. "Doc, I want you on the beach security team. You keep an eye on the raft. Keep in mind, this is a Biet Hai show, so Huan Van Nim calls the shots. You're an advisor. If he asks for advice, give it to him. If you think he ought to be asking for advice, give it to him anyway . . . but he's in charge. Got it?"

"Got it," Randolph acknowledged.

"Good. Sorry, Ong Thuy. Go on."

Thuy gave a curt nod. Randolph was surprised at the transformation in the man. There was an intensity there he hadn't seen before.

"Ong Steve and I will take Li Han and Tran Nhat as the third team," Thuy went on. "We will move overland toward Dong Hai and attempt to discover and eliminate the shipment of explosives which is supposed to be here this week. Since we do not know precisely what we are looking for, we will have to improvise along the way." He gave a thin smile. "Luckily, I have seen Ong Steve improvise before. I am sure we will be able to learn something of value before the night is over."

"The timetable is tight," Tangretti said. "When the beach survey is finished, I want those swimmers out of here and on their way back to the sub. Beach security pulls out as soon as the swimmers are clear. Take the raft and head for home. If there's any chance you might be seen or pursued, ditch the raft and the equipment and swim out to the sub. But I don't want anyone on this beach or anywhere close to it by the time the sun comes up."

"What about your team, Lieutenant?" Randolph said, frowning.

"Since we don't know how long it'll take to locate our target in Dong Hai, we'll have to be a little more open-ended about things. Ideally, we get in, take out the munitions, and get back here in time to pull out with you guys. But if we can't, we'll lie low and try to finish the job tomorrow night. If we haven't made it to the sub by dawn, day after tomorrow, we're not coming back. If you see we're not going to be back in time to swim out with you, bury our SCUBA gear and the radio at the foot of that stand of trees over there. That way it'll be there for us when we do make it back." Tangretti fixed Randolph with a glittering stare. "One thing, Doc. If we don't make it to the sub, you let the skipper head back for Subic Bay. No rescue missions. Understood?"

"Understood, Lieutenant," Randolph replied reluctantly.

"All right, then. Let's saddle up and get the hell out of here."

Randolph watched them disappear into the gloom, three Vietnamese and one American, all alone in the very heart of the enemy's land.

U.S. Airbase
Dong Ha, Republic of Vietnam
2358 hours

William Lattimore hesitated a moment before knocking on the door of his superior's temporary office. To coordinate the operation north of the DMZ, Dexter and Lattimore had commandeered a small, unused Quonset hut at the edge of the American airbase outside the South Vietnamese city of Dong Ha, setting up a communications shack and two rooms that did double duty as offices and quarters for the two CIA men. It was a far cry from their lavish surroundings in Da Nang, without staff of any kind to assist them or any of the comforts they had come to expect, but it would only be for a few days. And it was essential, as Dexter had frequently pointed out, that they closely monitor the progress of both the Biet Hai operation in the north and the search for signs of enemy infiltration around Dong Ha.

"Come," Dexter's voice sounded crisply from inside. Lattimore opened the door and entered, to find his boss sitting at a makeshift desk going over reports, still dapper in dark suit and white shirt as if it were the middle of the afternoon rather than two minutes before midnight.

"We've had contact with Tangretti," Lattimore said. "He's ashore with the Biet Hai and on the way to Dong Hai." He smiled. "I'd be a hell of a lot happier if the Vietnamese could have named these two damned towns differently. Between Dong Ha and Dong Hai and Biet Hai and all the rest, I'm starting to think my tongue's going to go on strike."

"What do you expect from a bunch of gooks?" Dexter asked. "Just be glad you didn't get posted to Taiwan. Every time I tried to say 'yes' to somebody I felt like I was swearing." He gave a humorless smile. "I'm glad Tangretti's doing what we wanted. I figured he couldn't pass up the chance to go in on the op. He may be a bit of a loose cannon, but I feel better with Tangretti riding heard on those gooks."

"I don't know. Some of them are pretty damned good."

"Yeah. But with everything so damned politicized in this damn country, we can't be sure anymore who's on our side and who isn't. But whatever else he may be, Tangretti's a patriot. And he carries a lot of weight with Thuy and some of the others. So he'll keep them on the straight and narrow."

"And if they run into trouble? We're running a big risk, letting Tangretti go in against standing orders."

Dexter shrugged. "Our asses are covered. Everybody knows how little Tangretti cares about any orders but his own. We can deny anything we have to deny."

"And we have the other SEALs close at hand if we need to cover our tracks or finish the mission," Lattimore said quietly. He wasn't sure that was Dexter's intent, but after over a year on the Da Nang station together they read each other fairly well. Lattimore was sure there was more to Dexter's bringing the SEALs north with their Biet Hai trainees than just helping out with Wallace's operations.

"Right," Dexter said. "The way I figure it, if Tangretti gets in over his head but looks extractable, a word to the other SEALs should be enough to involve them in another 'unauthorized' op to get him out. You know how thoroughly they stick together."

"I'm not sure about that," Lattimore said with a frown. "Gunn's pretty much a by-the-book man. Would he violate orders just to help Tangretti? They don't even get along all that well."

"But they're both SEALs, and they both came out of UDT before that," Dexter said. "I've seen them work before. These guys take *esprit de corps* to an all-time extreme. Lucky for our side. All we have to do is make sure we push the right buttons along the way."

Monday, 18 February 1963

Observation Post
Near Dong Hai
0135 hours

Tangretti hunkered down behind a fallen tree, scanning the terrain ahead through light-intensifier goggles. The commandos had found a position on top of a hill that commanded a wide view of the southern end of Dong Hai. Li Han and Tran Nhat had spread out to guard their flanks, while Tangretti and Thuy were observing their target from separate vantage points. With luck one of them might spot something worth looking at more closely.

As he studied the landscape unfolded like an untidy map below him, Tangretti found himself thinking uncharitable thoughts about the two CIA agents back in Da Nang who had so blithely set this operation in motion. Dexter and Lattimore had obviously thought that the commandos could imitate Gunn's Cuban operation, penetrating the harbor at Dong Hai from the sea and locating the store of explosives with a minimum of risk to the men involved.

That had probably sounded pretty good to them when they first came up with the notion. The problem was, it was completely impractical under field conditions. Tangretti had been sure of it from the start, but during the briefings he'd quickly learned to keep his mouth shut and go along with the Agency's ideas of what they should do here. He'd known from the start that he'd have to come up with a plan of his own to get the job done, but it had been awfully hard to plan when the object of the mission was as nebulous as what he'd been handed to work with.

Finding and eliminating those explosives wouldn't be easy. Dong Hai was a fair-sized town, and an approach from the sea would impose too many limits on the raiding party. It was considerably more risky to come in from the landward side, but Tangretti had been convinced that was the only way to go. Luckily Thuy had been agreeable.

So they'd humped their way overland from the beach, widely dispersed and moving with the utmost caution. Each man had changed into a camouflage uniform on the beach, and each was carrying a mix of weapons and a backpack with demolitions supplies. Li Han was carrying a second radio, a PRC-10. The lightweight radio had a very short range and a limited battery life, but was sufficient for maintaining contact with the unit at Beach Green.

At the end of their trek they'd discovered this vantage point. Now all they had to do was find something, anything, that would help them nail down their target with some degree of success. Then the fireworks could begin.

Tangretti's eyes came to rest on a fenced-off compound along the shore south of the town proper. It was plainly a military installation, from the uniformed guards and the parked trucks with NVA insignia clearly visible through the image-intensifier goggles. There was a long finger pier sticking out from that compound into the sea, and Tangretti was interested to note the presence of several fishing boats there, along with a pair of Komar-class patrol boats.

That looked promising. Fishing boats weren't likely to be tied up in a military compound . . . not unless the military had some specific use for them. Like transporting supplies south to VC agents in Quang Tri province, for example.

Tangretti watched for a while longer, taking note of the movements of the guards and the general lay of the land. Then he moved cautiously back from his hiding place to rejoin the others. His nerves felt taut with the suppressed excitement he always felt just before going into action.

This was his chance to show what SEALs could do.

Beach Green
Near Dong Hai
0210 hours

Randolph heard the patrol long before he saw it.

It began as the rumble of a motor in the distance, loud enough that all four of the beach security team were alerted almost simultaneously. Randolph had just finished double-checking the job he'd done of hiding the eight-foot-long IBS in a hollow under a camouflaged tarpaulin, heaped sand, and seaweed, and his immediate reaction was to reach inside the boat to draw out one of the AKs waiting there. All their weapons were foreign-made, on the theory that nothing the raiders carried into North Vietnam should be easily identified as South Vietnamese—or American. But most of their special equipment—night-vision devices, radios, and so forth—were American-made, drawn from the quartermaster's office at Subic Bay.

Thuy's orders echoed in his mind. They didn't want a firefight. But the automatic rifle was a comforting weight in his arms as Randolph slipped quietly up to the line of trees that dominated the beach. He slid into a clump of banana trees from which he could maintain surveillance of the area, and waited.

Out there beyond the booming surf, six Biet Hai were busy taking soundings, measuring depths and checking bottom compositions and marking off angles and bearings, recording everything on the slates that dangled from their wrists. He thought they should be very nearly finished with the job.

Brakes squealed and hissed somewhere off to the north. Randolph pressed himself more tightly against the tree he was using as a shield and kept up his watch through his night vision goggles. From somewhere off to his left he heard a faint birdcall, the signal his Biet Hai companions of the beach security unit had chosen to indicate *Enemy in Sight*.

It seemed to take forever for the situation to develop further. Then, just as Randolph was beginning to think he couldn't possibly wait any longer without doing *something*, a ragged line of uniformed soldiers appeared, walking along the beach. From the casual way they carried their weapons, it seemed evident that they weren't expecting any trouble. Probably just a routine patrol, checking the beaches for any sort of activity the army might take a dim view of. Usually that would be civilians trying to flee south, or RVN agents trying to slip into the country. *This morning*, Randolph thought sardonically, *it just happens to be frogmen reconnoitering the beach.*

He watched them pass, hardly daring to draw breath, but they seemed to be paying little attention to their surroundings. Clearly this was all just a formality, something the soldiers had to do because the brass required them to do it, but nothing to be taken particularly seriously.

Then it happened.

It was the last of the soldiers in the patrol, walking a little closer to the water than any of his friends. From Randolph's vantage point it was impossible to tell whether he had seen something that drew him to investigate more closely, or if it was just an accident. But in any event, he passed close by the hidden raft. Too close, as it turned out.

"O day!" he called out suddenly, stopping in his tracks and peering at the sand. *"Cai nay la gi?"* Randolph frowned, trying to translate. "Here! What's this?" was as close as he could render it.

That didn't sound good, not at all.

In moments the others had turned to join him, clustering around the oblong shape of the raft. Several of them crouched down and began to brush away sand and seaweed. Abruptly one of them, an officer or NCO from the sound of it, barked a couple of sharp orders that sent some of the NVA soldiers fanning out with weapons at the ready.

Randolph muttered a curse under his breath. With the raft found, they'd have to evade the patrol and swim for safety. All the equipment would be lost . . . and the NVA would be beating the bushes for them. Things were going to get way too hot for the beach survey, and soon.

And if they abandoned the gear now, how would Tangretti's party get out to the sub? The situation was rapidly turning into a first-class cluster fuck.

Randolph had just come to that conclusion when the night erupted in fire and thunder.

NVA Compound
Near Dong Hai
0224 hours

Tangretti waited motionless in the dark, hardly daring to breathe.

He wasn't sure how long he'd been standing with his back pressed up against the sandbagged wall that surrounded the building they'd identified as the munitions bunker, but it seemed like he'd been waiting for an eternity. Tangretti and Li Han had made their way down the hill to the target after a quick conference with the others. They carried all the demolitions gear with them, while Thuy and Tran Nhat, up at their hilltop observation post, had kept the PRC-10, the night-vision gear, and the extra weaponry they'd been packing.

From their earlier observations, it was fairly clear that there was only a single guard posted outside the one way into the bunker. More guards were deployed around the perimeter of the military compound, but it had been a relatively easy matter for the two commandos to slip past these, slipping in through a gap under the chain-link fence where an eroded gully gave just enough room for them to pass. Tangretti's clothes were still wet and clammy from sliding on his back through the brackish water, but they were starting to dry off in the light evening breeze.

Senses heightened by darkness and adrenaline, Tangretti could smell the pungent odor of *nuoc mam*, the Vietnamese fish sauce that was a staple of the diet in these parts, along with a whiff of cigarette smoke. He heard the guard grunt and shift his weight, and could mentally picture him rising from the log where he'd been sitting earlier, crush the cigarette out on the sandbag wall beside him, and flick the butt away. From the scuffling sound of boots against the dirt, Tangretti followed his progress. The man was walking toward Tangretti. In another moment he would round the corner that concealed the American commando . . .

Tangretti pressed himself back against the sandbags and drew his knife soundlessly, balancing it in his right hand.

The guard came around the corner, his AK-47 held casually. He passed Tangretti, barely three feet away, without noticing him. The American could hear him breathing. Taking two quick steps forward, Tangretti caught him from behind, his left hand circling the guard's face to yank his head back against the SEAL's left shoulder while smothering any outcry the man could have made. Bracing himself by jabbing his knee into the man's back, Tangretti drew the knife across his throat. A muffled gurgle was the only sound from the guard as he sagged against Tangretti. The American eased him to the ground, then dragged him back into the shadows at the base of the sandbag wall.

By the time he rose, Li Han was already at the entrance, AK-47 held at the ready as he scanned the space between the wall and the bunker it enclosed. Nodding once, Li Han gave a brief thumbs-up gesture and moved inside, with Tangretti close behind. The door to the bunker was locked, but Li Han produced a cutting tool from his backpack and made short work of the lock. Impenetrable darkness waited within.

They waited for their eyes to adjust, then split up, Tangretti going right while Li Han moved to the left. They had already prepared their charges up on the hill, so it took little time to set them. With all the explosives stored within the bunker, they didn't need to worry about planting large charges of C-4. All the two had to do was set smaller bombs where they would do the most good—or harm, from the enemy's point of view.

Li Han finished his side of the bunker first, signaling Tangretti with a soft whistle. Tangretti set his last charge, made sure the timer was set for 0300 hours, and joined the half-Chinese junk commando at the door.

All told, he'd spent more time waiting for a chance to take out the guard than he had carrying out the essential part of the mission. That was the way things worked, sometimes, even for commandos on a dangerous operation.

Now all they had to do was rejoin Thuy and Tran Nhat at the observation post and wait for the fireworks to begin . . .

Beach Green
Near Dong Hai
0230 hours

Randolph muttered a curse as the rattle of automatic weapons filled the night. The first shots had rung out from the tree line, which meant that one of the Biet Hai had violated the orders to lie low and hold their fire, but there was no way to tell who—and this was no time to be worried about blame anyway. Out on the beach the NVA soldiers were caught completely by surprise, and in that first moment of confusion they didn't have a chance to shoot back.

Other AKs did join in from the hidden Biet Hai, though, and after a further moment's hesitation Randolph raised his own weapon and added to the hail of metal sweeping the beach. Any hope of avoiding action was gone now, and the only option left was to make sure that every one of those NVA soldiers was taken out of action before any of them had a chance to sound the alarm.

They'd have to trust to luck that no one else was close enough to hear the firefight and spread the alarm.

The one-sided battle was over almost as suddenly as it had started. The NVA troopers were all down, though moans and cries made it clear that there were a few who were still alive out there. Randolph slung his weapon and charged down to the beach, heading straight for the raft. He needed to see if anything critical had been damaged in that brief firefight, either the raft itself or the radio, which he'd stowed back inside it while hiding the IBS. There were a pair of ragged holes in one of the inflatable compartments of the raft, but they looked easy enough to patch. The radio had escaped unscathed, thanks to the sand Randolph had heaped around the boat. One NVA soldier, the sharp-eyed one who had started the trouble in the first place, had fallen across the boat and the radio inside and left a pool of blood in the bottom of the raft, but none of the equipment had been damaged.

By the time he looked up, Randolph realized that the other Biet Hai commandos from the beach security team had also come down from the tree line, but with a grimmer job in mind. He caught sight of Huan Van Nim using a wicked-looking blade to slit the throat of one of the wounded soldiers. Randolph forced himself to choke back the angry protest that rose automatically to his lips. Nim was the NCO in charge, and he had no place rebuking the man for doing what was natural to the Biet Hai. They didn't wear those *Sat Cong* tattoos for nothing, after all. And there was no room on this op for taking prisoners or treating the wounded.

But as a corpsman, Randolph was horrified at what he was seeing. All his training before he became part of the Teams had been focused on saving lives, and though hospital corpsmen weren't real doctors, the principles of the Hippocratic Oath were still at the heart of their work. *First, do no harm . . .*

You couldn't reconcile medical ethics with the realities of being a commando, and Randolph forced the whole question out of his mind. There were more important things to worry about right now.

"Ong Nim!" he called. "Are any of your men checking on the truck we heard?"

Nim looked baffled for a moment. His English was about on the same level as Randolph's Vietnamese—adequate, but slow. After the briefest hesitation, Nim turned abruptly and bawled out an order in fluid Vietnamese. One of the other junk commandos started to run down the beach in the direction from which the patrol had first appeared.

But it was already too late. They could hear the engine roaring to life even as Nim finished his order.

Someone had stayed with the truck . . . someone had heard the firefight, and knew there were hostile forces on the beach. That someone was running, and that meant he would soon be able to report to his superiors.

This time Randolph didn't bother to keep his curses silent.

Chapter 16

NVA Compound
Near Dong Hai
0240 hours

More by instinct than from any specific clue, Tangretti
pulled up short just inside the opening in the sandbag wall,
holding up his hand to alert Li Han behind him. Someone
was moving out there, running by the sound of it, and Tangretti cursed under his breath. If somebody discovered the
guard was missing while they were still inside the munitions area, the two commandos would be trapped.

Tangretti didn't want to be anywhere nearby in twenty
minutes, when those charges went up.

He signaled for Li Han to join him. "You're a guard,"
Tangretti hissed in his ear. "Let them see you, but not well
enough for details to show. Act guardlike."

The Biet Hai's teeth gleamed in the moonlight, a quick
grin as he shed his backpack and gave it to Tangretti. He
moved forward slowly, holding his AK one-handed in the
same casual way they'd seen when the real guard was
walking around earlier. The junk commando sauntered
casually through the opening, then sat down on the log out-

329

side where the guard had been smoking earlier. Li Han even went through the motions of fumbling at his pockets as if in search of a cigarette, and Tangretti mentally crossed his fingers, hoping that whoever was out in the compound didn't decide to be a buddy and give him a smoke.

Voices sounded from out in the compound, the first one sharp, challenging, the tone enough to make Tangretti stiffen for fear it was addressed to Li Han. But a second voice answered excitedly, chattering on too fast for Tangretti to understand even isolated words. He was going to have to learn the language, he decided, if he ever got another assignment to Southeast Asia. The exchange went on, the voices fading with distance as the two North Vietnamese moved on. They sounded like they'd broken into a trot soon after the second voice had started his long, excited speech.

A moment later, Li Han was there, looking grim.

"Trouble," he said in a hushed voice. "A radio call has come in. A patrol was ambushed by hostile forces some-where south of here. One driver escaped and called it in. The two who were out there are on their way to fill in the base commander and ask for orders."

"Damn," Tangretti muttered. "Sounds like somebody found our boys. All hell's going to break out here any minute, Li Han. We've got to *move*."

He matched actions to words. With Tangretti in the lead, they hastened out of the sandbag enclosure and into the compound proper, trying to hug the shadows but moving as quickly as possible back toward the ditch they'd used to get under the fence. Tangretti knew they were violating every rule of a good exfiltration, but if they were caught inside the compound when the alarm went off . . .

And then it did.

Whistles screeched in the night, a tinny sound that reminded Tangretti of the shrilling of bobbies' whistles in London when he'd visited the city before D day. The two men broke into a run, but within moments a louder noise split the night, the grinding wail of a siren. The ear-piercing shriek seemed to reverberate through the compound, and in no time at all NVA soldiers were responding to it, erupting out of their barracks huts like angry wasps, some pulling on clothing as they ran. Lights began coming on everywhere, until the entire compound was ablaze, and the one ally the two raiders had relied on to protect, the concealing shadows, was gone.

"Ngung lai! Ngung lai!" That shout cut through the confused hubbub of voices, and it was one phrase Tangretti recognized. "Stop!"

Coming from behind him, Li Han smashed into Tangretti, knocking him to the ground as the first shot rang out.

Observation Post
Near Dong Hai
0244 hours

The wailing ululation of a siren rent the night, and Nguyen Thuy saw the NVA compound come alive with lights and sounds and figures boiling out of their barracks buildings like ants disturbed from their nest. Tran Nhat touched his arm and pointed toward the dock, where sailors had appeared on the decks of the two Komar patrol boats. Though plainly roused from sleep, they worked with practiced skill, casting off lines as the engines roared to life. Both boats backed out of their slips and turned into the main channel that led to the harbor mouth, gathering speed. A truck near the main gate revved its motor while NVA soldiers, some of them stumbling and half-asleep, clambered aboard the vehicle. Others were simply rushing out into the middle of the compound while officers shouted and tried to impose some kind of order out of the chaos.

Where were Li Han and Tangretti? If they were caught in the middle of this . . .

Shots rang out, singly at first, but quickly switching to the deadly rattle of automatic fire. From his vantage point on the hilltop, Thuy thought he could detect the bright flashes as someone's AK-47 pumped out round after round. Even from this distance, shouts and screams mingled.

There was only one reason for a firefight in that compound. Tangretti and Li Han were in trouble.

"Tran Nhat, you will stay here with the radio and be prepared to cover us," he ordered curtly. "I am going down to see if I can find the others."

The little commando nodded seriously. "Be careful, Ong Thuy," he said. "Do not allow one tragedy to lead to another."

"Never count a man out until you have seen the body," Thuy told him, a loose translation of a phrase Tangretti had been fond of using during training back at Da Nang. "Especially when it is Lieutenant Tangretti. That one, I think, could survive anything."

Thuy was up and running in one quick motion, leaving Tran Nhat behind him.

Beach Green
Near Dong Hai
0244 hours

"We cannot stay, Ong Doc. Lieutenant Thuy's orders were specific."

A great time for them to finally remember their orders, Randolph thought bitterly. If the Biet Hai had held their fire when the patrol was on the beach, it might have led to a heightened state of alert, but odds were the NVA wouldn't have mobilized everything in sight. As it was, they didn't have long before more hostiles would be showing up.

But Huan Van Nim was right. However they'd gotten into this mess, the way out was clear. It was time for the recon party to withdraw.

Reluctantly, Randolph nodded his assent. So did Vo Mung, the rather soggy-looking Biet Hai NCO who had joined the security party on the beach after the swimmers had heard the firefight. Mung was competent but unimaginative, a good man for the routine of survey work, but apt to follow the lead of a more aggressive personality like Nim.

"Okay, we get the hell off this beach," Randolph said. "Survey party first, right?"

"Yes," Nim agreed. "We will follow when they have had a chance to clear the area. Is the raft seaworthy?"

Randolph nodded. "Patched up, and the damaged chamber reinflated. But I wouldn't count on taking it all the way out. If I was the NVA officer in charge of this neighborhood, I'd be ordering patrol boats to look around if I had a report of bad guys on my beach. Wouldn't you?"

Nim nodded. "A good point. We will hope to salvage as much equipment as we can, but be ready to leave the boat if we have to."

"While Mung's boys are starting the swim home," Randolph said, "I think we should bury the cache Lieutenant Tangretti talked about. The radio and some SCUBA gear so they can extract when they make it back."

"If they make it back," Nim responded. "You know, Ong Doc, this beach will be covered with soldiers as soon as they get word of the fighting. I am afraid the raiding party may not be able to get through."

Randolph frowned and nodded. "I know. It's a tricky spot. I don't even dare break radio silence, for fear I might give them away by making noise at the wrong time. That's why I figure the only chance they've got is for me to hang around here until they call in or come back."

Nim's eyes went wide. "That is not what the orders were, Ong Doc. And it is very dangerous for you. I cannot let you do this."

"Look, Nim, you're in charge of the Biet Hai, and I was told not to overrule your orders . . . to them. But there ain't no way I'm in *your* chain of command, partner. And I aim to see to it that Lieutenant Tangretti and the others have a fighting chance of getting the hell out of Dodge. So I'm staying put. If I can get in touch with them, then I can swim out to the sub. But until they're warned of the situation here, I can't just abandon them. You understand?"

"And if you are caught?"

Randolph grinned. "Hey, I may not have done the Hell Week bit, but I put in time in the Escape and Evasion course in Panama last year. My group not only dodged the dogfaces looking for us, we evaded our way right into a local bar and had ourselves a couple of drinks before we checked in with our instructors. I'll dodge the bad guys, Nim. And if the boss doesn't get in touch by radio, I'll figure a way to spot him coming back and keep him from walking into any traps. Trust me."

Nim looked at him for a long moment before responding. "Very well, Ong Doc," he said at last. "If this is how you want to die . . ." He paused. "Ong Mung, get your party started on the way to the submarine." After the other Biet Hai had left, he looked at Randolph again. "What would you have us do, Ong Doc, before we withdraw?"

"Well, let's get some of this gear stowed under those trees. Then maybe you and your boys can help me figure out a good spot to hide out in. I'd really rather not meet any more of the colorful natives on this tour, if it's all the same to you."

NVA Compound
Near Dong Hai
0245 hours

A rifle shot shattered the night, followed by several more in close succession. Tangretti squirmed under Li Han, freeing up his AK. "Thanks, buddy," he said. "Close one."

The big Biet Hai NCO grunted a reply and got to one knee, leveling his own AK and cutting loose on full auto. The distinctive rattle of the Kalashnikov seemed wrong, somehow, after months of practice with American-made weapons, but the Russian-made assault rifle was just as lethal as any other. Tangretti joined in, and the two men kept up a continuous fire as they swept back and forth, each establishing his own kill zone as if they'd been practicing together all their lives. In seconds, the half dozen or so soldiers who had attacked them were all down, and Tangretti grasped Li Han by the elbow and jerked his head in the direction of their escape route through the gully.

"Let's go!" he hissed.

They started to run, with Li Han once again bringing up the rear. Once Tangretti heard him open fire, but he didn't look back to see what the junk commando was dealing with. He trusted the man to keep the enemy off his back, while Tangretti stayed alert for threats that might appear in their path.

More autofire disrupted the night, an angry clatter, punctuated by the sharp whines of ricocheting bullets and the whip-crack of rounds passing close enough for him to feel them rather than merely hearing them go by.

The fence was in sight up ahead when he heard a different sound, the impact of slugs hitting flesh. Li Han gave a cry and fell heavily behind him. Tangretti whirled around, cutting loose with the last of his magazine. NVA soldiers went down, and the American had time to drop to one knee beside the Vietnamese NCO. It didn't take Doc Randolph's skill to know that Li Han was dead. His chest and head had both been reduced to a bloody mangle by multiple hits.

He would feel sorry later, after this was over, as he had for so many comrades before this . . . if he was still alive to feel anything at all. Right now Tangretti had to concentrate on simple survival.

Scooping up Li Han's fallen AK, Tangretti turned to make a last sprint toward the fence. But more gunfire probed from behind him, and a searing pain flashed through his left arm, making him drop his own AK with its empty magazine. Yelling at the top of his lungs, Tangretti turned and opened fire one-handed, his aim poor but the sheer volume of autofire making up for it. "Hoo-YAH!" he shouted, the old UDT battle cry.

When his magazine ran dry again, he ran toward the corner of a nearby building, where a stack of crates and barrels would give him at least a little bit of cover. He dropped behind them, chest heaving with pain and exertion. His left arm hurt, and worse yet he couldn't make it work at all. It was as good as useless, maybe broken . . . maybe worse. Tangretti ignored that unhappy thought and focused on the immediate problem. With more NVA troops closing in on the firefight, he was as good as trapped. He wasn't sure he'd be able to slip under the fence anyway, not with his arm like it was.

It was awkward even swapping a fresh clip for the empty one, but he managed to do it one-handed. Then he peered cautiously around the barrier.

At that moment, it seemed as if every soldier in North Vietnam was gathering out there to attack him. Tangretti swallowed, knowing he had finally reached the end. It didn't seem right, somehow, that he should have survived everything the Nazis had thrown at him that day on Omaha

Beach, only to be taken down in some minor little raid in a
third-rate Communist country.

At least he'd be taking the same road as Li Han and old
Snake Richardson, he thought grimly. They'd make one
damn fine recon team on the road to whatever lay ahead.

NVA Compound
Near Dong Hai
0250 hours

As Thuy reached the section of the perimeter fence
where Tangretti and Li Han had penetrated the compound,
he spotted two running figures heading toward him, partly
silhouetted by the bright lights that illuminated everything.
More men appeared behind the first two, men in the familiar, hated uniforms of NVA regulars.

Horrified, Thuy watched as one of the two fugitives
turned to fire and was hit by a full-auto Kalashnikov burst.
He fell, lying in a crumpled heap on the ground. His partner turned and fired, then knelt by the body long enough to
pick up his weapon and ammo.

Thuy was about to hail him when more soldiers
appeared. He saw the second man wounded as he tried to
reach cover. From his position by the fence, he was fairly
well hidden, at least as long as the enemy was focused on
their quarry. They had learned a measure of respect for their
target, and were forming up for a carefully planned assault
with plenty of suppression fire to cover the advance of a
dozen or more men.

He raised his weapon, taking careful aim on the captain
who appeared to be in charge, but Thuy held his fire. He
had to make this count, and timing was all-important.

The captain shouted an order and five AKs opened up,
sending bullets smashing into the improvised barricade the

commando was hiding behind. Thuy could see the hail of splinters the onslaught raised, and hoped his man was keeping low.

Thuy squeezed the trigger, and the assault rifle bucked in his hand like a mad thing.

With all the firing already going on, it took long moments for the NVA soldiers to realize they were under attack. The captain went down at once, head smashed to a bloody pulp; a sergeant standing beside him looked startled as some of his superior's brain splattered across the front of his uniform, then died with the expression still frozen on his face. The NVA advance faltered, men diving for cover or shifting fire in whatever direction they imagined the attack might be coming from. Only one of them got off any shots that came close to Thuy, and the Biet Hai officer silenced that man with the last few rounds in his clip.

By this time the beleaguered commando inside the compound had realized there was a shift in the odds. Thuy saw him rear up and brace his weapon on top of the crates, firing with his good hand. He was glad to see Tangretti's craggy features, though that pleasure was tempered by the knowledge that the dead body on the ground in the midst of all those NVA troops must have been Li Han's.

Caught in an unexpected cross fire, the North Vietnamese troops died or broke and fled, and all at once there was quiet.

Thuy was aware of the gully the others had used to get through the fence—in fact, he had been the one who had first spotted it during their earlier recce, and pointed it out to Tangretti when they were putting together their improvised plan of attack. But he wasn't going to waste time using that approach now. His web gear was hung with four hand grenades, relics of World War II by American standards, but current issue in the ARVN. Thuy took one of the grenades and hung it in the chain links, pulling the pin and then running for the cover of the gully. The explosion tore the fence apart, and Thuy was up and moving before the dust and smoke even had time to settle. He was at Tangretti's side in seconds.

The American didn't look good. He was battered and cut, with one arm hanging useless at his side, the fatigue uniform's sleeve soaked in blood. Tangretti's face was pale, but his jaw was set in the determined look Thuy had come to know in the last few months.

"We must retreat, Ong Steve," Thuy said. "Can you travel?"

Tangretti nodded grimly. "Damn right I can," he said. "Let's get going before our friends invite more people to the party."

NVA Compound
Near Dong Hai
0255 hours

Tangretti gritted his teeth and tried to ignore the grating pain that shot up his arm with every pounding footstep. He still couldn't quite believe Thuy had shown up to bail him out. Part of him was afraid this was all some fever dream he was having in a hospital bed . . . or an NVA prison cell. But dream or reality, he was determined to make the most of it. A few minutes back, he'd been ready to die. Now he was very much ready to live, if only the North Vietnamese would cooperate.

They were well clear of the compound, running a zigzag course toward the hilltop observation post where Thuy had left Tran Nhat ready to lay down covering fire.

Away from the well-lit compound, the darkness both helped and hindered them. The night enclosed the two commandos to make them harder to spot, but by the same token it made it hard to navigate, harder still to move with any speed over the uneven ground, but Tangretti recognized the general lay of the land as they reached the foot of the hill.

It was there the pursuit caught up with them again.

The first Tangretti was aware of the new NVA arrivals was the sound of more shots being fired from behind them. Both men dived for cover in a fold in the ground. Tangretti was stunned momentarily by the agony that swept through his injured arm as he hit the ground awkwardly. In the seconds it took him to regain his equilibrium, Thuy was already returning fire. The Biet Hai officer was keeping up a running stream of chatter in Vietnamese, and Tangretti didn't have to know any of the words to recognize that he was swearing as he fired burst after burst in the direction of the enemy.

"Keep going!" Thuy broke off his cursing long enough to shout. "I will hold them while you get to Tran Nhat!"

Tangretti opened his mouth, ready to tell Thuy exactly how unlikely that was, but thought better of it. Wounded as he was, he slowed the two of them down. If Thuy could give him a head start and then break off the fight, he stood a better chance of getting clear of this battleground than he would trying to play nursemaid to a wounded SEAL.

"Just make sure you make it out of here, Thuy," Tangretti told him. "I intend to buy you all the Ba Me Ba you can drink for a week if we get back to Da Nang." He got to his feet, a little awkward, and started to run, crouching low.

It didn't help. Tangretti had gone no more than ten yards when something slammed into his right leg. At first it didn't hurt, it just knocked him off his feet into a damp patch of muddy ground. But when he tried to get up, it did start hurting, a searing pain almost as bad as the one in his arm.

He was cursing as he tried to turn over and around and at

least make himself useful by rejoining the firefight. Thuy had accounted for several of the enemy, but the rest were still coming. Tangretti fired, controlled three-round bursts this time to conserve the meager ammo he had left.

All at once, the scene was transformed.

The explosion lit up the night sky above the NVA compound, a gout of flame that leapt upward with a life of its own. The charges they had planted had finally gone off, taking those stockpiled explosives with them.

The enemy fire slacked off in the moment following the blast, and before they had a chance to recover two of them dropped without either Tangretti or Thuy firing at them.

"Didi mau! Didi mau!" With a shock Tangretti recognized the voice as Tran Nhat's and realized the little pirate had worked his way down to support them as the firefight had unfolded.

Thuy dropped his AK and ran to Tangretti's position. "How bad is it?" he asked.

"Bad enough," Tangretti responded. "But if you can help prop me up, I think I can make it to the OP."

"Right. We will hope the enemy stays sufficiently distracted by the fireworks." Thuy grinned. "And just the other day I was feeling disappointed that I had missed the Tet New Year celebration with all its fireworks."

Tangretti got his good arm around the lieutenant's shoulders and let the smaller man hoist him upright, tensing against the pain but forcing himself to ignore it. Slowly they started up the hill again, with Tran Nhat bringing up the rear. This time they weren't followed.

Observation Post
Near Dong Hai
0312 hours

"Green One, Green One, this is Alligator. Do you copy?"

Thuy heard the edge in Tangretti's voice as he tried to
make radio contact with the beach security team again, to
no avail. Ever since he and Tran Nhat had helped the
American to a reasonably well hidden hiding place on
the hilltop, Tangretti had been trying to raise the rest of
the Biet Hai team, but the radio remained stubbornly
silent. By now, Thuy reflected, it was possible that the
PRC-10's limited batteries had failed, and the whole exercise was pointless. But it had given Tangretti something to
do while Thuy had tended to his wounds, stopping the
bleeding by binding them tight with makeshift bandages
and rigging a splint for the SEAL's arm, which seemed to
be broken.

The American had taken three bullets, two in his leg, one
just above the elbow, and he'd lost a fair amount of blood.
None of the wounds was life-threatening, but Tangretti was
effectively immobilized, at least for a while, and that
spelled trouble. There was no way they were getting back
to the beach before daylight . . . and no guarantee Tangretti
would be in any shape to swim out to the sub.

He looked up as Tran Nhat materialized out of the darkness. The smaller Biet Hai commando was grinning
wolfishly. "No sign of any pursuit," he said in rapid-fire
Vietnamese. "There are some patrols beating the bushes
near where they caught you, but I think we're safe for the
moment. The explosion seems to have disrupted things for
a while, at least. We should be safe if we keep our heads
down during the day."

"Good," Thuy said. He hesitated. "Tran Nhat, I have an
important job for you . . . and a dangerous one, I'm afraid."

The enlisted man's eyes darted to Tangretti's radio, then back to Thuy. "There is no contact with the rest of the unit, is there?"

"No," Thuy admitted. "Ong Steve said that Li Han overheard talk of a disturbance on the beach. By now our people are either dead, captured, or withdrawn to the submarine. But we cannot get him out there without help. I need you to return to the beach, find the equipment cache they were supposed to leave, and swim out to the submarine to request help from the captain." Thuy frowned. "I fear he is not likely to give it. He was most firm on the subject of his orders. But do your best . . . and, at the very least, you will be able to return home."

"I cannot leave you here alone, Lieutenant," Tran Nhat protested.

"It is an order," Thuy said firmly. "I will remain with Ong Steve. If we can travel to the beach after sunset, we will do so. But if you can get assistance sent ashore, and you do not find us there, we will remain hidden here as long as we can. Be careful, and do not take any unnecessary risks." He smiled thinly. "If you do not call any of what I've already asked you to do unnecessary, that is."

Beach Green
Near Dong Hai
0418 hours

Something was moving on the beach.

Randolph had concealed himself in the small grove of banana trees where he'd buried the equipment the Biet Hai had left behind. It had all the makings of a good hideout, commanding a good view of the beach—at least through night-vision goggles—but providing concealment and fair cover for a prone man. So far his precautions hadn't been necessary. No North Vietnamese had put in an appearance following the loss of their first patrol, although he'd noticed the lights of what might have been a patrol boat moving parallel to the shore about an hour after the fire-fight. He had also thought he'd heard distant sounds like gunfire and an explosion, possibly the raiding party's handiwork. Perhaps that had kept the NVA occupied . . . but it had happened over an hour ago now, and there was no sign of Tangretti's party returning as yet. That didn't bode well.

But hard as it was to believe when his nerves were stretched tighter than a guitar string, after nearly two hours lying motionless, Randolph had been starting to worry that he might doze off. Even the tangy smell of blood in the air and the lingering horror of the earlier encounter were starting to fade with a combination of fatigue and reaction.

All fear of falling asleep vanished, though, when he caught the fleeting movement out of the corner of his eye, but when he looked he didn't see anything. The night-vision gear intensified available light, but it was after moonset, and there wasn't much to work with. His view of the beach was poor at best, and for a moment Randolph thought he might have imagined something in motion out there.

Then he spotted it again, and this time he was sure. It was a solitary figure moving cautiously along the beach, stopping now and then in a half-crouching posture that made him look more like an animal than a man. Randolph had to study him a long time through the goggles before he was sure he was looking at a familiar face. It was Tran Nhat.

He slid out from the cover of his hiding place and gave a low whistle, and the Vietnamese commando's head jerked around. Tran Nhat was close enough now for the relief to be plain on his face as he caught sight of Randolph.

"Ong Doc!" He gestured to the litter of corpses on the beach around him. "Trouble?"

"You might say that," Randolph said wryly. "Of course, you might also say that Ho Chi Minh's a bit of a rabble-rouser."

Tran Nhat gave him a blank look. He remembered that the little Biet Hai commando spoke English with some difficulty. "Ong Doc, we run into trouble, too. Ong Steve bad hurt. Li Han dead. Lieutenant Thuy send me here to find unit."

They both crouched down on the sand, close together so they could speak softly. "The rest of the Biet Hai went back to the sub," Randolph told him, speaking slowly. He didn't trust his Vietnamese enough to try it out now, so he'd stick with English and hope Tran Nhat didn't have too much trouble with it. "I stayed to watch out for you guys. After the NVA discovered us, I wanted to be sure you didn't blunder into a trap when you came back."

"Lieutenant Thuy say they not come back tonight. Try to come tomorrow night if Ong Steve can make trip. Wants to have men from sub come with raft to pick them up."

Randolph frowned. "Man, I don't know. The sub's skipper won't be eager to risk that. Hell, for all I know he's already packed up and left."

"What we do, Ong Doc?"

"Hmm." Randolph mulled it over. He was a hospital corpsman, not even a real SEAL, and neither tactics nor decision-making were supposed to be part of his MOS. But he had to come up with something. Tran Nhat was a good fighter, but it was clear he was placing his reliance on the *co van my,* the American military advisor.

"Okay," he said at last, a little reluctantly, "here's what

we do. You take one of the SCUBA rigs and swim out to the rendezvous. If you find the sub still there, go aboard and report to the captain. Try to get his go-ahead for a rescue mission. If he agrees, then either you or one of the other Biet Hai comes back ashore . . . say no later than 0600 hours . . . to let me know. We'll rendezvous with Thuy and the Boss and help them get back here to meet the rescue party tomorrow night."

"And if captain say no rescue?"

"If nobody's back here by 0600, I'll assume we're on our own. I'll find the others, and we'll figure out what we can do from there."

Tran Nhat looked doubtful. "Risky. Very risky."

"Yeah, but that's why they pay us the big bucks," Randolph said. He didn't feel nearly as cocky as he sounded.

"You have radio. Call for help?"

Randolph pursed his lips, letting out a soft sigh. "That had better be a last resort. I don't know if they can monitor our signals at all, but I'd rather not stir the bad guys up any worse than they already are . . . especially if Captain Lichter's going to agree to send a party ashore for a pickup. Best we leave the radio hidden until we absolutely have to use it."

The junk commando still looked worried, but he gave a nod. "I go," he said.

"Before you do, draw me a map so I can find where you left the others." Randolph handed over an extra slate for the beach survey he'd been carrying in the pocket of his fatigues. "While you do that I'll get the SCUBA gear out from the cache for you."

Randolph turned away, as much to hide his own bleak expression as to get the equipment. There was so much that could go wrong . . . so many things he could have missed.

He wondered how Steve Tangretti would have handled the situation.

USS *Perch*
Gulf of Tonkin
0455 hours

"Skipper, I've got two targets, bearing zero-one-five, range three miles, closing. From the sound of their screws I'd lay you good odds they're light patrol boats, maybe Komar-class, and whoever's running them has the throttles cracked wide open."

"Keep an eye on them," Captain Lichter ordered sharply before looking back at the short, dripping figure in front of him. The Vietnamese commando had only come aboard a few minutes ago, and he was still in swim trunks and bare feet, toweling himself off vigorously as he talked. "You hear that?" Lichter demanded. "You understand it? We've got two Russian-made boats out there heading our way. You expect me to try to mount a rescue mission while those guys are out there?"

Tran Nhat's voice was edged with anxiety. "They need help," he said, his English labored and accented, but clear enough. "My lieutenant and your two men. Ong Steve hurt bad. Cannot make pickup. You send raft ashore, men to help."

"Not on your life, mister," Lichter responded gruffly. "I have orders covering this. No unnecessary risk to my boat, and two Komars are all the unnecessary risk I need right about now."

The Biet Hai blinked at him, uncomprehending. "Please?"

"Go below," Lichter ordered, raising his voice in an effort to get through to the little foreigner. "I'm sorry, but there will be no rescue. None!" He waved to the UDT man who had trailed Tran Nhat to the control room. "Chief, take this man below to join the rest of his team."

George Marsh was frowning. "We're just leaving Gator and Doc . . . sir?"

"Don't you start with me, Chief. I gave you an order. Move!"

"Aye aye, sir," Marsh responded smartly, but his face was a thundercloud as he guided Tran Nhat out of the compartment.

Lichter turned to his Exec. "Get us out of here, Mr. Sanders. Shortest course out of North Vietnamese territorial waters, and flank speed. The last thing we need is for those two Komars to catch us here."

"Aye aye, sir," the Exec replied, turning to repeat the orders. At least Sanders had the sense not to argue with him, not like those crazy commando types. Nobody in their right mind would think about sending a rescue party in, not after what the little Vietnamese had described of the situation ashore.

It was a damned shame, Lichter told himself. Leaving those men behind was the only thing he could do under the circumstances, but it didn't make the decision come any easier or leave a better taste in his mouth.

As the sub began to turn and gather speed, Lichter motioned for the Exec to join him. "Once we're clear of NVA waters and sure those two Komars aren't on our tails, come to periscope depth and raise the antenna. We'll report in to the spooks from Da Nang and let them know their boys blew it big-time."

CIA Temporary HQ
U.S. Airbase, Dong Ha, RVN
0625 hours

Lieutenant Commander William Wallace was angry.

The original orders for the beach-survey mission had been handed down from the Pentagon, through Joe Galloway's office, where Navy Special Operations work was always coordinated. They had been clear and concise, a happy change from the way the Navy often worked, and Wallace had been looking forward to a straightforward UDT survey operation.

But that had been altered the moment the CIA had become involved.

The additions and complications introduced by the CIA officers in Da Nang had made things chaotic at best. Half the Marines who should have been handling beach security and surveying work above the high-tide line had been recruited to help the spooks hunt for signs of VC activity around Dong Ha, but Wallace's request to use his own men or the Biet Hai trainees to supplement the handful of Marines left to him had been turned down cold. That meant the inland part of the survey would be much slower than planned, which would leave the UDT twiddling their thumbs on the *Weiss* long after they should have been able to move on to the next set of beaches to the south.

Then there were the extra instructions for his own men. Dexter and Lattimore had the UDT contingent monitoring the movements of just about every fishing boat anywhere near Dong Ha, and the Biet Hai trainees who were supposed to supplement their work varied wildly in quality and reliability. In a way that was good, since it meant his men would have something to do while they waited for the Marines to get their part of the job done, but it was inefficient. And Wallace hated inefficiency.

That morning, though, his anger was far more focused than it had been through the long week of mounting annoyances that had led up to the beginning of the Dong Ha survey. He had been yanked out of a sound sleep and dreams of Alice and home, and summoned from the *Weiss* out to the American airbase at an ungodly hour on unspecified but apparently urgent orders from Dexter. The very fact that the CIA had decided to move their operation to the base during the survey operation had given Wallace a bad feeling right from the start.

To add insult to injury, he had been kept waiting for fifteen minutes, kicking his heels outside the temporary offices in the CIA's Quonset hut. No doubt the two spooks were inside, taking their time over coffee, entirely unconcerned about Bill Wallace.

Now, finally, Dexter had put in a belated appearance. The CIA officer waved him through the door to his office and gestured airily at a chair. "Have a seat, Commander," he said. Even so early in the morning he was carefully dressed and well groomed, though he had the slightly bleary look of someone who hadn't had much sleep the night before. Hell Week made that look all too familiar to Navy divers. They saw it in the mirror quite a lot before finishing the first week of UDT training.

Wallace sat down without comment, determined to let Dexter do all the work. The CIA man cleared his throat as he sat down behind the desk.

"Thank you for coming in this morning, Commander," he said. "Something has come up which requires a few changes in the routine of your survey group, and I would like to go over it with you so that you can begin implementing them this morning."

"Wonderful," Wallace said dryly.

Dexter plunged ahead as if he hadn't even spoken. "It has come to our attention that the North Vietnamese have started using a new and, if I may say it, novel method of transporting supplies to the Viet Cong." He pointed toward a table that ran along the side partition of the office. Wallace hadn't paid any special attention to when he first came in, but now that Dexter pointed it out he studied it with some interest.

There was a large cylinder on the tabletop, about five

feet long and perhaps two feet in diameter, made of metal. In front of this, various pieces of equipment were on display, including a pair of AK-47s and what might have been a backpack radio set.

"It seems that the NVA has conceived of the idea of simply packing supplies they want to slip south in watertight cylinders like this one, then releasing them in large numbers from their port of Dong Hai and allowing them to drift south past the DMZ," Dexter went on. "It's a terribly inefficient approach, since it's so hit-or-miss, but it's cheap, it's easy, and it doesn't put any of their people at risk." He paused. "Of course, for more important deliveries they must still use boats or cart things overland down the Ho Chi Minh Trail, but this does allow them considerable flexibility. We even found Communist literature and some simple guidelines to effective guerrilla warfare packed in this thing. Even if ordinary peasants or fishermen picked it up, there's every chance they'd find a use for the stuff that we wouldn't like at all."

Wallace nodded. "Okay," he said gruffly. "The Commies are floating care packages south. What, exactly, does that have to do with me?"

"We picked this one off one of the northern beaches late last night," Dexter said. "Or rather an LLDB patrol did. We want your men to keep an eye out for more of them as they're working on the survey today. If at all possible, I want to get an idea for the volume of this traffic, and also for the contents. Are they all like this? Or are there different packages?"

"You know, Mr. Dexter," Wallace responded tartly, "my divers aren't exactly equipped to salvage these things. If they have to stop what they're doing every time one of these bobs past, they'll never be able to do a coherent job on their soundings or bearings. This looks like a job for somebody from the black-shoe Navy. You know, guys with boats and boathooks who can snag the little suckers and haul them aboard?"

Dexter frowned. "Are you refusing the assignment, Commander?" he asked sharply.

For a moment Wallace was tempted to give him a resounding "yes," but his sense of duty won out over his anger. He'd been told to cooperate fully with the CIA agents based in Da Nang, and cooperate was exactly what he would do. But he didn't have to enjoy it. "No, sir, I'll pass the word to my men. Perhaps I can deploy some of the Biet Hai in IBLs to conduct an orderly search without disrupting the other divers."

"That would be fine, Commander. Just so you handle it."

Dexter broke off as the rear door to the office flew open and Lattimore burst in. It was the first time Wallace had seen either CIA man look anything but cool and unflappable. He didn't even seem to be aware of Wallace's presence.

"Frank, we've had word from the *Perch*. They were forced to withdraw from their rendezvous point by a couple of Komars, and they left Tangretti, Randolph, and Thuy stranded on shore. Apparently the beach team ran into trouble and took fire. One man's wounded—Lichter didn't say which one—and the whole neighborhood around Dong Hai's stirred up."

Dexter held up an imperious hand. "Damn it, Lattimore, don't you know better than to go spouting off in front of . . . *him*?" He jerked his head toward Wallace. The junior spook looked at the UDT officer, wide-eyed.

"Good God . . ."

His superior cut him off, turning to glare at Wallace. "Commander, you didn't hear anything just now. Do you understand that?"

Wallace didn't answer right away. Tangretti and Doc Randolph stranded in North Vietnam? What the hell were they doing there in the first place?

When he responded, he spoke slowly and deliberately. "If you say so, sir. But if what I didn't hear is true, what are you going to do about it?"

"That doesn't concern you, Commander," Dexter said. "I know Tangretti's a friend of yours, but he knows the rules of engagement. If he went in with the Biet Hai and got himself in trouble—and took Randolph, too, which is even more inexcusable—well, he knows it wasn't authorized or sanctioned by anyone."

"You're not going to do anything, are you?" Wallace said bitterly.

"That's enough, Commander. I think you had better leave now. But remember . . . this goes no further. There are serious penalties for disobedience. Keep them in mind."

"Oh, I'll do that, Mr. Dexter," Wallace said, surging to his feet.

He had no intention of heeding those orders.

Dexter's Office
0634 hours

Lattimore waited until Wallace had shut the door sharply behind him. Then he turned to Dexter. "Well, Frank?"

"Nice job, Bill," Dexter replied with a smile. "You had just the right touch of panic in your voice there."

"I'm not sure I like tricking our own people." Lattimore sat down heavily in his chair. "I mean, the real transmission came in over an hour ago. Staging this whole scene . . . it just doesn't seem right, you know?"

The senior officer shrugged. "We could have hauled

Gunn in and given him orders, I suppose. But Gunn's the
conscientious sort. He'd raise a stink, even if he went in
and helped those three. I don't need to tell you how many
complications that could cause if he started telling people
in Washington that we were mounting unsanctioned ops.
This way, Wallace will go running to Gunn and tell him
what he 'accidentally' overheard. Gunn will want to get his
SEALs out. And we have him in the position of mounting
an unauthorized raid of his own. As long as he stays quiet,
so do we. Otherwise, we haul his ass in front of a Navy
court-martial. Even that loudmouth Tangretti, assuming he
gets out, will think twice before letting his precious SEALs
take a hit like that."

"And if Wallace doesn't tell Gunn?"

"Well, there are other ways to leak information. But
Wallace will tell him. Count on it."

Chapter 17

Observation Post
Near Dong Hai
0947 hours

A squad of North Vietnamese passed by scant feet away from Doc Randolph, and he tried to still his breathing as they passed. Behind him, Lieutenant Tangretti stirred restlessly in his sleep, but Thuy leaned over with a guarding hand over the wounded SEAL's mouth in case he made a noise. A drizzle of rain helped to obscure sounds, but they couldn't afford to take any chances.

Minutes passed. The soldiers moved on, and Randolph finally breathed easy again.

He had waited until 0630, a half hour longer than he'd told Tran Nhat, before finally giving up his vigil on the beach. Leaving it that long had made the trip across country dicey, with the sun coming up and plenty of enemy activity to contend with, but Randolph had managed to follow Tran Nhat's crude map well enough to reach the hiding place behind the observation post on the hill that looked down over the NVA compound. He still wasn't entirely sure how he'd evaded contact with the enemy.

Remembering his boast to the Vietnamese about his time at E&E school in Panama, Randolph had to fight back a smile. *Sure wish there was a beer joint to duck into around here,* he told himself.

Tangretti stirred again. Randolph had followed up on Thuy's first-aid job soon after joining the two of them, but in fact there hadn't been much more he could do to help. The Biet Hai officer had done a thorough job with his bandages and splint. Most of what Tangretti needed now was rest, and he'd been sleeping fitfully ever since.

"Doc." Tangretti's voice startled him. The SEAL had opened his eyes and was looking at him with a look that mingled exasperation and relief. "Doc, I thought I gave you orders about getting the hell out of Dodge if things went bad." The voice was a whisper, but there was strength behind it. Tangretti wasn't done yet, not by a long shot.

"I had to stick around, Boss," Randolph told him. "There was too much of a chance you guys would walk into a trap. And you did, too, just not where I was expecting you to."

"Yeah. Screwed things up big-time." Tangretti sat up cautiously, looking surprised to find most of the parts working the way they were supposed to. "What's the situation?"

"Not good, Boss. I sent Tran Nhat out to the sub to arrange for a pickup, but he didn't come back. Either he bought it in the water, or the skipper decided discretion was the better part of valor and took off."

Tangretti nodded. "He chogied. He was none too happy with the whole op anyway, and I don't figure him for the kind to repeat a mistake if he can help it. And this little excursion was a mistake."

"You carried out the mission, Boss."

"Yeah, but if you and I get caught, or our bodies are found, Ho Chi Minh gets a propaganda coup handed to him on a silver platter. We've got to E and E, Doc."

"We're short on options, Boss," Randolph said. "You're not in any condition to do a lot of long-distance traveling."

"Did you get in touch with the spooks on the radio?"

Randolph bit his lip, then shook his head. "No. I figured I shouldn't make contact until I knew what was up with you guys, in case the NVA could track the signal or something. And I didn't bring it with me, either. Left it at the beach. Damn thing was too big and heavy to carry, when I already was humping some extra AKs and ammo. Tran Nhat told me you were running low."

He was expecting Tangretti to chew him out, but the lieutenant just nodded. "It was the right call. Even if we had the radio with us, there ain't no way it could do us much good, not this close to Dong Hai. Even if the bad guys didn't catch the transmission and track us down, you know we wouldn't have a chance of talking Dexter or Lattimore into any kind of an extraction when we're this close to a North Vietnamese town . . . and a military base, too."

"Yeah, but I don't see that leaves us with much in the way of solutions, Boss."

"Seems simple enough to me, Doc. Come nightfall, we hump it down to the beach, dig out the radio, and call for help. Who knows, maybe Tran Nhat was coming back to the beach after all and ran into trouble, and we'll find a bunch of guys waiting for us on the beach singing songs and roasting marshmallows around a bonfire."

"Yeah . . . and maybe I'll just grow wings and fly us out." Randolph shook his head. "You're not up to it, Lieutenant."

"I survived Omaha Beach, Okinawa, and Inchon, kid. And before any of them, I survived the first Hell Week there ever was. I can make it."

Thuy had been following the soft-voiced conversation without speaking. Now he leaned forward. "I do not think we have much choice, Ong Doc," he said quietly. "If we have to carry him there, we must try to get back to the beach. Ong Steve is right . . . if a rescue mission comes for us, it must come there, not to a place as close to danger as this."

Randolph looked away. They were right, of course. But only because there simply wasn't another option open to them.

U.S. Airbase
Dong Ha, RVN
1025 hours

Lieutenant Arthur Gunn shoved the door to Frank Dexter's temporary office open hard enough to shake the partition. With his jaw set and his back ramrod-straight, he strode into the room, ignoring Lattimore's attempt to head him off. He wasn't interested in anyone but Dexter himself.

"What is the meaning of this, Lieutenant?" the senior CIA man demanded, rising from behind his desk.

"I'm told that two of my SEALs are in trouble and you're not doing anything to help them," Gunn rasped. "I came here to see about changing your mind for you."

"Wallace was told not to speak about this matter with anyone," Dexter said. "You have no right—"

"*You* had no right sending my men into North Vietnam," Gunn cut him off. "Now cut the crap, Dexter, and tell me how we're going to get them out again!"

Wallace had paid him a visit in his quarters aboard the USS *Weiss*, riding at anchor just off the coast of Quang Tri province while the UDT beach surveys went forward. It had been a short conversation, and when it had ended Gunn had ordered his SEALs to prepare for action, while he headed ashore to confront Frank Dexter.

"We're not set up for a rescue mission," Dexter began. "I have no assets to use in the field . . ."

"You have SEALs. Next objection."

"Look, Gunn, I'm sorry, but Tangretti and Randolph got into this on their own. My hands are tied."

Gunn favored him with an evil smile. "Better tied than cut off at the wrists," he said. "Let's get to the nitty-gritty, Dexter. We both know Tangretti wouldn't have gone into North Vietnam unless you encouraged him to do it. Oh, I know, he wasn't ordered, he wasn't authorized, he knew the risks . . . Bill Wallace already filled me in on your lines. Well, two SEALs already went north without authorization. A few more aren't going to matter now, are they? What I want from you is a current sitrep and a way to get in there, pick up the survivors, and get the hell out before the North Vietnamese know what's going on. If you don't want a demonstration of what they teach SEALs about inflicting bodily harm, I'd suggest you start cooperating."

"You're out of line, Gunn," Dexter began. Then he seemed to think better of it. He held up both hands and went on in a quieter tone of voice. "Okay, okay, you're very intimidating. If you can hold off threatening me for a few minutes, maybe we can work something out."

"Now you're talking," Gunn said, smiling again. The expression was more frightening than friendly.

"Look, first off, we can't do a damned thing unless we get some kind of word from them. Nobody from Tangretti's gang has contacted us since I spoke to him last night, right after they hit the beach. You can't just charge in and search through all of North Vietnam hoping you'll stumble across him. You're going to have to accept the fact that we can't even *think* about pulling them out until and unless they get in touch with us."

Gunn nodded reluctantly. "Agreed," he said. "But just to make sure there's no shit from you spooks, my people will stand radio watch."

"All right," Dexter said. "Now . . . getting you in and

out. I think we may have a way. Have you ever heard of Air
America?"

Near Dong Hai
2108 hours

Pain lanced through Tangretti's leg, and he stumbled,
muttering a curse. Beside him, Doc Randolph managed to
catch him with a steadying hand and stop him from
falling.

"Thanks," Tangretti muttered. He gritted his teeth and
kept on walking.

It was night once again, and the three commandos were
on the move. Tangretti felt better for the day's rest, though
his wounds continued to cause him pain. What was worse,
they slowed him down, and tonight the very last thing
they needed was to be held back on their long, difficult
hike to Beach Green. The injuries to Tangretti's pride
were at least as bad as anything the NVA bullets had done
to him. He didn't like having to accept help from anyone,
and he hated showing weakness in front of Thuy and Randolph.

He was able to walk mostly under his own power,
though, thanks to a tree branch Randolph's diving knife
had shaped into an improvised crutch he could lean
against with his undamaged right arm. That, and all the
determination he was able to muster, had kept him going
since they'd left the observation post shortly after dark.
But Tangretti knew he was getting weaker. His head
swam, his vision blurred on him from time to time, and
his legs felt like they were made of rubber. Just in the last
few minutes he had noticed that he was starting to feel
cold, too, despite the muggy heat that lingered even after
nightfall.

At least the rain had stopped. But there was mud every-where, and pools of water obscured their footing in the dark.

Thuy had point, and was setting a pace Tangretti found hard to keep. But he didn't complain. He thought back to Hell Week, all those years ago, and told himself over and over again that what he and Snake had endured then made this seem like a stroll through the park.

With luck, he might start to believe it by the time this mission was over. If it ever ended, which Tangretti was beginning to doubt.

Ahead, Thuy made a quick hand signal to hold up, and Tangretti let out a happy sigh and leaned against a nearby tree. Thuy crept on into the darkness, reconnoitering the path ahead. Tangretti was aware of Doc's eyes resting on him, worried, and wanted to say something to reassure the corpsman. But he was too tired to come up with anything clever to say. So very tired . . .

He came suddenly awake as he hit the ground and jarred his injured arm. Doc was there in an instant, frowning down at him as he rolled Tangretti carefully over and checked his wounds. "You okay, Boss?"

"Asleep on m'feet," Tangretti mumbled. "Don't know what t'tell Ronnie . . . out all hours of the night . . ." He caught hold of himself and shook his head slowly, trying to clear the fatigue from his mind. "Sorry, Doc," he said, forc-ing himself to enunciate each word clearly. "Just a little tired."

"Tired, hell," Randolph said. "Looks to me like you've been bleeding pretty much steadily since we left the OP. You've had quite a bit of blood loss, and you're going into shock. You keep this up, and you'll kill yourself."

"Better'n letting the NVA kill me," he answered. "Quit fussing, Doc. You know I have to keep going. We sure as hell can't stop here."

Randolph gave him a reluctant nod, and helped him to

his feet. When Thuy returned, they were both ready to press on.

**Beach Green
Near Dong Hai
2123 hours**

Randolph was getting worried about Tangretti's condition.

They had finally made it back to the beach, and after Thuy had done a thorough recon job to make sure it was clear of enemy soldiers, Randolph helped Tangretti reach the clump of banana trees where the corpsman had spent much of the previous night. Too tired to put up more than a token protest, Tangretti allowed Randolph to help him this time. Thuy went to work digging up the cache of equipment while Randolph examined the wounded officer.

By the time Randolph had his patient stretched out on the ground, he was already fading out of consciousness. Checking him over carefully, the younger SEAL didn't like what he saw.

Tangretti was definitely giving in to shock. Not that it was a surprise. The amazing thing was how long the older man had held himself together on that tortuous march. He'd lost a lot of blood despite the bandages they'd applied, and he was at the very edge of his endurance. As Randolph looked down at him, he could see Tangretti starting to shiver.

Randolph manhandled a log into place and propped Tangretti's feet up on it, then found the tarp he'd used the night before to help conceal the raft. He folded it until it was roughly the size of a blanket and drew it over the wounded man. *Elevate the legs . . . keep the victim warm . . .* treatment for shock was second nature to Randolph by now. It was one of the first priorities for a hospital corpsman giving first aid.

Thuy had the radio set up before he finished and was able to help him with the tarp. When they were done, Randolph dropped to both knees by the PRC-74 and switched it on.

He wasn't sure what to expect. Official policy was to avoid anything that might put Americans in harm's way, so the CIA men would have a good excuse to leave them to fend for themselves. On the other hand, if they were desperate enough to keep the two SEALs from falling into enemy hands, perhaps they'd offer some sort of rescue plan. Not that the three commandos had many options open to them. They couldn't travel any farther with Tangretti the way he was. Even if the sub was still out there, Tangretti wouldn't be able to swim to it—not just because he was hurt, but because of shock. Immersion in the cool water of the South China Sea might well be enough to kill him then and there. Even a trip out on a raft would be dangerous.

He shook his head. There wasn't much point in listing all the things they couldn't do. What Randolph had to do now was discover if there was anything they could try to escape from enemy territory.

The corpsman raised the microphone.

"Bearclaw, Bearclaw, this is Alligator," he said slowly. "Come in, Bearclaw."

U.S. Airbase
Dong Ha, RVN
2127 hours

"Bearclaw, Bearclaw, this is Alligator. Come in, Bearclaw."

Gunn looked up sharply as the words crackled over the

speaker. Thor Halvorssen let out a whoop. "It's them, Lieutenant," he said, relinquishing his place at the radio so that Gunn could slide into the chair and grasp the microphone.

"Alligator, this . . . this is Mother Hen. Bearclaw can't make it right now."

"Copy that, Mother Hen," Randolph's voice responded. *"Good to hear you."*

"What's your sitrep, Alligator?"

"We're at our original insertion point, Mother Hen. Our ride's gone, and I'm afraid the Bossman's going to come unglued if he sneezes. I've got him held together with baling wire and chewing gum, but he needs proper care. Can you get us a taxi?"

"That's a roger, Alligator," Gunn told him. "We've got us a ride all lined up. ETA . . . twenty mikes, give or take. Think you can wait at the taxi stand that long?"

"No problem, Mother Hen. Thanks for the assist. The LZ's clear for the moment, but I can't vouch for a long-term forecast."

"That's okay. We'll handle whatever we find. We're on our way now. Keep your heads down and your weapons handy, Alligator. Mother Hen, clear."

Gunn was up and moving before Randolph finished signing off. With Halvorssen close behind him, he burst through the door and out onto the tarmac. An unmarked Huey helicopter sat there, with a cluster of men sitting or lying on the ground close by, weapons and field kits within easy reach. Chief Briggs stood up as he caught sight of Gunn. "What's the word, Lieutenant?" he asked.

"They're okay and asking for an extraction, boys. Let's saddle up and see what we can do to lend a hand."

The SEALs gave a shouted "Hoo-YAH!" and surged to their feet, grabbing their equipment and swarming to the side doors of the chopper.

It was an Air America helo, unmarked, unregistered,

owned and operated by the CIA's private air force. Gunn had never heard of the operation before, but according to Dexter and Lattimore it was a key part of the CIA presence in Indochina. Airplanes and helicopters belonging to Air America conducted plenty of legitimate business, transporting cargo and passengers from point to point within the region, often the only aircraft to fly into remote airstrips. And behind their legitimate facade, Air America carried out covert missions for El Cid. Dexter had grudgingly granted the SEALs the authority to use this helicopter for the rescue mission.

The pilot and copilot, a pair of rugged-looking CIA hirelings, were waiting a little apart from the SEALs. Charlie Becker was the pilot, a big, rawboned Texan who reminded Gunn of John Wayne. He stepped forward to meet Gunn.

"You really figure on flying into North Vietnamese airspace and putting down on a hostile beach, Lieutenant?" he asked, sounding a little belligerent.

"You'd better believe it, Becker," Gunn told him. "What's the matter? I thought you hotshots who flew for the CIA didn't let anything stop you flying."

Becker laughed. "We'll fly in low and fast, Lieutenant, and if I can set her down without getting shot up at the end of it I'll land. But if your passengers don't show up pronto, we're out of there. ¿Comprende?"

"You fly. We ride. Just get us there in one piece so we can get those guys out."

The Texan shook his head. "Shitfire, Lieutenant, people call us crazy, but you Navy guys, you take the cake. Hell, you take the whole goddamned birthday party."

**NVA Compound
Near Dong Hai
2135 hours**

The radio operator looked up from his equipment. "A transmission, Comrade Major," he said. "It was scrambled, so that I could not identify anything that was said, but from the strength of the signal and the general direction I was able to establish, it is within a few kilometers of here, and coming from the south."

The NVA major frowned. "I need a location," he said harshly. "Not a vague direction."

"Without multiple stations listening in, I cannot triangulate exactly, Comrade Major, but my best estimate places it somewhere near the beach where the original enemy incursion was reported. While I cannot be certain, that is the most likely place to find them."

The major nodded grimly. "Of course . . . they will be trying to get out the same way they came in. Very well, Comrade, you have earned a commendation for your work tonight. Now get on the radio and alert our patrols in that area to converge on that beach and sweep it clean of any enemies." He strode to the door of the radio room and threw it open, shouting orders. "I want as many troops as we can fit on the trucks ready to move out now!" he said. "And someone get those Navy bastards off their asses and into the patrol boats! We still may catch the saboteurs before they escape to the sea!"

John Randolph
Beach Green
2140 hours

"Lieutenant . . . you hear that?" Randolph cocked his head to one side, trying to pick up the sound he thought he'd heard more clearly. Beside him Thuy nodded.

"An engine . . ."

"Like the one I heard last night before that patrol showed up." Randolph felt his guts twist inside him. Their luck was running out fast.

They were still crouching together in the dense cluster of banana trees, with Tangretti's prone form stretched out between them and the radio nearby. Randolph had hoped they could simply lie low until the chopper showed up with Lieutenant Gunn and the rest of his buddies from SEAL One, but now it looked like trouble had caught up with them first. Even if an NVA patrol didn't locate them by beating the bushes along the tree line, they couldn't simply allow Gunn and the helo to fly right into the waiting arms of the NVA.

"You're the boss, Lieutenant Thuy," Randolph said. "What do you want to do?"

Thuy was silent for a long moment, while the engine in the distance growled louder, then abruptly stopped. The corpsman thought he could hear shouting and the sound of booted feet running, but it might have been the fruits of an overactive imagination.

"We must draw the enemy off," Thuy said slowly. "Away from the beach . . . away from Ong Steve." He picked up his AK and slapped a fresh clip into the receiver. "You must stay and look after him. I will go."

"Wait a minute, Lieutenant," Randolph said, gripping Thuy's arm to keep him from getting up. "I've done everything I can for him. I'm the grunt here—the enlisted man.

And I've had more E&E training, too. I should go. I've got
a better chance of drawing them off and then slipping back
here . . ."

Thuy shook his head. "And I have a better chance of
passing myself off as one of them, if I need to. You two
Americans need to stay hidden until Ong Arthur arrives to
fly you out."

Before Randolph could reply he became aware of another
set of eyes on him. Tangretti stirred, started to sit up, then
seemed to think better of it. "Both of you go," he said quietly, the first lucid thing he'd said for a long time. If it *was*
lucid, Randolph added inwardly. Maybe he was just picking
up their conversation and incorporating it into his delirium.

"One man might draw some of them off," Tangretti went
on, his voice less shaky. "But two of you can tie them in
knots. Split up, and when you see a chance nail the bastards. Hit them from different sides and keep 'em confused. That'll give Arty a chance to get here . . ."

"He can't come in on a hot LZ, Boss," Randolph said.

"Look, kid, he'll see a firefight and he'll make his own
evaluation. If he's smart, he'll run for the border, but since
when was any SEAL smart? It doesn't take brains to get
through Hell Week, you know."

"Ong Steve is right," Thuy said. "We can do better if we
both cause them trouble. But I do not like leaving you here,
Ong Steve. Helpless . . ."

Tangretti gave him a wicked grin. "Helpless, hell," he
said. He reached out to pat the AK-47 lying close by him.
"If anybody turns up, they'll get a hell of a surprise. And if
I run out of ammo for the AK, I've still got this." Tangretti
released the flap of his holster and drew out his Smith &
Wesson Model 19 Combat Magnum revolver. "You know
the story of Jim Bowie at the Alamo?"

Randolph nodded grimly; Thuy shook his head.

"Remind me to tell you about it sometime," Tangretti

said. "Like over drinks at the Green Parrot. Now get going, you two. And good luck to both of you."

Nguyen Thuy
Beach Green
2142 hours

Thuy dropped into a crouch behind the trunk of a tree and peered into the dark, sensing more than seeing the movement on the beach as NVA soldiers moved in. In a way the dark was comforting, because it obscured the odds against the raiding party tonight. In his mind, Thuy knew that their chances of surviving until the Americans arrived were slim at best, but without being able to see the forces arrayed against them he could at least ignore the hopelessness of the situation for a while.

Had it been like this that night when his family had run for the frontier? The incident had taken place not very far away, near the edge of the DMZ. He'd pictured it in his mind often enough, based on the half-coherent stories his sister told. It had been at night, like this, and the soldiers had been close behind, too close, and too many to dodge.

If Nguyen Thuy had been there, would he have put up a fight, perhaps saved his father's life? If he could have given his own life in exchange for that proud old man's, he would have done it gladly.

Tonight it looked as if he'd have a chance to play that same story out. Thuy had always believed he had only lost his father because he hadn't been there to help. Now he had to protect Steve Tangretti, the big, ugly American who somehow had become like a second father, or at least a respected elder brother, over the weeks they had been together in Da Nang.

Nguyen Thuy wasn't going to let Tangretti down. If the

SEAL died tonight, it would only be after Thuy himself was dead.

That was a vow as earnest as the tattoo on his chest.

The impenetrable darkness was suddenly, blindingly transformed as a flare lit up the night sky, throwing everything on the beach into stark relief. Thuy gritted his teeth and raised his rifle, training it on a cluster of North Vietnamese soldiers fifty yards away.

"Sat Cong!" he shouted, and squeezed the trigger of his AK-47.

Steve Tangretti
Beach Green
2144 hours

Don't pass out. Don't pass out.

The phrase was a drumbeat in Tangretti's throbbing head as he lay still under the cover of the banana trees and tried to follow the progress of the firefight that raged in the darkness that engulfed the beach. The periodic light from fresh flares only made the scene all the more surreal, like a series of isolated slides flashed on an enormous screen in some bizarre presentation for his benefit.

But the sounds of the fighting went on between those brief flashes of illumination, and in the dark he could see the strobing muzzle flashes of Kalashnikovs firing. It was hard for Tangretti to stay focused, tired and weak as he was, but he followed the progress of Thuy and Randolph as they moved along the tree line, sowing confusion among the enemy soldiers as they moved and fired, moved and fired, never staying put long enough to give the NVA troops a definite place to concentrate their return fire on. He doubted any of those enemy soldiers would have

believed that they faced only three men, one of them
wounded and staying out of the fighting.

Off to the left, the sounds of firing were growing more
sporadic. That was the direction Randolph had gone off in,
and Tangretti felt a knot of fear gripping his stomach as the
thought that the corpsman might have been hit or captured
took root. Creeping forward to the edge of his cover made
Tangretti's arm and leg throb painfully and threatened to
send him spinning off into unconsciousness again, but he
forced himself to hold on. Peering into the darkness, he
saw an exchange of fire and let out a sigh. Randolph was
still in the battle, then, but it looked as if he had switched to
single shots instead of full auto.

Probably running low on ammo, Tangretti mused. That
would mean his ability to make his foes keep their heads
down was diminishing to the point where he'd be in danger
of being surrounded and overwhelmed.

Unless Randolph's opposition was distracted.

"Time for the old man to get into it," Tangretti muttered.
He knew he was verging on delirium again, but he refused
to give in to his weakness. Not when another SEAL was in
danger.

He snagged his AK with his good arm and maneuvered
it into position in front of him, checked the magazine and
the action, and waited for the next Vietnamese flare to go
up. As the scene lit up, he picked a target and opened fire.
His man went down, screaming in anguish, and Tangretti
shifted to fire at a second Vietnamese soldier who had
dropped to one knee behind a rock outcropping that protected him from Doc . . . but not from Steve Tangretti.

He didn't have a chance to see what happened to his second target, though, because all at once Tangretti became
the center of unwelcome attention.

And unlike his two friends, Tangretti was in no condition to change his position between exchanges of fire. He was stuck in this position, a perfect target for the NVA.

John Randolph
Beach Green
2144 hours

Randolph threw down his AK-47, out of ammo, fast running out of luck. Crouching behind a rocky outcropping about twenty yards from the water's edge, he was momentarily protected from enemy fire, but not for long. They'd be able to outflank his position now, and without a usable weapon he couldn't even slow them down, much less stop them entirely.

It had been a good run while it had lasted, but there were too many enemy soldiers out there. He only hoped Thuy and Tangretti would last long enough for the rest of the SEALs to pull them out. Another flare lit up the sky, shining down on the battlefield as it drifted toward the ground.

An NVA soldier suddenly appeared above him, clambering to the top of the rocks. The man wore a surprised look, as if he hadn't really expected to find Randolph still here . . . or maybe he was just reacting to seeing an American. His AK-47 was pointed directly at Randolph's chest, but time just seemed to come to a halt as the corpsman looked up at him, frozen, awaiting whatever might come.

The man's body jerked, a puppet with its strings suddenly yanked by an unseen hand. The Vietnamese soldier swayed, then fell, with blood running dark and thick from the exit wound in his chest. Shouts and screams attested to an unexpected new threat that had caught the NVA off guard.

For a moment Randolph allowed himself to hope it was the SEALs, but then he realized he hadn't heard anything that sounded like a helicopter ... and surely the NVA wouldn't have been caught by surprise even if he had somehow missed the noise of rotors passing overhead. It must be Thuy ... or Tangretti.

Randolph pushed the thought from his mind. Whoever had helped him, he would only be out of danger for a few seconds before the enemy gathered their wits and launched a fresh assault. As the light of the flare died to nothing, the corpsman took his one chance. He sprang to his feet and sprinted across the sand as fast as he could run, heading for the water.

Hell Week or no, Doc Randolph was a SEAL. And SEALs were aquatic animals, when all was said and done.

Nguyen Thuy
Beach Green
2147 hours

Thuy's AK-47 fell silent, out of ammunition, and he tossed it away as he ran for the cover of a fallen log. Going down to one knee behind it, he drew his Makarov PM autopistol and chambered a round. It wasn't much compared with the discarded rifle, but it was all he had left ... except for three grenades that still hung from his web gear.

Not much to pit against the odds that faced the three commandos.

The NVA were focusing most of their attention on Tangretti's position, the original hiding place, since the SEAL had decided to join in the action. He hadn't heard any activity at all from Randolph's side of the beach for several minutes. The American enlisted man might be dead, or captured, or simply out of the fighting. Thuy knew Tangretti must have opened fire to relieve the pressure on Randolph, but he still wished the SEAL had lain low as he was supposed to. There was no way he could escape, not wounded as he was. The end would be inevitable. . . .

Which left Thuy with no options at all. He rose from his protected position and started working his way back toward Tangretti, hugging the tree line and staying in the shadows. Thuy stopped once, losing precious seconds while another flare burned itself out, before starting forward again.

At least the steady hammering of autofire from Tangretti's position made it clear the big-nosed American was still in the fight.

He reached the banana trees just in time to see an NVA soldier charging at Tangretti from behind. Thuy raised his pistol and fired. The hasty shot went low, catching the Vietnamese soldier just above the kneecap and sending him sprawling. The AK-47 fell out of his hands, and he scrabbled in the mud trying to back away from the Biet Hai officer.

Thuy didn't have the ammo to waste. He drew his knife and finished the man with one quick thrust. Then he picked up the AK-47, but a glance told him it was too fouled with mud to be of any use.

He shifted the Makarov to his left hand and pulled a grenade free, tugging out the pin with his teeth and lobbing it into the middle of the nearest cluster of enemy soldiers. It went off with a satisfying *boom* that added to the confusion. Thuy stepped forward, crouching close beside Tangretti with the pistol in one hand and another grenade ready in the other.

The two officers, American and South Vietnamese, would go down together, and they would go down fighting.

Beach Green
2149 hours

The NVA sergeant was a long-service professional soldier, a veteran of the fighting a decade before against the French at Dien Bien Phu, where he had earned a commendation from his commanding officer for his courage in the assault on one of the Foreign Legion redoubts near the end of the siege. This firefight was more confused than anything he'd encountered in past actions, but despite the chaos he knew that it was only a matter of time before the superior firepower and numbers of the People's Army would overcome the resistance of these fanatics.

He shouted encouragement to his men, waving his AK-47 and defying the enemy to turn their fire against him.

The sergeant didn't see a figure rise dripping from the ocean at his back, armed with nothing more than a knife.

Doc Randolph leapt on the NVA sergeant with a wordless scream, like a jungle animal striking its prey. The knife rose and fell three times, stabbing through the man's neck and back. Randolph released his target and watched him slump to the ground, dark blood staining the sand in the fading light of a flare overhead.

Randolph didn't contemplate his handiwork for long. Scooping up the fallen AK-47, he knelt beside the body to grab a pair of fresh clips for it. He could see the twin flashes that marked the position where Thuy and Tangretti were holding out, with the soldiers of the NVA closing in on them relentlessly. An explosion lit up the beach off to his left, one of Thuy's hand grenades, he thought. That made the enemy pause, but then they were back on the attack. John Randolph knew that opening fire now would merely turn their unwelcome attention on him, and this stretch of open beach was too damned exposed. He'd be lucky to buy the others more than a minute or two of extra life.

But he'd do what he had to, what he could, because he was a U.S. Navy SEAL, and his comrades were in danger. Randolph raised the gun.

Then he lowered it again as a new sound reached him over the chatter of gunfire and the explosion of a hand grenade near the tree line where Tangretti and Thuy were making their stand. A sound that started as a distant *whup-whup-whup*, but swelled to a roar as a wash of wind swirled around Randolph and a menacing dark shape swooped from the sky like the Angel of Death.

Bright lights probed the beach from the belly of the helicopter, and a heavier pounding drumbeat of machine-gun fire spoke out in counterpoint to the Kalashnikovs on the ground.

Randolph dropped to his knees. He wasn't sure if it was from fatigue, or reaction to the fierce wind of the chopper's passing, or a desire to offer up a prayer of thanksgiving— or perhaps it was all three.

He only knew that he might, after all, see the sun rise on a new day.

Air America Helicopter
Over Beach Green
2155 hours

Arthur Gunn braced himself against the frame of the open side door and peered out into the night. The beach below them was being sporadically lit up by muzzle flashes and the occasional brighter bursts of explosions. Then the pilot switched on a searchlight and swept its beam back and forth over a scene from hell.

Chaos reigned on Beach Green, a chaos that owed no small debt to the terror that stooped low over the North Vietnamese from out of the night sky.

The helo was fitted as a transport, not a gunship, but the SEALs had improvised. Briggs and Jackson were in the two open side doors, Jackson armed with one of the new AR-15 rifles, while Briggs was manhandling an M-60 light machine gun. Halvorssen and Carter crouched behind them, bracing against the inside of the chopper and hanging on to the SEALs' web gear to keep them from losing their balance and tumbling out of their bucking, heaving platform.

Gunn didn't like to think about the risks they were taking. He still hated helicopters, maybe worse than ever.

But they were certainly effective. As the hammering automatic fire moved over the NVA troops, the last vestiges of coherent formation vanished. Those who could, fled. Those who couldn't died. It was that simple.

"Hang on!" the pilot's voice sounded in Gunn's headphones. "I'm taking this puppy down!"

The chopper dipped alarmingly, dropping toward the beach. At the last moment Becker gave the rotors more power, and the Huey settled in for a landing. Before the skids had touched the sand, though, the SEALs were piling out, their guns blazing as they finished the job they had started from the air.

Gunn waited until the helicopter was on terra firma, than climbed out, head ducked to keep clear of the rotors. The battle, for all intents and purposes, was over.

The landscape was surreal, an engulfing darkness split by the brilliant glare of the searchlight, with swirls of blowing sand and smoke whipping past as the rotor wash continued to stir up the air around the chopper. Out of the scene that might have been framed by Dante, the wild-eyed figure of Lieutenant Thuy materialized, waving an autopistol and looking more dead than alive. He was shouting something incoherent in Vietnamese, but Gunn was hard-pressed to know if he was calling a greeting or yelling a battle cry.

Randolph, dripping wet and carrying an AK-47, came

running up from the sea. "It's sure good to see you guys, Lieutenant," he said, his face splitting into a wide but weary grin. "Think maybe you can cut things a little closer next time?"

"Hell, Doc," Jackson said from nearby. "What do you want from us? You go hogging all the fun and then yell because we're a little slow . . . it just ain't fair!"

Gunn looked from Randolph to Thuy, and back. "Where's . . . where's Gator?" he asked slowly. If they'd reached the beach too late to save the old warrior . . .

But he was there, wreathed in smoke, bloodstains on his clothes and his face pale and wan, but he was there. Tangretti was hobbling toward the helicopter, leaning heavily on an improvised crutch. Dubcek stepped forward, offering a shoulder to lean on, but Tangretti waved him away and kept on coming under his own power.

"Mount up, boys," Gunn shouted. "The meter's running!" He looked at Tangretti. "You wanted a lift to Fifth and Main, Mister?"

The older SEAL smiled wearily. "Next time you start talking about doing things by the book, Arty, I'm just going to remind you of this." He leaned heavily on his tree branch, looking like he was about to faint, but rallied his strength. "Thanks for coming for us. Even if it was against the rules."

"Just don't make a habit of it, Gator. You may still be young at heart, but I'm getting too damned old for this." Gunn gestured toward the helicopter, where the other SEALs were scrambling aboard. "After you, Gaston."

Tangretti shook his head. "No way. After *you*, Alphonse." He managed a parody of a gallant bow despite the crutch.

Gunn didn't argue the point. Tangretti had earned the right to be the last one onto the chopper. He'd paid for it in the costliest of all currencies, with his own blood. Gunn boarded the helo. Tangretti stood for a moment, looking around the now-silent battlefield, then stepped forward. The other SEALs all reached out to help him aboard, and at a shout from Gunn, Becker revved the rotors up and the chopper lifted slowly from Beach Green.

They turned south, heading for home.

Chapter 18

Base Hospital
Clark AFB, Republic of the Philippines
1015 hours

"Hey, Boss, how's it going?"

Tangretti turned over in bed and studied Doc Randolph's jaunty figure leaning against the doorframe. The corpsman looked fully recovered from the ordeal at Dong Hai, which was more than Tangretti could say for himself. His broken arm was in a cast that itched like the very devil, and the bullet wound in his leg still throbbed.

On the other hand he was alive, and free, and he'd be on a plane for home in a few more days. Things could so easily have been much, much worse, if not for Doc . . . and Arty Gunn . . . and, of course, Nguyen Thuy.

It had been more than two weeks since the fiasco at Dong Hai. The survivors from the raiding party had been shuttled to the Philippines to be treated; Lattimore had flown in from Da Nang to debrief them and swear everyone to absolute secrecy. As far as anyone apart from MTT 4-63 and a handful of others were concerned, Dong Hai had never happened.

Tangretti's wounds had been the most extensive of any of the survivors', but the doctors had assured him he'd be ready for release before too much more time went by. Lieutenant Thuy had flown back to Da Nang with Lattimore, already pronounced fit and ready to return to duty; Randolph had been held a few days longer, but was supposed to be getting his freedom today.

"Not too shabby, today, Doc," he said with a smile. "Come on in and park it."

"Thanks." Randolph closed the door and settled into a chair. Business was light at the Clark base hospital, and they had the double-occupancy room to themselves.

"Hear anything from the rest of the guys?" Tangretti asked.

"Yeah." There was something guarded about the way Doc said that. "Had a call from the lieutenant. He told me to tell you to take it easy. Said he didn't want you doing something stupid that would make him have to jump on another helo to come rescue you."

Tangretti laughed. "I don't think I can get into any trouble here. Even if I was inclined to chase the nurses, they're too fast for me until I get this goddamned leg healed up. How much trouble could I get into?"

"The mind boggles," Randolph told him dryly.

"So . . . are you shipping straight home from here? Or are they going to make you go back to Da Nang until the next MTT comes to town?"

Randolph didn't answer right away. "Well, it's like this," he said at length. "I'm heading back to Nam . . . and I won't be going home for a while."

"What's going on, Doc?" Tangretti asked, eyes narrowing.

Randolph took a deep breath. "The lieutenant filled me in on the latest news from Da Nang," he said. "The word came down a few days back. The Biet Hai have been disbanded."

"Disbanded?" Tangretti sat up in bed, then checked the angry impulse that made him want to jump up and do something—anything—to shake off his sudden surge of emotion. "After what those guys went through at Dong Hai? What the hell are they playing at down in Saigon?"

Randolph shrugged. "Politics as usual, I guess. The beach-survey project was scratched, and without any rousing success to point to, I guess Nhu finally got his way."

"Shit." Tangretti looked away. "So what happens to Thuy and the others?"

"According to the scuttlebutt the lieutenant passed along, most of them are being absorbed into the Lin Dei Nugel Nghia," Randolph told him. " 'Soldiers Who Swim in the Sea,' or something like that. They're basically the South Vietnamese equivalent of UDT. Less commando-type work than the Biet Hai, more clearing obstacles and that kind of thing. I guess some of them are being spread around to other units, but most of them at least get some familiar work."

"Thuy won't like it if he's not out there *Satting* the *Cong*," Tangretti said. "And it's probably a good thing for those idiots in Saigon that Li Han didn't make it back. He'd be tearing the place down brick by brick right now."

"Yeah," Randolph agreed. "Anyway, according to Lieutenant Gunn, everything's a mess in Da Nang now. Shutting down the Biet Hai means there's nothing left for our gang to do, not with a couple of weeks left before the end of the tour. There's a new MTT due in, but God only knows what they'll end up doing. Nobody seems to have a very clear idea of what's going on now. Looks like the LDNN will need SEAL training, but they'll have to start everything out from scratch."

"And our whole damned tour ends up wasted," Tangretti said harshly. "Even the Biet Hai we taught will get lost in the shuffle instead of getting a chance to pass on what they know to other Vietnamese units. By the time they get things sorted out, everything we tried to do will be forgotten."

"That's the way the lieutenant reads it, too," Randolph said. "Which is why he's putting out the word that anybody from our bunch who wants to can volunteer to stay on with the new MTT when it gets here. The brass has already approved expanding the size of the training team."

"And you're volunteering."

"Seems like the right thing to do, Gator," he said. "Maybe with a bigger team and some of us who've already put some time in, the new MTT can get up to speed faster and do some good getting the LDNN whipped into shape— preferably before some screwup in Saigon decides to pull the rug out from under *them.* I feel like I owe it to Li Han and the other guys to try to preserve something of what the Biet Hai was starting to achieve, if you know what I mean."

Tangretti nodded slowly. "Yeah. I know exactly what you mean." He paused. "Did Arty say how many others were staying on?"

"Well, he's sticking around at least for a couple of months," Randolph said. "And I guess all the others volunteered to stick with it, too, except for Chief Briggs. He's got some family problems back home, I guess, and didn't think he could extend for another tour."

"Well, with most of the team staying on, I'd say the LDNN's going to be in good hands," Tangretti said quietly.

Randolph studied him. "Guess you'll be glad to get back to Little Creek, huh, sir?" he asked. "After getting banged up like you did, a little peace and quiet Stateside's just what you need."

"Yeah," Tangretti said. "Yeah, I guess so." But inside he didn't feel much conviction behind the words.

Randolph stood up. "Well, guess I'd better go and start packing. Take care of yourself, Lieutenant." He paused. "And . . . look, sir, I can't tell you what it's meant to me to get a chance to serve with you. You may be *dien cau dau*, but you're okay in my book."

"Yeah, well, you're not so bad yourself, for a kid. And a West Coast puke."

"And for a corpsman who never did Hell Week," Randolph added.

"Listen to me, Doc. Hell Week's not just the experience, not just being trained alongside all the other UDT guys." Tangretti shifted uncomfortably in the bed. "We . . . I've always used it as the best measure I could find. You know—us versus them, guys who've lived through Hell Week against everybody else in the world. That's because I always knew I could automatically respect anybody who'd been through it, starting with Snake Richardson back at Fort Pierce.

"But Hell Week is something more than that. It's an attitude. It's being tested right over the very limit of everything you thought you could do, and proving you could take it. And by that measure, Doc, you've been through Hell Week. Because I couldn't respect you more if you'd been right there with me and Snake back at the very beginning."

Randolph drew himself up a little taller at that. "Thank you, sir," he said gravely. "Coming from you . . . well, I sure as hell don't need to win the Navy Cross, now."

Tangretti gave him a grin. "Don't let it go to your head, Doc. Don't forget . . . I'm just a dinky dau SEAL with a couple of holes in me. I doubt if anybody's going to take my opinions seriously for a while."

The corpsman took his leave, and Tangretti was alone in the room with his thoughts.

Respect . . . that really was at the heart of the SEAL spirit. Tangretti would never respect a Peter Howell or a Bill Lattimore or a Frank Dexter. Men like that had never been through Hell Week either literally or figuratively, and they wouldn't survive the experience if it was forced on them. Whereas Arty, neat, proper, sometimes almost prissy Arthur Gunn, had not just gone through Hell Week as part of his training, he'd lived it again that day at Dong Hai and proved himself worthy of Tangretti's respect. Just as Doc had done. And Li Han, and Thuy, and others of the Biet Hai with them. Those junk commandos had earned Tangretti's respect, even though their own government had chosen to treat them with contempt.

The idea of letting the whole tour go to waste because of political infighting in President Diem's inner circle made Tangretti almost physically sick. Starting from scratch and trying to build up the LDNN to replace the disbanded Biet Hai would take time and effort that could be better spent fighting the war against the Communists, Viet Cong and NVA alike. How long would it take for the LDNN to get to the same point the Biet Hai had already reached? And once they were there, how long would it be before their superiors understood how to use them properly? It was the same problem Tangretti had been fighting with his own lords and masters from the very beginning of the SEALs.

Gunn and the others could make a real difference by helping the incoming MTT.

And so, he thought, could Steve Tangretti.

He pictured Thuy dragging him to safety when he was too badly wounded to help himself . . . Li Han shielding him with his body and going down under a hail of automatic weapons fire. Tangretti understood exactly what Randolph had been talking about when he said he felt like he owed those men his help.

Tangretti owed them far more than Randolph did, and he was not the kind of man who would leave a debt unpaid. Especially not a debt of blood and honor.

But there was another debt that nagged him. What about Veronica and the kids? He hadn't written since the mission, so they didn't know about his wounds. But they expected

him home when the MTT's tour ended in April. And given
how Ronnie had felt about his coming over to Vietnam in
the first place, it might just turn out that a decision to stay
would be the very last straw for their marriage.

The thought loomed large in his mind, threatening, ominous. Life without Ronnie and the kids . . . that was no life
at all. He needed her. She was his wife, his friend, his companion . . . his partner. There was no Teammate—not even
Snake Richardson—who had ever been as important to his
happiness as Veronica.

But he hadn't told her that . . . not in a long, long time.
Maybe not since he'd proposed, all those years ago.

Would she give him another chance? Only time would
tell.

CIA Station
Da Nang
1345 hours

Lieutenant Arthur Gunn looked up as Nguyen Thuy
entered the small room that had been converted into a waiting area outside the CIA conference room. The Vietnamese
lieutenant looked crisp and alert, a veritable recruiting-
poster figure for the ARVN. It was a far cry from the way
he'd looked that morning on the beach near Dong Hai,
disheveled and wild-eyed, covered in grime and smeared
in blood as he held off the oncoming NVA troops with
nothing but an autopistol.

"Ong Arthur," Thuy said formally, with a respectful
inclination of his head. He took a seat in a chair across from
the sofa where Gunn was sitting. "It is good to see you
again."

"And you, Lieutenant," Gunn said. "Did our spooky
friends summon you, too?"

"No. I merely called here to pay my last respects. I leave for Saigon tonight."

"The LDNN?"

"Yes. There was some suggestion of posting me to a staff job, but I requested that I stay with the bulk of my men." He paused. "At least for the moment I will be back in Saigon, and closer to my sister. I will enjoy spending more time with her."

"I'm glad. And maybe we'll still end up working together, once everything gets sorted out."

"But . . . I thought your team was to return to the United States in a few weeks?"

"Most of us are extending our tour," Gunn told him. "We decided we wanted to be around to help rebuild after this mess over the Biet Hai." He paused. "I wish things had worked out better for you, Lieutenant. It's a damned shame what happened . . . first with Dong Hai, and then this nonsense about disbanding the Biet Hai. You had a good unit."

"Thank you, Ong Arthur," Thuy said quietly. "Perhaps with more practice and training, we might have rivaled your SEALs someday. Though I doubt it. We have—we had—many good fighters, Ong Arthur, but in all my time in the service I do not believe I have met anyone quite like your SEALs. And especially I have never met another one like Tangretti. With fighters like him, your SEALs will make a mark like no other unit."

Gunn smiled. "Yeah, there's only one Steve Tangretti. Thank God. I don't know if the Navy could survive two of him." He paused. "I wanted to thank you for what you did at Dong Hai, Lieutenant. It would have been easy enough to abandon Tangretti and head for cover. No one could have expected you to stick with him the way you did . . . especially since we abandoned you, first when the *Perch* withdrew, and then when Dexter ordered us not to try to extract you."

"Leaving Ong Steve was never an option," Thuy told him. "It was . . . something that I needed to do. Something I *had* to do. And *you*, at least, did not abandon us, Ong Arthur. You and your SEALs. You were there when we needed you."

"Okay, we'll call it even, then. But I just want you to know, Lieutenant, that I'd be pleased and proud to serve alongside you and your men anytime, anyplace, no matter what they're calling your outfit or how they're trying to use your people. You're probably getting pretty damned sick of having Americans looking down their noses at you, treating you guys like you're no good just because you're Orientals who only got your own country a few years ago."

It was Thuy's turn to smile as he interrupted Gunn. "Speaking as a gook, Lieutenant, we dinks are used to being called names. It doesn't matter that much, in the long run, what we're called or how much we are scorned. As long as we stay true to ourselves, it does not matter."

"Well, it matters to me. And as far as me and my men are concerned, you guys will never be slopes or dinks or gooks. You'll be the men we fought beside at Dong Hai. And you'll always be able to call the SEALs your comrades in arms."

Lattimore chose that moment to stick his head out of the conference room. "Lieutenant Gunn. Good. Mr. Dexter is ready to see you now."

Gunn shot him a look. "One moment, please." He turned his head back toward Thuy and stood up. The Vietnamese lieutenant did the same, and clasped the hand Gunn held out to him in a gesture that was purely American. "I hope I see you when this LDNN thing gets settled down into some kind of routine again. Take care of yourself until then."

"Thank you, Ong Arthur. And please . . . tell Ong Steve that I was proud to serve with him. I hope I see him again one day, too."

"I will, Lieutenant." Gunn walked across to the office door, which Lattimore held open for him.

The CIA man didn't follow him in. As the door closed behind him, Gunn heard Lattimore speaking. "I hope, Ong Thuy, that when you have a chance to talk to your new superiors you'll bring up the ideas we were discussing yesterday. A more active prosecution of the war in the north is the only way we can be sure of pinning their attention away from your country's internal politics . . ." *Some things*, Gunn reflected, *never change*.

Dexter was sitting at the conference table, studying a report. He absently waved Gunn to a seat as he continued to read, and the silence in the room became awkward. At last the senior Agency operative laid aside the report and met Gunn's expressionless gaze.

"Well, Lieutenant, I'm happy you could make it in on such short notice," he began.

"Not too hard to manage, sir," Gunn replied, keeping his tone carefully neutral. "After all, we don't have much to do down on China Beach at the moment. And won't, until somebody gets this mess with the Biet Hai and the LDNN sorted out."

"Yes, a bad business, that. Bad from start to finish." Dexter frowned. "I'm sure your decision to extend your tour and help shift the MTT program over to the LDNN will win you high praise from your superiors, Lieutenant."

"That's not why we did it, sir," Gunn told him. "We just don't like to see all the work we put in this past six months thrown away. None of us likes to leave a job half-done."

"Commendable, Lieutenant," Dexter said. There was another long silence before the CIA man spoke again. "I've had word that there won't be any disciplinary action for what happened at Dong Hai. The feeling at Langley is that despite everything that went wrong, the operation overall was a success. Thuy and Tangretti took care of a large stockpile of explosives, and even though the mission was compromised, no American involvement can be proven." He looked deep into Gunn's eyes as if seeking an answer to some great universal question there. "They're saying the lack of evidence of our direct involvement is mostly attributable to your successful extraction of Tangretti, so instead of demanding the Navy court-martial you and bury you under Leavenworth, they're praising your 'initiative and skilled improvisation.' " Gunn could hear the quotation marks in his sarcastic words.

"Nice to know we're appreciated," Gunn said with a faint smile. "No mention, I see, of the stuff that was screwed up a long time before we got on the scene. Like you guys encouraging Tangretti to go in against the 'no involvement' policy, for instance."

"We made sure he knew the score," Dexter told him. "Lieutenant Tangretti was well aware of the fact that we couldn't give him any official sanction if he chose to undertake the mission for us."

"Yeah, and being Steve Tangretti what other choice did you expect him to make?" Gunn shrugged. "It's over and done with. Recriminations aren't going to change much. But I hope to God that the next time around somebody shows a little more sense. You keep up this half-assed nonsense you've been doing, and we're going to be out of luck."

"I suppose you're another one of those who want to turn everything over to the military, eh, Lieutenant?" Dexter said. "Get the spooks out and the Pentagon in, and everything will be just fine. Pump the place full of troops and fight the Commies everywhere we find them . . . all the way to Hanoi, if need be."

"You're dead wrong," Gunn said. "Conventional warfare isn't going to win the day here, I think. You know, every time we get into a war we always find ourselves fighting the last one over again . . . and you'll almost always find

out you're in trouble when you do. World War I was fought
with the tactics that had worked back in the Civil War, but
new weapons turned the battlefields into slaughterhouses.
In World War II, everybody thought a big enough trench
line would stop the Germans cold, but the German tanks
went around the Maginot Line and France fell in a few
days. MacArthur wanted to fight Korea as if it was just a
continuation of his island-hopping campaign in the Pacific,
even though the political realities made the Korean War
something brand-new.

"If we try to fight in Vietnam the way we did in Korea,
we're going to be in for a tough time. Korea was a divided
nation, just like this one, but there's one important difference here. In South Korea the people were pretty much all
on our side. You had clear-cut front lines that armies could
fight along. Point in front of you and you're pointing at hostile territory. Point behind you, and that's your base. That's
not the way things are here. If simple military strength was
enough to knock out the Communists, Diem would have
done it years ago. The ARVN might not be the best army in
the world, but it's got some tough fighters, all the support
America can give, and plenty of will to win. Diem and Nhu
wouldn't think twice about launching an all-out attack on
the enemy. Trouble is, you can't *find* the enemy here. Tanks
and planes and heavy artillery is no good for a guerrilla war.
When the bad guys can blend in with the population, you
end up either slaughtering everybody indiscriminately, or
watching helpless while the enemy picks off the targets
they want to while you can't do anything to strike back."
Gunn leaned forward, animated now. "In World War II the
Nazis posted some of their best troops down in Yugoslavia,
but they were helpless against Tito's partisans. That's the
kind of war we're getting here, and if the U.S. responds by
trying to fight a conventional war, I guarantee you we'll end
up winning every stand-up fight we ever get into, and losing

the war in the end because conventional war techniques won't get at the underlying problem."

"So what's your answer, Lieutenant? Give up?"

"No way." Gunn shook his head. "No, I'd never consider turning this into a conventional war, but there's plenty of ways to win an unconventional one. What we need to do is to mobilize this country to go after the real enemy. Not the guerrilla soldiers in the field. Their leadership. Their infrastructure. Their supply lines from the north. Cut off the head, and the body won't carry on for long. But as long as there are leaders, and supplies, and ideology, they'll always be able to find more cannon fodder. In the long run we can't count on winning a war of attrition, not when the Viet Cong can turn their political movement into a religion and their casualties into martyrs."

"A good point," Dexter commented. "But you haven't told me how you'd hit their infrastructure."

"Not with an army, that's certain," Gunn said. "Vietnam is made for the kind of unconventional war Steve Tangretti was talking about when he argued for the SEALs. Small units, used aggressively to gather information and order surgical raids, will fight a hell of a lot more effectively than whole divisions in the field."

"Ah, another variant on Mr. Tangretti's old theme. Expand the role of the SEALs. Turn the war over to you, and you'll win it for us."

Gunn shook his head. "Actually, I'd say the Vietnamese are the ones who should carry the brunt of the fighting. Through it all, our original mission here, to help train the Biet Hai, was the one thing we've been doing right from the start. This is a civil war, and it's only right that the South Vietnamese do the fighting when they can. But by the same token, if we're going to claim that we're their allies, we have to stop being so wishy-washy about how much we're willing to do to support them. We shouldn't be

fighting their war for them . . . we should be doing everything we can to fight it *alongside* them. You saw the reports
on Dong Hai. Tangretti and Thuy's men ended up working
together, and as you said before, they did carry out the mission, no matter how much trouble they got into on the
way."

"I'd think you would be the last person I'd hear defending the status quo, Lieutenant," Dexter said. "I thought you
didn't approve of the way our operations were being handled."

"I don't. Right now we're splitting hairs about how far
we're willing to go to help our allies. We shouldn't be
improvising and sneaking around to support the Vietnamese
in the field. We should be working with them. The kind of
support work the Special Forces have been doing—or Doc
and his traveling medicine show, for that matter. But we
shouldn't back away from combat support when it's needed,
either. We have equipment, training, and tactics available to
us that the ARVN doesn't have. We shouldn't be holding
back from using it." He smiled. "A couple of Steve Tangrettis attached to every platoon of South Vietnamese commandos would probably be enough to make the Commies turn
tail and run just from hearing the news. And judicious use of
whole SEAL platoons or Green Beanie A-teams . . . they
could get damn near any job done. But the key is to mount a
genuine war effort. Not in size or scope, but in unity of purpose, in planning and preparation. Knowing what we want
to achieve and how we intend to get there. Until you have
those things lined up, I don't think South Vietnam has a
snowball's chance in hell of getting through this."

"It sounds nice enough, Lieutenant, but it's a dream. Do
you really think President Diem or his brother Nhu would
go along with it? They're more concerned with consolidat-
ing personal power than they are with real strategy. Otherwise, the Biet Hai wouldn't be getting the ax."

"Then find somebody else to back," Gunn said. "You don't have to go around setting up puppet governments to get things done . . . but you don't have to put up with Diem and his thugs, either. Find some real patriot and throw all of Uncle Sam's weight behind him. I'll bet you an honest leader with a solid program would break Uncle Ho's hold over the people faster than anything."

"If you could find an honest leader," Dexter said. "I imagine God would find it just as hard to find a righteous man in Saigon as He did in Sodom and Gomorrah."

"The honest men are out there," Gunn said. He was thinking of Thuy. "You just have to know where to look."

"Maybe. Thanks for the input, at least, Lieutenant. But I'll tell you the truth. I'm afraid you won't find too many people in Washington or in Saigon who'd go along with your program. Oh, we'll try new things. There'll be more talk, at least, about giving Tangretti his direct action SEALs, and maybe someday we'll even try it for real. Hell, it might be worthwhile to try out your notion of attaching American advisors from the SEALs or the Green Berets directly to Vietnamese units, instead of trying to run a little Special Warfare school and hoping the training takes and spreads. But I'm a realist, Lieutenant. And the way I see it, you're never going to convince anyone back home to give up on the notion of 'bigger is better.' We've got more than twelve thousand men in Vietnam now. The pressure's on to build up to even higher levels, although Kennedy's not willing to commit too many more troops. But when Kennedy's out of office . . . you watch how fast the tanks and planes and regular soldiers start pouring in."

"Well, if so, then all I can say is, God help us all," Gunn said, suddenly weary. "But the SEALs will do their best to lend a hand, too, whatever happens."

Dexter raised a sardonic eyebrow. "Then the watchword

really should be 'God help us all,' " he said. "Because I've never seen any fighting men anywhere who fought so hard but ignored so many of the rules to do it."

"Are you saying we don't do things by the book, Mr. Dexter?" Gunn asked innocently. "You're wrong, you know. SEALs always do things by the book." He paused, grinning suddenly. "Trouble is, our book was written by Steve Tangretti."

Friday, 22 March 1963

Tangretti Residence
Virginia Beach, Virginia
1820 hours

Veronica Tangretti slit open the envelope with the letter opener her son Bill had given her for Christmas. She was surprised to be getting a letter from Steve, when he'd grown so attached to mailing her those tapes. Frowning slightly, she drew out the pages covered with his untidy handwriting, unfolded them, and smoothed them out on the table in front of her.

She paused before starting to read, still frowning. These past months had taken their toll on her, and no doubt on Steve as well. For a time it had seemed as if they didn't have a future, not when every exchange ended in recriminations or resentment on one side or the other.

Some of it was her fault, she admitted. But only some of it. She had probably made a mistake marrying Steve in the first place, all those years ago. Veronica had known that he could never take Hank Richardson's place in her heart, but she'd been confused and vulnerable and struggling so hard to make things right for Hank Junior, and Steve had been there for her. First his letters, then his kindness and support in person . . . they'd lifted her spirits when everything had seemed bleak, and somehow she just hadn't been able to say "no" when he proposed.

And in the years since, for all of the clashes between two strong wills, she had learned to love him. Sometimes he fooled around, and that hurt. Sometimes he treated her like a second-class citizen, and if anything that hurt even more. But despite his faults, Steve Tangretti was basically a good man, and she only fought with him so often because she did love him. She hated to see him put himself in danger . . . and she felt it all too strongly when he ignored or neglected her. Veronica didn't care much what most people thought of her, but Steve's opinion mattered. That's why it hurt when she didn't seem to matter much to him.

Drawing a deep breath, she thrust the whirl of thoughts and doubts from her mind, and started to read.

My Dearest Ronnie,

I'm writing this from a hospital bed at Clark Air Force Base in the Philippines, where I'm being treated for some minor wounds I picked up on a mission last month. Stress goes on the word minor. I'm okay, and due to be released in a few days. You won't hear about the op on the evening news or see it in the wire services, because it's one of those things that we can't talk about outside the Teams. But it's nothing to worry about. It's over and done with now, and the odds are against my getting in harm's way again anytime soon.

She looked away for a moment. He'd claimed he wouldn't be getting into danger when he left for Vietnam, so this new assurance didn't carry much weight. But while Steve was well-known to downplay things when he was

sick or hurt, he wouldn't tell her he was all right if he didn't
mean it. She could take comfort in that much, at least.

*Now for the bad news. Things have gotten very
messy for our outfit in Vietnam. Nothing physically
dangerous, but messy politics. The unit we were
working with was disbanded for no good reason just
when we were wrapping up our training program,
and that meant that everything we've done since
November was pretty much pointless. It's really dis-
couraging to see a lot of hard work go by the boards
like this, and most of us feel like we can't come home
and leave things in the state they're in now. We've
been given the opportunity to stay on for a few
months more to help the next Mobile Training Team
try to set things right, and I've volunteered to be one
of the ones who sticks around for a while once I'm
released from this antiseptic prison I'm in and
allowed to return to full duty.*

"Oh, Steve, no," she said softly. This time there was
nothing of anger in her voice or in her heart. Veronica was
disappointed, and weary. Nothing ever seemed to change
with Steve. "Not again . . ."

She returned her attention to the letter.

*I know this isn't anything you want to hear, but it's
the only decision I could make and still look at
myself in the mirror to shave. It's just something I
have to do, even though I know I'm running the risk
of driving you away for good.*

*Ronnie, I've been thinking about us a lot since
they stuck me in here, and I've realized just how rot-
ten things have been for you for a long time. You've*

had to take second place to the Navy for years on end now, and I don't blame you for getting fed up. And I don't make things any easier when I get up on my high horse and treat the family as if you're all a bunch of my frogmen. You and they deserve a whole lot better.

Well, first and foremost, I guess you deserve a husband who is there with you instead of being off in the middle of nowhere. I'm asking you . . . no, I'm begging you, Ronnie, to hang on a little longer. If you do, you'll get that husband you deserve, but I can't turn my back on what I need to do here. I owe some people my help getting themselves back on their feet and back into the war, and it's something that has to be done now or not at all.

Maybe that's the case with saving our marriage— if it can be saved, if you want to try to save it. I hope you haven't given up on us yet, for all the things we've said to each other since I came over here. And I hope you'll give me a little more time before you do give up. I want to wrap up everything here, and come home and sort things out with you. You see, I've realized just how much I've come to need you there for me. Maybe I don't say it often enough, and I know I don't show it the way I should, but I can't picture a life that doesn't have you and the kids in it. I love you more than I can ever tell you, Ronnie. The Navy, the Teams, these are all important parts of my life, but you are my life, and if I ever lose you I'll lose the only anchor that's ever held me secure against all the tides and currents that have tossed me around all these years.

I can't make things work by myself. I've learned I can't expect to con you, or charm you, or map out a

*military campaign to conquer you. The only hope I
see for us is if we're both working together, in tandem.
Equal partners through the good times, and the bad
ones. In the past I haven't been very good at treating
you as an equal partner. Now I see that it's the only
way I'll ever have what I want above all else . . . you.*

*So I'm asking you to do this for me, Ronnie. It's
up to you to hold the family together, if you want to
do it, until I can come home again. I've made empty
promises about that before, but this is not another
one of those. When I can come home again, dear
Ronnie, I hope I find you waiting there for me,
because without you I just don't know how I'd ever
find my way again. You're the light that guides me
out of the darkness.*

*Give my love to the kids, Ronnie, but remember
that most of it is always reserved for you.*

> *All my love, dearest,*
> *Steve*

Veronica Tangretti sat still for a long time, looking down
at the letter and blinking back tears. He was staying in
Vietnam, and that should have made her angry. But he had
finally, after more years than she cared to think about,
offered her the one thing that made her think that there was
hope for them after all.

Respect.

Epilogue

Tuesday, 16 November 1982

Vietnam Veterans' Memorial
Washington, DC
1405 hours

Tangretti crouched by the Wall and reached out to touch the name of his old friend. For just a moment his eyes got misty as he blinked back unexpected tears at the memories that stark name set in granite had conjured up. Then he forced the emotion back down into the depths of his soul, where so many sad memories lived.

Arty Gunn had put in three more tours in Vietnam before a Viet Cong rocket attack finally claimed his life early in 1971. Ironically, he'd died aboard a Light SEAL Support Craft operating in the deep south of Vietnam while working in a combined SEAL/LDNN unit. After years of escalating American involvement in the war, they had finally gone back to the earliest concepts Gunn and Tangretti and the others from MTT 4-63 had tried to establish. By then it had been called "Vietnamization," and treated as a brand-new idea, but the cooperation between the SEALs and their Vietnamese counterparts had actually started long before, on that day when Lieutenant Nguyen

Thuy had saved the life of his American friend, and both in turn had been pulled out of harm's way by Gunn and his SEALs.

"Full circle," Tangretti said softly. "In the end, it always comes full circle."

"Sir?" Ensign Gunn looked down at him, cocking his head to one side in a way that recalled his father vividly.

"Nothing, kid," Tangretti told him.

Full circle. Sometimes Tangretti thought that all of his life was about circles. He'd been there for the birth of naval combat demolitions, and for the birth of the SEALs, and in each case he'd watched those outfits grow and change in the testing grounds of war. After Dong Hai the nature of the war in Vietnam had changed, with the CIA gradually pulling out of the business of running their covert war in favor of the military-run headquarters known as MACV-SOG. SEALs had continued as advisors, working out of China Beach and Saigon to assist the LDNN. Tangretti had played no small part in that, himself, before moving on to other jobs. He'd seen Diem's government mismanage the LDNN the same way it had mismanaged the Biet Hai, and watched as South Vietnam had steadily lost ground to the Communists until a cabal of military leaders—some claimed they'd received CIA backing, but no one knew the whole story even yet—had finally launched a coup that had claimed the lives of Diem and his brother. That had been in November 1963, a month when everything about the war in Vietnam had changed forever.

That had been the month of Kennedy's assassination, too. Just weeks before his death, in a letter to the chief of naval operations that had eventually been made public, the president had praised the SEALs and predicted they would have an expanding role to play in modern warfare. For a time it had seemed that his prediction might not come to pass, as the new administration escalated the American involvement and brought all the trappings of a conventional war to Southeast Asia. But the SEALs had adapted, and before long platoons from both Teams had been playing a role in the fighting in Vietnam—a role all out of proportion with the small numbers they sent to fight in the jungles of Vietnam. Only forty-eight other names, along with Arty Gunn's, represented SEAL casualties in the war, but SEALs had accounted for some of the most effective operations in the war. Three of them had won the Medal of Honor. And by the time America had pulled out of Vietnam, the character of the U.S. Navy SEALs had been forever altered. When Tangretti had created the Teams that first year, no one had known what to do with them; by the end of the Vietnam War, no one could picture a Navy without them.

Tangretti himself had stayed on through most of the war, finally retiring after things started winding down in 1972. Not that his connection with the Navy or the SEALs had really ended then, for he'd remained a government consultant thereafter, the man Washington turned to when they wanted to talk about Special Warfare. Ronnie had suffered through those war years somehow, and though their marriage had been through some rough seas, they'd stayed together after all . . . Tangretti wasn't entirely sure how or why, but he was glad it had worked out as it did. Both their sons had gone on to become SEALs as well, and continued to carry on the proud traditions begun by Gator and Snake back at old Fort Pierce all those years ago.

Just as young Ensign Gunn was about to follow in *his* father's footsteps.

Tangretti stood up slowly and clapped a hand on Gunn's shoulder. "Well, kid, if you're going to try to live up to your dad's reputation, you're going to have one damned tough time," he said with a grin. "He was one in a million, was Arty Gunn."

He'd been more than that, though, Tangretti thought as the two men took a last look at the Wall.

He'd been a SEAL.

SEALS
THE WARRIOR BREED

by H. Jay Riker

The face of war is rapidly changing, calling
America's soldiers into hellish regions where
conventional warriors dare not go.
This is the world of the SEALs.

SILVER STAR
0-380-76967-0/$6.99 US/$8.99 Can

PURPLE HEART
0-380-76969-7/$6.50 US/$8.99 Can

BRONZE STAR
0-380-76970-0/$5.99 US/$9.99 Can

NAVY CROSS
0-380-78555-2/$5.99 US/$7.99 Can

MEDAL OF HONOR
0-380-78556-0/$5.99 US/$7.99 Can

MARKS OF VALOR
0-380-78557-9/$5.99 US/$7.99 Can

IN HARM'S WAY
0-380-79507-8/$6.99 US/$9.99 Can

DUTY'S CALL
0-380-79508-6/$6.99 US/$9.99 Can